Escape Under
A Waning Crescent Moon

Book Two in The Blood Moon Series

By: Rhonda Partin-Sharp

2018

CLEEPs Authors

ISBN: 978-1-947216-02-0

Published By:
CLEEPs Authors
P. O. Box 5334
Cincinnati, OH 45205

Author's Information:
Facebook Page: Author Rhonda Partin-Sharp
Blog: *https://ronisharp.wixsite.com/mysite/blog/*

Cover Design by Rhonda Partin-Sharp

WARNING
This book contains adult topics and may not be appropriate for young readers.

Special Dedication

Precious few times in a lifetime does someone come along who understands you so well that you flow with them like water and everything they touch in your life is improved like a Midas-touch turning everything into gold. I was fortunate enough to have that with my friend Linde Grace White. Linde Grace passed away on January 24, 2017. It is with a broken heart but with deep appreciation of my friendship with this extraordinary person that I give this special dedication to her in this book.

I met Linde Grace at a transition point when I was starting to realize life had trained me to be a doormat, and it was imperative to break free from that if I intended to survive. I was in the early stages of that realization when I met Linde Grace. I was so backwards and awkward I'm still surprised she saw worth in me, but that was her way. She saw worth in everyone, even if she had to view that worth in some dangerous people from behind the safety of the very healthy boundaries she had. I was too passive rather than being dangerous, so boundaries never had to be an issue with us. Instead, she showed me a path, and then a road, and then a bridge – and had she lived long enough, she would have shown me how to fly.

I think the thing that solidified our relationship was our mutual love of writing, our shared Appalachian heritage (she always told me she could speak fluent Kentucky if she chose to), and her dedication to helping anyone who was as determined to help themselves as I was. In helping me help myself, she walked with me through personal growth, complicated caregiving situations, and grief, always finding the right balance between my needs and her own.

A few years into our relationship, she offered me the privilege of editing her book, "She Sits Up . . . After They've Gone." The writing and editing process took two years. During those two years, I escaped my passive state faster than I had with any other healing work I had done. During the editing process, she took time to answer any question I had and to help me through any memory that was triggered by the abuse recovery topic of her book. During that time, she also walked with me through writing the first two books of my "Blood Moon

Series," which included editing as well as emotional support when I was tackling the very painful parts of the story.

The trust we built during those two years showed in how comfortable we became with each other. She and I both have issues with being touched. I can handle a hug, and I respected that Linde Grace was not comfortable with hugs. One of the most meaningful memories I had of her was when she took me to see the movie "Inside Out," because she felt it would be meaningful to me. At one point during the movie, she snuggled into me a little bit (and before someone reads more into that than there is, it was only an affection between two close and heterosexual friends) and offered me one of her Swedish fish candies. I realized how much trust we really had built – there was no physical threat between us anymore. One of the things I'm most grateful for is that I saw her three days before her death. She gave me a birthday present, and she accepted a hug of gratitude. I cherish that final hug. That means a lot for people who were taught that touch can be threatening.

I will miss her for the rest of my life. In many ways, she was my heart. I have many other friends, and none of them can fill the void that Linde Grace left. They are all wonderful people and I love them all, but none of them can flow like water with me the way I felt Linde Grace and I did. One friend said to me that she couldn't take Linde Grace's place, and I thanked her for saying that. I told her the story of how after my Mom passed away several women in my Mom's age group, some of them my Mom's friends, offered to take her place in my life. I didn't let them know it because I knew their intentions were good, but I got mad and thought to myself: She's not a dog that when she dies I can just go out and buy another one! My friend pointed out that doesn't even work for dogs, so it surely doesn't work for humans. There will always be a void, and all I can fill it with are memories of our time together, gratitude that being valued by a quality person like her lets me know that I have great value, the writing and love of books we shared, and continued personal growth until I get to the point where I take the next step in the journey she and I were on together – that moment when I fly!

In this special dedication, I am also going to share what two pastors, who were good friends with Linde Grace, wrote about her life. They described her in ways that need to be said but that are beyond me to put into words at this time. Before I share this, I just want to end my portion of this special dedication by saying that I love Linde Grace with all my heart, and I will always miss her.

Pastor Robert Keefer wrote the following:
My thoughts on Linde Grace White
(Well, some of them; it would be quite a long document if I wrote all of them.)

When talking to some folks at church about Linde Grace and her death, I told them that a star had fallen from my sky. She may not have appreciated that image, however; she would probably rather be thought of as a starfish: crawling slowly on the bottom, the weight of the ocean above, but with the image of a light in the sky.

For she was a poet. She observed life with a keen eye and told us about it in carefully crafted words. Specifically, she observed her own life carefully and shared with us what she learned. In her 1992 poem, "How to Look at a Monster," she revealed what it was like to uncover the horror of her own childhood and what made that work possible:

You know it's there.
You feel it heaving, huge, invisible – so far.
You smell it like garbage three days old in July.
You distinguish some of the odors: musty hot newsprint,
Coffee grounds thrown out in grapefruit rinds,
Rotten vegetables, ant-encrusted pork chop bones.
You hear it lumbering about, breaking your valuables,
And your heart, snorting, farting, and growling
Low in its throat.
You step on some unidentified part of it – barefoot –
And draw back in shock.
It's cold, clammy, scaly, too hot, too soft, too squishy,
Wet, yet dry, confusing touch – but you're used to that.
How you need those 3-D glasses, two-toned,
From the movies thirty years ago,
You get a friend – someone you're sure of –
And looking over his shoulder, and holding on very tightly,
You open both eyes and have a look.

We Christians believe the Word of God is *incarnate,* made flesh: above all in Jesus of Nazareth. That implies that our own flesh – our own lives – can also embody the word of God. I think that Linde Grace discovered a great deal about the wonder and terror and tenderness and intimacy of God simply by the witness of her own life. Oh, she knew the Scriptures – for sure! – and she knew the Faith as we sing it. She rarely opened the hymnal, for she knew by heart all the verses of all the hymns. But the Christian Faith is meant to be lived, not merely known about, and so it was in the glory and darkness and ordinariness of her own life that Linde Grace knew God.

And she told us about that glory and darkness and ordinariness in her poetry and her books and in conversation. I don't remember her ever trying to teach me a lesson; I remember her telling me stories from which I learned something. If only I had written them all down! For example, I have often related to people how they can love others after a difficult breaking apart when I tell about her relationship with the family of her ex-husband. "I divorced only one Bates," she said. "Not all of you."

I've written as though her life were a lesson plan; that's wrong. Life is its own reward, as she discovered as she worked through pain and shadow and fear, and at the same time gave of herself in her work as a teacher and her service as an Elder in the Church, loved her children and adored her grandchildren, and was deeply devoted to her friends. Goodness, the woman knew how to love! She, who as a child was used when she should have been loved, loved us who were, I'm sure, stars in her sky. "Love one another as I have loved you," said the Lord Jesus. That is the word that was incarnate in the life of Linde Grace White.

Pastor Thom Shumann wrote the following:

I can't truly remember when I first met Linde Grace White. My best guess is that it had to do with some association through my dear friend, Robert Keefer. But I do remember when I came to value her as a person, and as a friend. That was when she came to work as the secretary at one of the churches I served in Cincinnati.

She was precisely what the church was looking for in a secretary. She was efficient. She was personable with folks who either came to the church or called. She was able to interpret my cramped handwriting. She understood the language of liturgy, worship, music, prayers. She was unflappable and was able to deal with any situation, any person, any problem that came into her office.

More importantly, though I didn't know it when she was hired, she was exactly what I needed at that time in my life and ministry. You see, church secretaries are filled with gifts which no one else realizes, notices, or needs – except for the pastor.

Though members may not know or understand, there are times when the pastor is in their office, but not really. Maybe it is time for prayer, maybe it is time for digging through files and books and memories for a sermon, maybe it is just those precious times of silence and peace which help one to recharge their batteries. Because of what she had experienced in her life, Linde Grace understood the need for boundaries and for protecting them. She was my bodyguard on many occasions, which helped me to be a better pastor.

Pastors deal with many people, many occasions; they deal with brokenness and loss, they deal with fears and doubts; they deal with questions that they cannot always answer, but struggle to find the words that might bring understanding to others. But so much is confidential, matters and things which cannot or should not be shared, especially with their family members. So, who does the pastor turn to, to try to process the words, the hurt, the thoughts, the struggles which have been handed to them? I was fortunate to have Linde Grace. Because of her own brokenness, because of the hurts and struggles she carried and dealt with, she was a much more compassionate person. A person who was willing to risk listening and caring and sharing in the pain of another. She was my therapist, my counselor, my listening ear on many occasions, which helped me to be a better person.

And as a writer, she was a gifted wordsmith. She was able to take her pain and sorrow, and speak about healing, to offer hope to others. She could look at what others were experiencing, and reflect that in her words and writings which enabled those who read her words, who heard her voice, who recognized her heart and soul, to grow as individuals. Her incredible ear, her shattered spirit put back together with hope and grace, her encouragement of what others tried to offer, served to make me a better writer.

All those years ago, so many years ago. And yet, they seem as fresh and real as yesterday. And even though she is no longer with us on this side of wonder, she is still as fresh, as real, as tough, as loving, as graceful as yesterday.

I give thanks to our God for the gift of Linde Grace White, who touched my life and ministry in ways which are beyond all imagining.

Dedication

I dedicate this book to my parents, Estil and Cloma Partin, because they taught me to have enough strength and compassion that I was able to hear and not just listen when I was told the stories that inspired this novel. I love them. Every ounce of good that resides in me is due to their love, both the profound effect that love had on me directly as well as how their love taught me that a loving Father in heaven could not be cruel and judgmental even if some of his followers portrayed him that way. Their love taught me to seek and find a God of love, mercy, and compassion. Since their passing, I miss them every day. I feel like I lost the only two people who see the world the same way I do because of our unique shared experiences. I love them both unconditionally. I truly am blessed to have the parents I had and still have in heaven.

The special dedication I wrote for Linde Grace helped me realize that out of respect for others who touched my life deeply, I should give the following dedications.

I credit my Mom for being that one person who I always knew cared about me. With that caring, she kept me on the straight and narrow and mostly on righteous paths even if they were passive paths. She and I were very different in many ways, but we would have died for each other. Our mutual understanding of our shared culture while living in a city with very different values is where we flowed like water. I thank my mother for always being the most stable influence in my life no matter what chaos surrounded us. She was my rock.

I thank my father for teaching me to never give up, even when no one seemed to be listening and no one seemed to care. In my father's latter years, our mutual understanding of the hard work of healing we were doing together and our shared heritage allowed us to flow like water in many ways. I am grateful to him for that gift of mutual healing.

I also dedicate this book to my aunt, Juanita. I cannot share your story in this dedication, but I can tell you that the person who shared the most stories about you loved you, I think sometimes more than he loved himself. Through the stories he told openly and the stories others let slip and then tried to erase, I feel like I know you. I sometimes feel as if your spirit watches out over us, even me. All of these things have made me love you.

I once had a boss named Rosemary who saw my value and got me on the road to better jobs, college and away from an abusive marriage and on the road to moving away from abusive men. I will never forget her and will always be grateful for what she did for me.

In the ways I wrote about in this dedication, all of these people had a Midas touch in my life in ways similar to the way Linde Grace did.

Acknowledgements

I am grateful to my father, Estil Partin, who encouraged me to write this story and who taught me that we can overcome anything. He epitomized the saying, "What doesn't kill us makes us strong." He was always better than where he started even when others didn't see it, and he soared above where he started in his last few years of life.

I am grateful to my mother, Cloma Partin, who encouraged me to write even when the many trials we experienced made it almost impossible to find time to do so. When she was alive, I told her the song "Wind Beneath My Wings" by Bette Midler must have been written to tell the story of the impact she had on my life. That was our song.

I am grateful that Juanita's story didn't die and that being exposed to it taught me deeper compassion and a greater sense of justice.

I am grateful to Dr. Deborah Andrews. She stood by me and some of my family as we learned to embrace the culture my family migrated to when they left the mountains. She also stood by us as we learned how to set boundaries that our new culture quickly taught us we were lacking.

I am grateful to Pastor Robert Keefer and his wife Kathleen and Pastor and Author Thom Shuman and his wife. They helped me release negative religious beliefs and grow to understand the love of Christ. That understanding increased my happiness and added flavor to this book.

I am grateful to Linde Grace White who was my dear friend and editor. To say she was my editor is not sufficient – she was an editor extraordinaire. My book flourished under her painful red ink marks that I sometimes feared and even resented, but she was usually right. My book was greatly improved under her guidance just as the quality of my life has improved due to her very patient, nurturing, and never-failing friendship. Her own writing against child abuse can be found at LindeGraceWhite.org.

I am grateful to Wayne Holmes of Religious Recovery Press for his literature, which helps people expand their minds beyond the religious boxes so many people get trapped in, for publishing the first book in this series, for his assistance with editing, and for his friendship. I am very impressed with his literary skills and his personal character. I am grateful for all I learned from him while publishing the first book in this series with his publishing house, which is now a 501(c)3 non-profit publishing house and thus is no longer carrying my book. I am also grateful for the lessons I learned about boundaries while visiting his religious recovery meetings and in personal conversations with him. My boundaries are much stronger now than they were before I began to work with Wayne on religious abuse recovery.

I am grateful to my husband, David Sharp, for assisting with computer issues, which included purchasing and setting up a new computer when my old one broke halfway through the writing process. I am also grateful for his dedication to learning how he can consistently be more of what I need him to be to allow me to dedicate more of myself to writing. I appreciate him supporting me in writing this trilogy and making this dream come true even when it took time away from him and other responsibilities.

I am grateful to the owner(s) and staff of College Hill Coffee Company in Cincinnati, Ohio. They allowed Linde Grace White and I to park there for hours each Wednesday afternoon for many months while we edited this book. Even though I have moved to another location since Linde Grace passed away (the memories are still too painful), I will always be grateful to them for all they did for us while we used their coffee house as a frequent meeting place.

Escape Under
A Waning Crescent Moon

CHAPTER ONE: IN THE CITY

Eamon was forced to escape the mountains of Appalachia and flee to Cincinnati for his own safety. The tragedy that forced him to flee started under a waning crescent moon. As Eamon stepped out of the car that drove him to freedom, in a manner similar to the abolitionists who delivered so many slaves to freedom in and around the Cincinnati area, that same moon watched over him. I watched over him, too.

My name is Sinead. I am Eamon's older sister. Even my tragic death fifteen long years ago in 1935 couldn't stop me, even after I became a ghost, from fulfilling my role as Eamon's protector. I will always protect him just like he protected this ghost dog that got out of the back seat of the car with me. That ol' dog is so grateful for all Eamon did for him that it is being loyal even in death.

Eamon gave that dog more respect than anyone ever had — he didn't even give the dog a name due to that respect. He wanted the dog to have the freedom to be who he was instead of what a name said he should be; therefore, Eamon just called him Dog.

No matter how much respect Eamon had for Dog, he couldn't keep Dog safe. Other than the love the three of us had for each other and a kind aunt and uncle back home, all any of us knew was violence — the violence that took Dog's and my lives and forced Eamon to run to the city before his life was taken, too. Dog and I would never leave Eamon. No matter how alone Eamon may have felt when he stepped out of that car into a strange city and an uncertain future, he most definitely was not.

When the car pulled away, a group of young people stepped out of the shadow of a three-story brick row house two doors down the street and walked toward Eamon. Only one woman was in the group of half a dozen boys. The boys all wore black leather jackets, blue jeans, and white t-shirts, and they all wore their hair greased back in a way I never saw men wear it in the mountains. Half of them smoked cigarettes.

The woman wore blue jeans that were so tight from ankle to waist that I wondered how she got into them, and the heels on her shiny black shoes were so high I wondered how she walked while wearing them. Her black shirt was cut so low that I could see parts of her body women back home only showed when they were feeding their babies. Her hair was stacked high on her head in a manner that looked more like a bird's nest than a hairstyle, and a blue band was tied around her head just above her bangs. Her make-up was so thick it was hard to tell what her face really looked like. She was the first woman I ever saw smoking a cigarette.

The group stopped in front of Eamon.

One of the boys looked at Eamon's short leg that was crippled by his abusive mother and asked, "Hey, Peg Leg, where do you think you're going?"

Eamon swallowed hard.

I think the girl was aware of Dog's and my ghost, because she backed into one of the boys when Dog growled. He put his arm across her shoulder and pulled her close to him.

His hand dangled in front of her breast as he said, "You didn't answer the question my friend George asked you. Where do you think you're going?"

Sweat glistened on Eamon's skin as he answered, "I reckon I be goin' into that there Goodwill® store. That be what the man who be drivin' me here be tellin' me I ought to be doin'."

"Ya reckon ya be goin'," George mocked before he laughed.

When he stopped laughing, the boy with his arm across the girl's shoulder drawled, "that there store." As they all laughed, he removed his arm from the girl's shoulder, pushed her toward Eamon and asked, "Why don't ya give this here country bumpkin' a proper welcome to the city, Imojean?"

Imojean stumbled toward Eamon. Eamon not only stepped away from her but raised his arms to keep from touching her as he did. I could imagine why. I wouldn't want to touch her either. She reminded me too much of our whore of a sister, Regan, who was evil enough to survive on that mountain. Touching her might spread some sex disease or, even worse, some of her evil might rub off.

When Imojean regained her footing, she turned to the boy and said, "Don't push me, Mark! Come on, guys, leave him alone! He ain't doing nothing to hurt you!"

"Oooohhhhhh," Mark said. "I think Imojean's taking a liking to our country friend here." He spun her around, placed his cupped hands over her breasts and asked, "Do you want some of these, country bumpkin? Do you want a nasty hot welcome to the city?"

Eamon began to shake.

My ghost body wanted to throw up but didn't have the organs to allow it. These folks were like the folks back home, and it was making me sick to realize people like that were everywhere. I was glad I decided to stay with Eamon, because it felt like there wasn't a safe place in the world. Dog's growls let me know he felt the same way.

Imojean spun around, slapped Mark's face, and yelled, "When Frankie hears you touched me, you'll be answering to him — you animal! Now, leave this boy alone!"

A bell rang and hinges squeaked when the door of the Goodwill® store opened. A dark-skinned man stood in the open door and yelled, "What in hell is going on out here?"

All of the people in the gang spun around to face the man.

The man cocked the shotgun he was holding before he yelled, "I'm damn tired of you punks! Get the hell out of here before I fill you full of lead!"

One of the boys who hadn't spoken yet walked toward the man as he said, "Well, don't you think you're the big man? You ain't nothing but a nigger, and I'm going to remind you of that." He pulled a knife out of the inside breast pocket of his leather jacket and pushed a button that made the blade pop out.

The man knocked the knife out of the boy's hand with the shotgun stock and hit the boy in the head with it so fast that it seemed like the man did both with one motion. He turned the gun and pointed the barrel at the other punks so fast I barely saw the gun move. He jerked the shotgun barrel toward the boy he had hit and said, "Get him outta here, and get yourselves on home. I've already called the police. It's your choice — go home or go to jail."

"The cops ain't goin' to believe nothing you got to say, nigger," George said. "They'll probably arrest you just for calling them about a white man."

"That boy you tried to hurt is a white man — and from the looks of him a crippled white man to boot. How do you think the police are going to feel about that?"

Two of the boys who hadn't spoken yet helped the injured boy to his feet, draped his arms across their shoulders, and led him away.

As the punks walked away, I stared at the man, feeling a deep admiration for his courageous spirit. He had a spirit like MawMaw Tierney. He used a shotgun to rescue Eamon just like MawMaw Tierney did yesterday before she sent him to the city for his safety. Maybe that waning crescent moon was watching out over Eamon.

"Get on in here!" the man said as he frantically motioned for Eamon to come inside. "Get on in here before they come back!"

Eamon, Dog, and I stood at the edge of the sidewalk and stared at the man. His skin was darker than I ever saw before, and the building he was trying to get us to enter was different from anything I ever saw, too. I was afraid to approach two things I didn't know anything about. I was more afraid to walk into that strange building with that strange man than I was of the punks coming back. If the punks came back, we could at least try to run. If that man locked us in like Pastor Skaggs used to do . . . I couldn't even finish the thought. Eamon's whole body was quivering and covered with sweat, and Dog was growling. I suspected they felt the same way.

The front of the building was made from the biggest pieces of glass I ever saw. They were being held together by metal frames, and the door was in a metal frame in the middle. A sign hung from a thin strip of yellow brick above the glass. The letters on the sign read G-o-o-d-w-i-l-l®, just like the man who drove us here said they would.

The man continued to motion frantically as he said again, "Hurry up and get on in here before they come back!"

The man was small compared to most mountain men. He was about the same size as Eamon, who due to malnutrition only grew to about 5'6" tall and was very thin even though lots of hard work made him muscular. The man was dressed similar to Eamon, too. They both wore faded overalls over a white t-shirt. Those were the only ways they resembled each other though. The man's skin was very dark, his lips were large, and his nose was wider than any I ever saw before.

The man looked in the direction the punks went. When he didn't see them, he stopped motioning, looked Eamon up and down, and said, "It looks like you can't hardly walk, and you're as skinny as a rail. When's the last time you ate, son?" Eamon didn't answer, so the man asked, "Does the cat got your tongue, son? I asked when's the last time you ate?"

Eamon touched his tongue before he said, "I nary be knowin' what a darn cat be wantin' with my tongue."

The man laughed and said, "It's just a saying, son. Now, tell me, when's the last time you ate?"

"Some man I nary be knowin' be buyin' me hamburgers 'round noon time. He be tellin' me to be comin' here, so I reckon h'it be the right thing to be doin' since he be so nice to me to be feedin' me an' all." Eamon looked up at the sign and asked, "This do be the Goodwill®, ain't h'it?"

Eamon pulled the piece of paper the man who drove him to the city wrote the name on out of the bib pocket of his overalls and compared it to the letters on the sign while the man answered, "Yes, this is the Goodwill®. You ain't from around here, are you, son?"

"Naw, sir."

"Where are you from?"

"I be comin' from the minin' compound. We jest be callin' h'it home," Eamon answered as he pulled a note out of the pants pocket of his overalls. "My cousin be writin' this down fer me. This be the address where I be from. MawMaw Tierney be tellin' me to be findin' myself a church and be askin' the preacher man to be writin' her to be lettin' her know I be a'right. I nary be too keen on findin' me no church though. Them there preachers nary be trustworthy where I be comin' from. Do ya reckon ya could be writin' to be lettin' her know I be a'right?" He limped toward the door with his hand extended like he was going to give the note to the man, but he stopped halfway and asked, "How do I be knowin' ya nary be goin' to be lockin' me up in there?"

"Why would I do something like that?" the man asked.

"I nary be knowin'. I reckon the same reason Pastor Skaggs —"

"What about this Pastor Skaggs?"

5

Eamon started shaking again as he said, "H'it nary be no never mind."

It seemed to me that the man's eyes changed when Eamon said that. I saw less fear and more, I don't know — warmth. I was beginning to feel less afraid of him.

The man looked Eamon up and down and asked, "Did you trust the man who drove you here?"

Eamon swallowed hard and said, "Nary at first. I be bein' more afraid my Pa be catchin' me than what might be happenin' to me if'n I be gettin' into that there man's car. Once he be buyin' me lunch, I reckon I be figurin' he be a'right about then."

"Since you figured out he was all right, do you think he would tell you to come here if he thought we would lock you up or do you any harm?"

Eamon looked at the man for several seconds before he said, "I reckon not." He took a couple of steps toward the door before he stopped and asked, "Do ya be workin' the fields?"

The skin above the man's nose wrinkled as he asked, "Why do you ask that?"

"My Uncle Teagan be gettin' mighty dark when he be workin' the fields, but he nary be gettin' as dark as ya be."

The man laughed out loud for several seconds before he asked, "Do you mean to tell me you've never seen a black man before?"

"I nary be knowin' what that be."

"I'm a black man. This is my skin color all the time. The sun can make me darker, but I'm dark all the time."

"No joshin'?"

"No kidding. Do you have a place to stay tonight?"

"Naw, sir. I nary be havin' no place to be stayin'. I nary be havin' no family 'round these here parts to be puttin' me up."

"Bring yourself on in here, son. Let's figure out what we can do for you." When Eamon didn't move, the man said, "That man who gave you a ride told you to come here. He wouldn't have told you that if he thought I was going to hurt you." When Eamon still didn't move, the man sighed and asked, "Are your feet glued to the concrete?"

Eamon lifted his crippled foot and looked at the bottom of his shoe before he said, "I nary be believin' my feet be bein' glued to — do concrete be what ya be callin' this here stuff I be standin' on?"

6

"You haven't ever seen concrete before?"

"Naw, sir."

The man laughed again and said, "Boy, you'd better get on in here and let me help you. You haven't ever seen a black man. You haven't ever seen concrete. This city's goin' to eat you alive if you don't let me teach you a few things. You've already seen the worst of it in those punks. There will be people like that preying on you every time you turn around if you don't learn a few things."

"My MawMaw Tierney done telled me h'it be a good thang to be havin' folks be prayin' on ya."

The man sighed heavier this time before he said, "No, son, I don't mean that kind of praying. I mean taking advantage of you."

"Folks done been takin' advantage of me all my life. That be why my MawMaw Tierney be sendin' me here."

"She must have wanted it to be different for you than where you were, so come on in here and let me show you how you can make it different."

Eamon took a couple of steps and stopped again.

The man stepped onto the sidewalk, held the door open, and gestured with a big sweep of his arm for Eamon to walk through the door. When Eamon didn't move, the man asked, "Are you afraid of me, because I'm black?"

"I reckon I can be gettin' used to h'it."

The man's face hardened as he asked with a serious tone, "What exactly happened to you that your MawMaw wanted to get you away from?"

Eamon swallowed hard and hesitated for a full minute before he said, "Pastor Skaggs be sayin' a Godly man nary be tellin' folks what done happened to him."

"You just answered my question," the man said as he shook his head. "I ain't goin' to hurt you, son. That nice man that bought you the hamburgers told you to come here, because he knows we help people. We're not here to hurt people. Come on in. You can share my supper with me. We can talk while you help me with some new donations that came in today. I don't believe you'd be much good at unloading trucks with that leg, but I bet you can sit in a chair and unpack the boxes."

"I can be unloadin' trucks. I be workin' the fields and ever thang back home."

"How about you help me work in whatever way you can in trade for some supper and some help. How do you feel about a trade?"

"That be right nice," Eamon said as he limped to the front door. He hesitated for a minute before he walked through it with me and Dog at his heels. The man followed us in and locked the door. Eamon spun around so fast that his bad leg almost caused him to fall and stammered, "Why ya be lockin' that there door fer?"

"Calm down, son. I'm just trying to keep us safe in here. It can be a bad neighborhood. You don't want those punks coming back and coming in here, do you?"

"When Pastor Skaggs locked the door — "

The man looked confused as he asked, "What's that?"

"H'it nary be important. A Godly man nary be whinin' to folks about what done happened to him."

I knew what Eamon started to say, because I was with him the day Pastor Skaggs locked the door of the church and touched Eamon in ways no young boy ought to be touched. I thought I knew how Eamon must be feeling, because the sound of that door locking ran through me like a jolt of lightning.

Eamon was trembling as he looked around the spacious front lobby. It ran the length of the front windows. It was long and narrow like Eamon's room at MawMaw Tierney's was. There was one door halfway along the back wall. A large desk sat to the right of that door, and there were chairs lining the window across from the desk. The linoleum floor was white, and the streetlights shining through the glass and reflecting off it combined with the sparse furnishings to make the room look bright and large.

The man extended his hand to Eamon and said, "My name is Jeb. Jeb Williams. Most everyone around here calls me Mr. Williams, but you can call me Jeb if you want to."

"I reckon I be callin' ya what ever'one else be callin' ya, Mr. Williams."

"Suit yourself," Mr. Williams said as he moved his hand a little closer to Eamon. "They just call me Mr. Williams, because I run the place. I'm just doing the Lord's work, but people around here seem to need to give anyone in charge extra respect."

Eamon looked at Mr. Williams hand and said, "I nary be knowin' why ya be pokin' yer hand at me like that."

"You've never shaken hands with anyone before?"

Eamon shook his head.

"That can be the first thing I teach you. In the city, men shake hands when they meet. Just reach out your hand and grab it like you would if you were pulling me to my feet after I fell down." When Eamon did, Mr. Williams continued, "That's right. Now just shake up and down a couple of times. Don't shake real hard but hold their hand firm. That makes people think you've got confidence." When Eamon followed those instructions, Mr. Williams finished by saying, "That's real good, son. You're a natural. Pretty soon no one will know you're not from around here."

When Mr. Williams released Eamon's hand, Eamon looked at it and asked, "Why do folks be doin' that?"

"Why do people do anything they do? We just do what everyone else does, so we don't stand out like a sore thumb. No one wants the whole world looking at them, because they're doing something different."

Eamon nodded.

Mr. Williams motioned for Eamon to follow him and said, "Come on in the back, son. I've got some fried chicken and okra my wife sent with me for supper tonight. There's plenty enough for two. I swear that woman finds more joy in feeding people than anyone I've ever known. I'm goin' to be as fat as a pig by the time I'm an old man."

Mr. Williams opened the wooden door that cut through the middle of the back wall and motioned for Eamon to go in ahead of him. Dog and I followed Eamon into a room that was bigger than MawMaw Tierney's barn. All three of us stopped just inside the door and looked around at the huge room. It had a concrete floor, and the walls were made of concrete blocks. They were all painted the same color of light gray. There was a large standing fan in each corner and in the middle of each wall. The middle of the room was filled with piles of clothing, blankets, pillows, toys, books, furniture, and more. There was more stuff than any of us ever saw before.

When Mr. Williams entered the room, he said, "Come on, son. My supper is over here."

Eamon followed him to a desk that sat halfway down the right wall. In the middle of the desk sat a paper sack with a greasy bottom and a bowl with a piece of waxed paper over it that was being held on by a rubber band. The man sat in a chair on the far side of the desk and motioned for Eamon to sit in a chair on the other side. Dog lay at Eamon's feet, and I stood behind him.

Mr. Williams opened the top drawer on the right side of the desk and pulled out two white plates with blue flowers on them. He closed that drawer, opened the one below it, and pulled out two forks. He lay a fork on one of the plates, sat the plate in front of Eamon, and said, "We're not much for luxury around here. Someone donated these plates, and I kept a few for the workers." He opened the bag and removed a big fried chicken breast. He lay it on Eamon's plate and put the next one he removed on his own plate. As he rolled the top of the bag down, he said, "There's two more pieces in there if you want some more." He sat the bag aside and removed the waxed paper from the big bowl of fried okra. He gave Eamon half before he put the rest on his own plate. He wadded up the waxed paper and threw it in the bowl as he said, "I know it's cold, but my wife cooks so good you won't even notice. Dig in."

Eamon took a big bite out of the chicken breast.

"Good, isn't it?" Mr. Williams asked.

Eamon nodded while he took a second bite. Eamon gobbled down his chicken and okra without saying a word. When he was finished, he stared at the bag.

Mr. Williams lay his half-eaten chicken breast on his plate and unrolled the bag as he asked, "Would you like the other piece?"

"If'n that be a'right with you."

Mr. Williams pulled out the two pieces of chicken that were still in the bag, laid them on Eamon's plate, and said, "You take the rest of it. I'm not that hungry tonight. I think you need it more than I do."

"Much obliged," Eamon said as he picked up one of the chicken legs and took a bite.

The two men finished eating at the same time.

Mr. Williams sat their plates and forks on top of the bowl and asked, "What do you need help with?"

Eamon swallowed hard and stared at Mr. Williams for a full minute before he said, "Ya's done been right nice to be feedin' me and all. I reckon I can be trustin' ya to be tellin' ya what I be needin'." Eamon looked at Mr. Williams for another minute before he said, "I reckon I be needin' help with ever thing. MawMaw Tierney be tellin'

10

me to be comin' to the city. She be tellin' me to be gettin' a job — says I be able to be buyin' me a car, and I to be usin' that car to be comin' home to be seein' her. She be tellin' me to be findin' me a church — sayin' church people be helpin' me if'n I be goin' to their church regular so they can be gettin' to know me. She be sayin' to be havin' the preacher be writin' home fer me so she be knowin' if'n I be a'right. I be agreein' with ever thang she be tellin' me to do, exceptin' I nary be wantin' to be findin' me nary church. Do ya reckon ya could be helpin' me to be writin' home and lettin' MawMaw Tierney be knowin' I be a'right?"

Why do you need someone to write home for you?"

"I nary be knowin' how to be doin' h'it fer myself."

"You can't read or write?"

"Naw, sir."

"Do you have any education?"

"My folks nary be lettin' me be goin' to school."

"I think I'm getting an idea of why your MawMaw told you to come to the city."

Eamon looked at his lap.

"What happened to your leg, son?"

Eamon continued to look at his lap.

"Did your folks do that to your leg?"

Eamon didn't look up as he said, "A Godly man nary be tellin' folks what done happened to him."

"I get the picture. That man who gave you a ride was right to send you here. I'm going to help you. Yes, I will write to your MawMaw and let her know you're okay. Can she read my letter when she gets it?"

"Naw, sir, she nary be readin' a'tall."

"How will she know what my letter says?"

"My cousins be livin' with her," Eamon answered as he looked at Mr. Williams. "My Uncle Teagan got his self three daughters. He be sendin' them all to school. They be readin' right fine. They be readin' yer letters to MawMaw Tierney fer her."

"I'll be happy to write to her," Mr. Williams said as he reached his hand toward Eamon. "You just give me that address you've been holding since you took it out of your pocket, and I'll make sure I write

11

her in the morning. Now that we've got that cleared up, would you like a job?"

"Yassir," Eamon said as he handed the grease stained piece of paper to Mr. Williams.

"I hate to make you do physical work with your leg like that, but I don't know what else I can give you if you can't read or write. How bad did it hurt your leg when you worked in the fields where you came from?"

"I be liftin' all the time at Uncle Teagan's farm."

"But, how bad did it hurt you?"

Eamon looked at his lap again and said, "I can be doin' anything ya be needin' me to be doin'."

"You aren't going to tell me if it hurt you or not, are you, son?"

"I be a right good worker."

"Would you like to start tonight? We've got a truck at the back door that I could use some help unloading. The job pays minimum wage."

"What do minimum wage be?"

"That's the least money the government tells us we can pay people. It's to make sure people make enough money to live on. That means I have to pay you at least seventy-five cents an hour."

Eamon smiled big and asked, "Seventy-five cents an hour?"

"Yes, son."

"I be right pleased to be havin' that."

"Then you've got a job. Follow me back to the truck, and we'll talk about the rest while we unload it."

Eamon, Dog and I followed Mr. Williams to a back door that we hadn't been able to see before, because so many piles were in front of it.

As we walked to the door, Mr. Williams said, "We don't usually work at night. Most of the time you'll come in early in the morning and be out of here in time to be home for supper. Today was just a crazy day. Three of my workers were too sick to come to work, and we got four extra trucks of donations. I wasn't feeling good about it at first, but now I'm thinking God wanted me to be here to help you tonight."

The door led to a back alley where a pick-up truck was backed up to the door. Mr. Williams opened the wooden double doors that were attached to the hand-made wooden frame someone made for the truck bed. After he opened the doors, he lowered the tailgate as he said,

"You get on up in the truck and hand me things down. I'll take them in and put them in the right pile."

"A'righty," Eamon said as he clumsily climbed onto the bed of the truck.

Dog and I stayed out of the way and watched them work.

Each time Mr. Williams returned to the truck, he had another question for Eamon. It took a while for Eamon to open up, but by the time the truck was empty, Mr. Williams knew everything Eamon felt comfortable telling about his rough beginnings and the abuse that left him handicapped. When Eamon tried to tell the story about how our father killed Dog, he became too upset to speak. One time he said my name, and I thought he was going to tell the story of how our parents killed me. Instead, he shook his head like he just walked into a cobweb and developed a blank stare. Mr. Williams said Eamon's name three times before he snapped out of it.

When they were finished, they sat on the tailgate of the truck. As they sat there, Mr. Williams said, "You're going to be needing to plan for the future, because that leg will only get worse with age. I sure wish there was a school that would take someone your age, so you could get an education. If there is one, I surely don't know where it is. Most folks around here came in from farming or mining towns, and most of them only have an eighth-grade education. Education just isn't that important to most people I know. As long as they can read and write, they seem to get by okay. I only have an eighth-grade education myself. That's why I'm still loading trucks. The only reason I'm the boss is people seem to like me, and I know enough to write the paychecks and sign them. Thank goodness we don't sell anything from here for me to have to watch the till. All we do is take it in, sort it, and send it out to the stores."

"I be gettin' along right fine up till now with nary book learnin', so I reckon I be keepin' on gettin' along without h'it. My Pa done be sayin' the only learnin' we be needin' be the Bible anyhow."

"The same Pa that beat you?"

Eamon nodded.

They were silent for several minutes before Mr. Williams continued, "You said your MawMaw wanted you to get a car and come home to visit. I hope we can make that happen, because you can't be walking every place on those legs like healthy folks do. I think I can help you get a driver's license. I have a friend down at the DMV who might work with me on this. If you can answer all the questions he asks you and then show him that you can drive, I think I just might be able to get you a driver's license without you having to take the written test. You'll have to catch the bus until you get that license and save enough for a car. I don't have a car, or I'd let you drive it."

"What do the DMV be?"

"It's the place that gives out driver's licenses."

"What do I be needin' a driver's license fer?"

Mr. Williams shook his head as he said, "Your parents really didn't teach you a damn thing, did they? It's a little card you carry with you to prove to the police that you earned the right to drive. The law says you have to have one before you drive a car."

"A'right. I be much obliged if'n ya be helpin' me be gettin' one. That nary be makin' no sense to me though. I nary be thinkin' my Pa nor my Uncle Teagan be havin' one of them there license things."

"The law might be different where you come from, but we've been required to have them here in Ohio since 1936. Don't worry about it. I'm sure I can help you get one."

"Much obliged."

"I'm sure you'll be wanting a car anyway. Most of the folks that work for me that came in from the mountains like you did go home every weekend to be with their families. I don't think they much like it here. Most of them seem to just come here for a job, but their hearts seem to still be in those mountains."

"I nary much be wantin' to be runnin' home ever weekend. There nary be nothing but bad memories be waitin' there fer me. If'n ya can just be helpin' me to be writin' home to MawMaw Tierney, I think that there will be enough."

"We'll see how it goes, son. You might change your mind once you have that car."

"Mays be."

Mr. Williams rubbed his forehead before he said, "You're going to be needing a place to live until you get on your feet. You can sleep on a cot at my apartment until you save enough money to get a place of your own."

"What do a 'partment be?"

"It's a place to live."

14

"Do h'it be like a house?"

"Yes, but it's smaller. There are usually several apartments in one building, but you have a door that separates you from the other apartments. It's like a house, because it's your own place."

"Will ya be helpin' me to be gettin' one of them there 'partments?"

"I'll be happy to help you when you have enough money. In the meantime, you can stay at my apartment. It won't do you no harm to have someone looking after you until you get settled in up here."

"Much obliged."

Mr. Williams stood up and said, "I think we've done enough work for one night. You did a good job. What do you say we go on home now, so I can show you where you'll be sleeping?"

"Much obliged," Eamon said before he got up and helped Mr. Williams close the tailgate and the doors on the truck frame.

Dog and I followed Eamon and Mr. Williams through the big room, into the narrow room, and out the front door. As we walked down the street together, I realized we could trust Mr. Williams. He was the only person, other than MawMaw Tierney and Uncle Teagan, who slowed down enough for Eamon to keep up without stumbling.

CHAPTER TWO: MOVING ON

From the first night Mr. Williams brought Eamon home, Mrs. Williams welcomed him as if he were family. She coaxed him into the apartment when he first arrived, repeatedly assured him he was not being a burden, and showed in her actions how welcome he was. She made breakfast for Mr. Williams and him each morning and sent them off to work with a bag lunch that was full enough to feed two people — she knew they would often share it with a person who came to them in need of help. Dinner was hot on the table when they got home from work. Whatever was left from supper went into two bags for the men to take with them the next day. She gave Eamon a snack and prepared a cot for him in the front room before she went to bed each night. Eamon thanked her for every kindness, and each thank you was followed by an apology for being a burden.

Dog and I could understand why Eamon apologized for being a burden all the time. When we were all alive on the mountain, we were reminded that we were a burden every day of our lives. Dog and I were whisked away to the land of the dead where we couldn't be a burden to the living anymore, and Eamon probably would have shared our fate if he wouldn't have escaped.

After a couple of weeks, Mrs. Williams sat on Eamon's freshly made cot and patted the mattress next to her as she said, "Come and sit with me for a minute."

Eamon joined her, but he sat far away from her at the other end of the cot.

Mrs. Williams smiled at him and said, "I don't know how people treated you where you came from, but you're not there anymore.

You're here, and you're not a burden. Mr. Williams and me are both glad you're here, and we want you to stay as long as you need to. You don't have to thank me for everything I do for you, and please stop apologizing for being a burden. You're not. You don't have to ask before you lay on the cot at night. I make it up for you. It's yours as long as you live here. If you get a hankering for some food or are thirsty, don't sit there hungry and thirsty until me or Mr. Williams asks you if you want something. Go ahead and help yourself. The food is yours, too, as long as you live here. Do you understand?"

Eamon nodded and said, "I surely do be sorry. I nary be familiar with takin' from folks — exceptin' MawMaw Tierney and Uncle Teagan, but I be workin' their farm for free to be earnin' my keep."

Mrs. Williams scooted over enough to allow her to pat Eamon's hand as she said, "You don't have to be saying you're sorry all the time either, child. Just be yourself, and we'll tell you if we need you to do anything different. Unless we say something to you, just assume everything is fine."

Eamon nodded.

Mrs. Williams stood up, nodded toward the bed, and asked, "What are you going to do now?"

"If'n h'it be a'right, I reckon I be goin' to bed."

"Why wouldn't it be alright to go to bed in your own bed?"

Eamon smiled and said, "I be goin' to bed now."

"Good night, dear," Mrs. Williams said before she left the room.

When Eamon, Mr. Williams, Dog, and I left for work the next morning, Eamon said thank you when Mrs. Williams gave him his lunch sack, but he didn't apologize for being a burden.

Mrs. Williams did a lot more for Eamon and Mr. Williams than feed them and prepare a bed for them. She was always on top of every domestic responsibility. The apartment was small, but Mrs. Williams kept it spotless even though she worked in the cafeteria at the neighborhood school four hours a day. She often said it was important to her to make sure all of the children got a good lunch in case they didn't get enough to eat at home.

Even though she was a tiny woman who was only five feet tall and weighed less than one-hundred pounds, she loved to feed people and had a hearty appetite herself. Mr. Williams often teased her that the food she ate must fall straight down into hollow legs, because she never gained a pound.

The apartment was in a large brick building that had six apartments in it. An apartment was on each side of the stairwell that rose through the middle of the building's three floors. Mr. and Mrs. Williams apartment was on the first floor. When you entered the building, their entry door was immediately to the left.

The entry door led to a large sitting room whose white walls needed painting and whose light brown linoleum had dark spots where it was wearing out. The front wall had two large windows where sun shined through during the day. There was a small plant on each windowsill, and a bird cage hung from a hook in the ceiling between the right window and the adjoining wall. The cage held a small, yellow canary. The adjoining wall had a couch that sat far enough away from the wall for the cot that had slept many people in need to slide behind it during the day. On the wall opposite the front windows was a General Electric standing radio. A card table sat along the wall next to the entry door, which had four folding chairs around it for eating supper as well as their frequent card games.

The rooms were laid out single file through the depth of the apartment. Next to the radio was a door that led to the kitchen. It was as sparse as the front room. When you entered the kitchen, you saw a shallow sink secured to the left corner of the opposite wall, and the pipes below were visible. One side of the sink was the water tub, and the other side was a flat section for draining. The refrigerator sat to the right of the sink. A small silver cube that was the freezer hung from the ceiling of the refrigerator, and Mrs. Williams had to defrost it every weekend. A small stove was on the opposite wall across from the sink. The wall that separated the kitchen from the stairwell had a small cupboard sitting against it that held the eating and cooking supplies. The wall opposite that cupboard was bare. There were no windows, and the room was only half the size of the other rooms in the house, which is why the card table where they ate was in the living room.

A door to the right of the refrigerator led to Mr. and Mrs. Williams bedroom. That was the only room in the house with a door, and they only closed it at night. Their room also had no windows, and Mr. Williams often teased that they had romantic lighting. The back wall held their bed. It had no headboard but was covered by a beautiful

18

quilt in many shades of blue. Mr. Williams told Eamon that Mrs. Williams made the quilt out of their deceased son's baby clothes. Their son was the only child they conceived. Each of them had their own dresser that sat on each side of the bed. There were no closets, so the dressers held all of their clothes. All of the other walls were bare.

Each floor had one bathroom that was shared by the residents of that floor. The bathroom was under the stairwell, and there was a door entering from each side of the stairwell. Along the back wall was a small bathtub. The front wall had a toilet and a small sink with a mirror hanging above it. The other two walls had only the doors. Mrs. Williams scrubbed the bathroom before every bath anyone who lived in her apartment took, because she did not know how good the hygiene of the people in the other apartment was.

Once you were inside their city home, it was similar to the mountain homes we were accustomed to — plain and sparse, except Mrs. Williams kept this apartment immaculate. MawMaw Tierney owned the only clean house I saw in the mountains. The mountain women said MawMaw Tierney was only able to keep her house so clean, because she had a daughter-in-law and four grand-daughters cleaning for her all the time — most of those gossipers had some type of daughter living with them as well. I think it was because Uncle Teagan, unlike most of the men back home, treated MawMaw Tierney so good that she felt like cleaning instead of feeling sad all the time. I believe this, because Mr. Williams treated Mrs. Williams very well, and this made her so happy that she sang while she bustled around keeping her house clean.

Mr. and Mrs. Williams both treated everyone well. Mrs. Williams always had a smile on her face and often sang gospel songs under her breath as she went about her day. Since I knew Eamon was safe in his new situation, I sometimes stayed with Mrs. Williams and listened to her singing instead of going to work with Eamon, Dog, and Mr. Williams.

The days I spent with her taught me that she lifted the window shades to let the sun in when the men left for work. She talked to each of her plants for a few minutes and put water on them every few days. She removed the cover from the bird cage and talked to her canary, Gabriel. He always came to the bars of the cage to greet her. When Mrs. Williams started singing, Gabriel chirped along with her. The singing continued while she cleaned up the breakfast dishes and put them away, while she swept the kitchen floor and around the table where they ate breakfast, while she folded the cot and slid it behind the couch, and while she made the bed she and her husband slept in, which always included hugging their quilt for several minutes while she sang, "Jesus Loves The Little Children." The only time she stopped singing was when she was talking to Gabriel, when she was talking lovingly to the children who came through her lunch line, and when she was listening to the men tell about their day. She was still singing as she prepared a comfortable cot for Eamon to sleep on, pulled down the window shades, and covered Gabriel for the night. I sometimes snuck into her room to see if she sang in her sleep. She didn't.

One night when I snuck into her room, she opened her eyes and said, "Hi, sweetheart. Do you need something?" She didn't seem to be afraid of me, but I still disappeared. I wasn't aware of any adult seeing me since I passed away, so I wasn't sure what I was supposed to do. Maybe I was the one who was afraid.

Mrs. Williams went to church every Wednesday night. The men stayed home — in this way, mountain men and city men were the same. One Wednesday night, Mr. Williams sat at the table flipping through the pages of a mail-order catalogue while Eamon sat on the couch listening to the Big Band Music Mr. Williams grew to love when he served his country during WWII. Dog sat at Eamon's feet like usual, and I sat on the couch next to Eamon.

As we all listened to the radio, Eamon said with a voice that retained an Appalachian accent even though he was learning to speak like the city people around him, "I surely do wish I could find me a woman like Mrs. Williams to have for a wife."

"She is a fine woman. I'm a lucky man." Mr. Williams smiled for a minute before he said, "It shouldn't be hard for you to find a good woman like my wife."

"Mrs. Williams is the only woman I ever met like that — except MawMaw Tierney. My MawMaw was nice to everyone like Mrs. Williams is. She keeps everything clean like Mrs. Williams does, too. She's not happy like Mrs. Williams is though. She doesn't sing all the time. There ain't much to be singin' about where I come from."

"I see," Mr. Williams said. After a long pause, he continued, "If there are two women like that in this world, there must be more. Why don't you go to church with my wife on Sunday? I bet you can meet a good woman there."

Eamon immediately answered, "I'm not much for church. I only met the worst kinds of women there."

"I see. Maybe one day the right woman will just walk into the Goodwill®."

"How will I know if she's the right woman?"

Mr. Williams smiled big and said, "You'll know, son. You'll just know."

He did know. While Eamon, Mr. Williams, Dog, and I waited for the bus a few days later, a woman who was about two inches taller than Eamon left an apartment on the opposite side of the street, carefully looked both ways before crossing, and joined them at the bus stop. She had short, curly, black hair and thick eyebrows the same color as her hair. Her skin was light, her eyes were deep brown, and she had high cheekbones in a beautifully sculpted face. The only make-up she wore was light pink lipstick, and her uniform suggested she was either a nurse or a waitress. She looked down when she got to the bus stop and said, "Howdy." After that, she stood quietly next to the two men as she stared in the direction the bus would approach from.

I wondered if anyone else saw the spark between them that I was sure I saw. The way Dog was sniffing at her legs made me think he had. I wasn't sure what I thought yet. I needed to see if she was someone I needed to protect him from before I decided how I felt about this.

Mr. Williams must have seen the spark between them, too, because he pushed his elbow gently into Eamon's ribs and said, "I told you you would know."

Eamon's face turned deep red, and he looked at his shoes. He obviously didn't know how to approach a woman, and I could understand why. MawMaw Tierney was the only woman he'd ever been able to safely talk to, and that hadn't prepared him to talk to a woman he had romantic feelings for.

The beautiful woman was at the bus stop every morning and rode the same bus Eamon rode home every night. Every time they saw her, Mr. Williams nudged Eamon with his elbow and nodded in her direction, but Eamon never approached her.

They never would have said more than "Howdy" if Mr. Williams hadn't taken the lead one morning and said, "Good morning, young lady. If we're going to be seeing you every morning, we should be properly introduced. My name is Mr. Williams."

She glanced at him before she said, "My name is Clara."

Mr. Williams smiled and said, "It's nice to meet you, Miss Clara. Nice to meet you, indeed. This is my friend Eamon."

Eamon looked at his shoes as he said, "Howdy. I'm right pleased to meet you."

Clara looked directly at him for the first time and said, "I haven't heard that accent much since I left home. Are you from Hilltop?"

Eamon looked at her and answered, "Naw. I'm from Middlesboro."

She smiled and said, "It sure is nice to meet someone from close to home. Did work bring you up here, too?"

"Among other things."

"Work brought me up here. There isn't any work back home since the mine closed."

"Your mine closed?" Eamon asked, shocked. "Did the company store let people move on?"

"I take money home to my folks every weekend to help them pay off their company store debt, but I reckon the minin' company may just forget the rest once they get all their stuff off the mountain. How often do you go home to see your folks?"

"I don't."

Mr. Williams chimed in, "Eamon doesn't have a car, yet."

"My brother has a car," Clara said. "I share an apartment with two of my brothers. We all drive home together every weekend."

"That sounds right nice," Mr. Williams said as the bus pulled up to their stop and opened the door.

Mr. Williams gestured for Clara to get on the bus, so she boarded first. She sat on a seat near the front of the bus, and Eamon, Dog, and I followed Mr. Williams to the back. Eamon sat down next to Mr. Williams, and Dog and I sat on the seat across the aisle from them.

Mr. Williams nudged Eamon and said, "I'm not allowed to sit in the front of the bus, but you are. You need to get on up there and sit next to that pretty young woman before somebody else does."

"I can't," Eamon said as he shook his head.

"The only thing you can't do, son, is choose when you're goin' to be born and when you're goin' to die. You surely do have a choice to go up there and sit next to a pretty young woman. If you don't, someone else will."

As Eamon shook his head, Mr. Williams put his hand on Eamon's back and tried to push Eamon to his feet.

An elderly black man sitting behind them grabbed Mr. Williams arm and said, "Don't be touching that white boy. You know what they'll do to you for touching a white boy."

Eamon turned and said, "He's my friend. He touches me all the time."

The elderly man held his hands up and said, "I'm sorry, son. I didn't know."

Mr. Williams goaded Eamon until the bus got to Clara's destination. When she pulled the cord to signal the next stop, Mr. Williams took his hand off Eamon's back and said, "It's too late now, son. I hope she doesn't meet anyone else at work today."

Eamon jerked his gaze toward Mr. Williams and asked, "Do you really think that could happen?"

Mr. Williams laughed as he watched her get off the bus and cross the street. As she walked into a restaurant on the other side of the street, the bus pulled away. Mr. Williams elbowed Eamon lightly and said, "At least you know where she works."

"A lot of good that's goin' to do me. She works when I work. It's not like I'm goin' to see her in there."

"Then I guess you'd better exercise your God given right to sit at the front of the bus tomorrow morning."

The following morning, Mr. Williams continued to the back of the bus when Eamon stopped by Clara's seat and asked, "Can I sit next to you?"

She scooted over to the window seat as she said, "Yes."

Dog and I sat on the seat across the aisle from them. I still wasn't sure if she was someone I needed to protect Eamon from. She seemed like a gentle soul like MawMaw Tierney and Uncle Teagan were, but I wasn't stupid. The hypocritical preacher Eamon left the mountains to get away from taught me that people weren't always what they seemed to be, so I made a decision to spend some time watching her. If she wasn't a gentle soul, I'd find a way to make Eamon see it.

He sat next to her. His body was so stiff it didn't look like he could turn his neck to look at her.

He jumped when Clara asked, "Where do you work at?"

He took a deep breath, which loosened his muscles a little bit, and said, "At the Goodwill®."

"I work at Everett's Eatery."

"I know. I see you get off the bus and go in there every day."

They were silent for the rest of the short bus ride to Clara's work, except for when Clara said, "Excuse me," as she maneuvered past him to get to the aisle.

They sat together the next day, and this time Eamon didn't jump when she asked, "What do you do at Goodwill®?"

"Whatever Mr. Williams tells me to do. I unload trucks, unpack boxes, sweep up — whatever he needs from me."

"Oh," Clara said before they both went silent and saved Clara's next comment for the next day. Shortly after Eamon sat next to her the following day, she said "I ain't never met a white man who works for a black man before."

"Mr. Williams is right nice. He's better to me than my own Pa was."

"I'm glad to hear that. We've got a black man workin' at the restaurant. He washes the dishes in the back room. They won't let him work out front where white folks can see him."

"Is that right?"

She nodded.

It was the next day before Eamon found the courage to ask, "Is that black man that washes dishes at your work good to you like Mr. Williams is good to me?"

"Yes. He's a real nice man. Right often I go back in the kitchen and eat lunch with him. I feel sorry for him. He looks so lonely back there. The other girls pick on me for doin' that though."

"The other girls?"

"The other waitresses," Clara said as she pulled the cord to signal the next stop. "My stop's comin' up. I don't have a long ride, but my legs get so tired waitin' on people all day that I take the bus."

Eamon patted his handicapped leg and said, "I can surely understand that."

It wasn't until the next day when Clara stood to get off the bus that she grabbed the handrail, turned back to Eamon, and asked, "What happened to your leg?"

He looked away from her and said, "I got hurt."

"I'm sorry," she said as the bus jolted to a stop. "I reckon I'll be seein' ya tomorrow."

He nodded before she walked down the aisle and got off the bus.

He did sit with her the next day, and the day after that, and the day after that. They continued to sit together for several weeks. Each day they talked a little more than the day before. Right around the time Eamon's body looked loose and comfortable around her, Mr. Williams helped him get a driver's license and a car. I assumed this meant their courtship would end, because Eamon wouldn't be seeing her on the bus anymore. If it took him this long to get comfortable talking to her on the bus, I didn't know how he would find the courage to talk to her any place else. I soon learned I didn't have anything to worry about. As usual, Mr. Williams guided Eamon to the next thing he should do to stay in touch with Clara.

CHAPTER THREE: TESTING LOVE

Getting a car was a dream come true for Eamon. He had dreamed about owning a car before he left home, but our father made that dream impossible. The company store took Eamon's paychecks to pay off our father's debt, and our father showed his gratitude by buying more stuff he didn't need. The dream come true shone on Eamon's face as he drove off the lot in a dark teal 1940 Plymouth Coupe.

Once I got in the car, I could understand why Eamon dreamed of owning one of these machines. Even my ghost body loved the feeling of the wind coming through the window and hitting me as I sat in the back seat with Dog. I could tell Dog loved that feeling, too, because he kept hanging his head out the window to better enjoy the feeling of the wind. It was exciting to watch the city passing by as we moved faster than the bus ever went.

While they looked at the car together, Mr. Williams assured Eamon that, even though the car was already over ten years old, it was in good enough shape for a young man who was gifted with fixing mechanical things to keep it in good repair. He said to Eamon, "After all the delivery trucks you've fixed, keeping this thing running ought to be a piece of cake."

As they drove home, Eamon said, "Mr. Williams, I surely have been wantin' me a car for a long time, but now that I have one, I think I'd rather be takin' the bus."

Mr. Williams looked at Eamon, smiled big, and said, "It wouldn't have anything to do with that pretty young girl, now, would it?"

Eamon blushed and answered, "Maybe a little."

"Well, I guess I've got something else to teach you, son. Women like a man with a car. You need to invite her to go for a ride with you. I suspect those women who make fun of her for eating in the kitchen with a black man would be right jealous if they saw her being dropped off at work by a man with a nice car. Why don't you drive on over to her apartment right now and show it to her?"

"I can't. She goes home every weekend to the mountains. She won't be back until Sunday night."

"Well, I guess we'll just have to park this fine automobile in front of her apartment where she crosses the street to get to the bus stop on Monday morning."

That is just what they did. When Clara looked in the car as she was walking around the front of it to cross the street, her eyes got wide and she gasped when she saw Eamon sitting in the driver's seat. She smiled at Eamon before she looked at Mr. Williams in the back seat and said, "This isn't the bus. You're allowed to sit in the front seat."

Dog and I were in the back seat next to Mr. Williams. As usual, she didn't see us.

Mr. Williams smiled and said, "I left the front seat open for you, Miss Clara. Would you like a ride?"

She nodded. She sat on the passenger seat and asked, "When did you get a car?"

Eamon kept his eyes on the steering wheel as he stammered, "Me and Mr. Williams went to the car lot near the Goodwill® on Saturday. Stayin' with Mr. Williams let me save enough to buy it. She's an old one, but she's a good one."

Clara closed the car door and asked, "Now that you've got a car, did you go home this weekend to see your family?"

"Naw," Mr. Williams interjected. "He just got the car on Saturday. Half the weekend is gone by then."

Clara leaned back in her seat, hugged her purse, and said, "It sure is pretty."

They didn't talk any more until Eamon parked across the street from her work.

"Thank you for the ride," she said as she opened the car door.

"Can I pick you up after work?" Eamon stammered.

"I'd be much obliged," Clara said as she got out of the car and closed the door.

And he did pick her up after work that day, and the next day, and the day after that, and the day after that. Mr. Williams always sat in the back seat with Dog and me. He never spoke. It seemed as if he was staying quiet to force Eamon and Clara to talk. After a while, it worked.

One night after they rode together long enough that they were talking comfortably with each other, Mr. Williams leaned forward and said, "Drop me off at our apartment first, and you young people can go for a nice ride together. Pretty soon the weather will be too cold to enjoy a ride, so you should enjoy it while you can."

"Is that ok with you?" Eamon glanced at Clara and asked.

When she nodded, he quickly looked away.

A few minutes later, Eamon parked in front of Mr. Williams' apartment. Mr. Williams got out of the car, but Dog and I stayed in the back seat. We still needed to make sure Eamon didn't need to be protected from this woman, although I have to admit I was starting to like her.

As they pulled away from the curb, Clara said, "Now that you've got a car, you can go home on the weekends and see yer folks."

"Not everyone wants to see their folks," Eamon blurted out in an angry tone.

I understood why he sounded so angry. Even though I wanted to see MawMaw Tierney and Uncle Teagan, my ghost body wretched from a stomach that didn't exist anymore at the thought of seeing everyone else.

Clara looked at him and asked, "Why not?" When he didn't answer, she asked again.

Eamon tightened his grip on the steering wheel and said, "Some people's folks aren't so nice."

"What did your folks do to you?"

Eamon gripped the steering wheel so tight his knuckles turned white and his breathing became shallow and fast as he answered, "You know how you asked what happened to my leg, and I told you it was an accident. My folks caused that accident."

"But, it was an accident —"

"It wasn't an accident," Eamon said as he gripped the steering wheel even tighter and accelerated. "She did it out of pure, spiteful meanness."

Clara put her palm on the dashboard and said, "You're drivin' awfully fast."

He slowed the car down and said, "I'm sorry. I just get so mad when I think about it."

She grasped the arm rest and said, "Maybe we ought to go back to my apartment and sit on the stoop and talk. I've got some Coca-Cola® in the refrigerator. I think I've even got some salty peanuts we could dump in it. We could each have a bottle."

Eamon didn't answer. He drove to the next side street, used it to turn around, and drove back to Clara's apartment. He didn't speak again until Clara joined him on her stoop after going to her apartment to get them each a bottle of Coca-Cola® and some peanuts. Dog and I stayed in the back seat of the car, but since the windows were down, we could still hear them.

After Eamon dumped some peanuts in his Coca-Cola®, he took a long drink, wiped his mouth on his sleeve, and said, "I'm sorry. I didn't mean to scare you in the car. I just don't like to talk about it."

Clara dumped some peanuts in her Coca-Cola®, took a drink, rested the bottle on her knee, and stared straight ahead.

Their bottles were almost empty before Eamon spoke again to ask, "Are you mad at me?"

I willed my ghost body from the back seat of the car and lay my hand on his shoulder to try to bring him some comfort. I thought this was going to be a difficult conversation.

"Naw. I just don't know what to say."

"I don't know what to say either."

After several more minutes, Clara asked, "Was she punishin' you?"

"For bein' alive," he answered. After a long pause, he asked, "Haven't you ever know'd anybody who hit people for no particular reason?"

Clara sat her pop bottle on the step between them, cleared her throat, and said, "Well, yes. My older brother, well, he beats his wife. People say she brings it on herself — but he's really big and she's not." She shook her head like she was trying to release it from cobwebs and said, "I don't know."

"Everybody said I brought it on myself. My MawMaw was the only person who was ever kind to me, and she said it wasn't my fault. She sent me up here to the Goodwill® to keep me alive."

Clara looked at him for the first time since they sat down and said, "I'm real sorry that happened to you."

Eamon nodded.

After a long silence, Clara said, "I'd better get back in. My brothers are goin' to be wonderin' what I'm doin' out here for so long."

"I reckon you don't want to be talkin' to someone like me no more."

"I still want to talk to you," she said as she stood up.

"Winter's just around the corner," he said as he looked up at her. "Would you like to continue ridin' to work with me and Mr. Williams, so you can stay out of the cold?"

"I would like that," she said as she pulled her sweater around herself and crossed her arms to keep it closed.

They smiled at each other before she walked to the entry door on the side of her building. He watched her until she was in the building before he picked up the empty pop bottles and carried them to Mr. and Mrs. Williams' building across the street.

Eamon, Mr. Williams, Dog, and I waited in the car in front of her building the next morning like we always did, and she came out and got in the car like she always did. Things were not like they always were. The tension that existed between them while they were getting to know each other was back. They didn't say anything to each other until she thanked him for the ride before getting out of the car at her job. It remained that way until the first bad snowstorm of the season.

The first snowstorm of the winter season kept Clara and her brothers from going home to the mountains. They called home to let their parents know and to remind a brother who still lived at home to stay sober and keep a close eye on them during the bad weather. Once that was settled, Clara accepted her boss, Everett's, offer of extra hours. He thought the weekend might be busier than usual, because so many of the Appalachian families were staying in the city that weekend.

Eamon agreed to drive Clara to and from work on Saturday, but the day was so cold his car wouldn't start when it was time to pick her up. Dog and I sat in the back seat while he tried to get the car to start.

He worked on it for so long that Mrs. Williams came out and said, "Son, you've got to come in and get warm. You're going to catch your death out here trying to start that car in this rain and snow."

Eamon closed the hood and said, "I don't think it's goin' to start, but I can't just leave her stranded at work. Things haven't been the same between us since I told her what my folks did to me. If I don't pick her up, she'll probably never speak to me again."

"I'm sure someone from her work will help her. She won't be stranded."

Eamon pulled the collar of Mrs. Williams' coat tighter around her neck and said, "You go on inside and get warm before you catch your death of cold. I'll give up on the car, but I'm goin' to catch the bus to her work and make sure she gets home okay. In just a few minutes, I'll be on a warm bus, so you don't need to worry."

"I'd really rather you didn't."

"I'll be okay. I promise. I'll be home before you know it, so you make sure you have some water on the boil for some coffee. Okay?"

"Okay," she sat as she patted his arm. "You be careful now."

He watched her until she was in the building before he walked over to the bus stop. Dog and I waited for the bus with him. After an hour, I wasn't sure if the bus was even running in this weather. I was getting as worried about him as Mrs. Williams was.

I willed my ghost body to Clara's work. I hoped if I found her safe that I could somehow help Eamon understand that and persuade him to follow Mrs. Williams' advice. When I got there, Clara was staring out the window. The restaurant was closed. The only light that was on was the one behind the counter, and her boss, Everett, stood in front of it and blocked most of the light. He was a tall, broad-shouldered, dark-haired man who might have looked scary in this dim lighting to a woman who didn't know him. As he stepped from behind the counter, he said, "I don't think he's going to show up."

When Everett moved from in front of the light bulb, light washed over Clara as she turned to him. Her stone features and tight lips revealed her anger before her voice did. She remained calm even though her voice was tight when she said, "I can't believe he didn't show up. He promised me he would be here."

"Maybe he got stuck in the snow."

Clara walked to the counter, lay her purse on it, and pulled her coat tighter around herself before she sat down.

"I'm sorry it's cold in here," Everett said. "I try to keep it at this temperature, because it gets too hot when the restaurant is full of customers if it's set any higher. It will be a waste of money to turn it up just before we leave. A furnace uses twice as much energy to increase the heat as it does to keep it the same temperature."

"That's okay," she said as she took her gloves off and lay them on her purse.

Everett sat next to her, cleared his throat, and said, "Maybe you're too hard on men. Like that Mike boy — "

She turned to Everett and said, "He still lived with his mother and was always askin' me for money. Where I come from, a man doesn't ask a woman for money. He stopped at home ten times durin' one walk to ask his Mom for a cigarette, because he couldn't buy his own."

"What about that red-haired —"

"He's one of the men who used to sleep with loose Imojean," Clara said as she looked forward again. She sat so stiff she looked like the cold had frozen her in place.

"What about that airline pilot. You'd be a rich woman today — "

"He was ten years older than me and cared more about that plane than he did me — but I guess this one doesn't care much either!"

Everett patted her shoulder before he said, "Please don't get mad at me for saying this, but maybe if you talked to them and let them know how you feel instead of just walking away. Your needs matter in a relationship, too. You're allowed to speak up and tell them what you want."

"Tellin' someone how you feel or what you want isn't goin' to change who they are," Clara said softly. She released enough tightness from her body to pick up her gloves and play with the fingers. It almost seemed as if playing with the gloves was taking her into a state of meditation as she said, "My brother's wife was the only woman back home who spoke up and said what she needed, and my brother —" She jolted out of her relaxed state of mind and hurriedly picked up her purse as she said, "Listen to me! What am I talkin' about? I just ramble sometimes." She walked to the front door, turned to Everett, and said, "Will you give me a ride home? I don't know if the buses are even runnin' in this weather. I'll be happy to give you some money for gas."

Everett stood as he said, "Of course I'll give you a ride home, and I don't want any money. I stayed with you, so I could make sure you made it home okay. You're like a daughter to me. What kind of person would I be if I made you pay me to drive you home?"

Clara walked outside and waited in front of the building while Everett put his coat on and turned off the light. I followed her outside and immediately willed my ghost body into the back seat of Everett's car. I couldn't feel the cold, but the snow blowing around me was disorienting, so I got in the car and out of the snow as fast as I could.

I watched them as they approached the car. Everett tried to take Clara's arm to make sure she didn't slip on the ice, but she pulled away. She also opened the passenger door as he reached for the handle to do it for her.

When they were on the road, Everett said, "These roads are mighty bad tonight. Please just hear what Eamon has to say before you break up with him."

"I'll see what he has to say." After a long silence, Clara hugged her purse and continued, "The Wednesday night before you hired me, I told my congregation I was goin' home. I told them it was just too hard up here. I couldn't find a job, and I didn't have any hope of marryin' if I had to choose from these city slickers. After the service, one of the Elders pulled me aside and told me the Holy Spirit told him I needed to stay here, because the job I needed and the man I wanted were both here. You hired me two days later, and that made my doubts go away. When I met Eamon at the bus stop a few months later, I thought I surely made the right decision to stay here. Now, I wonder if I should have just gone back home like I planned on doin'. There's a reason we all go home every weekend. We don't belong here."

"I don't know if the Holy Spirit gives messages like that. I don't know if you were supposed to stay or go back home. All I know is I'm glad you stayed. You're the best waitress and the hardest worker I ever had. You feel like a daughter to me. I'll sure miss you if go back home. I hope you'll think twice about it before you up and leave. You came here, because there weren't any jobs back home. What are going to do if you go back there now?"

They drove the rest of the way in silence. Every time the car skidded, Clara put her palm on the dashboard. A trip that usually took less than ten minutes took over half an hour, but they made it home safely.

After Clara got out of the car, she leaned over so she could see Everett in the car and said, "Call me and let me know when you get home safely — or have Crystal call me."

"I will."

Clara closed the door, put her purse strap over her shoulder, pulled her coat tighter around herself, and checked both ways several times before she walked across the street toward her apartment with her hand held in front of her face to protect her eyes from the stinging wind. I stayed with her even though this wind disoriented me, because I knew Eamon was waiting on the other side of the street for her.

When she got to her steps, Eamon said, "Clara."

She looked up, saw Eamon, and asked, "What are you doin' here?"

"I'm sorry. I said I'd pick you up, but my car wouldn't start. I tried to fix it, but it was so cold I could barely touch the parts. I was waitin' for the bus, so I could come down to your work and make sure you were okay. After a while, I realized the bus wasn't comin'. I decided to wait and make sure you made it home okay and let you know what happened. I didn't want you to be mad at me."

"Oh my goodness! Have you been out here all this time?"

"About two hours."

"Oh, my goodness," Clara said as she grabbed his arm. "You have to come into the apartment with me and warm up. You must be about froze to death."

She started walking with Eamon's arm in her hand, but he couldn't move his crippled leg and said, "Wait a minute, Clara. My knee froze up."

When I saw how much the cold affected his leg, I felt bad that I willed my ghost body to Clara instead of staying with him. What if something would have happened to him while I was gone?

Clara stopped while he moved his leg for several minutes. When it was loosened up, they walked to the side door and entered the building.

"Oh," Eamon said when she closed the door. "That heat feels mighty good."

"My apartment is on the third floor. Can you make it up there?"

"I can, but I might be movin' slow."

Clara held onto Eamon's arm as he limped up the stairs. By the second floor, he warmed up enough that he was walking better. By the

34

time they reached her apartment, he was walking with his normal limp. She released his arm to get the apartment key out of her purse.

After Clara opened the door, she asked, "Emmet, Morgan, are you home?"

"I'm here," Emmett answered. "I'm in the kitchen."

"I brought someone home," Clara said as she grasped Eamon's arm and led him into the apartment. Dog and I followed them in.

After she closed the door, Eamon, Dog, and I looked around. Clara's apartment looked a lot like Mr. and Mrs. Williams' apartment. It was the same floor plan as well as the same sparse furnishings and cleanliness. The only difference was the two roll-away beds in the middle of the living room that were both decorated with colorful quilts we would later learn Clara made.

Clara saw Eamon looking at the apartment and asked, "Do you like it?"

"It's very nice and very clean. I'm just surprised that it looks exactly like Mr. and Mrs. Williams' apartment across the street. Are all of the apartments in the city the same?"

"I don't know. I haven't been in any apartments other than this one and my sister's down the street."

Emmett walked out of the kitchen holding a sandwich. He was a tall, thin man who looked so much like Johnny Cash that Eamon asked, "Aren't you that famous singer, Johnny — yeah, Johnny Cash?"

Emmett laughed and said, "Naw. I can't sing a lick. Our sister Lana's apartment does look like this one. I don't think Clara would notice though, because when the two of them get together, they're too focused on the dozen doughnuts they split between them every time they're both off work at the same time."

"Aw, hush now. We don't do it that often."

Emmett took a bite of the sandwich, chewed, and swallowed before he said, "Yeah, the last time they both had a day off at the same time, they sat in Lana's kitchen from the crack of dawn until after dark drinkin' coffee and eatin' doughnuts. They didn't quit until the whole dozen was gone."

"You hush, now. You're goin' to have Eamon here thinkin' I'm a pig or somethin'."

"Nobody as skinny as you could be a pig," Emmett said as he walked toward Eamon. "I guess you're this Eamon that's been courtin' my sister out on the stoop since the end of the summer. It's nice to finally meet you."

Eamon took the hand Emmett extended and said, "I reckon it must be me. I think I'm the only Eamon around these here parts."

Emmett laughed and said, "I think you're the only Eamon courtin' my sister, too."

Clara took off her coat and lay it on the couch as she said, "He's been standin' out front in this cold waitin' for me. He's about froze to death. Why don't you take his coat, Emmet, and I'll make him a cup of coffee and something to eat. He's about froze stiff."

She disappeared into the kitchen as Emmett asked, "Can I take your coat?"

"I reckon I'm still cold enough to be needin' it," Eamon said and pulled the coat closer around him.

"Suit yourself," Emmett said as he walked over to the couch and sat on Clara's coat. When Eamon didn't move, Emmett said, "You're welcome to have a seat."

Eamon sat on the other end of the couch. He ran his hand along the brown floral fabric that covered the couch arm and said, "This be a right pretty couch. I've never seen one this nice before."

"We got it at the Goodwill®."

Eamon looked at Emmett and asked, "At the Goodwill®? That's where I work."

"We didn't see you there."

"I work at the distribution center. I unload the trucks."

Emmett looked at Eamon's leg for a minute before he said, "I don't mean to be pryin', but how can you unload trucks with your leg twisted up like that?"

"It don't bother me none. I'm right happy unloadin' trucks. I'm stronger than I look."

"I reckon you must be."

Clara returned with a cup of coffee. She sat it on the dark wood of the rustic coffee table that sat in front of the couch and said, "I hope this makes you feel better."

"I'm sure it will," Eamon said as he scooted forward to the edge of the couch, picked up the cup, and took a drink. He held the steaming cup under his face for a minute before he said, "That sure does hit the spot."

36

Clara hurried back to the kitchen and returned a few minutes later with a sandwich. She sat the plate on the coffee table and said, "I reckon you must be hungry after standin' out in that cold for two hours."

"You stood out there for two hours?" Emmett asked as Eamon sat the coffee cup down and picked up the sandwich.

Eamon nodded as he took a bite.

Emmett sat forward on the couch and, always the kidder, asked, "You stood out there for two hours in this weather for my sister?"

"Yes, he did," Clara answered.

Emmett looked at Clara and teased, "Now, that's devotion. Have you two been doin' anything I need to be tellin' Mommy about next weekend?"

"Don't you dare go gettin' her upset over nothing. The most we've done is sit out there on the stoop."

"Don't I know it," Emmett teased. "That stoop has a groove in it that didn't used to be there before y'all started sittin' out there all the time."

Eamon ate his sandwich and drank his coffee while the siblings teased each other. Even though his red face showed that he was still cold, he didn't ask for another cup of coffee until it was offered to him.

After three cups, he left. Clara watched from the front window as Eamon limped across the street to Mr. and Mrs. Williams' apartment. I watched from the window with her, because I wanted to know what they said about Eamon after he left.

When Eamon was safely in Mr. and Mrs. Williams' building, Clara turned to Emmett and said, "Can you believe he stood out there for two hours to make sure I made it home okay when his car wouldn't start to pick me up?"

"I reckon he's what they call a gentleman around these here parts."

She turned and looked out the window again before she said, "I'm goin' to marry him."

I willed my ghost body back to Mr. and Mrs. Williams' apartment and spent the night thinking about how I was going to figure out if this woman was someone Eamon would be safe spending the rest of his life with.

CHAPTER FOUR: YOUNG AND IN LOVE

Since I knew Clara's plan was to marry my brother, I decided to go to work with her on Monday. I wanted to make sure she was really what she appeared to be instead of a hypocrite like that mountain preacher Eamon ran to the city to get away from. When Clara got out of Eamon's car at her job, my ghost body followed her. Dog stayed in the car, because I asked him to keep an eye on Eamon.

Everett and all of the employees were standing at the window watching her cross the street. When she came in the door, they all turned to her as Everett said, "Well, I guess you didn't break up with him."

I stood just inside the door. I wanted to see what this place was like before I decided where I would spend the day.

"I reckon I didn't," Clara said as she took off her coat.

"Does this mean one of your boyfriends is finally going to cut the mustard?" Everett asked as all of the waitresses left the window and returned to their work.

Clara walked to the employee coat rack that stood by the back wall near the double doors that led to the kitchen and hung up her coat without answering. On her way back, she went behind the counter, filled a cup with coffee and a little cream, carried it to a table near the middle of the room, and sat it in front of an old man who was smiling as he watched her approach.

"Thank you, Mrs. — uh, what is his last name?" the old man said when Clara sat the cup of coffee in front of him.

"You're the same dirty ol' goat you always are, L.C.," Clara answered. "If you're goin' to take up this table all day every day, maybe we ought to put you to work."

L.C. ran his hand through his white beard as he said, "They don't make facial hair nets, so Everett won't let me work. Besides, it's a full-time job keeping up with your boyfriends."

"Can I get you anything else, or are you just goin' to drink up all of our coffee again like you do every day?"

"I've told you once, and I'll tell you again. If you'd just let me be your boyfriend, all of your romantic troubles would be over."

Clara laughed and said, "Now, how will I explain that to my folks when I bring you home? They'll think you're Santa Claus, and I haven't been feedin' you."

L.C. laughed as she walked away. He obviously wasn't offended by her description of him, so he must have known it was accurate. He was a tiny little man with white hair and a white beard, both of which were just a bit too long without being scruffy. The deep blue eyes that sat in his wrinkled face expressed kindness, and he seemed like he was always ready to laugh. He had most of the physical and all of the personality traits of a good Santa, except he dressed more like an old west undertaker. He wore a casual black suit with a white tee shirt under the jacket, and from the tattered look of the jacket, it seemed he wore it often.

As Clara went behind the counter, retrieved a pink apron like all of the other waitresses wore from a shelf under the counter and put it on, L.C. asked, "Did you give him a little kissy on the jaw before you got out of the car?"

"That ain't none of your business," Clara answered.

I sat across from L.C., but he wasn't any more aware of my ghost body than the rest of them were. He spent the entire day teasing all of the waitresses. Some of them seemed annoyed with him, and some of them teased him back. Clara alternated between annoyance and putting him in his place in a teasing manner. Sometimes he made me feel annoyed, but I kept sitting with him because I liked his bright blue eyes, his frequent smile, and his uninhibited laughter. I had never met a man who expressed happiness like he did, and I wanted to be near him. When he moved to the counter during the lunch rush, I followed him and sat next to him.

39

About an hour before Clara's shift ended, a young man came in and sat at the counter on the other side of L.C.. He was such an attractive young man that I peeked around L.C. several times just to get a look at his curly golden-brown hair that hung almost to his shoulders in the back and curled around his face in the front. He was tall, muscular, and wore his work uniform well even though it was dirty in the same way Eamon's clothes were dirty when he worked on the delivery trucks. Each time Clara interacted with him, his flirting was so blatant that it left her cheeks red.

After about a half hour, L.C. smiled big and said, "Mister, you're wasting your time flirting with that one. She's got a boyfriend. She's so head over heels it's almost shameful. You should have seen the kiss she placed on his jaw this morning when he dropped her off. When he picks her up at night, she gets so excited she pert near runs into the wall racing to the door to meet him."

The man turned to Clara and said, "I'm sorry. I didn't know."

About fifteen minutes later, Eamon parked his car in front of the restaurant. As L.C. predicted, Clara ran to the front door to meet him.

L.C. guffawed and yelled, "Do you see what I mean? Watch out for that wall, Clara. You won't be no good pouring my coffee if you hurt yourself."

"Very funny," Clara said as she opened the door to let Eamon in.

Of course, there was no display of affection as L.C. predicted. They were both too shy and proper to show affection in public.

As the door closed, Clara said, "I've got another fifteen minutes before I get off work. Go have a seat at the counter, and I'll get you a cup of coffee."

Eamon nodded and sat near the front window at the other end of the counter from L.C. and the curly-haired young man.

L.C. looked around the curly-haired young man, laughed and said, "You're welcome to sit here with me and this young man, Eamon. I think the two of you have quite a bit in common."

Before Eamon could answer, L.C.'s gaze turned to a woman who walked in wearing skin tight jeans, a low-cut shirt, and shiny black high-heeled shoes. She sat at the counter next to Eamon, asked Everett for a cup of coffee, and lit a cigarette.

Eamon noticed her out of the corner of his eye and immediately jerked his head in her direction. He stared at her for several seconds

40

before she said, "Take a picture. It'll last longer." He looked away, but he kept peeking at her out of the corner of his eye. After several minutes, she asked, "Okay, buddy, what gives? Why do you keep looking at me?"

Eamon looked at the counter and answered, "I know you."

"And just where do you think you know me from?"

"Never mind," Eamon said as Clara sat a cup of black coffee in front of him while looking suspiciously at the woman.

Eamon stopped glancing at the woman, but she kept glancing at him as she drank the coffee Everett got for her. She chain smoked three cigarettes during the fifteen minutes before Clara got off work.

When Clara's shift was over, she took her coat off the coat rack as she said, "Okay, Eamon, my shift's over. We can go now."

Eamon took the last sip of coffee in his cup, got up, and limped to the back of the restaurant to help Clara put her coat on.

As Eamon and Clara walked toward the front door, the woman spun around and said, "I do know you. You're that crippled boy my friends were picking on that night in front of the Goodwill®."

Eamon looked at his shoes as he said, "Yes, that was me."

She stood up and walked to him as she said, "I'm so sorry. You remember I tried to get them to stop. I didn't want them to be treating you like that. They're always doing stuff like that, and it makes me so mad."

When the woman got to them, she reached for Eamon's hands, but Clara stepped between them and said, "We've got to be goin' now."

As they walked toward the door, the woman said, "You're looking better than you did that night. You've gained some weight, and you've got better clothes now. I'm glad to see it."

They left the restaurant without answering her. I followed them to the car and joined Dog in the back seat. Clara didn't say anything during the ride home.

When Eamon parked in front of her apartment, he asked, "You're not mad at me over that woman, are you?"

"I saw the way you were lookin' at her."

"I was only lookin' at her, because I remembered her. She and her friends attacked me the first night I came to Cincinnati. I don't know what they would have done to me if Mr. Williams wouldn't have pulled out his shotgun and saved me from them. I didn't think I'd ever see any of them again, so I was right uncomfortable when she sat down next to me."

"So there wasn't ever anything between the two of you?"

"No. Besides, she's got a boyfriend. One of them touched her in a bad way, and she told him Frankie would kill him."

"Yeah, Frankie. He was her boyfriend last month. She's got a new one this month, and she'll have another one by next month. She goes through men like most people go through toothpaste. Her name is Imojean. Everyone around here knows all about her. She's the town whore. She sleeps with other men when she has a boyfriend, and she sleeps with married men all of the time. It's true that Everett isn't married to Crystal, and I can't say I agree with them livin' in sin the way they do, but they are livin' together. He is taken. Imojean still tries to sleep with him all the time. She probably came in the restaurant tonight to flirt with him."

"You ain't got to worry about me. Women like that ain't nothing but trouble, and I've had enough trouble in my life. She reminds me too much of my Pa's Ma, and I've had my fill of those kinds of connivin' women. Believe me, you're the only woman I want. You're one of the few good women I've met in my life."

Clara smiled, kissed him on the cheek, and got out of the car. The next morning when he dropped her off at work, she kissed him on the cheek again. The kissing was making me feel embarrassed, but that didn't stop me from keeping an eye on Eamon and those who wanted to be close to him. I got out of the car and followed Clara into the restaurant when he dropped her off, and Dog stayed in the car again to keep an eye on Eamon.

When Clara entered the restaurant, L.C. was sitting at the same table as the previous morning. He looked at Clara and said, "I knew you gave him a little kissy on the jaw before you got out of that car every morning."

Clara smiled and said, "I already told you that ain't none of your business."

L.C. guffawed as Imojean spun around on her seat at the counter and said, "Maybe you ought to make it his business. Maybe he can give you some tips on how to keep that man, because he sure couldn't keep his eyes off of me yesterday. I guess you just look too pure and innocent to keep a man like that interested for long."

I sat across from L.C. and stared hard at Imojean while Clara walked to the employee coat rack and hung up her coat.

As Clara walked to the counter to get L.C.'s coffee, Imojean said, "I guess you aren't saying anything, because you know I'm right."

Clara carried the coffee to L.C.'s table. When she sat it in front of him, L.C. whispered, "Don't let her get away with talking to you like that, or you'll never get rid of her. She'll be in here gloating like that every morning."

Clara smiled and whispered, "I don't even want to give that woman the time of day."

When Clara walked away, L.C. grabbed her hand and said, "I'm not kidding. Stand up for yourself. I've known that woman in a carnal way, so believe me when I say you can't let her get the better of you. Do you understand?"

Clara nodded, returned to the counter, and retrieved her apron from the counter shelf.

As she put her apron on, Imojean said, "I guess I'd be too choked up to talk, too, if I knew my man wanted another woman."

L.C. laughed.

Imojean turned to him and asked, "What are you laughing at?"

L.C. kept laughing as he said, "I think that's the other way around. You're the one who is always wanting another man."

"Shut your mouth, you old bastard!"

Clara looked at Imojean and said, "Don't talk to him like that! As a matter of fact, don't use that kind of language in this restaurant — this is a family place. And, you ought to know that my man was lookin' at you, because you made him so uncomfortable. How was he supposed to act when someone who assaulted him his first night in town sat right next to him? He told me last night you were a connivin' woman who reminded him of one of the worst women he'd ever known."

"You were a waitress and not a preacher the last time I checked," Imojean said. "How about stepping down from the pulpit and pouring me a cup of coffee?" As Clara filled a coffee cup, Imojean asked, "Are you engaged to that man?" When Clara sat the coffee in front of Imojean without answering, Imojean said, "Well, you never are going to be unless you open those legs a little bit. No man is going to marry a woman before he test drives the car."

As Clara walked away, she answered, "If that's what it takes to get married, I'll gladly stay single for the rest of my life. It would kill my mother if I ignored everything she taught me about sexual immorality growin' up. Besides, how many men have you been with? I don't see a ring on your hand."

L.C. guffawed loudly for nearly a minute before he said, "That's all right, Imojean. I'm still here for you. Come on over here and give an old man some sugar."

Imojean threw a quarter on the counter and ran to the front door. She knocked the coat tree that stood by the door over as she yanked her coat off it before storming out of the restaurant.

As Clara walked to the coat tree to pick it up, L.C. said, 'I'm proud of you, young lady! I knew you had it in you to stand up for yourself if you had to!'

Clara's busy work day ended with the usual teasing when Eamon picked her up. When he parked the car in front of her house, I felt embarrassed that I would have to watch her kiss him again, but that kiss didn't happen. Instead, she looked across the street and asked, "What is Imojean doin' standin' in front of your building?"

Eamon looked across the street and said, "I don't rightly know. Maybe she's here to visit Mr. and Mrs. Williams."

"Mr. and Mrs. Williams wouldn't have anything to do with the likes of her."

"I don't rightly know then."

"Is she here to see you?"

"I swear to you she isn't here to see me. Why would I want to have anything to do with her when she was one of that gang that attacked me?"

"She'd better not be here to see you," Clara said as she got out of the car and slammed the door.

"Wait, Clara," Eamon said as he got out of the car and ran to her so fast that his bad leg almost made him fall several times. When he got to her, he grabbed her upper arms, looked into her eyes, and said, "Please don't punish me for what she's doin'. I don't want anything to do with the likes of her."

Clara looked across the street at Imojean and said, "I'm not goin' to have this conversation with her standin' over there watchin'. Get rid of her, and we can talk about this later."

44

Clara pulled away from Eamon and walked to the side door of her building. Instead of going inside, she watched Eamon as he turned the car around and parked across the street in front of Mr. and Mrs. Williams' building. Before he could get out of the car, Imojean rested her forearms on the open passenger window, which better revealed what her low-cut shirt was meant to reveal, and started talking to Eamon. He didn't look at or answer her, so she met him in front of the car and blocked him. When he tried to step around her, she put her arms around his neck and tried to give him a hug. He started shaking, which got worse when he looked over his shoulder and saw Clara watching. I guess his fear of losing Clara made him more aggressive then I'd ever seen him before, because he pulled Imojean's arms from around his neck, pushed her away, and yelled loudly enough for Clara to hear, "Stay away from me! Why would I have anything to do with the likes of you when I already know I want to marry Clara?"

From the back seat of the car, I looked across the street and saw Clara smile before she entered her building.

When I looked back at Imojean and saw the look on her face, I remembered one other time Eamon had been that aggressive — the last time he protected himself from that nasty mountain preacher. Maybe Imojean acting as sexually aggressive as the preacher brought up memories that caused Eamon to be so much more assertive than he normally was.

Eamon walked past Imojean and entered Mr. and Mrs. Williams' building. Dog and I got out of the car and followed him. By the time he got inside their apartment, his breathing was getting labored and his shakiness was getting worse. He leaned against the door and lay his palms on his chest as he gasped for air.

Mr. and Mrs. Williams were sitting at the card table. Mr. Williams was listening to the radio and looking at a catalogue that came in the mail, and Mrs. Williams was darning a sock. They both jumped up and ran to Eamon. Mr. Williams put Eamon's arm over his shoulder and helped Eamon to the couch while Mrs. Williams walked beside them asking repeatedly if he was okay. When Mr. Williams had Eamon seated comfortably, Eamon leaned back and started shaking harder. Dog lay at his feet as he watched his every move, so I sat next to Dog and petted him, which calmed both of us a little bit.

Mrs. Williams took one of Eamon's shaking hands and said, "Lord Almighty, child. What happened to you?"

Between gasping breaths, Eamon said, "I don't rightly know."

Mr. Williams took Eamon's other shaking hand and said, "Take deep breaths, son." Then, he looked at Mrs. Williams and said, "I think we should take him to the hospital."

Eamon sat up and said, "No, No, I'm okay. I'm startin' to feel a little better now."

"What happened?" Mr. Williams asked.

Eamon took several deep breaths and stammered, "I don't rightly know. This lady named Imojean came into Clara's work yesterday. It turns out she's that girl who was with those punks the first night I got into town — the ones who attacked me in front of your store. She followed me home tonight and was waitin' outside. She was tryin' to hug me, and, well, I don't know. I remembered my first night in town and those boys. Then, I remembered how they reminded me of my people back home, and, well, I started havin' a hard time breathin'. I barely made it into your apartment."

Mr. Williams looked at Mrs. Williams and said, "Get the boy a glass of water."

Mrs. Williams got up and went to the kitchen.

While she was gone, Mr. Williams said, "I don't know what causes it, but a spell like this has happened to me from time to time. Nigh on about fifteen years ago, a bunch of white men beat me almost to death for no reason other than bein' black. For years after that, this very same thing happened to me every time I came upon a large group of white men. My shotgun was the only thing that made me brave enough to stand up to those punks for you that first night I met you. Without that gun, I might have been shaking like this myself."

Mrs. Williams returned with the water. As she handed it to Eamon, she asked, "Is there anything else I can get you?"

"There's this drink Clara gives me sometimes at the restaurant. They call it hot chocolate. It's hot milk with chocolate in it. Do you have the fixin's to make something like that?"

"Yes, son, I do believe I do. I think we've got half a can of Hershey's® syrup in the refrigerator right now. I'll be happy to make you some."

When Mrs. Williams left the room, Eamon leaned back and said, "I surely do hope Clara didn't see any of what happened outside. I surely do hope she didn't see me fall apart like this. I told Imojean to get her hands off of me, because I was goin' to marry Clara. If Clara saw me fall apart like this, she won't ever want to marry me."

"Well, Lord have mercy, if that isn't good news," Mr. Williams said. "Wife! Wife! Make that three cups of hot chocolate. We've got some celebratin' to do. Our Eamon here is goin' to get himself hitched."

Dog jumped when Mr. Williams screamed for his wife, but he calmed down right away.

Mrs. Williams came out of the kitchen wiping her hands on her apron and said, "Lord have mercy, do it be true?"

Eamon sat up again and said, "I haven't even asked her yet. She's probably goin' to say no."

Mrs. Williams squealed like an excited child before she said, "Three hot chocolates coming up. We do certainly have something to celebrate."

A few minutes later, Mrs. Williams came in carrying two cups of hot chocolate that she sat on the card table. While she went back to get her own cup, Mr. Williams helped Eamon to the table.

As they walked, Eamon said, "You don't need to hold onto me no more. I'm feelin' a right smart better than I was."

Dog and I saw that Mr. Williams had everything under control, so we moved to the couch and watched.

"I'll just hold onto you until after supper. You might need some food in you. Mrs. Williams has a nice roast and vegetables baking in the oven right now."

When Mrs. Williams returned, she sat her hot chocolate on the table, picked up the sock and magazine they dropped when they ran to Eamon's aide, laid them on the side of the table by the wall, and sat down with the two men. Once she was seated, she said, "Well, gettin' married, are you? That's enough to give anyone the jitters. When do you plan on asking her?"

"I don't rightly know. I think I just tonight decided for sure I was goin' to ask her."

"Do you have a ring, son?" Mr. Williams asked, opening up a father and son type conversation between the two men.

"Naw, sir."

"We need to be gettin' you a ring before you ask her."

"But you don't need the ring until the wedding."

"You need to have an engagement ring to give her when she says yes," Mr. Williams said as Mrs. Williams nodded.

Eamon took a sip of hot chocolate and said, "Back home we just wear a weddin' band."

"Around here a woman expects an engagement ring," Mr. Williams said.

"Where do I get something like that?"

"At the jewelry store. You might have to buy it on time, but that's okay. You have a good job, and I'll vouch for you."

They talked about the engagement ring and the proposal all the way through the hot chocolate, supper, and the card game after supper. It was finally decided that Mr. Williams would take Eamon to the jewelry store the next day. The following Saturday, Mrs. Williams would make a nice picnic basket, and Eamon would take Clara for a picnic at Mt. Echo park just up the hill from where they lived on State Avenue. That is when he would propose.

CHAPTER FIVE: ENGAGED

Mrs. Williams was up at the crack of dawn on Saturday. Dog and I watched her prepare a picnic basket for the proposal. She wrapped the white velvet ring box in a napkin that she tied a pink ribbon around, so Eamon would know which napkin to give to Clara. That basket was sitting next to Dog and I in the back seat of the car when Eamon did a U-turn to pick Clara up in front of her building at eleven o'clock that morning.

When they got to the park, Eamon spread out a blanket on the grass while Clara held the picnic basket. Once the blanket was in place, all four of us sat on the blanket while Clara unpacked the basket. When she got to the napkins, Eamon didn't have to make sure she took the one with the pink ribbon tied around it like Mrs. Williams had instructed him to do, because the box fell out and landed on her lap when she picked the napkins up.

She picked up the box, opened it, and stared at the ring for a full minute before she looked at Eamon and asked, "What's this?"

Eamon took the box out of her hand, removed the ring, and reached it toward her as he stammered, "I was hopin' you would agree to be my wife."

Clara stared at the ring for so long that I was starting to fear she would say no and hurt Eamon again, but finally she stammered, "Okay."

They smiled at each other, and Eamon put the ring on her finger.

She stared at her newly adorned finger as she said, "You've got to go home with us this weekend, so you can meet my folks. We need to drive over and meet your folks, too. You said they were just on the other side of our mountain, right?"

Eamon's voice quivered as he answered, "They're about four hours away from your folks." By the time he finished speaking, he was gasping for air and shaking like he did after escaping Imojean's advances.

Clara looked at him and asked, "Are you okay?"

Eamon put his palms on his chest and stammered, "I think so. I'm havin' a hard time breathin'."

Clara walked on her knees until she was sitting next to him. She rubbed his back as she asked, "Do you need to go to the hospital?"

Between gasps, Eamon answered, "I don't think so. This happened earlier this week, and it went away."

"If it keeps happening, you should go to the doctor."

"Mr. Williams said this happens to him sometimes when he's reminded of —"

When he didn't finish the sentence after several seconds, Clara asked, "Reminded of what?"

"It doesn't matter."

"Are you bein' reminded of something?"

Eamon took several deep breaths before he answered, "I don't want nothing else to do with that mountain. I ain't been back on it since I left, and I don't want to see it no more."

She rubbed his back more vigorously as she asked, "What exactly happened to you on that mountain?"

He pushed himself to his feet with his strong arms and paced as he took deep breaths.

Clara walked beside him and held onto his arm as she asked, "Don't you want to see your MawMaw Tierney and Uncle Teagan?"

Eamon stopped pacing, looked at her, and smiled. His breathing slowed down after a couple of minutes, and he sat on the blanket again.

Clara sat next to him and said, "You told me your MawMaw wanted you to come back down and see her, but you never have. Don't you want to go see her?"

"I reckon it would be right nice to see MawMaw Tierney and Uncle Teagan."

"So, we'll go this weekend?"

Eamon smiled and said, "I reckon I will."

When they left for the mountains on Friday night, Eamon drove his car, Clara rode in the passenger seat, and Clara's brothers, Emmett and Morgan, rode in the back seat. They didn't seem to realize I was sitting between them with Dog on my lap.

It was the first time Eamon met Morgan. He looked a lot like Emmet, except Morgan was tall, thin, and wiry while Emmett was tall and muscular. Morgan's thin stature made his cheekbones and features more prominent than Emmet's, but they both had the same dark brown hair and thick eyebrows. Despite their differences, it was obvious they were brothers.

Another way they were different was Morgan didn't talk a lot while Emmett was cracking jokes during the entire trip. Half of the time Clara laughed along with Emmet. The other half of the time he was trying to find a way to get her to laugh again after he embarrassed her so badly that her cheeks turned red and she got quiet. Clara talked easily with Emmet, but she didn't say much to the other two unless it was to ask a question that I assumed was designed to get them talking. Each time she asked them a question, Eamon and Morgan answered and stopped talking again. That is the way we traveled for two-hundred miles.

When we arrived, Clara's Ma met us at the car and herded us toward the kitchen and the full table she had waiting for us as she said, "I be so happy y'all be makin' h'it safely. Y'all must be about starved stiff after that there long drive. Bring yourselves on into the house and be gettin' yourselves some vittles. Y'all can be tellin' me about yer trip whilst ya be feedin' yourselves."

No one spoke as she herded us through a front room that had a couch along every wall except the wall opposite the front door where the pot-bellied stove sat. She hustled everyone past the pot-bellied stove and through a door to the right of it that led into the kitchen.

Eamon stopped and gasped when he saw the kitchen. It was a large room that was more than twice as long as it was wide, and just inside the door was a table that was half as long as the room. There was a plate in front of every chair, and the middle of the table was filled with bowls and plates full of steaming food — a big plate of fried chicken, a big plate of cornbread, and large bowls filled with mashed potatoes, gravy, stewed tomatoes, green beans, dumplings, succotash, and poke sallet.

51

Clara's mother must have seen how the spread affected Eamon, because she lay her palm on his back and pushed him toward the table as she said, "Nary use in bein' shy, young man. Ya be sittin' yourself on down, and ya be helpin' yourself to as much as ya be wantin'."

"Thank you, ma'am," Eamon said as he walked toward the table.

"My name be Darina. Pleased to be meetin' ya."

"Pleased to be meetin' ya, Darina," Eamon said as he sat down next to Clara, who was sitting about half way down the long table.

"Ya must be Eamon."

"Yas'm. I'm Eamon."

"Well, ya be diggin' right on in there and et yer fill."

By that time, everyone was sitting around the table and filling their plates, so Eamon filled his plate as Darina took her seat at one end of the table. Dog lay at Eamon's feet, and I stood behind him like I often did.

A few minutes later, Clara's Pa came in, walked to the sink at the far end of the kitchen, washed his hands, and took his seat at the other end of the table from Darina. When he was seated, he looked around the table and said, "There be bein' a new face amongst y'all. Who do he be?"

"This is Eamon," Clara answered.

"The one ya be tellin' us about," her Pa said as he scooped food onto his plate. When his plate was full, he said, "My name be Faolan."

"Pleased to meet you, Faolan," Eamon said between bites.

Everyone ate in near silence. The only reason anyone spoke was to ask for something to be passed to them.

When everyone was finished eating, Faolan stood up and said, "Whilst some of the women folk be cleanin' up the kitchen, some of y'all be needin' to be goin' out back and be bringin' in some firewood. That there fire be needin' to be stoked before the last one of y'all be goin' to yer rest."

As Faolan walked toward the living room, Eamon said, "I'll be right happy to go get some firewood."

"Suit yourself," Faolan said as he entered the living room, sat on one of the couches, and pulled a bag of tobacco out of his pocket for an evening chew.

A young girl came around from the other side of the table and shook Eamon's hand as she said, "Howdy, my name be Olivia. I be

Clara's niece. I be stayin' here with MawMaw and PawPaw fer a while. I reckon I can be helpin' ya with the firewood."

The girl was wearing blue jeans that were cut off and rolled up to just above her knee and held up by suspenders, a flannel shirt, tube socks, and cowboy boots. She hadn't developed womanly curves yet and could easily have been mistaken for a boy, except her face was so dainty and pretty it was obvious she was a girl.

"Much obliged," Eamon said as he followed her to the front door with Dog and me close behind.

As they walked around the side of the house, Olivia said, "I's be seein' yer leg be game. No need to be worryin' about carryin' back any firewood. I mays be a girl, but I be strappin'. I can be carryin' the wood back around."

There was a big weeping willow behind the house, and the wood pile sat next to it. The pile consisted of mostly stumps that needed to be split.

"Well, shucks," Olivia said. "We's be a-havin' to be splittin' some before we can be takin' h'it back."

"That ain't no problem," Eamon said. "I can split a few."

Olivia guffawed before she said, "Ya be thinkin' ya can be splittin' wood. Ya just be a city boy."

Eamon pointed at the mountains in the distance and said, "I ain't no city boy. My people come from just on the other side of that there ridge, about four hours from here, down in Middlesboro."

"Boy, howdy, I surely did be takin' ya fer a city boy. I's be wonderin' what my aunt be wantin' herself a city boy fer. I surely do be feelin' better about ya gettin' hitched to my cousin now." Olivia gasped in amazement when Eamon lowered the axe to cut the first stump. "Boy howdy," she said. "Ya nary be doin' bad at all fer a boy who be sportin' a game leg. Ya really ain't no city boy."

Eamon insisted on carrying as much wood as Olivia when they returned to the house. They stacked it by the pot-bellied stove before Olivia threw a few pieces in. As she stoked the fire, she said, "Ya be a'right in my book, city boy."

Eamon laughed for the first time since the trip began and said, "Thank you."

When the kitchen was clean and the fire was stoked for the night, Darina came out of the kitchen and said, "Most nights we be sittin' around the fire here just jawin' fer a spell, but ya two young'uns needs to be gettin' an early start to be drivin' over to be seein' Eamon's people. Clara, ya can be sleepin' with me, and Eamon and Faolan can be sleepin' on these here couches by the nice, warm stove. Emmett and Morgan can be sleepin' on the spare beds up there in the attic where Joshua be sleepin'." Darina stopped, looked at the front door, and crinkled her brow. She shook it off after a few seconds and said, "I hope Joshua nary be disturbin' y'all too much if'n he be stumblin' in tonight. Olivia, can ya be goin' and gettin' some extra blankets and pillows out of the chifforobe that be in yer room?"

"Yes'm," Olivia said as she left the room with the sound of Darina saying "Much obliged" following her.

After Eamon and Faolan chose the couches they wanted, Dog and I took one of the couches that was left and lay on it. It seemed like hardly any time had passed when we heard the noises of women making breakfast.

Darina sent Eamon and Clara on their way with a good breakfast in their bellies and a hearty goodbye from everyone in the family—except the mysterious Joshua who never came home the night before. I was surprised they let them travel alone since they'd been so worried about them coming in too close of contact during the night, especially since they didn't know Dog and I were riding along with them as chaperones.

It must have been hard for Eamon and Clara's mortal bodies to travel another four hours to Middlesboro when they had traveled four hours the night before. I wondered how much harder their silence made that four hours, because four hours of silence was difficult for me to bear. No matter what Clara asked Eamon, she couldn't get him to talk. In spite of the silence, I was enjoying being back on the mountain and seeing the beauty I had rarely noticed when I lived here in a state of constant stress.

The closer we got to Middlesboro, the harder Eamon gripped the steering wheel. I also noticed his body looked stiff and his arms were quivering. From time to time, he breathed several deep breaths in a row like the ones that had helped him the two times he experienced what everyone was now calling a spell.

Dog lay his head on my lap, and I noticed he was stiff and quivering as well. I remembered the times I was surprised by the physical reactions my ghost body could have, and I wondered if I would look stiff and quivering if someone could see me.

We arrived around eleven in the morning. I saw Eamon wipe a tear from under his eye as we rounded the Rose of Sharon bushes at the end of MawMaw Tierney's and Uncle Teagan's driveway. If my ghost body was able to release a tear, I would have, too. It was good to see the only safe place from our childhood again. He parked at the bottom of the porch steps.

MawMaw Tierney ran down the steps, pulled Eamon out of the car, hugged him so hard she picked him up off the ground, and said, "Ya done made h'it boy. Ya done made h'it to the big city and ya done bought yourself a car — just like them letters yer boss be writin' to me be sayin' ya done. I be so happy to be seein' ya."

When his feet touched the ground again, he pulled away from MawMaw Tierney's embrace and said, "I'm right happy to see you, MawMaw. This is Clara. We're gettin' married. I wanted you to meet her before we do."

MawMaw Tierney walked around the car, gave Clara a quick hug, and said, "I be right happy to be meetin' ya. Ya be comin' on in the house. Ya must be bein' about starved stiff after that long drive. I be havin' some lunch a-waitin' fer ya."

Dog and I followed MawMaw Tierney, Clara, and Eamon across the well-tended porch and into the house. The house was exactly the way I remembered it. Inside the door, there were steps that led to the second floor to the right of a hallway that ran the length of the house. The hallway was lined with doors that led to the various first floor rooms. We followed MawMaw Tierney down that hallway to the last door on the right and into the kitchen. Her kitchen was smaller and fancier than Darina's was. It had white curtains with yellow flowers on them, yellow walls, and a much smaller table than the one in Darina's kitchen sat in the middle of the room. Ham, mashed potatoes and green beans sat in bowls on the middle of the table.

I remembered that MawMaw Tierney always served a meat, potatoes or bread, and a vegetable from her garden or her canning. She called it a well-rounded meal. She always served a dessert after each meal, too, but it wasn't on the table yet. I couldn't believe I remembered that since I had passed away at such a young age.

As MawMaw Tierney motioned for Eamon and Clara to take a seat at the table, she said, "Yer Uncle Teagan be right sorry he nary be able to be seein' ya today. He and the girl's Ma be takin' his oldest girl down to Berea College. She done been accepted to be studyin' there. Can ya be believin' that one of our own is goin' to be goin' to college? The other two girls be goin' with them to see what h'it be like. They be sayin' maybe they be wantin' to be goin' there, too."

"I'm right sorry to miss seein' them," Eamon said as all three of them took a seat at the table.

As we often did, Dog lay at Eamon's feet, and I stood behind his chair.

While they ate, MawMaw Tierney asked Eamon a hundred questions about what it was like to live in the city. Eamon and Clara took turns answering. The questions continued through the white cake with chocolate frosting MawMaw Tierney sat on the table when they were finished eating the main course.

Eamon didn't ask any questions until dessert was over and Clara stood at the sink washing dishes while MawMaw Tierney dried them and put them away. As he watched the women-folk at work, he swallowed hard and asked, "Do you ever hear from Caelan and Mabon?"

MawMaw Tierney crinkled her brow before she turned to Eamon. As she wiped her hands on her apron, she asked, "You nary be hearin'?"

"I didn't hear anythin'."

"Yer Ma and Pa nary be livin' on this here mountain no more."

"What happened to 'em?"

"Regan went and found herself a man who be havin' a good job, and he done moved her on up to the city —"

Eamon twitched like a scared bunny as he stammered, "Is she livin' in Cincinnati?"

"H'it be near to Cincinnati, but h'it nary be in Cincinnati. H'it be some little town close by, but I nary be rememberin' the name of h'it right now. Regan be livin' there with this man what be havin' a good job. I be hearin' tell his job nary be good enough for her though, because she be spendin' his money like h'it be water. She be workin' in some good office job, too, but I be hearin' tell they still be runnin' outta money right often. I reckon I be hearin' right about her spendin',

56

because she done up and bought a second house up there and done moved yer folks into h'it."

"Well, I'll be," Eamon stammered.

"Ya nary be thinkin' about visitin' them now that they be livin' up yer way, does ya?"

"Naw. I don't see any reason to visit them."

Clara turned away from the sink, cleared her throat, and asked, "Are they really so bad that we shouldn't visit them before we get married?"

MawMaw Tierney turned her whole body toward Clara, looked deep into Clara's eyes, and said, "Ya be wantin' to be stayin' as far away from them there folks as ya can be stayin'. If'n the good Lord be blessin' ya with young'uns, ya be keepin' them young'uns far away from them there folks. Do ya be hearin' what I be sayin' to ya?"

Clara nodded.

"Good," MawMaw Tierney said. "I be glad to be seein' y'all be agreein' with me. I be an old woman, and I nary be knowin' how much longer I goin' to be amongst the livin'. I nary be wantin' to be worryin' about what be goin' to be happenin' to yer young'uns once I be passin' on."

MawMaw Tierney turned to Eamon and patted his hand before she said, "I nary be carin' what Eamon be tellin' ya 'bout what done happened to him on this here mountain, ya be needin' to be believin' him. Even if'n h'it be soundin' so terrible no one could be believin' h'it, ya be needin' to be knowin' h'it probably be even worse than what Eamon be tellin' ya. He be havin' his self a way of bein' too easy on them there folks. Nary be lettin' yer young'uns around them."

Clara wiped her hands on the apron MawMaw Tierney tied around her waist before they started washing the dishes as she said, "It is hard to believe anyone could be that bad. Sometimes I'm miserable up in the city, because I miss my Ma and Pa so much. The only thing that has made it tolerable for me is that my sister and my two brothers are up there with me, and I really like my church. To be honest, I was gettin' ready to come back home and tough it out with the lack of jobs, but one of the Elders at my church convinced me to stay. I figured he was right when I found a good job and then met Eamon shortly after that. I liked Eamon right from the start, but I didn't think he was ever goin' to get the courage to talk to me. When he finally did start talkin', I knew my Elder was right."

"H'it be seemin' like y'all be movin' perty fast once he be findin' the courage to be talkin' to ya. He only be in the city for nigh on a year h'it seems and already he be bringin' ya home to be tellin' me y'all be gettin' married." Eamon and Clara both blushed until MawMaw Tierney said, "Aww, h'it be a'right. Ain't nothing more blessed than young folks who be fallin' in love. Y'all be doin' the right thing to be gettin' hitched."

Clara looked at her watch and said, "Good Lord, Eamon, it's already almost supper time. We've sat around this table talkin' from lunch to supper. We'd better be gettin' back, or my Pa's goin' to be thinkin' we've been up to no good."

MawMaw Tierney untied the apron from around Clara's waist as she said, "Now that I done met ya, don't ya be bein' no stranger. I be wantin' ya to be visitin' regular, and I be wantin' to be meetin' them babies once they start a-comin'."

Eamon stood and grasped MawMaw Tierney's hands before he said, "MawMaw, I'm awful sorry I didn't come home when I got a car. I surely did want to see you, but sometimes I just about choke on the memories of what happened on this here mountain. That makes it right hard to get the gumption up to drive in this direction."

MawMaw Tierney patted his hands as she said, "I know, darlin'. I know h'it be right hard to be facin' what done happened here. I be hopin' now that ya be gettin' married that Clara comin' along with ya will be makin' h'it easier for ya."

Clara stopped at the kitchen door, turned, and said, "I come home every weekend. We'll be comin' back around this way more often."

"I be right glad to be hearin' that," MawMaw Tierney said as she lay the palm of her hand on Eamon's back and led him to the door. "Yer Uncle Teagan will be right pleased to be hearin' he'll be seein' y'all soon."

MawMaw Tierney walked us to the car. While Dog and I got in the back seat, she gave Clara a quick hug. When she hugged Eamon, I saw a tear stream down her cheek. That is the first time I ever saw that strong woman cry. She stood on the bottom porch step and waved until Eamon got the car turned around. Then, she walked to the middle of the driveway and waved until our car drove around the bend in the driveway and out of sight.

As Eamon drove past the Rose of Sharon bushes, Clara said, "I hope Pa ain't too mad when I get home so late. It's goin' to be nearly ten o'clock by the time we get there."

"I'm sure he'll understand. He knows it's a long drive."

Faolan might have understood if they would have gotten home around 10:00, but halfway home, Eamon got lost. By the time he found his way, it was almost midnight before they got back. When they pulled up in front of Faolan and Darina's house, Faolan was standing on the porch steps with his arms crossed over his chest and his foot tapping. Before the car was parked, he was running toward it.

When Eamon got out of the car, Faolan put his face right in Eamon's and said, "Where y'all been to? H'it be bein' nearly midnight."

Eamon crossed his arms over his face and hunkered down like a dog that was about to be beat, but Faolan grabbed Eamon's forearms and slammed them back to Eamon's sides as he yelled, 'Ya best be tellin' me ya nary be stoppin' at no motel with my daughter. Y'all nary be hitched yet, and they nary be no cause to be actin' that way before y'all be hitched." Eamon moved his arms back to his head as Faolan yelled, "I be knowin' how men be. Ya best be tellin' me ya nary be stoppin' at no motel room whilst ya be out on the road with my daughter."

Clara ran around the car and said, "Pa, Pa, calm down! We weren't doin' nothing we shouldn't be doin'. We didn't leave his MawMaw's house until supper time, and then we got lost on the way back. We know we were out too late, but we didn't do nothing we shouldn't have been doin'."

Faolan stepped away from Eamon, looked at Clara, and asked, "Y'all be willin' to be swearin' on the Bible that y'all nary be stoppin' at no motel on the way home?"

"I swear it, Pa. If you don't believe us, you can call his MawMaw tomorrow and ask her. We were enjoyin' talkin' to her so much that we didn't leave her house until after supper time. She'll tell you. Besides, the roads from their house to our house don't hardly have anything on them we could stop at anyway. That's why we had such a hard time findin' our way back when we got lost. We didn't see a soul we could ask for help. Ask his MawMaw if you call her. She'll tell you that there ain't even no motel over in their part of the country for us to be stoppin' at. The roads be just about empty all the way from their place all the way back over here."

"Well, I reckon everythin' be a'right then. I just be knowin' how men be. I nary be wantin' one of 'em to be takin' liberties with ya and be ruinin' yer life." He motioned to Eamon and said, "Y'all be comin' on in the house. I reckon y'all must be hungry since there nary be places to be stoppin' on the road. H'it be way past supper time. Yer Ma, she be havin' plenty of vittles left over from supper."

"We are feelin' mighty hungry," Clara said as she turned to Eamon.

Eamon was holding himself up by leaning on the door of the car. He was as white as a sheet, his skin was clammy, and he was gasping for breath again. Clara ran to him and tried to help him stand up straight, but he had to grab onto the back of the car seat and sit down again.

Clara knelt in front of him and asked, "Are ya all right?"

"The people on these mountains always be bringin' this kind of thing on me," Eamon said between gasps.

"Take deep breaths like you did in the car." She ran her palm up and down his arm as she said, "You're safe. He ain't goin' to hurt you. That's just how my Pa is. He's got my best interest at heart, but sometimes he gets a little mean when he's been into the shine. He's a good man, but sometimes he drinks a little too much. He fell off the swingin' bridge and into the river one night when he was drunk. To this day, no one knows how he dragged himself to the shore without drownin', because he was so drunk he could hardly walk by the time he got home."

Eamon had to take deep breaths for several minutes before his breathing returned to normal and he stopped shaking enough to be able to stand. When he was able to stand, Clara held onto one of his arms as she helped him walk to the house. Dog and I got out of the back seat of the car and followed them.

Darina had pinto beans and cornbread heating in a cast iron skillet on top of the pot-bellied stove for when they arrived. She made a plate for each of them. It seemed like Eamon shook a little less with each bite he took.

While they ate, Dog and I made ourselves comfortable on the same couch we passed the previous night on. After Eamon and Clara ate, everyone retired to the same sleeping arrangements they had the night before.

Once again, it seemed like hardly any time had passed when we heard the noises of women making breakfast. When everyone sat down to eat, Dog lay in his usual position by Eamon's feet, and I stood in my usual position behind his chair. As I looked around the table, I noticed a new face. A man I hadn't met before was sitting on the other side of the table. I assumed this was Joshua. He didn't look much like the other children. He was shorter than this tall group, he had a round almost impish face that made him look friendly, his hair was a lighter shade of brown, and he was thin but muscular.

When Joshua excused himself from going to church with the rest of us after breakfast, I smelled alcohol on his breath as he walked past us to get to the hallway on the other side of the pot-bellied stove. The bawdy song he sang as he walked down the hallway to get to his attic room made me suspect he was still drunk.

Faolan also chose to stay home. He said he worked hard all week, and Sunday was his day to relax on the porch with a Mason® jar of shine. Dog and I followed the rest of them when they passed Faolan on the porch as they left the house and walked in what I assumed was the direction of the church.

As they walked, Eamon whispered to Clara, "I don't much like goin' to church."

"Why wouldn't you like goin' to church? Church is a really nice place."

"I got a lot of reasons for not likin' church."

"Tell me one of them."

"I guess one of my biggest reasons is I can't stand all the snakes."

Clara crinkled her brow before she stopped, looked at him, and asked, "Why on earth would there be snakes in the church?"

Eamon stopped, looked at her, and said, "I never rightly understood why we had to have snakes in the church either, but we always did."

You're joshin' me," Clara said so loud that the rest of the family stopped and walked back to them.

"What do y'all be talkin' about?" Darina asked.

"He just told me they have snakes inside his church."

"Ever buildin' be gettin' snakes in h'it from time to time," Darina said. "Y'all just be havin' to be carryin' 'em out on a stick. Ya nary be wantin' 'em to be livin' with ya if'n ya can be helpin' h'it."

"Naw," Eamon said. "We had them in cages in the front of the church. The preacher took them out during the service, and people held them to prove they had enough faith in God for the snake not to bite 'em and for them not to die if they did get bit."

"Well, I'll be dogged," Darina said. "I be hearin' about churches what be doin' that, but I be thinkin' h'it just be talk."

"It's nary be just talk. They really do be playin' with snakes durin' church."

"Do any folks ever be gettin' bit?" Darina asked.

"Yes'm. People got bit all the time.'

"And them there snakes be poisonous?"

"Yes'm"

Everyone was silent for a minute before Clara asked, "Did anyone ever die?"

Eamon nodded as he answered, "Yes, there were a few people who died when I was a child."

"Did ya ever be gettin' bit?" Olivia asked.

"Naw, but my Pa got bit a time or two."

"Did he up and die?" Olivia asked.

"Naw, he's just plain too mean to die.'

"But, I thought you said the Lord kept those who have faith from dyin', so why would the Good Lord be savin' your Pa if he's mean?" Clara asked.

"I said that's what they believe. I didn't see a lot of God in that church. My MawMaw told me the snake was the devil in the Garden of Eden, so I always thought that's why they brought those snakes into the church – I thought they were bringin' the devil into the church."

"That nary be no way to be talkin' about God's people," Darina said.

"If you met them, you'd be sayin' the same thing."

Darina shook her head for several seconds before she said, "Well, I reckon we ought to be gettin' on to our own church before we be gettin' there late. We nary be wantin' to be disturbin' ever one else when we be comin' in late."

When they started walking again, Eamon asked, "You mean I nary have to be worryin' about no snakes?"

"Not in the church anyway," Clara answered.

Emmett chimed in with his typical humor and said, "I don't think Preacher's got it much in mind to be savin' no snakes. They can be awful hard to baptize."

Everyone laughed, and then they walked the rest of the way to church in silence.

The church didn't have steps like the church Eamon grew up in. It was all on ground level, and several people could walk through the open double doors that resembled barn doors at the same time. Everyone else walked through the welcoming open doors, but Eamon stopped just outside of them. He started breathing heavy and looking around like something was after him. Several people whispered about him as they walked past, but no one stopped to see what was wrong until Clara came back out of the church to see if he was alright.

Dog paced back and forth while I rubbed Eamon's back.

Eamon placed his palms on his thighs and said, "I can't breathe. I don't rightly know what's wrong, but I can't breathe."

Clara looked at a man who was walking through the door in his Sunday best and asked, "Get my Ma, won't ya, please?"

The man ran into the church.

A few minutes later, Darina came to the back door and asked, "What be the matter?"

"He says he can't breathe," Clara answered.

"He be needin' to be sittin' down," Darina said as she took his arm and tried to lead him into the church. "Ya be comin' on in here and be sittin' on this here back pew until ya can be catchin' yer breath."

They pulled him until he crossed the threshold. Dog tried to block them from dragging him into the church, but no one could see Dog. Once Eamon was inside, he followed them to the back pew and sat down. He leaned forward with his head practically between his knees and kept trying to breathe.

Emmett was standing at the end of the pew where the family sat near the front of the church. Darina motioned for him to come back. When he got to them, she said, "Get on out to the well and be gettin' Eamon a drink of water. Mays be that'll be helpin' him."

"Yas'm," Emmett said before he ran out the door.

When Emmett came back a few minutes later with a ladle full of water, Eamon was sitting up, but his breathing was still labored. Emmett handed the ladle to Darina, and she tried to help Eamon drink.

Eamon pushed the ladle away and said, "I don't rightly think I can drink that. I think I just need to go on back to your house if that's okay with y'all."

"There nary be no point to be walkin' back when ya be feelin' this poorly," Darina said. "Ya be comin' on up and be sittin' with the rest of the family, and we be havin' the congregation to be prayin' fer ya."

Darina nodded to Emmet, and Emmett helped Eamon to his feet. Once Eamon was standing, he said, "I'd like to walk down by myself. I'll be all right."

Eamon stumbled down the aisle. When everyone got seated, the Pastor took his place in front of the church and started preaching about forgiveness. During the entire sermon, Eamon kept having waves of the same symptoms. He would feel better for a few minutes, but then it would come back again. I sat behind him with Dog on my lap and rubbed Eamon's back through the entire service, but it didn't seem to help.

After the service, the pastor had an altar call. Darina raised her hand and said, "Clara's intended be feelin' right poorly. I'd be much obliged if'n y'all could be prayin' fer him."

Eamon breathed harder when the Pastor approached him and laid hands on him, and it got worse when many members of the congregation gathered around as well. After a prayer that was so long I thought Eamon would pass out before they were done, the pastor removed his hands and said, "I be believin' the Good Lord will be workin' a miracle soon. He ought to be feelin' a right smart better real soon."

After the family ate at a potluck the women set up in the churchyard, they walked home. Even with the exertion from the walk home, Eamon's breathing returned to normal by the time they reached Darina and Faolan's house. Eamon sat on the bottom step of the porch when they got there.

As Darina walked past him, she said, "I reckon the Good Lord done healed ya, son. I reckon ya be feelin' right happy that ya done stayed through the service now."

After the rest of the family walked past him, Clara sat next to him and asked, "Did you hear all that the preacher talked about durin' the service?"

"I don't remember much of it. I was feelin' too bad to pay attention."

"You look to be feelin' better now."

"I reckon I do. I seemed to start feelin' better when I walked out of that church, and eatin' at the potluck really helped a lot. To tell you the truth, I didn't want to go in and sit on that back pew like your Ma made me do. Everything in me was tellin' me to run away. I didn't want to make a fuss and make your Ma mad at me, so I found the strength to let her lead me in."

"I'm glad you're feelin' better now. The pastor today kept talkin' about forgiveness, and that got me to thinkin'. I think we need to visit your folks once we get back to Cincinnati and let them know we're gettin' married. I think you'll probably agree after the Good Lord healed you and all."

"You heard what MawMaw Tierney said yesterday. She said to stay away from all of them. She told you to believe everything I told you about them even if it seemed too bad to be believed."

"I don't doubt you or your MawMaw Tierney. I just think it's important for you to forgive. We can go and see them next weekend, and then we can get married right after that." She stood up as she said, "I'm goin' to go help Ma get lunch together for Pa and Joshua."

Eamon leaned his forehead on the porch rail and slumped forward like every bit of energy was leaving his body. Dog lay at his feet, and I sat next to Eamon. I rubbed his back again, but it didn't help this time any more than it helped the other times I'd done it that day. I just sat there, worried, and hoped my presence was helping in some small way.

CHAPTER SIX: VISITING THE FOLKS

While Eamon and Clara drove to Eamon's parent's house the next Saturday, Clara said, "I didn't know if I would be able to find them or not. They haven't lived up here long enough to be in the phone book. Everett told me I could call the operator to get new phone numbers. It was Wednesday before I learned that, but they still seemed right pleased to know we were comin' to visit today. I don't think it's goin' to be a problem."

Dog and I were sitting on the back seat. I could see that Eamon's arms were shaking as he tried to hold onto the steering wheel, and he kept wiping his sweaty palms on his pant legs. Dog kept putting his front paws on the back of Eamon's seat so he could lay his head on Eamon's shoulder, but it didn't seem to ease Eamon's tension. Clara took the nervousness she felt about meeting the parents she'd heard so many bad stories about out on the handkerchief she kept wringing between her hands. I kept fighting for breath even though my lungs were those of a ghost. I suspected if one of us would have calmed down that we all would have calmed down, but we were keeping each other agitated.

When Eamon didn't respond, Clara asked, "Aren't you excited to see them?"

"I think you should have listened to MawMaw Tierney."

"I don't think it's right to get married without them meetin' me, especially since they only live an hour outside Cincinnati."

Eamon snapped at her for the first time when he said, "It don't matter if it's right or wrong now. We're doin' it, so let's just get it done and over with."

Clara hugged her purse and leaned back in her seat.

After a few minutes of silence, Eamon said, "I'm sorry. I didn't mean to snap at you. I just get so nervous at the thought of seein' them again. I honestly think my Pa had it in his mind to kill me the last time I saw him, and that's not an easy thing to walk back into."

"I didn't know . . ."

"Well, now you know. Can we please not talk about it anymore? It's takin' every bit of concentration I have just to drive this car right now."

"All right," Clara said and hugged her purse tighter.

When they parked in front of Eamon's folks' house a half hour later, the sweat Eamon was wiping off his palms during the whole trip was beading on his face and staining under the arms of his shirt. Clara got out of the car and stood next to it while Eamon leaned his forehead onto the steering wheel he continued to grip and breathed in the same way he had at the church on the previous weekend.

Clara walked around to his side of the car and asked, "What's wrong?"

"I'm havin' that feelin' like I can't breathe again."

"Do you want me to get you a glass of water?"

"That won't help. Just give me a minute."

He took several deep breaths before he lifted his head and looked at the house. I listened to his thoughts, and this time they were calming him. 'Maybe they have changed. Not only did they move up here to the city, but that house isn't gray and run down like our house on the mountain was. Everything's white washed, and the yard is green instead of dead and dirt like it was back home. I've changed since I moved up here. Maybe they have, too." By the time he got finished thinking about how the house was different and better, his breathing had almost returned to normal. He got out of the car.

As Eamon came around the back of the car, he opened the trunk and said, "Clara, put your purse in here just in case we have to make a quick getaway."

Clara hugged her purse to her chest and asked, "Are you serious?"

Eamon nodded, so Clara handed him her purse. He locked it in the trunk before they walked across the front yard.

As Dog and I followed them to the house, I took inventory of the many ways this house was better than the one we had lived in on the mountain. The only flaw I saw was that it was small. There was a door on the far-right side of the house that had a small porch just big enough to stand on to knock. There was a natural wood deck that extended the entire length of the left side of the house that was much larger than that small porch. All of the deck rails were in good repair. The house and porch rails were all painted white. There were several types of flowers planted along the front of the house from the edge of the deck to the edge of the porch, and there was a large picture window centered above the flower bed. The shutters on each side of the window were painted dark blue. There was a carport on the right side of the house that covered the end of a gravel driveway. A narrow strip of rooms extended from the back of the house behind the small porch and the carport. You could see the right corner of a storage shed behind those rooms. It was also painted white with blue trim. The yard covered the front, back, and left sides of the house and was healthy, bright green, and freshly mowed.

This house was so much better than the one they lived in back home. The house back home had never seen a coat of paint and was as gray on the inside as it was on the outside. Even the barn that sat across from the old house was unpainted, gray, and rotting away. The grayness seemed to have conquered the land around that house as well. It felt like their meanness killed the plants and forced us to live in a dustbowl. It seemed like a miracle that they had evolved from that house to this one. Maybe they had changed.

When we reached the front door, Eamon raised his fist to knock, but it froze about two inches from the door and didn't move.

After a couple of minutes, Clara asked, "Aren't you goin' to knock?"

"I can't."

Clara knocked, and he lowered his fist when she did.

A few minutes later Mabon came to the door. Suddenly, I understood what Eamon felt when he had a spell in the car and why he couldn't knock on the door. I expected to feel numb when I saw her. I was surprised when my ghost body had difficulty breathing, my heart started race, I felt dizzy, and my stomach was lurching. If I would have been in a living body, I would have passed out. Dog growling at her snapped me out of it enough that I could follow them into the house.

Mabon, who I had long ago started calling by her name since she was never a Ma to any of us, offered no warmth – no hug or handshake. She just ushered us into the house and told Eamon and Clara to have a seat.

They sat on a light blue couch with slightly darker blue flowers on it that sat under the front window. There were two chairs that matched the couch facing it, and they had a rectangular end table that had a raised shelf in the back that extended half the length of the table sitting between them. There was a light blue doily on the shelf and on the front of the end table, and two phone books sat under the shelf. A small lamp sat on the shelf's doily. There wasn't a coffee table. There were two rustic-looking dark wood end tables on each end of the couch. Matching lamps with huge white shades that were too large for the tables sat on each one. The end tables looked out of place among the fancy couch, chairs, lamps, and light blue walls. Maybe those rustic-looking tables allowed them to hold onto a little bit of the mountain. This house was much nicer than anything I thought any of us would ever have when we were trapped inside the gray walls with the gray wood furniture that was our mountain home.

Dog and I stood inside the front door. We couldn't stand to get any closer to Mabon, and I wondered how Eamon could stand being that close to her when one of her beatings had left him crippled.

Mabon sat on a chair across from them, looked at Clara, and said, "I reckon ya be the Clara I done talked to on the phone earlier this week?"

Clara nodded as she answered, "Yes'm."

"So, ya be plannin' to marry this here boy of ours?"

"Yes'm."

"Well, God help ya then."

Clara crinkled her brow and looked at Eamon. He shrugged.

I wanted to scream, "How can you try to make him look bad when you're the one who crippled him?" What was the use in screaming? No one could hear me. If anyone could hear me, she would have gone to prison for murdering me a long time ago. The whole world would know how evil she was. She wouldn't be able to make anyone else look bad to hide her own crimes anymore. Maybe that's why she had killed me. Dead children can't talk. I suddenly realized that was what she always did — try to make other people look bad, so no one would see

69

how bad she was. I wished I had a way of telling that epiphany to Eamon, so she couldn't tear his self-esteem down more than she already had. Unfortunately, Eamon hadn't been able to see or hear me after he outgrew being a child.

Eamon and Clara sat quietly, fidgeting, for several minutes before Mabon said, "Yer Pa'll be back in a minute. Regan took him down to the store to get some Coca-Cola®. We thought y'all might be wantin' somethin' to be drinkin'."

When Mabon mentioned Caelan, Eamon jolted up in the seat like he'd just got an electric shock and pushed his back into the couch like he was trying to back away from something. I didn't know if his reaction was because he was nervous about that mean old man returning or if he was offended to hear the word Pa used. Eamon and I both started calling our Pa by his name, Caelan, when we realized he'd never been a Pa to either of us.

Nobody said anything else while they waited for Caelan and Regan to return. While they waited, Mabon looked around the room like she'd never seen it before, and Eamon and Clara stared straight ahead. When the front door opened about ten minutes later, Eamon grabbed Clara's hand.

Caelan sat on the empty chair next to Mabon while Regan carried a bag of groceries into the kitchen. The door to the kitchen was on the wall behind Mabon just a little to the left of Mabon's chair. The living room area extended from the deck to the porch. On the left side of the kitchen door, a hallway was created by a white, wrought iron fence that sat as far away from the kitchen wall as the width of the door at the end of that hallway. On the other side of the wrought iron fence sat a large, oval, dining room table that had two chairs on each side of it and one on each end. The table was so large that it took up the whole area, so the china cabinet sat next to the end table. It covered a portion of the window and the light blue curtain that matched the light blue carpeting. That carpeting covered all of the living area except the hallway the railing created. That hallway was covered in white linoleum. The blue carpet even went as far as I could see down the hallway that was directly across from the linoleum-covered hallway. That must have been the rooms I saw extending from the house behind the carport while we were knocking on the door. There was a large curio cabinet along the carport wall next to the front entry door and a

70

smaller one on the front wall near the door. Everything in the house was spotless except there were pill bottles, needles, and various medical supplies littering the top of the small curio cabinet.

As we listened to Regan loudly slamming around in the kitchen, Caelan said, "I didn't reckon I'd ever be seein' ya again."

Eamon just cleared his throat and stared at Caelan, but I thought, "You're darn lucky to be seeing him again since the last time he saw you MawMaw Tierney had to save him from you tearing his back up with a whip.'

Caelan returned Eamon's stare until Eamon looked down before Caelan asked, "Well, are ya just goin' to sit there lookin' stupid, or are ya goin' to tell me what ya came here for?"

Eamon squeezed Clara's hand tighter.

Clara looked at Eamon and then their entwined hands before she said, "We wanted to let you know that we're gettin' married."

Caelan looked at their hands and said, "Well, I should hope so considerin' how familiar y'all seem to be with each other. Are ya with child or somethin'?"

Clara's mouth fell open before she answered, "I most certainly am not! I'm a Christian woman, and I'm not goin' to be actin' like that before I get married!"

"Get off'n yer high horse," Caelan said. "We're good Christian folk, too, and Mabon here was pregnant when we got married."

I remembered what my Uncles had accused Caelan of the night Mabon killed me and wanted to scream, "Because you raped her!" What was the point? No one would hear me.

Caelan stared at Clara until she looked down before he yelled, "Regan, ya needs to be gettin' that Coca-Cola® out here now."

Regan came out of the kitchen carrying a tray that had five glasses of Coca-Cola® on ice on it. Eamon leaned forward and whispered to Clara, "The bottle's done been opened. Don't drink it."

Clara crinkled her brow and looked at Eamon for a second before she took a glass from Regan. She started to take a drink, but Eamon took it out of her hand and sat it on the end table. When Regan carried the tray to him, he shook his head no.

Mabon looked at Clara's glass and said, "Lord Almighty, now he thinks he's too good for what we be servin' him."

Clara cleared her throat before she said, "We had a Coca-Cola® before we came, so we're not thirsty yet."

"You could have told us that before Caelan went to the store to buy some," Mabon sneered.

Clara shook her head like she was trying to escape a small spider web before she said, "He was gone before we got here, so how could we —"

"We ain't made of money. If you would have told us before he left, we could have saved the money."

Eamon lightly tugged Clara's hand. When Clara looked at him, he shook his head no. Clara looked down and dropped the conversation.

After Regan gave Caelan and Mabon their drinks, she came to the side of the couch Clara was sitting on and said, "I reckon I need some place to sit."

Caelan said, "Get one of the kitchen chairs."

"They're not comfortable. These two are engaged, so why don't Clara just sit on Eamon's lap, and then I can sit where she's sittin'."

"I don't reckon that's a good idea," Eamon said.

"You're goin' to marry the woman, but she can't sit on your lap?" Regan asked.

Clara looked at Eamon and said, "It's not worth arguin' about. I don't mind sittin' on your lap."

When Clara moved to Eamon's lap, Regan sat on the couch, looked at Clara, and asked, "You're a might old to be gettin' married, aren't you?"

"What?" Clara asked, obviously confused.

"You should have got married when you were young like me. Ma weren't much older than me when she got married. Besides, when a man with as much money as my husband makes asks you to marry him, you do it. Not only do we have a nice house of our own, but he bought this nice house for Ma and Pa. And, he bought me this nice dress I'm wearin'. What can Eamon afford to buy for you?"

Eamon and Clara stared at her without saying anything, but I wanted to scream, "So, he buys you presents for sex just like Pa did. It's a wonder Pa let you go, or did you just get too old for him? You're already looking older than your years just like Ma always did."

That thought made me look at Mabon. She still looked the same as she did on the night she had killed me — 5 feet of tornado in wrinkled skin and gray hair. The only difference was she got her hair cut short and permed instead of having that bun on the back of her head. I did have to admit that not having her hair pulled straight back kept her from looking older than she was like she used to, but she probably would look older if she hadn't changed her hair. She also wore a nice store-bought dress that flattered a figure that was still somewhat thin for a woman of her age. This woman had murdered me, so the store-bought dress and curly hair just looked like lipstick on a pig to me.

I looked over at Caelan. He was still tall and lean with strong, prominent features. His dark hair was starting to get a few flecks of gray in it. His clothes had improved from overalls to a tan plaid dress shirt and tan dress pants. He also wore a pair of dark brown loafers instead of work boots. The memories of how badly he beat Eamon as a child wouldn't allow me to appreciate his improved appearance either.

"Why don't we go out in the yard and sit on the deck," Mabon recommended. "It's gettin' a bit stuffy in here."

Clara ignored the veiled insult, stood, and said, "Okay."

Everyone followed Caelan down the linoleum paved hallway to the door that led to the deck. Eamon and Clara were the last ones to leave the house with Dog and me close behind. Eamon's breathing had improved, but he was still clammy and his hands were starting to shake.

There was a picnic table on the deck as well as several chairs. Caelan, Mabon and Regan sat at the picnic table, but Eamon and Clara pulled chairs up to the end of the table and sat away from the others. Dog and I stood just outside the door.

They must have sat there for ten minutes without saying a word before Mabon said, "Regan got some fixins for sandwiches at the store." Mabon looked at Regan and nodded before she said, "We'll go in and make the sandwiches."

Eamon grasped Clara's hand again and said, "You don't need to make any for us. We ate on the way out."

"Well, I'll be," Mabon sneered as she walked toward the door. "He's too good for our food now, too."

Regan followed Mabon as she said, "Let him sit and watch us eat then. Why should we go hungry because he's so prideful?"

When the door closed behind the women, Eamon leaned closer to Clara and whispered, "Don't take any food or drink from 'em. I wouldn't put it past them to put rat poison in it." Clara jerked her head in Eamon's direction, but before she could say anything he whispered, "Shhh! Just remember what MawMaw Tierney said."

Eamon, Clara, and Caelan didn't say anything else. The silence allowed us to hear everything the two women said through the kitchen window.

"Did you see the way she was just sittin' on Eamon's lap like they was already married?" Regan said.

"I seen it. They was holdin' hands just as shameless from the time they walked in the door. It's obvious she ain't nothing but a whore. I reckon I can see why Eamon would be wantin' a woman like that when his Pa's first love was that whore Ruby. Your Pa ain't never treated any of us right cuz that whore got in his blood and stayed there."

"I reckon Eamon will be gettin' just what he deserves."

Caelan got up and stomped into the house, slamming the door behind him. A few seconds after the door slammed, he screamed, "We can hear what y'all be sayin' out there on the deck. How dare you say that about me. I've always done right by y'all."

Clara looked at Eamon and whispered, "Regan told me to sit on your lap."

"You can't listen to a thing these people say," Eamon answered.

Honey could have dripped off Mabon's tongue as she said, "I never meant you no harm, old man. I'm just upset that Eamon brought that whore home. She done me dirty, she's always done me dirty, and now I guess that's what I've got to look forward to for the rest of my life."

Clara looked at Eamon and asked, "How could I have done her dirty when I've never met her before?"

"Remember what MawMaw Tierney told you," Eamon said as he stood. "Let's go. I told you there was no point in comin' out here. I hope you believe me now."

Clara nodded, stood, and followed Eamon down the deck's stairs and across the yard to the car.

Even though Eamon's hands were shaking bad by then, Clara seemed more upset by the things that happened that day than Eamon was, probably because she never saw people act like that before and wasn't used to it.

They stopped at Frisch's® on the way home and ate hamburgers in the car. While they ate, Clara expressed her surprise that there were people in the world who acted the way Eamon's family did that day. By the time they were finished, Eamon stopped shaking

When we got home, I told Dog to stay with Eamon, and I went with Clara to make sure she was all right. Emmett and Morgan were sitting on the couch, their arms crossed over their chests, staring at the phone they sat on the middle of the coffee table.

Clara looked at them and asked, "What's wrong?"

"The phone's been ringin' off the hook for over an hour," Morgan answered as he motioned toward the phone when it started ringing again.

"Why?" Clara asked as she walked toward the phone and answered it.

"Don't answer it," Morgan hurriedly said. "It's probably Eamon's family callin' again to cuss you out."

Clara gasped and asked, "Why would they do that?"

"It appears you just had a wonderful visit with Eamon's folks today, and they've been tellin' all of the relatives about it," Morgan answered and sighed.

Emmett said, "Apparently Eamon's Ma is mad that y'all left without sayin' anything. Why would y'all do something like that?"

"If you would have seen how badly they treated us, you would understand."

"That is kind of rude," Emmett said. "How would our Mom feel if someone did something like that to her."

"Can you imagine our Mom spreadin' rumors to get everyone in an uproar like this?" Clara asked.

Emmett and Morgan both shook their heads.

"That just goes to show you that this woman isn't like our Ma. She was as nasty as she could be, she called me bad names, she accused me of doin' her dirty when I'd never met her before, and Eamon was so afraid they'd poisoned our food that he wouldn't let me eat or drink while we were there."

"Why would he think they would poison your food?" Morgan asked.

"Maybe because she's the one who left Eamon crippled. She beat him almost to death, but just her spreadin' rumors like this ought to tell you what she's like."

The phone rang again. Clara looked at it for a second before she said, "Unplug it and go to bed. I'm goin' to bed. I've had enough nonsense for one day."

Dog and I followed Clara into her room. She sat on her bed, put her face in her palms, and cried. Dog sat on one side of her and I sat on the other side, but there was nothing we could do to make her feel better. Clara didn't understand that this had nothing to do with her. I saw these people act like this so many times when we were back on the mountain and still around them on a regular basis. The people who were calling didn't care that Mabon and Regan were spreading lies, and they didn't know that similar lies got spread about each one of them on a regular basis. That was how this family communicated.

Sadly, there were people who would talk about Clara behind her back and treat her badly for her entire marriage to Eamon based on the lies Mabon and Regan spread that night. If those people were mature enough to know that gossip says more about the person speaking than the person being spoken about, they might have gotten to know Clara enough to know that most people called her an angel. They entertained an angel that day but made her out to be a devil, and Clara felt the sting of it for many years to come.

CHAPTER SEVEN: THE WEDDING

Most of our family in the mountains didn't make much of a wedding. Often it happened in the living room of the bride's parent's house with only two witnesses, who were often the bride's parents, and the pastor in attendance. On a rare occasion, it was held at the church. Even then, there would still be sparse attendance. If it was held at the church, the reception would be potluck style refreshments that were provided by the congregation's women. Most of the time, the women would drop them off earlier in the day and return to the responsibilities of their own families instead of staying for the celebration.

It was rare that someone got married by a Justice of the Peace. A couple was not considered married unless the union was blessed by a man of God. Even in the case of those rushed weddings that occurred due to pregnancy or disapproving parents, the couple usually went to Jellico, Tennessee, where a pastor performed the ceremony.

Eamon and Clara had Clara's pastor marry them in the church even though the only people who would be attending were her two brothers, a sister who lived in the city, Mr. and Mrs. Williams, Everett and Crystal, and, of course, Dog and me. The wedding was held right after Sunday services, so a few friends from the congregation stayed for the ceremony.

It was understandable that relatives who lived in the mountains weren't able to travel all the way to Cincinnati for the ceremony, especially since weddings weren't typically a big celebration. The union itself was important enough that Clara's family, MawMaw Tierney, and Uncle Teagan called early that Sunday morning to extend their best wishes. What was not understandable was that no one from Eamon's family attended or called, not even the ones who lived in the Cincinnati area. I assumed it was because of the rumors Mabon and Regan were spreading. I couldn't understand why they didn't want to come, because I saw it as a privilege for Dog and me to stand next to Eamon while he exchanged vows with Clara.

Poverty and culture had taught our people not to think about a big, fancy wedding, but Eamon and Clara both got new clothes. Eamon wore a nice black suit, white shirt, and black tie. He was clean shaven and his hair was greased back. Clara wore a beautiful blush-colored dress, new black pumps, and a lightweight blush-colored coat she needed for spring and fall anyway. She got her hair cut and permed and wore make-up even though she rarely wore anything other than lipstick.

New clothes didn't dress up the pain inside Eamon. When they entered the foyer of the church, he started having a hard time breathing, which quickly developed into one of his spells. Clara sent Emmett to get a chair from one of the downstairs classrooms, and Eamon was so clammy and weak by the time Emmett returned that he flopped onto the chair like he was about to pass out.

Mr. Williams held Clara's hands, looked into her eyes, and said, "He'll be all right. I'll stay with him and make sure of it. You go on in and get a seat before the service starts, and I'll make sure he gets in there for the wedding."

Clara nodded, and Emmett and Morgan each took one of her arms and led her into the sanctuary.

Mr. Williams knelt in front of Eamon and asked, "Is there anything I can get for you?"

"Maybe something to drink," Eamon said.

"There's punch downstairs for the party after the wedding. Will you be okay if I leave you here to go get some?"

Eamon nodded, so Mr. Williams left him and returned a few minutes later with two cups of punch. Eamon quickly drank the first one, and within in a few minutes, he stopped shaking. He slowly became less clammy as he sipped the second cup. By the time the service was over, he was feeling much better.

As he stood to walk down the aisle, Mr. Williams asked, "Are you going to be okay?"

Eamon nodded and said, "I'm feelin' much less weak, but my stomach is lurchin' at the thought of walkin' into that church."

"What is it with you and churches?" Mr. Williams asked.

"You don't want to know," Eamon said as the two men walked side by side toward the aisle that cut through the middle of the pews and led to the front of the church.

As the two men walked toward the front of the church, the Pastor stepped down from the pulpit and stood at the front of the aisle. Clara stepped out from a front pew and stood to the left of the pastor, and Eamon joined her and stood to the right of the pastor a couple of seconds later. Once the couple were in place, Emmet, Morgan, and Lana, the sister Dog and I had not met until that morning, came out of the pew they were sitting on and stood next to Clara. Both of the brothers were dressed in nice black suits, and Lana wore a nice pair of black dress slacks and a white top whose collar tied in a bow. Everett and Crystal moved to the pew next to Clara's siblings, and Mr. and Mrs. Williams moved to the pew next to Eamon. Once all of the invited attendees were situated, several members of the congregation who were staying for the ceremony moved closer to the front of the church.

Everyone stared at Eamon and Clara as they answered the pastor's questions with "I do". Once all of the questions were answered, the pastor invited Eamon to kiss his bride. Eamon looked around at all of the faces in the church before he gave Clara a quick peck on the cheek.

The pastor giggled and said, "I now pronounce you man and wife. Turn and face your guests."

Eamon and Clara turned to face the pews as the pastor said, "Some of the ladies of the congregation have been kind enough to bring food and a cake for a celebration after the ceremony. Let's all go downstairs and enjoy what they brought."

Dog and I followed behind everyone else as Eamon and Clara led the group down the aisle and down the stairs to the classroom area where a party was arranged in the largest classroom. There was a coffee percolator and cups sitting on a table inside the door of the classroom. All of the men stopped and got coffee while the women went to a long table with many types of food on it and filled their plates. The men sipped their coffee as they walked to the seats they chose around the guest table, set their cups down, and went to the food table. After Eamon sat down, Dog and I took our usual places of Dog at his feet and me standing behind him.

When everyone was seated, with Eamon and Clara sitting next to each other at the head of the table, Lana looked at Eamon and said, "I can't believe I haven't met you yet when you live just down the street from us."

Emmett looked at her, smiled and said, "You were afraid to invite him down, because he might eat some of yours and Clara's doughnuts."

"Hush, now," Lana said in a tone that sounded harsh, but her smile revealed a different story. "Truth is, I guess I don't have much time for visitin' since I have a job. Me and Clara try to get together as often as we can to share a box of doughnuts and a pot of coffee at my kitchen table. Other than that, I'm usually workin' or takin' care of my children and my house."

It wasn't surprising that she worked outside the home. There was a strength about her that few women I'd met had. She was tall, thin, and pretty with short curly hair that had a tint of red in it, unlike her dark-haired brothers and sisters, but she carried herself like she had the power of a man. Her back was straight, her gait was confident and powerful, and she didn't hesitate to look the world in the eye. She had to have some type of inner strength to wear pants to church and get away with it at a time when that seemed to be forbidden.

"Is your husband out of work?" Eamon asked.

Clara leaned closer to Eamon and whispered, "Her husband hasn't been in the best of health since he was in the TB hospital a few years ago. He works when he can, but he's not always able to."

Lana smiled at Clara and said, "Yes, he was in the hospital for quite a while, but he's doin' much better now."

"I'm sorry he couldn't come today," Eamon said. "It would have been nice to meet him."

"I left him home with the young'uns. I won't be able to stay long myself. I'm goin' to have to leave when I'm done eatin'. His patience with young'uns can be short-lived."

"I understand," Eamon said as he nodded.

The table got quiet while everyone ate.

When everyone was finished, Clara looked at Lana and said, "Since you have to leave soon, let's get us some of that dessert and coffee."

As Lana followed Clara to the dessert table, Emmett said loud enough for his sisters to hear, "If y'all want some doughnuts, you best get 'em now before they eat 'em all."

Lana turned to Emmet, smiled, and said, "Hush now!"

The other women at the table followed the sisters. When the women returned, the men got their dessert and refilled their coffee cups. Once everyone was situated with dessert and coffee, the conversation continued.

"So, tonight's the weddin' night," Lana said, proving how opposite in personality the two sisters were. "Everyone's goin' to know what you two will be up to."

"Lana," Clara chastised as her face turned red.

Several people giggled, Eamon started using his fork to play with the food that was still on his plate, and Morgan put down his fork and cleared his throat.

Lana laughed and said, "I'm just speakin' the truth."

Emmett smirked, "If you're goin' to work for a living, Lana, you ought to be a truck driver. You already know how to talk like one. You'd fit right in."

Clara leaned closer to Lana and scolded, "We're in a church!"

Lana laughed and said, "The good Lord knows what y'all are goin' to be doin' tonight. He invented it."

Emmett laughed while Clara looked over her shoulder, turned back to Lana, and said, "Shhh, the pastor's here now."

Lana laughed again and said, "He's married, ain't he? I think he knows."

Clara looked from face to face before she said, "Would everyone please just eat your dessert?"

Lana and Emmett laughed.

When everyone was finished eating, Lana stood up, threw her napkin on her plate, and said, "I really have to be gettin' back to the children. If y'all need anything, let me know."

"Thank you," Clara said. "Be careful goin' home."

Each person slowly left the room in the same manner — they stood, announced their departure, and left without ceremony, handshakes, or hugs.

After the wedding, Eamon and Clara were as shy about consummating their marriage as they were those first weeks of courting when they could barely talk with each other. They decided to go to a movie together before returning to Clara's apartment that was now their apartment.

Dog and I sat in the seats behind them at the movie. Even though our ghost bodies couldn't enjoy the popcorn, sodas, and candy they treated themselves to in celebration of their wedding, it was nice to watch the movie. I had never been in a movie theater before. I was so amazed as I watched the pictures flash on the big lighted screen in the dark room that I could barely follow the story the movie was trying to tell. It was good no one could see Dog and me, because Dog had his feet on the back of Eamon's seat through the movie and was not suppressing the panting and yipping that showed his excitement.

When Eamon and Clara returned to their busy apartment that Emmett and Morgan were still living in, Eamon whispered to Clara, "I'm happy we went to the movies and had some time alone together as husband and wife."

It seemed to me that when people are used to living in the cramped conditions poverty can necessitate, some social graces are just not understandable any more even after a rise out of poverty begins. Clara's brothers were still living in the apartment even though they now had factory jobs that paid more than Clara's restaurant job. It seemed like they were so used to living in poverty that they hadn't yet figured out they could make it on their own.

The brothers took a few pictures of Eamon and Clara in the living room before the siblings returned to their normal routine. In half the pictures, Clara continued to wear her blush-colored coat before she remembered to take it off. I wondered if the chaos of such a busy apartment on such a special day caused her to forget.

Eamon was not used to the sibling's routine, so he continued to stand where the pictures were taken when Clara went to the kitchen to make supper for all of them. He looked around the apartment for several minutes like he was confused before he joined the brothers who were sitting on the couch talking. When he joined them, Emmett made off-color jokes about the wedding night every time Clara was out of hearing range, and Eamon blushed and looked away each time a joke was made.

When Eamon and Clara did retire to the bedroom, Clara whispered to Eamon, "I can still hear them out there, so I bet they can hear us."

That was all that was needed to quell the passions of this shy couple that night and for the rest of the week. It wasn't until the next weekend when both brothers had dates that Eamon and Clara were finally alone long enough to feel comfortable touching each other in ways they never had before. After a few tentative kisses that were more than they had shared until that moment, nature finally took control and became stronger than their modesty. Fortunately, sex was not the focus of their relationship, because the only time they were alone during their first months of marriage was when Emmett and Morgan went on their Saturday night dates. Dog and I got in the habit of visiting Mr. and Mrs. Williams on Saturday nights.

Despite the rarity of their contact, Clara quickly became pregnant. Marriage didn't seem to hold the importance pregnancy did. Maybe that's why so many of the marriages from our culture had problems. Marriage was treated more like a chore that was required rather than something to be nurtured. Expecting a child seemed to be a different story. When Clara knew she was pregnant, she quit her job, and the brothers found an apartment of their own to share. Marriage didn't warrant a reason for the newlyweds to be alone, but parenthood did — maybe because of the cultural belief that children are the property of the father to do with as he sees fit. Having someone else aware of and involved in parental discipline would have been seen as highly inappropriate. Therefore, Eamon and Clara were alone as expectant parents, except for Dog and me.

I hadn't witnessed how Clara's parents handled their marriage, but I was happy to see that Eamon was doing a better job than our parents did. Despite the fact that he wasn't an abusive husband like our father was, Dog and I were still sometimes concerned about the growing tension. Any time two people live together they're going to get on each other's nerves. What concerned Dog and me was how Clara and Eamon handled this when it happened. Clara turned away from Eamon, rolled her eyes, and tightened her facial muscles, but she never told him how she felt. Eamon walked into the next room and sulked, but he never told her how he felt. Since they didn't seem to know how to resolve conflict, I was afraid it would get worse.

Clara was home doing laundry the day it got worse. Her belly was already big with child, so she was sitting on the bed folding the clothes she just took off the line and carried up from the basement where there was a wringer washing machine and clothes lines that the tenants shared. There were six apartments, so each person had a day of the week they were allowed to do their laundry, with no one assigned Sunday since that was the Lord 's Day.

Dog and I were staying with Clara more since she got pregnant, so we were sitting on the bed with her when Eamon stormed into the house, stomped to the bedroom, and started yelling. Clara's eyes got wide and her mouth fell open, but she didn't say anything.

He paused, and blushed, before he yelled, "Why are you lookin' at me like that?"

She continued to stare at him with the same look on her face without answering.

He grabbed the shirt she was folding out of her hands, ripped it into several pieces, threw it on the floor, and stormed out of the apartment. Dog and I followed him. He stormed out of the building so fast that his handicapped leg almost made him fall down the steps several times. When he got outside, he ran as well as his crippled leg would allow him to across the street to Mr. Williams' apartment.

Mr. Williams looked concerned when he saw Eamon standing on the other side of the apartment door. He ushered Eamon inside as he asked, "What happened, son? What's wrong?"

"I messed everything up," Eamon said as he walked across the living room and sat on the couch.

Mr. Williams sat next to him and asked, "What did you mess up, son?"

Eamon covered his face with his palms before he pushed his palms through his hair. He then sat up quickly and said, "I really messed up. One of the guys down at the store talked me into goin' to a poker game with him, and I lost most of my paycheck. I was so mad that I went home and yelled at Clara and tore up a shirt she was foldin'."

Mr. Williams gasped before he asked, "You didn't hit her, did you?"

"Naw, I didn't hit her."

"Did you want to hit her?"

Eamon looked into Mr. Williams eyes and said, "I promised God when I was a child that if he'd get me out of that hell I was livin' in that I'd never hit another person like I was bein' hit. It nary matters whether I wanted to hit her or not. I ain't got no choice."

"Whew," Mr. Williams said as he exhaled deeply.

Eamon rested his elbows on his knees, rested his face in his palms, and shook his head as he asked, "What am I goin' to do?"

"I don't know what you're goin' to do about losin' all of that money. What caused you to do that, son?"

"I don't know. It just felt good while I was doin' it. I usually feel like everything is out of control and about to cave in on me, but I felt like I had some control while I was winnin' early on. Then, when I started losin', I felt like I'd get back on top if I kept tryin'. Then, I felt like I'd lost so much that I couldn't afford to stop until I won it back. When it was all gone and I couldn't even get back in the game, that feelin' like everything is out of control was ten times worse than it normally is. I went home and took it out on Clara."

"I'm sorry to hear that, son. You've got to stay away from that gambling. Don't be doing that no more. I need some time to think on how you might fix the money part, but right now you've got to go home and fix things with your wife. You know what the good book says — don't let the sun go down on your anger. Get on out of here and fix things with Clara. I'll try to figure out what to do about the money and talk to you more tomorrow."

"I can't go back and face her."

"What other option do you have? Are you going to just run out on her and leave a pregnant wife? Are you just going to run away from your baby? Your only choice is to go home and talk to that woman."

"I just can't."

"You can and you will. I'm throwing you out, so you won't have any place else to go but home to fix this. Get on out of my apartment. You're not welcome back here until you fix this."

Eamon stormed out of Mr. Williams' apartment, but he didn't go home. He limped around the block as he mumbled to himself, "How dare him tell me to do what the good book says! That so called good book ain't never brought me nothing but trouble! How could he say that to me after what that nasty preacher back home did to me! Not only did that nasty preacher stick his dick in me like I was a woman, but then he told my Pa lies to keep from gettin' caught! I'll never forget the beatin' those lies brought down on me! That old son of a bitch! He knew how my folks beat on me! Everyone knew how my folks beat on all of us! Did anyone help us? Hell no! Instead of helpin' us, that ol' bastard used what he knew to cover his own ass! I'll never forget the beatin' that brought down on me! I was already crippled and that ol' bastard lied to get my body beat on some more! If I hadn't gotten strong enough to overpower that ol' bastard when I was a teenager, he would have probably stuck his dick in me for the rest of my life! That ol' bastard!"

By the time Eamon was finished ranting, he had circled the block and was back at Clara's and his apartment. He sat on the stoop, buried his face in his palms, and cried until it looked to me like he was too tired to cry anymore. He rubbed his crippled leg for several minutes before he got up. As he walked to the side door of their apartment building, he mumbled, "If the good book tells me not to go to bed angry, I'm goin' to make good and damn sure I'm mad as hell when I lay down to go to sleep. That so called good book ain't never done nothing but cause me trouble, so I'll be damned if I'm goin' to start listenin' to it now."

He walked up the stairs to their apartment much slower and safer than when he went down them earlier in the evening. When he got into the apartment, he went straight to the bedroom, crawled under the blankets on his side of the bed without changing out of his day clothes, and lay on his side facing away from Clara. She was already in bed and laying on her side facing away from him. She stayed in that position and didn't say anything when he lay down.

Dog and I sat on the end of the bed and watched them ignoring each other. I knew this was the beginning of a problem. When I was alive, Eamon and I never ignored each other. No matter how hard it got, we always looked each other in the eye. That assured us that we were not alone even when it wasn't safe to speak. We knew it wasn't good to look away from someone you needed to rely on for survival. It frightened me that they seemed to be developing a habit of ignoring each other — and so soon after they got married. If they didn't make eye contact, they would start to feel alone and unsafe like I would have felt if Eamon would have ever ignored me. If they didn't stop this, they were in danger of their love becoming buried so deep they wouldn't realize how deep it was until they were separated in an irreparable way like Eamon and I were separated — by death. I didn't want that for them.

The next morning, Clara worked on fixing the financial situation Eamon's gambling created. She had been good at saving money when she was working, so she had some in the bank. She used some of it to pay the bills that were due that week. When he did it for several more weeks in a row, that fix became increasingly less feasible.

Dog and I spent enough time with Clara by then that I was starting to be able to listen to her thoughts like I was able to do with Eamon. She was starting to feel out of control, and that was a very uncomfortable feeling for her. When they ran out of food, she spent a day experiencing a hunger that was more intense than any hunger she knew before pregnancy. When that was made more difficult by the baby kicking in protest at what I can only imagine was it feeling hunger, Clara found a courage that was rare for her – she spoke up instead of quietly trying to fix it. Even when speaking up, she was so kind that the impact was minimal.

The next day was Friday, so she asked a neighbor to drive her to Eamon's work. She was waiting in the passenger seat of his car when he left the Goodwill®.

When he saw her, he walked over to the passenger side of the car and asked, "What are you doin' here?"

"It's payday. I came to see where your paycheck is goin'."

His blush showed his embarrassment even though he walked around the car, got in, and said, "I don't think that's any of your business. I'm the bread winner in this family. It's my money to do with as I see fit."

"You put this baby in my belly and then ran through my savings so that I can't feed myself to feed the baby. You told me you knew hunger when you still lived at home. You know what it feels like, so why are you makin' me and this baby feel it now?"

"Don't you dare make it sound like I'm like my folks!"

"I reckon it's your choice whether you're goin' to be like your folks or not. Are you goin' to feed me and this child, or are you goin' to let us go hungry like your folks made you go hungry?"

He leaned his forehead on the steering wheel and asked, "What am I supposed to do?

"I'm pretty good with money. I had enough saved from when I was working to get us through these last few weeks. I want you to give me your check every Friday night and let me pay the bills."

He looked at her and said, "So you can take all my money like my Pa did! I don't think so!"

Tears welled in her eyes as she said, "Okay. I won't take your whole paycheck. I'll meet you here on Friday night and get it. I'll pay whatever bills are due and get some groceries in the house. With whatever is left, let's be fair to both of us. It's awful hard for me to be trapped in that apartment all the time when I'm used to workin'. Take me out to eat, and you can have whatever's left to do with as you see fit. If you waste the rest of it, you'll be the one goin' to work with no money in your pocket."

"What if I don't agree to this?"

"I can't let this child starve before it even comes out of my belly. If you don't agree to this, I reckon I won't have any other choice than to go home to the mountains and live with my Ma and Pa."

"That's what you've wanted all along anyway, isn't it?"

"Where do you even come up with the things you say? I left the mountains, because there wasn't any work. If I go back with a child in tow, about the only thing I'm ever goin' to have is a room at my folks' house and food in our bellies. There won't be nothin' more to look forward to."

His body got stiffer at first, but then he relaxed it, leaned back in the seat, and said, "Okay. I agree."

"Everett came by today and asked me if I could return to work. I told him I didn't have anyone up here to watch the baby while I was at work, so I couldn't. He said he only needs me for a few weeks. One of his waitresses needs to go home and take care of her sick Mom for a while. He wants me to work until she returns, or if she doesn't return, he wants me to work until he can find a replacement. I told him I would. That will make us enough money to get our bills caught up and get a little money back in the bank. I'll be done workin' in plenty of time to be home for the baby when it comes."

Eamon sighed and nodded.

I was afraid I was seeing them create another problem in their marriage. If Eamon continued to push Clara into corners until she was forced to fight back with meek threats and ultimatums, his relationship with her would be like Dog's had been with Caelan. It might not be as violent, but being cornered is being cornered. Dog and I looked at each other, and I sensed that Dog was as scared as I was that things might become as bad here in the city as they had been back home.

CHAPTER EIGHT: IMPLEMENTING THE PLAN

Clara started working for Everett again on Monday morning. Eamon drove her to work and picked her up like he did when they were dating. When he dropped her off in the morning, I stayed with her and Dog went with Eamon. I was glad to see that Everett gave her easy jobs, so she wouldn't be on her feet too much while she was pregnant. The only time he had her waiting tables or cleaning up was during busy times. The rest of the time he had her sitting behind the cash register doing some of his paperwork between checking out customers. This freed him to do some of the physical work Clara would have normally done.

Everett didn't schedule Clara to work on Fridays, because that was the day she went to Eamon's work to get his check before he spent it. Since she didn't have to be there until the end of Eamon's shift, this meant she had to catch the bus. Catching the bus became more difficult as Clara's pregnancy progressed, so Lana traded days off with a co-worker and started riding the bus with her. Lana got on the bus a few blocks up the street at her house, and Clara joined her on the bus when it stopped in front of Clara and Eamon's apartment building. Lana knocked on the window to let Clara know which bus she was on, and then Clara got on that one.

One Friday as Dog and I followed Clara onto the bus and down the aisle to where Lana was sitting, Lana said loudly enough for everyone to hear, "Well, my, my, look at you. Who got you in that shape? Everyone knows what you've been doin'."

Clara sat next to Lana and said, "Shush, now. You're embarrassin' me."

"That was the plan," Lana said as Dog and I sat in the seat behind them.

"I don't know where you get that from. Ma and Pa surely don't act that way."

"I guess I got it from the same place Emmett did."

"You both need to leave it wherever you got it from."

Lana laughed and said, "Y'all have a car. You need to let Eamon teach you how to drive, so you can use it on the days you need it. You could drop him off at work from time to time, do what you need to do, and then pick him up. It would take some pressure off of him, too. He wouldn't have to come home with his legs hurtin' like they do and drive you to the grocery store."

"He doesn't seem to mind. He sits in the car while I go in shoppin'."

"I'm sure he'd be much more comfortable sittin' at home listenin' to the radio."

"He listens to the radio in the car," Clara said as she grabbed the back of the seat in front of her when the bus hit a pothole.

"Is there a reason you don't want to learn to drive?"

Clara shook her head.

"Okay, we'll ask Eamon about it when we get to his work."

"You don't know how to drive."

"I don't have a car, but that doesn't mean I don't know how to drive. I got my license shortly after I moved up here."

Clara looked at her and said, "I didn't know you had a driver's license."

"There ain't much point in lettin' people know when I don't have a car to drive. It's not hard to drive. You can do it."

"All right. I guess we can at least talk to him about it."

Lana talked about her children and her job for the rest of the ride, and Clara seemed content to listen. When the bus approached their destination, Lana pulled the cord to signal a stop. Clara didn't get up until the bus was at a complete stop.

As Clara waddled down the aisle, the bus driver said, "I've got a schedule to keep. You could have started walking up here when you pulled the cord."

91

Lana, Dog and I were behind Clara. Dog growled when she started walking faster, but Lana lay her hand on Clara's shoulder and said, "You take your time."

While Clara waddled down the three steps she had to go down to get to the sidewalk, Lana looked at the bus driver and said, "Don't you ever talk to a pregnant woman like that again, and most especially don't you ever talk to my sister like that again. It wasn't safe for her to stand while the bus was still movin', because you drive like a maniac. This bus was jumpin' all over the place. She had to hold onto the seat in front of her most of the way here to keep from fallin' off the seat. We'll be on this bus every Friday, and you will treat us both with respect. If not, I'll be talkin' to your boss. Do you understand me?"

The bus driver swallowed hard and said, "Yes ma'am. I'm sorry, ma'am."

"That's better," Lana said before she joined Clara, Dog, and me on the sidewalk.

As the bus pulled away, Clara said, "I don't know how you get away with talkin' to folks like that. No one takes me seriously when I do."

"You can't stand like a mouse and talk like a lion. That never works. You let them know you've got something to back up that roar, and they'll back down every time."

"I don't think I'll ever be able to do that."

They walked the half block from the bus stop to Goodwill® in silence. When they went inside, Lana ushered Clara to one of the lobby chairs and helped her sit down before Lana sat down herself. When Eamon wasn't around, Dog lay at Clara's feet like he did at Eamon's feet, and I stood behind her like I did for Eamon. We were growing to love her, too.

Eamon entered the lobby about ten minutes later with his check in his hand. He handed it to Clara, and she put it in her purse.

While Lana helped Clara stand, she said, "Eamon, Clara and I were talkin' on the way over here. I think you should teach Clara to drive, so she doesn't have to take the bus in this condition or be haulin' a little baby on the bus once it's born."

"Women don't drive," Eamon answered.

"Is that a law?"

"I don't know if it is or not, but I ain't never known of a woman who drove before."

"Women drive all the time. I have a driver's license myself."

"Well, I don't think Clara needs one."

"You want your wife draggin' a baby over here on the bus in the snow this winter. You know this child is due in January, and that's one of the coldest months around these parts. She wouldn't have to be on this bus at all every Friday if it wasn't for what you did with the —"

"Okay, okay," Eamon interrupted her. "I'll start teachin' her to drive."

"When?" Lana asked.

"I don't rightly know."

"This weekend," Lana demanded. "The snow could start hittin' any day now, and she only has two months until this baby is born. There isn't any time to wait."

Eamon pulled the keys out of his pocket and said, "Come on, let's go home."

While Lana and Clara followed Eamon to the car, Lana asked, "Does that mean you'll start teachin' her this weekend?"

Dog and I ran ahead and got in the back seat.

"Okay, okay," Eamon said. "I'll start teachin' her this weekend."

The car was parked in front of the store. Eamon got in the driver's seat while Lana helped Clara into the passenger seat. Clara scooted over to make room for Lana, but Lana said, "No. You just stay where you are. I'll get in the back." She was already sitting in the back seat next to Dog and me by the time she finished the sentence.

Just as promised, Eamon started teaching Clara to drive the next morning. She got up early and made breakfast for both of them. After three cups of coffee, Eamon picked up the keys and said, "Come on then. Let's go drive."

Clara followed him down the stairs and got in the car on the driver's side, Dog and I got in the back seat, and Eamon got in on the passenger side before he gave her the keys. She put the keys in the ignition without being told what to do, and Eamon said, "That's good."

"I watch you do it every day. It's pretty easy to figure out."

Eamon nodded and said, "You've got four peddles down on the floor. The one on the far left is the emergency brake, that little one. The one next to that is the clutch. You have to press that in any time you shift gears. You'll use your left foot for that one. The one in the middle is the brake. You press that one with your right foot when you want to stop the car. The one on the right is the gas pedal, and, of course, you use your right foot for that one. You press that one down when you want the car to go or to go faster. Does that make sense?"

Clara nodded.

"You have to keep your foot on the clutch while you shift gears. The emergency brake is already on, so the car will stay still. If the emergency brake isn't on and you press down on the clutch when the car is sitting still, the car will roll. The emergency brake is on now, so it's safe to press down the clutch. Put your left foot on the clutch and press it down, and I'll show you where the gears are."

She did what he said, and he demonstrated on the shifter as he said, "This here is first gear. This here is second. This here is third. This here is fourth. This here is reverse. The lowest gear is for the lowest speed and the higher gears are for the higher speeds. You'll hear the engine start to sound like it's strainin' as you go faster, and that's when you want to shift to a higher gear. Does that make sense?"

Clara nodded.

"Is your foot still on the clutch?"

"Yes."

"Keep your foot on the clutch and put the car in first gear."

She did as he asked.

"Now, press in the brake so the car won't roll and pull that lever above the emergency brake to release it. You do know how to steer, right? You just hold the steerin' wheel straight unless you want to turn, and then you just turn it the way you want to go."

Clara nodded.

"Oh, and one more thing," he said as he touched a lever on the steering column. "You want to signal to let people know when you're goin' to turn. Push that up to signal a right turn, and pull it down to signal a left turn. Do you got that?"

Clara nodded.

"I think that's as much as you need to get started. Go ahead and pull out. Let's go for a drive."

As she pulled forward, the car stalled.

I was feeling very proud of Eamon for being so patient and so good at explaining everything to her, but that feeling was damaged when he yelled, "Damnit. I knew women shouldn't drive."

"Let me try it again," Clara said.

Eamon sighed and said, "Press the clutch in and let it out slowly as the car starts to move."

He sighed loudly each of the three times she stalled the car, but she got it moving on the fourth try. After about a half hour of driving, she was doing pretty good. I thought she was a natural.

When she seemed comfortable enough driving that she didn't need a lot of direction, Eamon asked, "Why did you want to learn to drive anyway? Your Ma never drove, did she?"

"Naw, she never drove. I just reckon Lana's right that it'll make it easier on both of us if I learn to drive. I won't have to be draggin' a baby on the bus to meet you on Friday, and you won't have to drive me around. You can stay home and listen to the radio on the comfortable couch while I drive myself to the grocery store."

He leaned forward and tried to look into her front-facing eyes as he asked, "So, you won't be needin' me no more?"

"I won't be needin' you to be drivin' me around no more. You can stay home and rest, and I can take myself where I need to go."

He huffed loudly and fell back into his seat. He ran his palm through his greased hair and fidgeted as he said, "You're already takin' my paycheck and doin' with it what you think ought to be done. You're meetin' me at my work to take it like I'm a child or something. Now, you want to learn to drive, so you won't even need me for that anymore. The next thing I know you'll be takin' this car and drivin' back to the mountains to live with yer Ma and Pa like you done threatened to do, and there won't be a thing I can do about it."

Clara glanced at him and looked back at the road. She gripped the steering wheel tight and said, "If I ever wanted to go back home, my brothers would drive me. That ain't got nothing to do with why I want to drive."

Eamon stretched his leg across the car and pressed his foot on the gas pedal. As the car went faster and faster, he yelled, "Since you're such a good damn driver, tell me what you're goin' to do now!"

Clara gripped the steering wheel so tight the muscles in her arms bulged. It took her several seconds to realize she needed to press the brake. When she did, the car fought being braked and accelerated at the same time.

Clara screamed, "You're just breakin' your own car!"

Eamon removed his foot from the pedal. Since Clara's foot was still on the brake. The car jerked to a stop and stalled.

Clara got out of the car and said, "I'm never gettin' behind the wheel of a car again. I'll drag my pregnant belly and then a baby on the bus, and you can wear yourself out drivin' me any place I need to go."

She slammed the car door and started walking.

Eamon slammed the side of his fist on the dashboard several times before he leaned his forehead on it and cried. By the time he was cried out, Clara was several blocks up the street. He slid over to the driver's seat, turned the car around, and drove it to her. He drove slowly next to her as she walked and said, "Get in the car."

She kept walking without answering him.

"Get in the car!" he yelled.

When she didn't get in the car, he stopped it, got out, and ran to her as fast as his crippled leg would carry him. He stopped in front of her, grabbed her upper arms, and said, "Please, just come on back home. I'm just so afraid you're goin' to leave me like my brothers and sisters did."

Clara looked into his eyes and asked, "What are you talkin' about?"

Eamon let go of her arms and paced back and forth as he said, "I haven't talked to my brothers and sisters since I left home. MawMaw Tierney told me none of them want to talk to me, because they believe everything Regan said about me. She told me not to even try to talk to them, because they'd only hurt me more than I've already been hurt."

Clara walked over to him and ran her hand up and down his back as she said, "Calm down, now. Let's get in the car and go on home. We'll figure it out from there."

As they drove home, Clara said, "I'm sorry you're goin' through so much, but you can't keep takin' it out on me, especially not after the baby comes."

"I'm sorry. I didn't mean it. It won't happen again. I won't let it."

After a long silence, Clara said, "You really haven't talked to any of your brothers and sisters since you left home?"

"I haven't talked to any of them since I went to live with MawMaw Tierney and Uncle Teagan. MawMaw told me none of them want to talk to me."

"Do you have any of their phone numbers?"

"I reckon I could get them."

"Maybe you ought to try callin' them. Maybe they would understand if you told them what happened."

"But MawMaw Tierney said —"

"Your MawMaw is a fine woman, but maybe she loves you so much she's tryin' to protect you from something you don't need protectin' from. Maybe if you call one of them and tell them your side of the story —"

"I reckon it's worth a try."

When we got home, Dog and I sat on the couch next to Eamon as he called MawMaw Tierney. After a lot of persuading, he convinced her to give him the only phone number she had — his sister Darcy. She was the one Caelan called Legs, because she was the only sister who was tall. Hand-me-downs from the other sisters were always too short for her, so she had spent her childhood tugging at the hem of her dress. MawMaw Tierney explained that most of his brothers and sisters who still lived on the mountain didn't have phones, but Darcy got one when she moved to Cincinnati.

Eamon dialed Darcy's number when he hung up. The phone rang three times before she answered. I was sitting close enough that I could hear what she said.

"Darcy?" he asked.

"Yes. Who is this?"

"This is Eamon. MawMaw Tierney told me you moved to the city." Darcy didn't say anything for so long that Eamon asked, "Are you still there?"

"Unlike you, I'm still here."

"What's that supposed to mean?"

"You left us!"

"I had to. Pa tried to kill me."

"Regan told us you'd say that. She told us everythin'. I know you left because you had to take care of us for so long you were sick of us. You ran away so you wouldn't have to take care of us no more."

"That isn't what happened. Ask MawMaw Tierney. She'll tell you."

"And just what did you and MawMaw Tierney think was goin' to happen to us when you ran away and left us with th —"

"Don't you realize how much I cared about y'all by how much I took care of you when we were little? I wouldn't have left if I'd had any other choice. You know how Regan is —"

"Don't ever call here again," she screamed before she slammed down the phone receiver.

Eamon put his elbows on his knees and leaned his face into his hands. I think he was trying to hide his tears.

Clara came out of the kitchen, sat next to him, and rubbed his back as she said, "I'm sorry. It's goin' to be okay."

Eamon's voice came from behind his hands as he said, "They don't even remember that I cared enough about them to do as much as I was able to do. They think I just left them, but I couldn't take them with me. How can I make them understand that?"

Clara put her arm across his shoulders, and he fell into her lap and cried. The tears must have cleansed something that needed to be cleansed, because they got along like they had when they were dating after that — for a while anyway.

CHAPTER NINE: IT'S A BOY

The birth of Eamon and Clara's first child blessed them with a son they named Mitchell. Although Eamon left the work for Clara to do, he did spend most of his free time holding the baby. Dog and I also spent a lot of time with Mitchell, and part of the reason was that it sometimes seemed like he could see us.

Mitchell made Eamon so happy that the happiness alone seemed to have put some of Eamon and Clara's problems on hold. Eamon was so focused on the present that he rarely visited the past, so his mood was much more stable and predictable. This allowed Clara to be open to Eamon instead of reserved and tentative. It was a lot of responsibility to put on a baby, but Mitchell brought a lot of healing into this home when he was born.

Mitchell was only home a few days when Clara carried a baby bottle into the living room, leaned over to take Mitchell from Eamon's arms, and Eamon said, "Wait a minute, Clara. Just watch him for a minute."

"What's he doing?" Clara asked

Dog and I snuggled up to Mitchell, and he smiled like he was aware of us.

"Look!" Eamon said. "He looks like he's lookin' at something, and it's makin' him smile."

"He's probably just got gas. Babies smile for no reason all the time."

I tickled the bottom of one of Mitchell's feet while Dog licked the other one, and Mitchell squealed with glee.

Eamon looked up at Clara and said, "Don't tell me you didn't see that?"

"I saw it. It's just him bein' a baby. That's what all babies do."

She placed her arm under the back of Mitchell's head and the other under his legs and lifted him as Eamon said, "I could just swear he's seein' something we're not seein'."

"There's always a logical explanation."

"I don't know. I sort of remember when I was a little kid — oh, never mind. It was probably just my imagination."

Dog and I looked at each other and back at Eamon when he mentioned remembering something from when he was a child. I wondered if he remembered seein' my ghost when I stayed to protect him.

Clara sat on the other end of the couch, put the bottle in Mitchell's mouth, and said, "Probably."

As with all babies, one day of diapers, bottles, and holding fingers blended into the next day of diapers, bottles, and holding fingers until Mitchell was old enough to begin doing some things on his own. In the interim, lots of hugs, cuddles, and giggles kept any of it from being boring.

When Mitchell started to walk, he became a real handful for Eamon, who discovered it was even more difficult to stand on his handicapped leg when he was bending over to meet the needs of a child. This proved particularly true one day when Mitchell was about two years old. Eamon usually went to the passenger side of the car to get Mitchell out, because Eamon was afraid his bad leg wouldn't allow him to safely hold a child in oncoming traffic. On this day, Mitchell ran across the front seat and jumped into Eamon's arms. Eamon would have stumbled into a passing car if he hadn't grabbed Mitchell with one hand and the car door with the other one.

From the back seat of the car, Dog barked and I screamed, "Mitchell, be careful!"

Mitchell looked at me when I said that. He continued to look at me while Eamon closed the door and carried Mitchell around the front of the car.

When Eamon knelt and sat Mitchell on the sidewalk, Dog and I got out of the car and stood next to them as Eamon said, "You hurt Daddy when you jump on him like that, little boy. I'm goin' to have to let you walk from here. Daddy's back and hip really hurt now."

Eamon took Mitchell's hand, and they walked about a half block down the street before Mitchell pointed to a cat across the street and yelled, "Kitty cat!"

Eamon rubbed his hip with his free hand while he looked across the street and said, "Yes, that's a kitty cat."

Mitchell yanked his hand out of Eamon's hand and ran toward the cat.

"No, Mitchell!" Eamon screamed as he chased Mitchell into the street without looking. In spite of his crippled leg, Eamon ran so fast that he grabbed Mitchell before he got to the center line.

A car's tires squealed as it stopped inches from them. Dog growled at the car as Eamon fell to his good knee in front of the car, pulled Mitchell into a hug, and started crying.

The man who was driving got out of the car and ran to them as he yelled, "Are you okay? Are you okay?"

Eamon continued to hold Mitchell and cry.

The man lay his hand on Eamon's shoulder and asked, "Are you okay, buddy?"

Eamon looked up at the car's driver, wiped his eyes, and said, "Yeah. Yeah. We're a'right. I'm sorry."

"Not to worry," the man said. When he saw Eamon was having a hard time standing with Mitchell in his arms, the man grasped Eamon's arm and helped him to his feet. "I've got a little guy at home myself. You can't let them out of your sight for a second."

The man continued to hold onto Eamon's arm while we all walked to the sidewalk. As we walked, Eamon stammered, "He just yanked his hand right out of mine — I don't know what — oh, yeah, he saw a cat. He saw a cat and yanked his hand away and was in the street before I could get him. What if your car would have —"

Once they were on the sidewalk, the man patted Eamon on the back and said, "Everyone's okay. That's all that matters. Don't beat yourself up." The man looked at Eamon's leg and asked, "How could you catch him that fast with your leg hurt?"

Eamon shrugged.

"Do you live far from here?"

"Just in that buildin' right there," Eamon stammered as he pointed at it. "I was walkin' him to our side door when he —"

The man patted Eamon on the back again and said, "Why don't you get on in there and try to relax. My boy has given me a scare before. It's goin' to take a while before you feel like yourself again."

Eamon nodded before he carried Mitchell toward the door of their apartment building with Dog and I following him. As he walked, Mitchell said, "Down, Daddy. Down."

"I don't care how much it hurts to carry you, boy. You ain't gettin' down."

When Eamon carried Mitchell into the apartment, Clara laid the clothes she was folding on the couch, went to Eamon, took Mitchell out of his arms, and asked, "You didn't carry him all the way up the stairs did you?

Eamon nodded.

"Why?" Clara asked while Eamon closed the door seconds after Dog and I entered.

Tears welled in Eamon's eyes as he said, "He yanked his hand out of mine and ran into the street. We both almost got hit by a car."

"Oh my word," Clara said as she put her hand on Mitchell's head, pushed his head on to her shoulder, and hugged him tight. "Are you both okay?"

"Yes," Eamon said as he limped to the couch and sat down. "My back and hip are hurtin' me something awful now though. I need to just sit here for a while."

"Okay," Clara said as she followed him to the couch and sat next to him.

Mitchell started to wiggle, so Clara sat him down. He ran to a small box of toys that sat under the front window, pulled out a wooden truck Mr. Williams' had whittled for him, plopped down so hard that it was good he had a diaper and plastic pants on to protect his butt, and pushed the truck across the floor in front of him. Dog and I followed him. He pushed the train toward Dog several times and giggled when Dog backed away.

Clara lay her hand on Eamon's arm and asked, "Are you sure you're a'right?"

Eamon nodded as he said, "Yes, I'm a'right, but I sure could use a cup of coffee."

Clara got up and went to the kitchen. While she was gone, Eamon watched Mitchell play. As Eamon watched, he had tears in his eyes but also a smile on his face.

When Clara returned with the coffee, Eamon took a sip, sat it on the coffee table, and said, "It feels like I almost lost him like I lost my brothers and sisters. I'm still shaken up."

"You can't blame yourself for any of it. You risked your life for your brothers and sisters just like you risked your life for Mitchell today. Just because they were too young or are too angry to remember doesn't mean they never will. God knows what you did for them. Maybe he'll bring you a miracle."

"Maybe," Eamon said before he wiped tears from his eyes and took another drink of coffee.

As Eamon drank his coffee, Clara said, "Eamon, I've been meanin' to ask you something, and it seems twice as important now. I know money is mighty tight, but I would like to get Mitchell an Easter present."

"What did you have in mind?"

"He put it in my mind. The other day when we were walkin' by a store, there was an Easter display in the window that had a bunny in it. I can understand how he pulled his hand out of yours today, because he almost pulled his hand out of mine to get to the window to see that bunny. I let him look at it for a minute, and when I tried to pull him away so we could get home, he waved at it and said, 'Bye, Bye, Bunny, see you later at home.' I just felt like I needed to get it for him after that."

"He's a smart one," Eamon said as he looked over at Mitchell and smiled again. "How much did it cost?"

"It was nearly $3."

Eamon looked at the toy box and said, "He really doesn't have many toys. Go ahead and get it for him. We'll make it somehow this week."

Clara smiled and said, "I'll go over and get it tomorrow."

Clara purchased the bunny for him the next day. Mitchell was sitting on the couch holding it when Eamon got home from work.

Dog and I moved out of the way, so Eamon could sit on the couch next to Mitchell. We sat at Mitchell's feet and watched as Eamon asked, "Who's your little friend?"

"Wabbit," Mitchell said as he handed the bunny to Eamon.

Eamon looked at the bunny for a minute before he gave it back to Mitchell and asked, "Does your bunny have a name?"

"Wabbit," Mitchell said as he hugged it.

"I'm just glad you're here today to hug that bunny," Eamon said.

Mitchell was lucky he got the bunny when he did, because a few days later Clara found out she was pregnant. They were so worried about money that a stuffed toy would have seemed like too big of a luxury when another mouth to feed was on the way.

"Mitchell will be three years old by the time the baby comes," Clara explained to Eamon. "He can start sleepin' on the cot we have for company, and the baby can have his bed. I've still got all of Mitchell's baby clothes, cloth diapers, diaper pins, and plastic pants, so the baby can use those. I've still got all of his baby bottles. We'll make it somehow."

"If you breast fed instead of usin' the bottles, we wouldn't have to buy formula."

"Oh, no," Clara answered, obviously shocked. "I can't do that. Pastor says it's a sin for a woman to display and use her breasts in that way. He says Godly women use bottles."

Eamon sighed and said, "I don't remember women usin' bottles back home."

"Pastor said the companies that started makin' bottles so available to women in the last ten years or so were sent by God. He said they save us from yet another way Satan uses our bodies to lead us into sins of the flesh."

"How much money are those baby bottle companies makin' — "

"Pastor said people would use that argument to side-track us, but that ain't got nothing to do with it. If it did, Pastor said he'd be tellin' us to use those new disposable diapers, but he's tellin' us to stay away from those. He said those are a trick of the devil to make our little boys sterile, so they won't be bringin' up Godly households in the next generation. That way the sinners will take over the country."

"How can diapers hurt little boys like that?"

"Pastor says because of all the chemicals in them. This is all about whether we're goin' to commit sins of the flesh or not. I'll figure out a way to afford formula. We'll make it somehow. You'll see."

Clara almost had Eamon convinced they could make it financially until their baby girl, who they named Rebecca, was born with a clubfoot. Dog and I stayed with Rebecca in the room with all of the babies until she came home from the hospital, so we saw Clara when she came to the nursery, looked through the window at her daughter, and said, "I'm so sorry. Life is hard enough, especially for women, and now you have this countin' against you, too. It knocked the wind out of me when the doctor told me. I guess we've just got to pick up and go on from here — somehow."

Rebecca's first night home, Eamon sat on the couch and rocked her in his arms as he said, "I know what it's like, baby girl. I'm crippled, too. I promise you that I'll do everything in my power to make life better for you than it was for me. You'll never suffer like I have."

Mitchell wasn't as supportive of Rebecca's special needs as his parents were. He kept trying to push her out of Eamon's arms. Eamon gently helped Mitchell sit on the couch next to him, but Mitchell continued to try to take Rebecca's place. He did this every time Eamon or Clara held her. Each time Mitchell did this, Dog would get in between the two children while I told Mitchell to stop. He looked at me each time I scolded him, but he didn't listen.

Fortunately, the expensive operations Rebecca needed wouldn't start right away, but the expense of routine medical care did. The first step was to buy orthopedic shoes that had a bar brace connecting them. The bar was tightened weekly to slowly train the clubfoot to be in a position that was closer to normal. Due to Eamon's work schedule combined with Clara's inability to drive, they had to go to the doctor on Saturday. This meant they couldn't go home every weekend anymore, so they experienced Rebecca's medical trials without much support from Clara's family, MawMaw Tierney, and Uncle Teagan.

The doctor was so popular and so many people needed Saturday appointments that the wait was often long. Eamon dropped Clara off with the children, Dog, and me in the morning and picked us up four hours later, because they quickly learned that was the typical wait time. Eamon worked during those hours to earn the overtime needed for the medical bills.

Dog and I sat with Clara, Rebecca, and Mitchell as they waited patiently Saturday after Saturday even though many other patients complained loudly to the receptionist or each other. Clara never complained. I was learning she didn't like to draw attention to herself. Even worse, we witnessed some parents blaming the children for the wait or for being handicapped.

One of the worst episodes we witnessed happened when Rebecca was around 18 months old. A child Mitchell was playing with, who appeared to be from a rich family, was yanked away from the play area as the mother chastised, "Act like a lady, young lady! You're already going to have a hard time presenting yourself as a lady with that foot of yours, so it's even more important for you to act the way society expects you to. I don't know how I'm ever going to present you to society when you have to wear those ugly orthopedic shoes with a beautiful, white, debutante dress. Maybe I'll be lucky enough to have a normal daughter one day, so she can save this family's reputation."

When Clara realized her children were watching the scene the mother was making, she called Mitchell away from the play area and encouraged him to help Rebecca with the picture book Rebecca had been looking at before the scene started. Mitchell normally didn't seem to like books or playing with Rebecca, but he did what he was told this time even though he kept glancing up from the book to look at the mom who kept being so hard on her child.

I wished Clara could see me and Dog to call us away as well, because I couldn't quit looking. I hoped Eamon realized how well he was keeping the promise I heard him make to his daughter about doing everything he could for her. Against all odds, Eamon and Clara were doing their best for their child while this woman who seemed to have everything couldn't find the compassion to do the same thing for hers.

Although the lobby was similar to any doctor's office, the hallway that led to the examination rooms was decorated with strange statues none of us understood. Clara and the children walked tentatively past the decorative dragons and the golden man with a big belly who sat Indian-style in front of wallpaper with big-leafed flowers on it like none of us ever saw before, but no one ever asked the doctor about them. Maybe it was because the doctor wasn't a talkative man.

The doctor greeted them when he entered the examination room, but beyond that, he only told them what Clara needed to know about her daughter's health. It wasn't that he was unfriendly, and the family seemed to like him. I don't think they would have waited four hours every Saturday if they didn't like him. Rebecca was often shy outside her own home, but she seemed comfortable with this doctor even though she was as reserved with him as he was with her. It seemed he was just quiet — peaceful. He was so peaceful he didn't seem to need words, yet he still seemed to communicate what needed to be said both medically and socially.

One Saturday when Rebecca was about two years old was particularly difficult for everyone. The family waited six hours at Rebecca's weekly doctor's appointment. While Eamon waited the last two hours with them after he came to pick them up, Mitchell crawled onto Eamon's lap, lay his head on Eamon's chest, and said, "I don't feel good, Daddy."

Eamon lay his hand on Mitchell's forehead, looked at Clara, and said, "He's warm."

"We should be out of here soon," Clara said.

Mitchell feel asleep on Eamon's lap, so Clara, Rebecca, Dog, and I went back to the land of the golden statues to see the doctor without them when Rebecca was called. Fifteen minutes later, the brace was tightened.

Halfway home, Mitchell threw up in the car.

Clara leaned over the back seat and placed her palm on Mitchell's forehead before she said, "He's burnin' up. I think we'd better take him to the hospital. It almost burned my hand to touch him."

"What a day!" Eamon said before he turned the car around and drove to the hospital.

They arrived around supper time. By 8:00, Mitchell was passed out in Clara's arms.

Clara looked at Eamon and said, "He's so hot that holdin' him is makin' me sweat. I hope they call him back soon."

Clara's talking woke Rebecca up, and she started to cry.

"She's probably hungry," Clara said. "There's some powdered formula and a bottle in the diaper bag, but I don't know how to heat up some water here to make it for her. There's a box of animal crackers in there, too. See if she'll eat those."

As Eamon searched through the diaper bag for those items, Clara noticed his hands were shaking.

"Why are your hands shakin'?" Clara asked. "Are you gettin' ready to have another spell like you used to have?"

"I don't know. I hope not."

"I wish they'd hurry up."

Eamon found the animal crackers. Rebecca grabbed the first one and ate it so fast that she was ready for another one before Eamon's shaking hands could get it out of the small box.

"Calm down," Eamon snapped at her as she reached for a second cracker.

Eamon became more and more impatient as he fed her the animal crackers. Clara watched it for several minutes before she asked, "Why are you bein' so impatient with her?"

"I just feel so damned shaky," he snapped. "I don't know what's wrong."

The nurse who checked them in got up from her desk on the far side of the room and came over to Eamon. She knelt in front of him, grasped one of his shaking hands and asked, "Has it been a while since you've had something to eat?"

Eamon nodded and said, "We've been in doctor's offices all day — first for my little girl and now for my boy."

"Does this happen to you often — getting shaky and impatient when you don't eat?"

Eamon nodded.

"The same thing happens to me. You need to talk to the doctor about it. In the meantime, let me see what I can do," the nurse said before she stood.

"Do you know how much longer it's goin' to be," Clara asked. "My son's so hot that I feel like I'm holdin' a small furnace. I'm really worried about him."

"It shouldn't be much longer," the nurse answered.

The nurse returned to her desk and made a phone call. About ten minutes later, a man in a white coat brought a tray to her desk. She carried it over to Eamon, who by then was leaning against the wall gasping for shallow breaths.

The nurse sat the tray on the chair next to Eamon before she knelt in front of him, peeled the top off a juice container, and said, "Sir, I need you to drink this right away."

Eamon sat up to drink the juice, and Rebecca tried to take it from him. The nurse pushed her tiny hands away and held them as she said,

"Daddy needs this juice. You'll get some in a minute." When Eamon finished, the nurse said, "You should start to feel better soon."

She peeled the top off another juice container and gave Rebecca a drink as she said, "The cafeteria sent up juice and a sandwich for each of you. I can't promise the sandwiches will be good, but at least they'll make you feel better."

When Rebecca finished her juice, the nurse gave Eamon a sandwich that he shared with Rebecca. Clara accepted the juice but waved the sandwich away.

Shortly after the nurse returned to her desk, the family fell asleep. At three o'clock in the morning, the nurse woke them to take them back to see the doctor.

When Clara woke up, she said, "I don't feel hot from holdin' him anymore. She lay her hand on his forehead and said, "His fever broke while we were waitin'."

"He probably should see the doctor anyway," the nurse said. "Follow me."

Eamon and Clara followed the nurse through a door that was near where they were sitting, each of them carrying a sleeping child. Dog and I, of course, followed. She led them down a white hallway that was glaring from the harsh light. About halfway down the hallway, she opened a curtain to reveal a small room that housed only a bed that had a chair on each side of it and some medical equipment behind the headboard. Clara lay Mitchell on the bed, sat on a chair, wiped his hair off his forehead, and held his hand. Eamon sat on the chair on the other side of the bed and held Rebecca.

Before the nurse closed the curtain, she said, "The doctor should be with you soon."

Two hours later, a paunch, elderly doctor who wore the typical white coat and stethoscope around his neck pushed the curtain back and entered the room while he looked at the chart. As he closed the curtain, he asked, "What seems to be the problem here?"

"Our son had a very high fever," Clara answered. "It seems to have broken while we were waitin' to be seen, but the nurse said we should let you check him anyway."

The doctor walked to the bed and lay his hand on Mitchell's forehead. He removed his hand and wrote on the chart as he said,

"There's nothing wrong with this child. He's as cool as a cucumber. I don't even know why you brought him in."

"I don't mean no disrespect," Clara said. "I know you're the doctor and you have more book learnin' than we do. Normally, I wouldn't say anythin', but I'm worried for my son even though he's cool now. He was burnin' up with fever when we first got here. He was makin' me sweat just holdin' him. Will you please take a look at him and make sure he's okay?"

The doctor lowered the chart to his side and said, "Ma'am, do you know how busy we've been tonight? We have patients in here who are really ill and need my attention, so it angers me that you brought in a child who isn't even sick."

Dog growled at the doctor, so I knelt next to Dog and petted him as we watched the rest of the conversation.

"We never meant to waste your time," Clara said. "I swear to you he really was sick when we got here. We waited ten hours in the waitin' room and another two hours back here in this room. That seems to have been enough time for the fever to have broken. Can you please take a look at him and make sure he really is okay now?"

The doctor cleared his throat and said, "I've seen the likes of you in here before. Unfortunately, this city's getting over run with your type since some of the mines closed down South. You come up here and live off the system and expect everyone to cater to you, and I for one am not going to do it."

Tears welled in Clara's eyes as she said, "We wouldn't have suffered through sittin' in the waitin' room for that long if our child wasn't sick. We sat out there for so long that my husband started shakin' — oh, yes, the nurse gave him juice and food to make it stop and said we should tell you about that and have you examine my husband, too."

The doctor looked at Eamon and said, "You look to be fine, too — just like your son is. Anyone who goes a while without eating is likely to have problems. It's not anything to talk to a doctor about. I recommend that the two of you go home. If you need attention in the future, look for it from each other, a pastor, or a whore for all I care. Don't come here again with stories of a sick child and a husband who can't miss a meal. Doctors have real healing work to do."

The doctor left the room so quickly that Eamon or Clara couldn't say anything else, but they wouldn't have been able to anyway since both of their mouths were hanging wide open in shock. Dog chased the doctor down the hallway biting at his ankles, but the doctor didn't notice. After Clara and Eamon bundled up the children and left the room, Dog rejoined us in the hallway, and we left the hospital together.

Shortly after we got home, Clara heard a knock on the door.

When she answered it, Mrs. Williams asked, "I came over to check on y'all. Your car was gone from early morning until early morning."

"Yesterday was a hard day," Clara said as she stepped out of Mrs. Williams way and gestured for her to enter. "We sat at the doctor's office all day for Rebecca's appointment and then took Mitchell to the hospital on the way home. We sat over there for so long that the boy's body healed itself while we waited. That doctor acted like we were wastin' his time or somethin'."

"Doctors," Mrs. Williams harrumphed. "They don't know everything."

Rebecca was sitting on the couch holding Mitchell's bunny. Mrs. Williams sat next to her, picked her up, and snuggled her like Rebecca was snuggling the bunny. Mrs. Williams looked into Rebecca's eyes and said, "This child is one of God's wonders. She's gifted; she's able. She's going to be fine even if she's crippled and has to spend her Saturdays sitting in doctor's offices instead of playing. Play will never be that important to her anyway. She's going to find much greater things important. Don't you be worryin' about this baby. That bad leg is the mark of God, because God makes his special people especially able. She is able."

Mitchell woke up, sat up on his cot, and looked around. When he saw Rebecca sitting on Mrs. Williams' lap holding his bunny, he ran to them, grabbed the bunny out of Rebecca's hands, went back to his cot, and lay down.

When he got back to his cot, Clara said, "He's grumpy. He was so sick last night, and they kept us at the hospital all night. He's tired. I don't rightly know how Rebecca's still up. She has to be tired, too."

"Why don't you put her in her crib?"

"I did. She's so spunky I can barely keep up with her. Even with a bar connectin' her shoes, she climbs out of the crib if she's not ready to sleep and runs around the house. She's already climbed out twice since she got home."

"I don't know how you're still up," Mrs. Williams said. "Is Eamon in bed?"

"Yes. Eamon went to bed when we got home. When Rebecca finally goes to sleep, I'm goin' to lay down."

Mrs. Williams looked into Rebecca's eyes and said, "Well, I'd better get out of here and let you all go to sleep. You go to sleep for your Mom now, okay."

Rebecca looked at Mitchell, reached toward him, and said, "Wabbit."

Mrs. Williams took her soft, hand-knitted jacket off and said, "This is softer than that bunny. You hug this while you go to sleep. That bunny doesn't matter at all, child. You just let Mitchell have it. Get used to people acting like that. People will try to grab things from you, because they will think your leg makes you weak. You're not. You will have all of the protection you ever need. I promise no one will hold you down for long." She lay Rebecca on the couch next to her and said, "Now, get some sleep."

Rebecca was curled up around the jacket, sucking her thumb, and falling asleep by the time Mrs. Williams got to the door to leave.

CHAPTER TEN: A LOVING GRANDFATHER

The fiasco at the hospital during the previous weekend hurt Eamon and Clara so deeply that neither one of them trusted doctors anymore. That lack of trust became a big issue when Darina called mid-week to tell them Faolan was sick, and the doctors didn't know if the treatments would help him recover. At first, Eamon and Clara were torn between their daughter's condition and Faolan's medical care. The bad experience in the emergency room ended up being the deciding factor. They decided Rebecca would be okay with fewer doctor's appointments, because Faolan might need them to be closer if any of his doctors were as heartless as the one they'd met in the emergency room. They cancelled Rebecca's appointment and went home for the weekend.

When Eamon parked the car in front of Clara's parents' house on Friday night, it was already dark. Darina and Faolan came to the car and helped Clara and Eamon get the children and their suitcases. Dog and I watched until it was time to follow them into the house. Darina was so busy herding everyone toward the house that she was the last to enter. When she did, she set the suitcase she was carrying on the couch just inside the front door before herding everyone into the kitchen.

While the family settled at the table for the huge supper Darina had prepared, Clara said, "It surely is nice to be home. Havin' those doctor's appointments every Saturday keeps us from gettin' home every weekend, and we need to get out of the city."

Eamon sat on the side of the table by the outside wall. Dog lay at his feet, and I stood behind him like always. Mitchell sat next to Eamon, and Rebecca sat next to Clara on the other side of the table. This seating arrangement made sure each child had help with their meal if they needed it. Faolan and Darina sat at each end of the table, and Faolan prayed over the food before everyone filled their plates.

"We surely do be missin' ya when ya nary be able to be visitin'," Darina said as she filled a plate and sat it in front of Mitchell.

Clara filled a plate and sat it in front of Rebecca as she said, "We surely do miss you, too."

The adults filled plates for themselves as Faolan asked, "How do them there young'uns be doin'? Yer Ma done told me y'all be havin' a terrible week with illness."

"They're fine now," Clara answered. "Mitchell went to the hospital last week after Rebecca's doctor's appointment – an appointment we waited six hours to get in for. Mitchell was just burnin' up with fever. We sat in that waitin' room for so long that the fever broke while we were waitin'. The doctor was right rude with us. He said we were wastin' his time."

"Doctors nary be knowin' ever thing," Faolan said. "I be happy to be hearin' the boy be a'right. I nary be knowin' how y'all can be standin' them long waits at the doctor ever' week. A six-hour wait! Lord A'mighty! Things surely do be bein' different up there in the city than they be bein' down here. What do he be needin' to be seein' her ever' weekend fer anyhow? The child do be havin' a bum leg, but she be doin' fine otherwise."

"He tightens up her brace to pull her foot in," Clara answered. "He says with time he'll train her foot to point forward. If he does that before she starts havin' the operations, the operations will be more of a success."

Eamon cleared his throat and said, "Clara talked with the doctor on Monday and told him one weekend a month we'd be out of town and couldn't bring her in."

"Do that there doctor be obligin' to that?" Darina asked.

"Yas'm," Eamon answered as he nodded.

"If'n he be obligin' to that, I reckon ya ought to be askin' him if'n ever other week be bein' enough to be seein' her. Y'all be needin' to be gettin' out of that there city more before h'it be suckin' the life right outta y'all. We be understandin' y'all be needin' to be workin' up there, but h'it nary be no place fer a soul to be livin'," Darina said.

Faolan shook his head as he said, 'Yer Ma surely do be right about that there. Y'all be keepin' yer heart and soul on this here mountain, so yer soul be comin' back to h'it when ya be passin' on. Ya nary be wantin' to be leavin' yer ghost in that there city."

Clara nodded and said, "My heart and soul will always be on this mountain, and I'm teachin' my young'uns to do the same. Our souls will join the ancestors on this mountain one day. I'm afraid it's not so easy for Eamon though. His time on this mountain wasn't as pleasurable as ours has been."

Faolan lay his spoon on his plate and asked, "What done be happenin' to ya son?"

"My folks weren't always so nice," Eamon said before he laid his spoon on his plate.

"What they done to ya, son?" Faolan asked.

"I don't much like to talk about it."

"H'it be a'right, son," Faolan said. "Ya be with family. What done happened to ya?"

"I wasn't born with my leg like this," Eamon stammered. "My Ma did this to me. It wasn't a one-time thing either. They beat on me so much that I don't know how I'm alive."

Darina lay her spoon on her plate, looked at Eamon, and said, "We be knowin' yer time on yer mountain nary be bringin' ya no pleasure, son. We be awful sorry about all what done happened to ya."

Eamon nodded at her and stammered, "Much obliged. I fear my soul returnin' to the mountain and my ancestors. I try to take the mountain out of my heart and soul. I'd just as soon leave my ghost in that there city."

Darina sighed and said, "I be awful sorry to be hearin' that, child. If'n the spirit world be obligin', please be knowin' ya can be joinin' our ancestors on this here mountain in the line of yer young'uns."

Eamon looked down at his plate and stammered, "I hope the spirit world will be obligin'."

"So do we, son," Faolan said. "So do we."

Faolan and Darina picked up their spoons and started eating again, but it was a full ten minutes before Eamon did the same.

After supper was over, the men sat on the porch sipping shine and rolling their own cigarettes while the women cleaned up the kitchen and got the children in bed. Once all of that was done, the adults were ready for bed as well.

After breakfast the next morning, Faolan returned to the porch and sat on his rocking chair. As he rocked, Rebecca toddled out to her Grandpa even though she was wearing her braces and climbed onto his lap. Dog and I followed her. Dog lay at Faolan's feet, and I sat on a wooden bench that sat along the wall behind the rocking chair.

Rebecca lay her head on Faolan's chest, and he lay his hand on her leg. As they rocked, he said, "Child, yer leg be bein' beautiful. Nary be lettin' nobody be a-tellin' ya that ya be bein' less than cuz of that there leg. Ya be bein' marked by God, child. God be pickin' his special children to be marked by him, because he be havin' a special purpose fer ya. Ya nary be forgettin' that, child."

"Okay, PawPaw," Rebecca said before she put her thumb in her mouth and curled up even closer to him.

She fell asleep on his lap. Even though she slept for over an hour, he kept his hand on her leg and rocked her the entire time.

When she woke up, he sat her on the floor and said, "Child, ya be seein' that there wood box over yonder?"

"Yes," Rebecca answered as she nodded.

"I be needin' ya to be goin' over there and be openin' that there box fer yer ol' Grand Daddy."

Faolan sat her on the ground, and she toddled over to the box. After she lifted the lid, she looked into the box and squealed, "Cookies!"

Faolan laughed and said, "Yes, child. Them there cookies be fer ya. I be buyin' 'em fer ya."

Rebecca pulled out a box of Hi Ho® cookies and carried them back to Faolan.

He opened the box and handed one to her before he took one out for himself. As he separated the two outer chocolate cookies from each other, he said, "I only be likin' the white stuff that be in the middle."

Rebecca already took a bite of her cookie, but she separated the two outer cookies and said, "Me, too, PawPaw."

They ate the white crème in the middle of their cookies, and Faolan threw his cookies over the porch railing into the yard.

Rebecca looked at him and said, "PawPaw make a mess."

"Naw, child. Them there dawgs be eatin' up anything I be throwin' over that there railin'."

Rebecca toddled to the railing, pointed, and said, "Dog."

Dog jumped up like he thought she called him. After a few seconds of standing erect and wagging his tail, he lay back down.

Faolan nodded and said, "Them there do be dawgs."

Rebecca threw her cookies to the dogs, too. That started a game of Faolan and Rebecca eating the white crème middles and throwing the cookies to the dogs. When Faolan's older stomach had all he could handle, Rebecca continued the game alone.

About halfway through the box of cookies, Darina stepped through the door and yelled, "Oh, my word, child, ya nary be needin' to be wastin' food like that. Them there dawgs done be gettin' enough of our leftovers to be eatin'."

Faolan looked at Darina and said, "I done buyed them there cookies for that there child, and she can be doin' with them whatever she darn well be pleasin' to be doin' with them."

"But —"

"I nary be wantin' to be hearin' another word about h'it, woman. Leave that child be!"

Darina huffed and said, "Well, I'll be," before she turned and walked back into the house.

Faolan laughed and said, "The world nary be havin' a lot of breaks fer people what be different. Ya be enjoyin' life ever chance ya be gettin', child."

Rebecca giggled and threw two more cookies to the dogs. As they gobbled them up, she squealed and yelled, "Dog!"

Dog got up and walked to Rebecca. She ate the middle of another cookie before she petted Dog and handed the chocolate cookies to him. He sniffed them, but his ghost body couldn't eat them. She threw them to the dogs on the ground below before she started petting Dog again. Just like all children, she could see us, but for how long?

Rebecca clung to Faolan all weekend. When the weekend was over and we were all getting in the car to leave, Rebecca jumped out of Clara's lap before Clara could close the passenger door and ran toward her PawPaw as fast as she could with a bar between her shoes. Her arms were outstretched as she ran toward Faolan screaming, "PawPaw!

PawPaw!" When she got about halfway to him, her braces caused her to fall onto her belly and face instead of her knees.

Clara was already chasing her by the time she fell, so Clara got to her before Faolan, who had knelt down to allow the child to run into his arms. When Faolan got to them, Rebecca reached for him and through the tears that ran down her dirty face said, "PawPaw."

Faolan took her and hugged her body while she hugged his neck. As he bounced her, he whispered, "Ya nary be forgettin' what I done telled ya. Yer leg nary be makin' ya less than anybody else. Yer braces nary be makin' ya less than anybody else. Yer able. Ya be pickin' yourself up and dustin' yourself off. Yer able."

She let go of his neck, looked into his eyes, and said, "Okay, PawPaw."

When Darina got to them, she asked, "How does that child do that with those braces on her legs?"

"I don't know," Clara said as she took Rebecca from Faolan. "She climbs out of the crib and runs across the house all the time even with those braces on. I have a harder time keepin' up with her than I ever had keepin' up with Mitchell."

As Eamon approached, he said, "I'm not so sure about that. Remember when Mitchell ran out in front of a car."

"That was a lot scarier, but it was also only one time," Clara said. "This child does this every day."

Faolan kissed Rebecca on the cheek and said, "She be able. Nary a-body ever goin' to be holdin' her down."

As Eamon and Clara walked back to the car, Rebecca looked over Clara's shoulder, waved, and yelled, "Bye, PawPaw! Bye, PawPaw!

A few days after they arrived home, a package came in the mail for Rebecca. It was her first mail. Clara sat on the couch with Rebecca next to her and opened the small box. Dog lay at Rebecca's feet, but I stood next to Clara and waited impatiently to see what was in the box. Rebecca gasped when Clara removed the lid and revealed a black and white gingham dress designed with a smocked bodice and a few little red roses at the waistline just underneath the bodice.

Clara removed the dress from the box and held it up in front of Rebecca. Rebecca touched it gently, her mouth hanging open in awe. After picking up pieces of the fabric between her fingers several times, she stroked it like she sometimes stroked Dog.

"Do you like it?" Clara asked.

Rebecca nodded as she continued to stroke the dress.

"It's from your PawPaw."

"PawPaw!" Rebecca squealed as she grabbed the dress from Clara and hugged it like she sometimes hugged Mitchell's bunny.

"Do you want to call PawPaw and thank him for the dress?"

Rebecca nodded.

Clara picked up the phone receiver and dialed. After a few seconds, we all heard Faolan's voice say, "Hello."

"Daddy?"

"Clara, is that you?"

"Yes."

"How do y'all be doin'?"

"We're doin' good. Rebecca just got the dress you sent her. She just loves it. You should see how excited she is. She wanted to call and say thank you. Hold on just a minute, and I'll hold the phone up to her ear."

Clara moved the phone to Rebecca's ear, and Rebecca said, 'PawPaw.'

"Hi, Sweetheart."

"Hi."

They were silent for a few seconds, so Clara said, "Say thank you to PawPaw.'

Rebecca did.

"You be welcome, Pumpkin. I be sure ya be lookin' right perty in that there dress."

Rebecca giggled as Clara said, "Let me talk to PawPaw now." Rebecca let go of the phone and Clara put it back to her own ear and said, "Daddy."

"I be here."

"Thank you for the dress. This is the nicest dress she owns. This can be her church dress. That was right nice of you."

"Ya be knowin' I be willin' to be doin' anythin' for that lil' crippled girl. She be my own heart."

"I know, Daddy."

Faolan coughed before he said, "Clara, I nary be meanin' to be bein' rude, but I reckon I ought not be talkin' too long today. I be feelin' a might bit poorly this week."

"Are you okay?"

"I be bein' a'right soon enough. I just be bein' a bit under the weather. Do ya be wantin' to be talkin' to yer Ma?"

"Yes, I'll talk to Mommy. I hope you feel better soon."

"Thank you, Darlin'."

Darina came to the phone, and they talked for a long time. Little did they know they would talk again the next day when Darina called to let them know that the first time Rebecca wore that dress it would be to her PawPaw's funeral.

Dog and I knew before the call came. Faolan stopped by to visit with Rebecca before he went with the Angel. Even though it was a different Angel than the one that came for me and Dog, she still offered for us to come with them. Dog and I shook our heads, and she disappeared with Faolan as fast as she came.

Dog and I rode back to the mountains for the funeral with Eamon, Clara, and the children. During the entire trip, Rebecca sat on Clara's lap and sucked one thumb while she twirled her hair around the other one. She didn't speak even to answer people who spoke to her during the entire trip and during their entire visit to the mountains. Because of this, Dog and I stayed with her.

This meant we had to go with the family when they went to the undertaker to plan the funeral. Part of planning the funeral was picking out the casket. As Darina, Clara, Mitchell, and Rebecca walked around a room that was lined with decorative caskets, Darina stopped at one and started crying in a high-pitched scream that was out of character for her. Rebecca backed away from the screaming while she pointed at the casket and said, "PawPaw!" Dog and I saw him, too. Faolan's ghost was laying in that casket like he was trying it on for size. Maybe Darina's grief allowed her to see him, too. Maybe Faolan wanted her to see him one last time.

The next evening at the wake, Clara carried Rebecca to the casket and told her to say goodbye to her PawPaw. Rebecca kissed him on the cheek and then wiggled until Clara sat her down. In spite of the braces that connected her shoes, Rebecca ran to the coat rack and hid in the coats. Dog and I followed her. Shortly after she hid, Faolan appeared.

Dog and I looked at him, and I stammered, "But, you went with the Angel."

"The gates of heaven nary be locked. Ya can be comin' and goin' as ya be pleasin'," he said before he knelt down in front of Rebecca and said, "I be here, sweet baby."

Rebecca looked at him through her tears and said, "PawPaw."

"Yer PawPaw will always be bein' with ya. I will always be lookin' out fer ya."

"No go, PawPaw."

"I've got to be goin', but I nary be far away. I will always be bein' here when ya be needin' me." He touched her shoes, and they turned into black, patent-leather Mary Janes. Rebecca looked at them and gasped before he said, "Ya can be havin' anything ya be wantin' in yer own mind. Ya should be goin' there any time folks be tryin' to be makin' ya be feelin' bad about bein' crippled. Whilst ya be bein' there, ya be havin' anything ya be wantin'." The shoes disappeared when he said that, but Rebecca continued to smile even after her PawPaw disappeared. Maybe that's why Rebecca loved books and writing so much. These things lived in her imagination.

The next day at the funeral, Faolan stood next to Clara, who was holding Rebecca, and held Rebecca's hand during the entire service. Since Faolan was tending to Rebecca, Dog and I returned to Eamon's side. He was having one of his spells, so he was sitting in the lobby by himself. He was more upset by Faolan's passing than Dog and I could understand until he whispered, "Next to Uncle Teagan, he was the closest thing to a Pa I ever had." I thought he was talking to himself until I noticed he was looking at me. I remembered Darina acting like she saw Faolan yesterday, and I wondered if people who were grieving could see us like children could. I kissed Eamon on the cheek, and he started crying.

Everything was happening so fast that I felt like I was getting lost in the confusion of places, events, and emotions, so I was glad when the funeral was over and we were all back at what would now be Darina's house. Clara told Darina to take it easy and went to the kitchen to cook supper. She sat Rebecca at the table with one of the many books Rebecca liked to look at and began cooking. Dog lay at Rebecca's feet, but I sat on the seat that was closest to her and looked at the pictures while she flipped through the pages of the book.

Darina soon came into the kitchen and helped. As they cooked, Darina said, "If'n only he nary would of gone chasin' after them there stupid pigs like he done. They done got outta the truck when he be tryin' to be takin' 'em to the pig sticker, and he nary be in the mood to be takin' help from nary a soul. I reckon he done been wantin' to be convincin' his self he still be bein' spry. He done chased down them stupid pigs even though he be feelin' right poorly."

"At least we know he's in a better place now," Clara said.

"I reckon he done be makin' h'it into heaven. He done been a rowdy one when he be bein' young, but after he be findin' out he be bein' sick, he be tellin' me he nary be understandin' why people be wantin' to be runnin' around and be drinkin' till they be bein' drunk and such. Findin' out he be bein' sick sure enough did be turnin' him around."

Rebecca pointed at Faolan as he stood behind Darina and tried to comfort her. She kept pointing as she chanted, "PawPaw.'

Darina and Clara started crying.

Clara tried to stir a steaming pot of dumplings with tears blurring her vision, so she didn't clearly see how thick the steam was rising up out of the pot and burned her wrist. She yanked her hand away and held it as Darina grabbed some butter off the table and started smearing it on the burn.

"This ought to be helpin' right soon," Darina said as she smeared the butter into the burn.

"I'll be a'right," Clara said as Darina led her to the table and helped her sit on the chair on the other side of Rebecca from me.

"Ya just be sittin' here, and I'll be finishin' up the supper."

As Clara sat holding her wrist, Faolan knelt beside her and tried to comfort her.

Rebecca waved and said, "Hi, PawPaw."

Clara looked at Rebecca and then looked in the direction Rebecca was waving at the same time Darina stopped stirring and looked in that direction.

"You nary be reckonin'?" Darina asked as she stood holding a dripping spoon.

"I don't rightly know," Clara said. She looked back at her wrist and said, "This is startin' to blister. Whether he's here now or not, it looks like I'm goin' to have a scar to remind me of this day for the rest of my life."

Darina returned to her stirring as she said, "Whether or not ya be havin' a physical scar, yer Pa's passin' will be leavin' a scar with ya fer the rest of yer days."

CHAPTER ELEVEN:
THINGS ARE GETTING BETTER

When the family returned to Cincinnati from Faolan's funeral, everything went on as if nothing had happened. Dog and I saw Clara privately wiping tears from her eyes when she was alone. It happened a lot when she was cooking or making the bed, because the children were usually in the front room when she completed those chores. We also caught Eamon doing the same thing when he was alone. We never saw Mitchell cry. Rebecca cried a lot until Clara told her not to. Rebecca was too young to understand this meant she was expected to cry where no one could see it, so she turned off her tears and sat quietly.

At first, Rebecca sat and stared at the wall. Dog and I sat with her, but we couldn't help much even though she was still young enough to see us. At her next Saturday doctor's appointment, she carried a picture book to the corner of the toy area and sat alone looking at the pictures for the entire four-hour wait. She did this for a few weeks before she sat with Clara again, but she still looked at books instead of interacting with her mother. It was a few more weeks before she shared the books with Clara. When she shared them, she demonstrated that she had taught herself how to read several words when she was looking at the books alone. Although Eamon never went to school, Clara went through the eighth grade and was able to read. She taught Rebecca new words. Just from reading at those Saturday morning doctor's appointments, Rebecca was reading fluently by herself by the time she was three years old.

Even though books were not an important part of Rebecca's family's culture on either side of the family tree, Clara noticed how much Rebecca loved to read and tried to help her get books. There wasn't a library in their neighborhood. Since their family had never used libraries before, Clara didn't know there was one downtown they could have ridden the bus to. Therefore, Clara looked for opportunities to get books for Rebecca. When a grocery store began giving away a different children's book each week for sales over $20, Clara shopped there until Rebecca had the entire collection. When people from the church Eamon and Clara were married in learned how much Rebecca liked to read, they started giving Clara their children's old books even though Eamon's distaste for church meant the family only went on Easter and Christmas — or when Clara was so mad at Eamon she didn't care how he felt about her attending church. Rebecca's Aunt Lana also passed her children's books down to Rebecca. Slowly, Rebecca developed a collection of books that she read repeatedly.

Around the time Rebecca began to read fluently, Mr. Williams retired from his job at the Goodwill®. Even though everyone spoke their surprise since he never smoked, Mr. Williams developed emphysema. The job was becoming too much for him, and he was eligible for social security retirement. Everyone was sad to see him go, even Dog and I.

Even though Mr. Williams told Eamon everything would be all right, that didn't end up being the case. The new boss reminded Eamon and Clara of Eamon's father, Caelan. He reminded Dog and me of Caelan, too. Dog spent so much time growling at the new manager that he would have had a sore throat if he were still in a physical body. The new boss was critical of everything his workers did. He punished them for perceived mistakes by making them work longer hours and Saturdays even though several of them had special needs or were working their way out of stressful situations and didn't need the added stress.

Being around that every day seemed to be turning Eamon into a different person. He came home from work yelling at Clara when the children weren't where they could hear it, and he snuck away from work one Friday before Clara got there to pick up his check and gambled their money away again. That made Clara get there earlier the next week, which made Eamon even grumpier when he got home.

On the Saturday when Rebecca's foot was found to be straight enough that her braces could be removed and her operations begin, Rebecca followed Eamon from the front door toward the bedroom when they got home from her doctor's appointment. She mimicked his limp as she followed him.

Clara ran to Rebecca, knelt in front of her, and asked, "What are you doin'?"

"Walkin' like Daddy."

"You shouldn't walk like Daddy. He'll think you're makin' fun of him."

Rebecca looked at her feet and whispered, "I just want to be like my Daddy."

Clara rubbed Rebecca's arm as she said, "That's nice, but Daddy might not understand that. He might think you're makin' fun of him. A lot of people already make fun of him, so that might hurt his feelin's. We don't want to hurt his feelin's at home, do we?"

Rebecca shook her head.

"We don't want to make Daddy mad either. Daddy's havin' a hard time lately. That's why he was in a bad mood when he picked us up at the doctor today. If he thinks you're makin' fun of him, he'll get even madder. We don't want to make Daddy mad, do we?"

Rebecca shook her head.

"Good. So, you're not goin' to do that anymore?"

"No," Rebecca answered.

"Good. Go back in the livin' room and look at your books. Daddy's just changin' out of his work clothes. He'll be back out in a few minutes."

Fortunately, Eamon wasn't destined to be in a bad mood for very long. A few weeks later, an heiress named Mrs. Reynolds, who often made donations to the Goodwill® store, saw the new manager yelling at Eamon when she came in to donate some antiques. She was so appalled that she marched over to the manager and asked, "Why are you treating this man so badly?"

"Because he's an incompetent idiot. I'm already making concessions for how much his crippled leg slows him down. You would think he would understand that and try harder."

"That is not what Mr. Williams said about him. Mr. Williams said he was a good worker, and I've seen how hard he works myself. You need to stop treating people this way."

The man turned to Mrs. Reynolds and said, "With all due respect, this is none of your business."

Mrs. Reynolds straightened her back, looked into the manager's eyes, and said, "When I donate thousands of dollars a year to an organization that I believe is supposed to help vulnerable people have a better life, how am I supposed to feel when I see those vulnerable people be treated this way instead of being helped? That makes it my business. I'll be reporting you to the corporate office."

The new manager swallowed hard.

Mrs. Reynolds looked at Eamon and said, "You're coming with me. You work for me now."

Eamon and the manager glanced at each other before they watched Mrs. Reynolds walk away. When she was halfway across the sorting room, she turned to Eamon and said so loudly that it echoed off the walls of the huge concrete room, "Don't just stand there! Come on!"

Eamon stumbled several times, because he was walking so fast to catch up with her. Dog and I followed him. We didn't know where she was taking him, and we wanted to make sure he was going to be all right. We all followed her out of the room and through the lobby to a pale blue, convertible, Jaguar XK-E that was parked out front. Mrs. Reynolds walked to the driver's side of the car and got in. Eamon stood on the sidewalk until she told him to get in.

He walked to the passenger side of the car, looked in, and said, "I've never seen a car with two seats before."

Mrs. Reynolds looked at him, smiled big, and said, "Now you have."

"Where do your children ride?"

"I don't have any children."

"Oh," Eamon said. "Where do you put your groceries?"

"The maid picks them up in my other car."

Eamon's brow wrinkled as he asked, "You've got two cars?"

Mrs. Reynolds nodded as she patted the passenger seat and said, "Get in, and I'll show you when we get to my house."

"I'll lose my job if I leave with you."

"You don't need that job. I'm giving you a job. Get in the car."

Eamon opened the car door and asked, "What about my car? It's parked here."

"I'll have my butler drive you back tonight to get your car."

"But, my manager might . . . "

"He won't do anything to your car, Eamon. Now he knows who I am, and he's already afraid I'm going to report him for what I saw today."

Eamon got in the car and closed the door before he asked, "How did you know my name?"

Dog and I looked at each other, because we didn't know where to sit. When Mrs. Reynolds started the engine, we jumped on the passenger side hood of the car and leaned on the window. The hood was huge, but the back end of the car was barely even big enough for two ghosts to sit on. We'd never seen anything like it before.

"Mr. Williams told me your name," she answered as she put the car in gear and pulled out. "He talked about you like you were his son."

Mrs. Reynolds talked easily all the way to her house about things that were unfamiliar to Eamon, Dog, or me. I wondered what Eamon thought about this new experience, because I thought all of her talk seemed silly compared to what the three of us went through back on the mountain and what Eamon and Clara still went through every day of their lives. In spite of whatever he might have been thinking, he politely listened to her talk about cars, clothes, antiques, and artwork. Just when I was losing hope that she was the good person she had appeared to be when she rescued Eamon earlier that day, she said, "These things make me feel happy, but I know they're not the only things that are important in life. I work with the Goodwill® and other charities to help other people find something in life that makes them feel happy, too. That is why I could not stand listening to that horrible man scream at you like that. Everyone deserves to be happy."

Eamon smiled, but his smile soon surrendered to his mouth falling open in surprise when Mrs. Reynolds turned the car into her driveway and they drove toward a big white house that was the size of six of Clara and his apartment building. It was easy to imagine a row of six apartment buildings occupying that space, because the house was a long rectangle with a pillared porch that extended the entire front of the house. The house and pillars were painted white, and the woodwork and shutters were painted black. The driveway was a semi-circle that came in one entrance, circled around in front of the porch, and back out an exit on the other side of the front yard. On the other side of the semi-circle from the porch, a fountain sat in the middle of the freshly mowed grass that was cut off from the rest of the yard by the driveway. The rest of the property was freshly mowed grass with perfectly trimmed bushes that made a fence around the edge of the property, except for the driveway. Various types of flowers grew in neat rows in front of the bushes. It appeared that most of the yard was in front of the house, because the bushes in the rear appeared to be close to the house. As Mrs. Reynolds parked the car, a strange sound caused Eamon to look toward the fountain. A colorful bird with a big tail was standing on the edge of the fountain just out of reach of the water that was cascading down behind it.

"What's that?" Eamon asked.

"That's a peacock," Mrs. Reynolds answered. "He just showed up one day. I guess he likes it here, because he stayed. He probably belonged to one of the neighbors. I call him George."

"He's pretty," Eamon said, still looking at the peacock as he got out of the car and closed the door.

Mrs. Reynolds closed her car door and said, "Follow me. I'll show you the house."

Eamon stood beside his closed car door and asked, "What could I possibly do for work in a fancy house like this?"

"I'll show you — after I show you the house."

Dog and I jumped off the hood of the car and followed Eamon inside.

Mrs. Reynolds showed us through three floors of fancy carpets, fancy furniture, and walls that were filled with fancy pictures. I couldn't stop myself from thinking this was more than any one person needed, and I wondered if Dog and Eamon were thinking the same thing.

I learned that Eamon was thinking the same thing when we got home and he told Clara about the new job. Within the first few sentences, he said, "I don't know why any one person needs so much, but at least she can afford to give me a job. I'm sure happy to get away from that hateful man who took Mr. Williams place."

Clara made hot chocolate to celebrate Eamon's new job. Once a cup was sitting on the coffee table in front of each of the four family members, she asked, "What's she goin' to have you doin'?"

I sat on the cushion between Eamon and Clara, and Dog lay between the two children who sat on the floor on the other side of the coffee table.

"She'll have me doin' some of the same things I did for Mr. Williams. I'll do any kind of odd job she needs around the house or property, and I'll be maintainin' the cars and gardenin' equipment she has. When I'm not busy with that, I'll be takin' care of an attic full of family antiques. She wants to fix them and clean them up so they can either be donated or sold. She said she'll sell enough to pay my salary and the rest she'll give to charity to make life better for those who don't have as much as she does."

"She sounds like a nice lady," Clara said before she took a drink of hot chocolate.

"She seems nice enough," Eamon said. "I guess I'll find out in time. The best part is she's goin' to raise my salary from $1.25 an hour to an even $2.00. She said she prefers even numbers. I think she can be a little odd, but I'm grateful for the extra money."

"She's goin' to pay you 75 cents over minimum wage?" Clara asked, obviously surprised.

"Yes," Eamon answered. "Maybe this would be a good time to move to another apartment."

"Why?" Clara asked.

"This one's too small for two children."

"We're getting' by."

"We're gettin' by, but it would be nice to have something not so crowded. Most of all, walkin' up three flights of steps every day is hard on my legs. I was thinkin' maybe we could find a place on the first floor."

"That's probably a good idea, but what about Mr. and Mrs. Williams. They're right across the street now, and we can check on them whenever we want to. What are they goin' to do if we move away?"

"Mr. Williams didn't think about me when he left his job," Eamon said.

"Eamon," Clara said, shocked. "How can you say that after everything Mr. Williams did for you — after everything both of them did for us?"

Eamon glared at her for several seconds before he said, "Yes, he did do a lot for us, didn't he? It's not like I'm never goin' to check on them again though. I've got a car. We can drive over here and check on them any time we want to."

"That's true. Okay. If you want to find another apartment, we can do that. We'll start lookin' when you get your first paycheck."

"That reminds me. She sent some things home with me today. She said she didn't need them anymore, and we might need them."

"She's payin' you seventy-five cents more an hour and givin' you things too?"

"Yes. There's a box in the car. Would you mind bringin' it up. My legs are pretty sore tonight."

Clara got up and left the apartment without saying anything. A few minutes later, she returned with the box. She sat it on the floor next to Eamon and returned to her seat on the couch. As she picked up her hot chocolate and sipped it again, Eamon looked through the box.

He pulled out a three-ring binder full of paper and lay it on the floor in front of the box. He pulled out some pencils and crayons and laid them on the table. Several cars and a sock monkey soon joined the pencils and crayons. He pulled out several kitchen utensils, including a big stirring spoon, a butcher knife, a set of steak knives still in the box, and a set of salt and pepper shakers that looked like roosters, and laid them on the coffee table in front of Clara.

While Clara gathered up the kitchen things and carried them into the kitchen, Mitchell grabbed the cars and the sock monkey, yelled "Mine," and ran into Eamon and Clara's bedroom with his new treasures.

When Mitchell jumped up and grabbed the toys, Dog crawled under the table and onto my lap.

While Rebecca watched Mitchell run out of the room, Eamon said, "I'm sorry, Rebecca. Did you want those things?" She didn't answer. She just kept staring in the direction Mitchell went with the toys.

When Clara returned, she asked, "What's wrong?"

"Mitchell took the toys and ran into our room with them," Eamon answered.

Clara sat on the couch and said, "Eamon, reach me that notebook of paper."

Eamon picked the notebook up off the floor and gave it to Clara.

Clara laid the notebook on the table and opened it before she pointed to the box of crayons and said, "Rebecca, bring those over to me."

Rebecca picked up the crayons and walked on her knees to the end of the coffee table where Clara sat. Clara took the crayons from her, removed one from the box, and drew squiggly lines on the paper. Rebecca took a crayon from the box and started drawing squiggly lines, too.

"See," Clara said. "These are much better than those toys Mitchell took."

Rebecca smiled while she kept drawing. I craned my neck as far as I could with Dog on my lap to see what she was drawing. I didn't know what it was, but the colors were pretty.

When the paper was filled with crayon marks, Clara turned the page and said, "Eamon, will you reach me one of those pencils?"

Eamon gave Clara a pencil, and she drew with it as she said, "You can use these pencils to draw, too."

Rebecca grabbed a pencil from the pile in front of Eamon and started to draw.

Clara leaned back on the couch and said, "I think everyone's happy now. As much as she likes books, I thought she'd like that stuff better anyway."

Rebecca drew until it was time for Clara to unfold the cots and get the children ready for bed. Rebecca usually took one of the free grocery store books to bed with her and looked at it until she fell asleep. That night, she took the binder of paper and a pencil too. She sat up long after everyone else went to sleep and copied the words from her free grocery store book onto the paper. Dog and I sat on the bed and watched. I never learned to read or write when I was alive. I thought maybe I could learn a few words if I watched Rebecca enough.

She did this every night for the rest of the time they lived in their third-floor apartment. She continued to do it when Eamon and Clara found a house that was inexpensive enough for them to buy on Eamon's new salary. When they discovered that houses sell inexpensively for a reason, and often those reasons are crime and drugs that lead to bad neighbors, needed repairs, or both, Rebecca used her books and writing to survive.

CHAPTER TWELVE: OWNING A HOUSE

Eamon, Clara, and the children toured their new house during the day, and the neighborhood appeared to be calm and peaceful. Dog and I were with them, and we got the same impression. The street the house was on ran parallel to a highway that ran along the Ohio River, but there was a strip of forest between the two streets that in addition to muffling traffic sounds was beautiful. The side of the street the house was on also had trees covering a hill that extended the length of the street. The house they were looking at and a house to the left of it were the only ones that were close together, because houses were built intermittently where there were large enough flat spaces to accommodate building on the hill. Due to this, there was forest between most of the houses. This house would have been as isolated in nature as homes in the mountains were if it wouldn't have been for the house next door that was separated only by a chain link fence and the steps that led up to the side door of the house they were considering. Since the houses cut into a tree-topped hill, trees covered the hill behind the back yards, creating a scene reminiscent of the mountain beauty Eamon and Clara had come from.

The only concern Eamon had were the steps that went up to the door on the left side of the house. Since the entrance was on the second floor, there were almost as many steps as there were to the third-floor apartment they lived in. There were no entrances on the first floor of this house. The street level of the house was mostly buried in the hill, and the small portion in front that wasn't didn't have an entrance or windows. The first-floor front wall was made of stone that merged into a stone retaining wall of the same height on the right side of the house.

The retaining wall made entry from that side of the house impossible as well. This meant Eamon would not escape steps, which was the main reason for moving. After discussing it with Clara while they stood at the top of the steps after the first climb, Eamon decided he could manage the steps since the house payment would be less expensive than the rent they had been paying.

The layout of the house made me more comfortable with that decision. Everything Eamon needed could be accessed from the entry door that opened onto the kitchen. The portion of the kitchen inside the door was half as wide as the rest of the room, and the appliances lined the wall opposite the door. The bathroom was on the other side of that wall. The bathroom was a quarter the size of the kitchen and sat in the corner behind the appliances, creating an L-shaped room. The rest of the house was a perfect square of four square rooms. From the kitchen, doors created a path through a square of large rooms that would have circled the bathroom except for the final wall didn't have a door that opened to the kitchen. The room that stopped the circle at the kitchen wall was the only one that had privacy, because all of the other rooms had two doors to allow people to walk through to the next room.

This was a double-edged sword for Rebecca. When the family moved in, the room next to the kitchen became the living room, the room next to that became Eamon and Clara's room, and the room that didn't have a second door became Rebecca's room. Since Mitchell had to walk through Eamon and Clara's room to get to the one door that led to Rebecca's room, I hoped this would protect her from his teasing. In some cases, it did. In other cases, it meant she was trapped. Maybe that is why she eventually spent so much time on the first floor.

Mitchell's room was on the other side of Eamon's and Clara's in a two-room annex on the back of the house. A small bathroom in the center of its back wall could be entered from both rooms, and a door on the outside wall of Eamon's room led to the back yard. The back door remained locked most of the time, because Mitchell didn't like people coming through his room to go outside. The annex room next to Mitchell's room was another that only had one door, meaning whoever occupied that room had to walk through Mitchell's room to get to the main house. Thank goodness Eamon and Clara didn't put Rebecca in that room, because it was far enough away from Eamon and Clara's room that she would have been more vulnerable.

The door to the first floor was on your right when you left the kitchen to go into the living room. That door opened onto a flight of descending stairs. The wall that separated the stairs from the living room cut the room in a way that made the kitchen and the living room the only rooms in the main house that weren't perfectly square.

The living room was high enough that you could look over the trees from the front windows and see a train bridge that cut into the mountain on the other side of the river. Rebecca ran to the window when she heard a train whistle. Eamon and Clara looked at each other and smiled. It appeared her obvious joy at seeing the train would be a selling point.

The addition made the house look lopsided from the backyard, because the kitchen stood alone to the right of the house. This gave the impression that the addition was trying to escape. The yard was flat and covered in concrete immediately behind the house. The concrete ended at a retaining wall that was about the same height as a chair's seat. Behind it was a grass covered hill that led to the forest of trees that towered above the houses. The side of the house opposite the stairs was a grass covered hill that ended at the retaining wall.

Dog and I followed Clara and Rebecca as they maneuvered the narrow steps to the first floor. It was one big room that could have been called a basement, because it was dug into the hill, was concrete, and the back of the room was underground. After they moved in, they bought a wringer-type washing machine like the one in the basement of the apartment they had been renting and put it in the underground portion of the first-floor room. They also hung clotheslines in front of that machine for the winter months.

The front of the first-floor room started out as a place to put Mitchell's and Rebecca's toys, but it slowly ended up being a private refuge for Rebecca. Mitchell rarely went downstairs, so it was a place where she could escape Mitchell picking on her, grabbing her toys, or making fun of her for being handicapped or different than him in any way that gave him ammunition to pick on her. Rebecca spent a lot of time alone in that room reading, writing, and drawing. She spent so much time there that Clara set up a cot for her to sleep there once Rebecca proved she didn't have any problems maneuvering the stairs with her handicapped leg.

Their first day as home owners passed in the peaceful way they anticipated when the house tour led them to believe it was a peaceful neighborhood. When night shadowed the house, the darkness seemed to bring with it evil forces. Eamon and Clara weren't prepared to handle the noise of a neighborhood that came awake at night, and they were less prepared to handle the lack of sleep it caused. Night after night, Dog lay on the floor at Eamon's feet while I sat at the kitchen table with Eamon and Clara. Clara wore her robe, but Eamon stopped getting out of his day clothes by the end of the third week. They both drank coffee, but the caffeine wasn't what was keeping them awake. They often rested their heads on the table and nodded off for a few minutes, but when they fell asleep, someone who was partying at the house next door would scream, turn the music up louder, start arguing, or shoot a gun.

Calling the police proved ineffective, so they stopped doing it. Ignoring it was easier to take than watching a police officer tell the neighbors to keep it down and then walk away while the party was still going on in full force. The times the police blamed Eamon and Clara or refused to come out after admitting it was a bad neighborhood and the police didn't risk the safety of their officers coming there were even worse

The way the neighbors acted when they were fighting reminded me of our family back in the mountains. When the fights started, Dog cowered under Eamon's chair, and Eamon jumped every time there was a loud noise. He then looked around like he was watching for what was going to hurt him like he had done when we were children. He also got up and limped to the bathroom a lot, and I remembered how he had pee'd on himself every time Caelan scared him when he was a child.

One day, I realized Dog kept sniffing Eamon when the people next door were being noisy and violent. I wanted to know why, but when Spirit bodies stay close to humans instead of going with the Angel, dogs bark like they do when they are in physical bodies. He couldn't tell me. One night when the neighbors were acting exceptionally bad and we were all very upset, I sniffed Eamon. I kept my nose close to him and puzzled about the familiar smell for several minutes. Suddenly, I realized what Dog was smelling, and tears welled up in my ghost eyes. That is how I smelled in the last hours of my life. That is how Eamon often smelled when we were children. We smell different when we're afraid. I wondered if our parents noticed that smell, and if they did, why didn't they stop hurting us? Did they enjoy that smell? Did it entice them to act even worse, so they could smell it more?

When I was alive, I tried to protect Eamon even though I was in danger myself. When Dog was alive, Eamon and Dog tried to protect each other even though they were both in danger. When Mitchell ran into the street, Eamon risked his own life to save the child. Why weren't we like Caelan and Mabon? Why did we show caring for each other and protect each other when Caelan and Mabon seemed to enjoy inflicting pain? Were Caelan and Mabon monsters?

The next evening, Mrs. Reynolds kept Eamon late at work. The family needed groceries so badly they couldn't wait another day.to go to the grocery store, so we ended up rushing there an hour before the store closed. Dog and I went with them, because I loved grocery stores. We never had them in the mountains, so I walked through them thinking how wonderful it would be to be alive and eat all of the food that looked so good and was so plentiful. By the time we returned, it was already dark. While the family carried the groceries up the side steps with Dog and I following close behind, the party next door was already going on.

A young man with long blonde hair halfway down his back whose shirt was open to reveal the skinny, bare chest above his cut-off, blue jean shorts approached the chain-link fence between the two houses and yelled, "Hey there pretty lady!"

Eamon stepped between Clara and the man and said, "Just keep walkin'."

The man took a drink from the beer bottle he was holding and said, "Damn, girl! You're mighty fine looking! You've got the biggest tits for a skinny girl I've ever seen!"

Eamon handed the bag of groceries he was carrying to Clara and said, "Take the children in the house." Eamon turned back to the man and said, "Don't ever talk to my wife like that again, and don't you dare ever talk to her like that in front of our children!"

The man took another drink of beer and said, "Those are your children. Whoo-eeee! That's a good-looking woman! You must have had a lot of fun makin' them children with her, puttin' your hands all over those big tits."

Eamon started walking toward the fence as he yelled, "You stupid son-of-a-bitch! You've kept us awake all night every night since we moved in here, and now you insult my wife! I've had about as much of your shit as I'm goin' to take! If you don't get your ass back over to your house and keep the noise down and let us get some sleep tonight, I swear to God, I'll — "

The man started laughing as he backed away from the fence while pointing at Eamon and screaming, "Look, everyone! We've got a crazy man living next door!"

Clara came out of the house and said, "Eamon, come on in. Arguin' with people like that ain't goin' to make a bit of difference."

Eamon picked up a beer bottle that was on our side of the fence and threw it at the man before he allowed Clara to lead him into the house.

When they got inside, Eamon said, "Well, ignorin' them hasn't calmed them down. Maybe standin' up to them will."

I was proud of him for standing up to that man, because he was protecting Clara like I had protected him when I was alive. He smelled Clara's fear and responded by protecting her instead of making her more afraid. He couldn't have been more wrong about how the neighbors would react to it though. Not only were they louder than usual for the rest of the night, but several times they gathered at the fence to throw things at the house and scream insults at the family. Eamon and Clara called the police, but it had the same effect it always did — nothing was done.

What Eamon and the rest of the family didn't understand was that the kind of people who turn to addiction can't be reasoned with whether it be ignoring them, standing up to them, or talking reasonably with them. The only way standing up to them will have any effect is if you have enough power behind you to make them feel afraid. If you don't have police support or belong to a gang, standing up to them only provokes them. Eamon was from an uneducated family and culture and was still trying to learn the unfamiliar culture of the city, so he needed the police to educate him on his options and guide him to the appropriate legal resources. When they failed to do that, the family was left feeling hopeless.

After another night with very little sleep, Eamon and Clara woke up early. Clara made breakfast for Eamon before he went to work. After he left, she started making breakfast for the children. When she was halfway finished, someone knocked on the door. Dog lifted his head and growled, so I crawled under the table with him and petted him.

Clara turned off the burner under the eggs and bacon and went to the door. She looked out the small peephole and apparently saw someone she didn't know, because she asked, "Who are you and what do you want?"

"I'm Louie, Regan's husband. May I come in?"

Clara crinkled her brow and tentatively asked, "Regan, Eamon's sister? You're her husband?"

"Yes."

"What do you want?"

"I want to talk to you."

"What about?" Clara asked as she leaned her ear against the door to hear him better.

"Can I please come in?"

"I don't know. I don't know you."

After a long pause, Louie said, "Look out your peep hole. I'm holding up my wallet with a picture of me and Regan on our wedding day. That will prove to you that I'm her husband." They were both quiet for so long that Louie asked, "Are you still there?"

"Yes."

"Did you see the picture?"

"Yes, but I don't know if that makes me feel any better about lettin' you in my house. Regan isn't a very nice person. How do I know she didn't send you to do something to me? How do I know you're not like her?"

"You're not like what they say Eamon is like. You're not like any of the rest of them. Please believe I can be different than them just like you are."

"I reckon I can believe that, but what are you doin' in this neighborhood so early in the mornin'?"

"I'm sorry to bother you, Clara. You see, we live down the street from you now. I got a job doing accounting for one of the barge companies, and my office is down here by the river. Regan ran through our money so bad that we are having a hard time affording her house and her folks' house, so we sold her house and moved down here. It's closer to her job, too. She works downtown."

"I thought Eamon's folks got money through the Minin' Act, because Caelan was a coal miner."

"They did, but Regan has them living higher than their means, too. I think growing up so poor did something to her. She's always got to be putting on airs. It seems nothing is ever good enough for her."

"Why did you come here to tell me all this?"

"Please don't laugh."

"I'm not findin' any of this funny."

"Well, you see, Regan takes my whole check and gives me 50 cents a day allowance. She left today without giving me my 50 cents, and I was wondering if I could borrow it from you until tomorrow."

"What? Why would I believe somethin' like that?"

Louie cleared his throat and said, "Because you've met Regan, and you know how her family is."

Clara leaned on the door for several seconds before she opened it and said, "Come on in."

Louie came in and stood just inside the front door. He was a tall, thin, handsome man with well groomed, dark hair and chiseled features. He was wearing a dark suit, white shirt, and tie and was holding a hat that matched his suit. He was obviously a business man.

Clara motioned toward the table and said, "You may as well have a seat since you're here."

Louie sat at the table while Clara asked, "Did she feed you any breakfast before you left the house this mornin'?"

"No," Louie answered.

"Are you hungry?"

"It seems I'm hungry most of the time."

Clara turned the heat back on under the eggs and bacon and sat the plate she put them on in front of Louie once they were cooked. While he ate, she poured both of them a cup of coffee and sat across from him.

She took a sip of her coffee and watched him eat as she asked, "Why did you come to me?"

Louie lay his fork on the half-eaten food and said, "To be honest, you live the closest. But, that's not the only reason. I never asked her Mom or Dad for anything the entire time we lived up the street from

141

them. I don't think I'd ask any of the other brothers or sisters even if they lived right next door. I don't think I'd even ask Eamon. I think I'd do without if I had to ask any of them."

Clara took another sip of coffee and asked, "Then why are you askin' me?"

"To be honest, the way Regan talks about you behind your back lets me know you're a really nice person."

"What? She hates me. I'm not sure why, but she hates me. I spent the entire week of our weddin' gettin' nasty phone calls from Eamon's family because of the horrible things she was sayin' about me to everyone. Even the people who live up here didn't come to the weddin' because of that."

"She's jealous of you," Louie said. "She's so hateful she has to try to fool people into liking her, and most of the time she still gets figured out for who she is — eventually. You're genuine. You have an ease about you. You put people at ease. What you see is what you get. Who you are now is who you're always going to be, because it's who you really are. That scares her. Even when she's talking bad about you, she says a lot of things that makes me realize you're a good person. She makes fun of your innocence. She calls you goody-two-shoes, Sandra Dee, and Donna Reed. It's like she's the devil and you're an angel and that makes her mad. She goes out of her way to make you look bad. If people are judging you instead of her, it will take them longer to realize she's bad."

Clara shook her head almost the entire time Louie was talking. When he stopped, she looked into his eyes and asked, "If that's how you feel about her, why don't you leave her?"

He shrugged and said, "I don't know. She seems to have the same allure as the devil, and you know what a hard time God has getting converts away from him. I've heard that the Bible says the devil is actually beautiful instead of being a monster with horns. I guess that's why I stay, and I guess that's why she still attracts so many men."

Clara shook her head like she was trying to shake cobwebs off of it before she said, "But, she's not beautiful. She looks like a younger version of her Ma, and she's obviously agin' before her time."

Louie sighed heavily and said, "I guess I know that. Hell, I know I know that. I still see her attracting men like flies, and I'm thinking as I watch her in action that she isn't beautiful enough to succeed, but she always does – and then she comes back and succeeds with me again, too. Maybe it's that she's attractive more than beautiful — she can convince people to see her however she needs to be seen to attract them. She's like a spider luring in the flies, and once you're caught in her web, it's really hard to get free. She's able to make herself look the way she wants people to see her even when she does the most evil things. Like I said — the devil."

Clara shook her head and asked, "You came here for fifty cents?"

Louie nodded.

Clara went into the living room and returned a few minutes later with fifty cents. She laid two quarters on the table in front of Louie and said, "I hope this helps."

Louie thanked her, finished his breakfast, and left.

The rest of the day was peaceful until Clara was preparing supper. When she heard a knock on the door, she sighed and whispered, "Not again." She turned the burners off before answering the knock. When she opened the door, she was noticeably startled when she saw Regan standing there.

"What are you doin' here?" Clara asked.

Regan smiled big and said in a charming voice, "Louie told me you were kind enough to loan him fifty cents when my silly self forgot to give him his daily allowance this morning. I told him I would come by to thank you for your kindness and pay you back the money."

Clara extended her palm and allowed Regan to drop the two quarters Regan held between her fingers onto it. When the coins hit Clara's palm, she wrapped her fist around them and said, "Thank you for payin' us back. Good night."

Regan pushed on the door to keep Clara from closing it and said, "I'm awful sorry about the way we started out. I knew you lived here when we rented down the street. I thought it would be good to live next to you, so we can all get close again. Family is so important, don't you think? Don't you think it would be a good idea to mend bridges?"

"I'm not so sure I do."

"You mean you really don't think family's important?" Regan asked, acting shocked.

"That's not what I said."

"But, I just asked you if you think family is important?"

"What do you want?" Clara asked before she sighed.

"Well, I was thinkin' it would be awful nice if all of the children got together again —"

"We've got two children now. We don't have much opportunity to go out."

"Perfect! Then, we'll all come here Saturday night. I'll let everyone know."

"What?"

"Tootles. We'll see y'all Saturday night," Regan said before she walked away.

Clara stuck her head out the door and called Regan's name three times, but Regan kept on walking without answering.

Clara closed the door, leaned against it, and said out loud, "Saturday night is goin' to be extremely interestin' — fightin' inside and outside the house."

CHAPTER THIRTEEN: FAMILY REUNION

Clara was waiting at the door for Eamon when he got home from work, and she started telling him about Louie's and Regan's visits and the party Regan volunteered their house for before he was even in the house.

Eamon sat at the kitchen table and said, "That stupid bitch. She always sets people up like this. These kind of games is how she got all of my brothers and sisters turned against me. I can guarantee she has something in mind, and it's not good."

Clara sat across from him and said, "I wanted to call everyone and tell them not to come, but the only phone number we have is Darcy's and she made it very clear she doesn't want us to call her again."

Eamon sighed heavily and said, "Let's not worry about this anymore. This may be a blessin' in disguise. I can tell Regan in front of all of my brothers and sisters that she lied about everything she said about me. That might fix everything."

"Okay," Clara answered. "I guess I'll get the house ready for a party."

Clara spent the rest of the week making sure everything was put away from their recent move, cleaning the house, and baking. She spent the entire day on Saturday making a big pot of chili to go with the cornbread she baked the day before, and Eamon went to the store and bought more pop and potato chips than they could afford.

When Eamon got home with the party supplies, he asked Clara to help him carry them up to the house. She walked down to the car to help him, and Dog and I followed. We couldn't help carry anything, but I felt comforted being close to them. I assumed Dog was clinging to them for the same reason. I had never been to a party before, and I didn't know what to expect. I really didn't know what to expect with this party where so much old animosity was on the invitation list.

When Clara saw how much pop was in the car, she asked, "Can we afford all of this?"

"Probably not, but I wanted to make sure we didn't run out. They already think badly enough of me. Whatever is left, our children can drink next week."

"Okay," Clara said as she grasped the handles of two six packs of pop bottles in each hand and carried them up to the house.

The first people arrived around six o'clock. It was Eamon's brother, Bobby, and his wife and children. Clara answered the door, introduced herself, and invited them in.

Once they were in the house, Clara looked at the children and said, "I have two children about your age, and they are a boy and a girl like you two. They're playin' right through that door in the living room if you want to go play with them. Their names are Mitchell and Rebecca." As the children ran toward the living room, Clara looked at Bobby and his wife, Bertha, who was holding a baby in her arms, and said, "If you'd like to lay the baby down, you can lay her on our bed and put pillows around her."

"I'll hold her for now," Bertha answered. "Maybe later."

Bobby and Bertha were both about 5'6" tall. Both had dark hair, and Bertha had short curly hair that those who used them could tell were rolled on bobby pins to create a tight, neat look. Bertha was thin and wore an A-line dress that only went about halfway down her thigh. The two women had similar taste in hair and clothing styles, but Clara's dress ended just below her knee, which was the shortest length Clara would ever wear.

Clara looked at Bobby and said, "It's amazin' how much you look like Eamon. The two of you could almost be twins."

"I reckon," Bobby said. "I haven't seen him in a long time."

Eamon entered the kitchen and said, "I saw some children come into the livin' room, so I knew someone was here."

Clara turned and said, "Your brother, Bobby, and his wife, Bertha, are here."

The look on Clara's face made me think she was afraid he wouldn't recognize which brother it was after all these years. Eamon seemed to

146

recognize that look too, because he mouthed the words "Thank you" before he walked over to his brother and said, "It's good to see you. I haven't seen you in a while."

"Whose fault is that?" Bobby asked.

I could hear the wrath in Bobby's voice, and I didn't like it. These people had a weird tension about them that was making the air in the house feel tense. I assumed Eamon was feeling it, too, because he was shifting from one foot to the other. I got closer to Eamon, because I thought we could both use the comfort. Dog stayed very close to me, so I think he felt the tension, too.

Clara quickly motioned to the table and said, "We've got chili and cornbread. Why don't you sit down before a crowd gets here and have a bowl? Once everyone gets here, there probably won't be an empty chair around this table."

Bobby and Bertha looked at each other, nodded, and took a seat. Clara dished up two bowls of chili and sat them in front of Bobby and Bertha before she gave each of them a piece of cornbread on a dessert plate. After the first bite, they both complimented the chili, but they were quiet while they finished eating.

Shortly after they were finished eating, Bertha said, "I think my baby needs to be changed? Where can I change her?"

"You can take her to our bed to change her," Clara answered. "I'll get a towel to lay under her. Just follow me." As they walked through the living room to the bedroom, Clara said, "Young'uns, there's chili in the kitchen when you get hungry. If I'm not back yet, Eamon will put some in a bowl for you."

"Okay," a couple of the children answered without interrupting their play.

While Clara and Bertha were changing the baby, all of Eamon's brothers and sisters, except Regan and Garnett, arrived. It was as if Eamon's siblings were cloned instead of being birthed by the same parents. All of the boys looked alike, and all of the girl's, except Darcy, were short and looked like Mabon. Darcy had been tall and thin and looked more like the boys since she was a child. Because of this, she spent most of her childhood pulling her too-short, hand-me-down dresses down to keep from showing her underwear. In addition to looking alike, they all entered the house in the same way, had children

147

of similar ages, ate a bowl of chili, and stood close to the living room wall without talking much.

It seemed like the tension Bobby and Bertha brought into the house got thicker when the other siblings arrived. As the evening progressed, the air kept feeling thicker and thicker — almost as if the tension had a life of its own. Even my ghost lungs were having a hard time with what it was doing to the air, and Dog was panting even though I hadn't seen him pant since he had crossed over into the ghost realm.

Clara was shy, but she kept trying to get conversations started. Those attempts failed until Eamon asked about his brother, Garnett. The siblings explained, through sordid remarks that were disguised by fake pleasantries, that Garnett was living in Tennessee with a Catholic wife whose religion made her unacceptable — and Eamon would know this if he hadn't left the mountains and left his favored Garnett behind. This opened the door to an evening's worth of gossip about anyone who wasn't at the party or was too far away to hear what was being said.

The liveliest part of the evening was when all of the women ended up in the bedroom changing baby diapers at the same time. Rebecca stood in the doorway watching them change the babies, so Clara went over to her and asked what she was doing.

"I like the babies," Rebecca answered.

"Do you know how to tell if the babies are boys or girls?" Clara asked.

"When you change their diapers."

Clara smiled for a second, but her smile quickly faded before she asked, "How do you know that?"

"I don't know," Rebecca said as she continued to watch the babies.

Clara opened her mouth to say something, but she stopped when she became aware of the noise next door.

"Here we go again," she said as she walked toward the kitchen. Eamon was already standing in the open door watching the escalating party when Clara entered the room. She walked over to him and asked, "Should we call the police?"

"What good will it do? Let's just hope they don't disturb my family too much while they're visitin'," Eamon said as he closed and locked the door.

When they turned back to the kitchen, a couple of Eamon's siblings asked, "What's happenin'?"

Clara smiled and said, "It looks like our neighbors are havin' a party tonight, too."

Clara returned to Rebecca and started to say something, but her words were drowned out by one of the women loudly saying, "Mama said she really did her dirty. She acts like she's nice and all, but we've heard enough about what she's really like."

Clara leaned against the wall outside the door and listened to all the women talk about her. She became the main topic of conversation. She only listened for a few minutes before she grasped Rebecca's hand and said, "Let's go to the kitchen and get a pop. Would you like a pop?"

Rebecca nodded and followed her to the kitchen with Dog and I close behind. Dog and I sat under the kitchen table together and watched Clara get a bottle of pop out of the refrigerator, open it on an opener that hung on the woodwork by the front door, and sit at the kitchen table with Rebecca on her lap. The two of them sat there and sipped on the soda for the rest of the night. Clara returned nice pleasantries if people talked to her first, but she didn't try to start any more conversations.

When Clara sat stock-still for over an hour, I became concerned. Even Rebecca's movements weren't disturbing Clara's statue-like pose. I became so concerned that I listened to Clara's thoughts: 'Maybe I should stand up to them, but what's the point? They'll just start spreadin' rumors about me like Mabon and Regan did — the phone will ring off the hook all night like it did the first time I met them. Standin' up to this kind of people is like standin' up to the people next door. It's like standin' up to Eamon when he's in the middle of one of his rages. It's like when my brother was beatin' his wife — him beatin' her was okay but her tryin' to get people to admit what they saw him doin' was something that deserved punishment. Life will be a lot more peaceful for me and my kids if I just keep my mouth shut.'

Under the table, I petted Dog while we watched the party go on around us. One by one, the brothers and sisters left with their spouses and children. The air got noticeably lighter each time a family left. The only family who hadn't left when Rebecca got tired and fussy were

Bobby and Bertha. Clara said her good nights to them and went to put Mitchell and Rebecca to bed.

After the children were asleep, Clara returned to the kitchen. Everyone was gone, and Eamon was sitting at the kitchen table alone.

"They're all gone, now?" Clara asked.

"Yes," Eamon answered.

"Is something wrong?"

"You were gone longer than I expected you to be, so I came back to peek in on you. When I returned, Bertha was puttin' the pop that was left into her big diaper bag. I started to say somethin', but then I heard Bobby say, 'It's the least he can give us after walkin' off like that and leavin' us with nothin'.' I just went back into the livin' room and sat on the couch and let them do whatever they were goin' to do. They walked out the door with all that pop without even sayin' goodbye."

"They stole from us?"

"I guess you could call it that. They'd probably call it takin' home some left overs. It seems none of them can see when they've done wrong — just like Ma and Pa."

Clara sat across from Eamon.

They were both silent for several minutes before Eamon said, "Regan started this whole thing and didn't even come for me to stand up to her in front of everyone. They still believe everything she said about me."

"They believe everything she said about me, too," Clara said. "I heard all of your sisters talkin' about me behind my back while they were in the bedroom changin' their babies. From what I can see, Eamon, they all seem to be like Regan. It's probably a miracle you didn't turn out like your folks. Your Uncle Teagan and MawMaw Tierney gettin' you away from them is probably the only thing that saved you. We probably shouldn't be surprised that the younger ones who came up under Regan would turn out like her."

"I reckon."

"I don't think any of them are good people, Eamon. When I was puttin' Rebecca to bed, she told me those were some cute damn babies. She had to pick that up from them. I don't really want those people around my children anymore."

"Neither do I."

Clara cocked her head and said, "It sounds like the party's still goin' on next door. Do you want some coffee?'

Eamon nodded, and Clara got up and brewed another pot.

When Mitchell and Rebecca came in for breakfast the next morning, Eamon and Clara were asleep at the table. Both of them had folded their arms on the table and used them as a pillow. Dog and I were still sitting under the table in that twilight state of rest that isn't quite sleep that we ghosts experience.

When the children woke them up, Clara asked, "Is cereal okay for breakfast?"

Rebecca nodded while Mitchell said, "Yes."

"Lucky Charms®?"

Both children said, "Yes."

Clara poured four bowls of cereal and put milk on them. She sat a bowl and a spoon in front of Eamon and Mitchell. Then, she picked up the other two bowls and asked, "Rebecca, would you like to eat our bowl outside? Maybe we'll see a bunny run across the yard again."

Rebecca nodded before she took her bowl and followed Clara outside. Dog and I went with them.

When they got outside, Clara sat on the retaining wall. Dog ran around the grassy hill, and I sat next to Clara. When Rebecca sat on the other side of her, Clara gave Rebecca a spoon.

After they both took a couple of bites, Clara asked, "Do you remember when I asked you how you know which babies are girls and which babies are boys last night?"

Rebecca nodded as she took another bite.

"You never did answer my question. How did you know that?"

"I don't know."

"Did anyone ever show you they were different from you, you know, between your legs?"

Rebecca shook her head as she took another bite.

"Did anyone ever touch you down there?"

Rebecca stopped eating and asked, "Why?"

"I just don't understand how you know the difference between boys and girls."

"I don't know. I just do."

"Someone must have shown you the difference," Clara said, frustrated.

"Did I do something bad?"

"I just want to know how you know the difference," Clara said, sternly.

Tears welled in Rebecca's eyes as she asked, "Why are you mad at me? I didn't do anything."

Clara took a couple of deep breaths before she answered, "I'm not mad at you. I just wish you'd tell me how you know the difference."

Rebecca cried and said, "I don't know. I already said I don't know."

As Rebecca sat her half-eaten bowl of cereal on the retaining wall and wiped her eyes, Clara asked, "If anyone makes you feel uncomfortable about down there, will you tell me?"

"Like you're doin' now?"

"I'm not doin' anything but tryin' to make sure you grow up right," Clara snapped.

Rebecca cried harder.

"There's no need to cry," Clara said. "It's okay. Will you just promise me that if anyone ever tries to do anything to you down there or shows you their down there that you will tell me?

Rebecca wiped her eyes on her sleeve and said, "Yes."

"If anyone ever tries to hurt you, I want you to tell me."

Rebecca watched Clara finish her cereal. When Clara was done, she asked, "Aren't you goin' to finish your cereal?"

Rebecca shook her head and said, "Mitchell hurts me."

Clara sat her bowl next to Rebecca's and asked, "What do you mean?"

"Can you make Mitchell stop bein' mean to me?"

"Why are you tellin' me this now?"

"You told me to tell you if anyone ever hurts me."

Clara smiled and said, "I know he picks on you a lot. I'm sorry. I'll talk to him, but I don't know if it'll do any good. That's just the way boys are. People say 'boys will be boys' for a reason. Just take comfort in the fact that girls are sweeter than boys. My Mom used to tell me that girls are sugar and spice and everything nice, but boys are snakes and snails and puppy dog tails."

"Is that why he's so mean to me?"

"I'm afraid that's just how boys are. That can be how men are, too. Sometimes we have to save our strength for the big battles, like if

152

someone touched — I don't want you to go through what I — well, listen to me ramble when there are dishes to do. Will you bring your bowl in the house for me to wash when you're done?"

Rebecca nodded and watched Clara until she was in the house. I stayed with Rebecca while Dog continued to play on the hill. Once Clara was inside, Rebecca picked up her bowl and started eating her cereal again. A few minutes later, a baby from the yard next door crawled to the fence, plopped down on its big wet diapered butt, and reached through the fence toward Rebecca. She looked at the baby, and I could see her eyes change as compassion filled them. She and I walked over to the fence, and Dog ran down the hill and joined us.

Rebecca sat down across from the baby, and asked, "Are you hungry?"

The baby reached for the bowl.

Rebecca put some cereal on her spoon and stuck it through the chain link fence for the baby to take a bite. When she did, some of the cereal fell off. She was picking it up and handing it to the baby when Eamon opened the door to check on her.

When he saw what she was doing, he yelled, "Rebecca, get your ass in here right now!" Rebecca looked at him and started shaking when he yelled again, "I said get your ass in here!"

By the time Rebecca, Dog, and I got in the house, Clara was in the kitchen and asked, "What's goin' on?"

"This child of yours was feedin' that baby next door. She has no respect for how hard I work on crippled legs to make money. She just takes the food I buy with it and feeds it to the enemy."

Clara glared at Rebecca as hard as Eamon was and asked, "You didn't do that, did you?"

"Yes, she did!" Eamon screamed.

Rebecca just stood in front of them looking like a cornered rabbit.

"I ought to beat your ass like my Dad used to beat mine," Eamon screamed, "but I can't stand to look at you long enough to even do that. Get your ass in your room and go to bed. You can come back out tomorrow after I go to work."

Rebecca stood there so long that Eamon took a step toward her. When he did, Clara intercepted, grabbed Rebecca's hand, and led her to Eamon and Clara's room. As she did, she said, "I can't believe you did that after the way those people have treated us."

153

Dog and I followed her. When Rebecca was tucked into Eamon and Clara's bed, Dog and I lay next to her. Shortly after she cried herself to sleep, she started twitching and whining. I listened to her thoughts and found myself watching her dream. Clara and Mitchell were sitting halfway up the backyard hill, and each of them had a bucket in their lap. Rebecca was trying to climb up the hill toward them, but Mitchell and Clara were both taking caterpillars out of their buckets, peeling the black faces off of them, and throwing them at Rebecca. Rebecca was crying. After a couple of dozen caterpillars, she stopped climbing toward them, sat down, and cried while they continued to throw faceless caterpillars at her. When their buckets were empty, Clara got up, grabbed Rebecca by the wrist, and drug her kicking and screaming into the kitchen. She put Rebecca into a pot of boiling stones to cleanse her.

Rebecca woke up screaming. Clara ran to her, but Rebecca backed away toward the headboard when Clara entered the room. Clara sat on the edge of the bed and said, "You don't have to stay in bed all day. Go downstairs with your books and crayons, and I'll bring you some lunch later."

Rebecca veered past Clara and ran to the door that led downstairs as fast as her crippled leg would allow her to move. Dog and I followed her. Clara brought Rebecca's meals to her, and Rebecca, Dog, and I stayed in the downstairs room until Eamon came home from work the following day.

When Eamon entered the house after work the following day, he was carrying a television. As he walked across the kitchen, he yelled, "Look what Mrs. Reynolds gave me! She got a new one today, and she said I could have the old one to thank me for the nights I work late."

Clara came to the kitchen and said, "Are you serious? A television? We actually have a television now?"

"Yes," Eamon said as he carried it into the living room and plugged it into the socket on the wall that separated the first-floor stairs from the living room.

The family watched television shows for the rest of the evening. They even ate the fried chicken Clara made for supper on the couch in front of the television. Rebecca joined them, and no one said anything about what happened the day before.

That night after Rebecca went to sleep, she started twitching and whining, so I watched her dreams again. She was dreaming about military men from a show they watched that night called Hogan's Heroes. The military men were trying to catch her to take her away. She ran into the backyard and hid under a picnic table the previous owners had left when they moved away. She was cowering there while the men looked for her. When one of them found her, she woke up screaming again, but she stifled her scream, curled up in a ball, and covered her head with her blanket. Rebecca repeatedly had the same two dreams for several weeks.

About two weeks after the dreams started, Clara took the children outside with her while she hung their laundry on a clothesline whose poles were anchored in the narrow strip of concrete along the edge of the retaining wall behind the annex rooms. Rebecca was wandering around the grassy hill behind the clotheslines with Dog and me. She was picking dandelions and trying to ignore Mitchell, who kept teasing her. When Clara hung a sheet between herself and the children, Mitchell seemed to become bolder when Clara couldn't see him. After several pranks, he pushed Rebecca hard enough to make her fall. Dog growled at him while I told him to stop picking on his sister, but he wasn't always aware of us. She sat on the ground and looked at the dandelions she already had in her hand through her tears. It seemed she was not going to defend herself until Mitchell sat behind her and started pulling handfuls of grass and throwing them on her.

When he did, she struggled to her feet as she screamed, "No caterpillars! No!"

When she got to her feet, she ran down the hill faster than her crippled leg could manage, so she fell halfway down. Mitchell started throwing grass at her again.

"No caterpillars!" she screamed. "Stop it!"

Clara walked to the other side of the clothes she was hanging. When she was able to see the children, she asked, "What's wrong?"

Rebecca held her arms behind her head and screamed, "Mitchell's throwin' caterpillars!"

Clara went to Rebecca and helped her stand as she said, "It's just grass. There aren't any caterpillars."

When Clara took Rebecca's hand and tried to lead her down the hill, Rebecca fought so hard to pull away that she fell when she broke free. When Clara picked her up and carried her down the hill, Rebecca continued to fight so hard that she fell again when Clara put her down on the concrete at the bottom of the hill.

Clara helped Rebecca up, knelt in front of her, and held her upper arms firmly as Clara said, "There are no caterpillars, so please calm down. Ride your tricycle here on the concrete where I can see you." She looked at Mitchell and said, "And Mitchell won't be throwin' anything else at you, or he'll spend the rest of the day in his room."

Rebecca stopped fighting and asked, "We're not goin' to the kitchen?"

Clara shook her head and said, "No. Just ride your tricycle, so I can finish hangin' the laundry."

Rebecca got on the tricycle Mrs. Reynolds gave them a few months before when Eamon found it in her attic while working on the antiques she stored there. Mitchell watched Clara while he followed Rebecca on the tricycle. Each time Clara looked away, he threw a twig at Rebecca. While Clara was busy struggling with a big blanket, Rebecca peddled unnoticed between the clothesline and the annex in what appeared to be an attempt to get away from Mitchell. When she got to the top of the hill on the side of the house, Mitchell pushed her tricycle and sent it spiraling toward the retaining wall. When she started screaming, Dog and I chased her over the hill, but Dog barking at her seemed to be the only thing we could do. Clara looked up from hanging laundry, saw what was happening, dropped the blanket and clothespins she was holding, and ran toward Rebecca screaming, "Jump off! Jump off!" Rebecca was three-fourths of the way to the high retaining wall before she understood what Clara was asking her to do and jumped off. A few seconds later, the bicycle tumbled over the wall and hit the concrete below with a loud crash.

As I watched, I was flabbergasted. I wondered if Mitchell intended to hurt her or if it was a childish prank gone wrong. I knew I would never know the answer to that question. Clara was so busy hanging clothes that she hadn't seen what Mitchell did, and I doubted Rebecca would be brave enough to tell on him. He'd done so many similar things, albeit less dangerous, that Rebecca never told anyone about in the past due to Mitchell threatening to hurt her if she did. Mitchell had been training her not to tell for a long time.

Clara ran to Rebecca, grabbed Rebecca up in her arms, hugged her close, and started crying as she asked, "Are you okay? Are you okay?" Clara sat Rebecca down and spun her around while looking her up and down while asking, "Are you okay?"

When she was convinced Rebecca was okay, Clara picked her up and carried her toward the house as she yelled, "Mitchell, come on. It's past time to take a nap. After all of this excitement, I'm sure she needs one."

"I don't want to take a nap!" Mitchell yelled.

"Come on anyway."

Mitchell threw down the handful of grass and twigs he'd been teasing Rebecca with and followed Clara into the house with Dog and me close behind.

When they got in the house, Clara sat Rebecca down, looked in her eyes, and asked again, "Are you okay?"

Rebecca nodded.

"It's past time for our nap. Do you want a snack first?"

Rebecca nodded.

"What do you want?"

"Apple."

"Okay," Clara answered. "Go sit at the table, and I'll get an apple for you."

When Mitchell entered the room, Clara said, "Sit with your sister at the table, and I'll get you a snack before you take your nap, too."

Mitchell sat across from Rebecca. While Clara sliced the apples, he leaned across the table and whispered, "You better not tell Mom I pushed you."

Rebecca swallowed hard and nodded.

When Clara sat a plate of apple slices in front of each of them, Mitchell whined, "Why do I have to eat what she wanted? Why didn't you ask me what I wanted?"

Clara sighed and asked, "What do you want?"

"Cookies.'

Clara went to the cabinet, got each of the children a chocolate chip cookie, and sat them on their plates next to their apple slices. She then got them each a small glass of milk.

She sat at the table while they ate. When they were finished, she instructed the children to follow her to Clara and Eamon's bed for their nap.

Dog and I had watched Clara take a nap with the children every day since they were born. Clara lay in the middle of the bed, Mitchell lay next to her near the outside edge of the bed since he was older and less likely to roll off — and since he couldn't lay next to Rebecca without picking on her, and Rebecca lay on Clara's other side between Clara and the wall. Now that Mitchell was in school, he only joined them in the summer and on the weekend. He complained that he was too old for naps, but Clara answered that he was also too young to be left alone when everyone else was napping. He always fell asleep anyway.

Dog and I followed them to the bedroom, so we could lay on the foot of the bed like we always did while they took their nap. When Clara walked through the bedroom door, she gasped. I walked around her and saw that a heavy vent that was usually in the wall high above the bed had fallen onto the spot where Rebecca slept each time they took a nap.

Clara fell to her knees, pulled Rebecca into her arms, and said, "Oh, my word. If we would have taken our nap on time today — "

Clara gave Rebecca a kiss on the cheek and said, "We don't need a nap today. There's been too much excitement. Why don't you go read your books, Rebecca? And, Mitchell, you can go play, but stay in the house."

Clara went to the kitchen and sat at the table. She was still sitting there when Eamon got home.

"What's for supper?" Eamon asked as he entered the house.

Clara looked up at him and answered, "I haven't started makin' anything yet."

"Is something wrong?"

"Yes," Clara said. "I think we need to get out of this house. Rebecca almost rode her tricycle over the retainin' wall today, and then the vent fell out of the wall above our bed right around the time we usually take our nap. If we would have been nappin' when it happened, Rebecca would probably be dead right now. It landed right where she usually lays. If it would have fallen out while we were in bed tonight, one of us would probably be dead."

Eamon sat across from her and said, "This house is a piece of junk, but I never thought that vent would fall even though I always wondered why it was so high up on the wall. It seems like whoever built this or someone who lived here before did a whole lot of riggin' things."

"What are we goin' to do?" Clara asked.

"I've been afraid to try to sell it," Eamon answered. "We might have to take a loss on it, and money is always so tight. It's only goin' to get tighter when we start payin' for Rebecca's operations. I've been afraid we'd end up with no place to live at all. At least while we're here, we know we have a roof over our heads. What if we lose money givin' it up and find we don't have a roof over our heads at all? I was as good as homeless several times growin' up, and it was scary enough then. How scary is it goin' to be with a wife and children?"

"Money may be tight, but at least you have a job and we have money comin' in. If we lose money on the house, we could go back to an apartment like we had before or go home to the mountains if we thought we were goin' to end up homeless."

"I've thought about that," Eamon said. "I can't go back to where I come from. If your folks would take me in too, maybe that would keep us safe. I've been so poor before that it isn't hard for me imagine losin' enough money sellin' this house that we won't even have enough for gas to get back to your folk's place."

"Since you have a job, I think the worst that will happen is we'll end up back in a small apartment like we had before. Or, Mr. and Mrs. Williams might take us in for a while until we can figure it out."

"We just don't come from places where you give up what you have, because anything you have wasn't easy to come by."

"I know, but we have to do something. It's bad enough that the neighbors have kept us up almost every night since we moved here, but now it feels like the place isn't safe. I feel like today was a series of omens, and my folks always told me to never ignore an omen."

Eamon sighed loudly and tears welled in his eyes before he said, "You're right about the omen. Maybe we've been gettin' omens all along and not recognizin' them. I haven't wanted to tell you this, because I didn't want you to be worryin' about it, too, but I noticed a crack in the back wall of the foundation when I was installin' the washin' machine. I've been worried about how bad it might get. I've been afraid if we tried to sell the house to get out from under it and a realtor saw it, she might report us or somethin'. We can't afford to fix that. We've got to listen to omens though, don't we?" Eamon paused for a long time before he said, "I hate to do it, but this weekend, I'm goin' to build a wooden wall in front of the cracked foundation to hide it, and then we're goin' to sell this house to someone as unsuspectin' as we were when we bought it. Then we can work on gettin' out of here." After another long pause, he stammered, "Besides, even without all the problems buyin' this house has brought on us, Regan livin' nearby is enough of a reason to move. I'm sure you're tired of Louie stoppin' by all the time, and I learned a long time ago that the less Regan knows about your life the better off you are. She can make your best quality look bad to the whole world if she sets her mind to it. I don't want my kids raised around that."

Clara nodded.

"Why don't we make this the night I take you out to eat instead of Friday when I get my check? We'll go to Frisch's® and get some hamburgers at the car hop?"

"Thank you," Clara said as she got up and pushed in her chair. "I'll go get the children ready."

When they got home from Frisch's® that night, Clara went to each of the children's beds, gave them a hug, and kissed them goodnight even though neither Eamon nor Clara came from an affectionate family to teach them to do that. On that first night of displaying affection, Clara said to both of them, "Today was pretty scary, but thank God we're all still together."

"Why wouldn't we all be together?" Rebecca asked when Clara said that at her bedside.

Clara cleared her throat several times before she said, "You might be with your PawPaw now if you would have been on the tricycle when it went over the wall. We're goin' to move when we can, and please stay away from that retainin' wall until we do. I need you here with me more than PawPaw needs you right now."

Rebecca answered, "Does that mean you care as much about me as you do Mitchell?"

"Of course I do," Clara answered. "Why would you ask that?"

"I'm a girl. You said boys are more important than girls."

"What? When did I say that?"

"You said girls just have to take stuff off boys cuz their stronger and make the money."

Clara hugged Rebecca again and said, "That doesn't mean I like boys better."

"Even if I know how to tell which babies are boys and which babies are girls when you change their diapers?"

Clara wrinkled her brow and said, "Of course."

"Even if I feed the enemy?"

"What?"

"You said I was feedin' the enemy when I gave that baby some cereal."

"Just because we get mad at you doesn't mean we don't care about you."

"Even if someone touched me down there?"

"Did someone?" Clara asked, tentatively.

"You said boys are just mean to girls because they are snakes and snails and puppy dog tails."

Clara smiled and said, "I think you've just had too much excitement today. I also said that girls are sugar and spice and everything nice, and people always like nice best, so don't you be worryin'". She tickled Rebecca and during the giggles kissed Rebecca on the forehead, pulled the blanket up over her, and left the room.

Rebecca's bad dreams stopped that night, and even though Eamon and Clara were raised around people who didn't show a lot of affection, Clara continued to kiss the children good night for the rest of the time they lived at home.

CHAPTER FOURTEEN: STONED NEIGHBORHOOD

The years it took to sell the house were filled with trying to ignore neighbors who partied all night and then trying to survive the day with hardly any sleep. The stress of the situation evolved the family into one where the father was always grumpy, the big brother was taking his frustrations out on the little sister, the little sister was trying to disappear among personalities she didn't have the strength to compete with, and the Mom was the eternal peacekeeper. Even Dog's and my ghost bodies were feeling the effects of all the stress. Only a few events need to be told to emphasize the pattern that emerged over those years.

Eamon and Clara grew to distrust the neighborhood and the school during the previous school year. Although Mitchell made it through unscathed, probably due to his propensity to be the bully, he shared many stories about abused and neglected students. Those kids were receiving no more help than Eamon had received in the mountain culture he grew up in where laws to protect children hadn't existed. Instead of helping these students, Mitchell told stories of teachers scapegoating the victims and being harsh with all of the students. It seemed that drugs in the neighborhood had seeped into the school, causing the teachers to be suspicious, guarded, and quick to judge.

On some level, Eamon and Clara must have known that Mitchell was a bully who could take care of himself, because they didn't fuss over him when he came home with distressing stories — or maybe that was only because he wasn't handicapped. Those stories convinced Clara to walk to school and pick Rebecca up after her morning kindergarten classes, because the school bus only ran in the morning and the evening. Those walks convinced Clara of the growing drug problem in the neighborhood — people didn't seem to see the need to hide suspicious transactions. She became so concerned that she started waiting in front of their house for the school bus, both in the morning when it picked both children up and in the evening when it dropped Mitchell off. The family's needs were becoming so great that Dog and I were having a hard time keeping up with them. Eamon, Clara, and Rebecca all needed protection, but there were only two of us. Even if the most we could do was get angry enough to scare them with slamming doors like we had once done to Mabon back home, we felt they were safer when we were with them.

At the beginning of the school year, I stayed home with Clara and sent Dog to school with Rebecca. All I could do was pray that Eamon would be okay. I noticed Louie was developing a habit of knocking on the door every time Regan didn't give him his daily allowance — or at least every time he said she didn't. He always arrived late enough to avoid Eamon and the children but early enough to spend some time talking to Clara. His timing combined with the way he looked at Clara made me suspect he had a crush on her, so I didn't trust him. I wanted to make sure Clara was safe. While he was there, he often told Clara about neighbor problems at their end of the street that were similar to the ones we were having, and he said he suspected those were also drug related.

Eamon and Clara's concerns about the neighborhood and the school increased when Rebecca became withdrawn in the first grade. Their first concern was that she was succumbing to the easy access to drugs at her young age, because she was steadily evolving into a child who didn't read her books, didn't write and draw in her binder, and was losing her appetite. At that point, I became more concerned about Rebecca than I was about Clara or Eamon, so I started going to school with Rebecca and Dog every day.

Rebecca's teacher was tall and burly while not being heavyset. Beyond that, she didn't need a description, because what she looked like was rarely noticed due to the way her body language displayed her demeanor. She was like watching a stone statue that developed movement. She also possessed the ability to freeze people in stone fear just by looking at them. One of her looks let people know when she didn't approve of them; another made it clear to everyone around her that they should conform to her displeasure — and most did. She didn't seem to like children, and she especially didn't like special needs children, children who came from families she saw as questionable, or students she saw as weak.

Unfortunately, Rebecca fell into all of those categories. Shortly after Clara left from dropping Rebecca off on the first day I went to school with her, Mrs. Stone looked at Rebecca and asked, "Why are you wearing baby shoes? My daughter wore those white, high-top shoes when she was a baby. You're grown. Is your hillbilly Mama so poor she has to make you wear baby shoes because she can't afford to get you a pair of big girl shoes?"

"I have a clubfoot," Rebecca answered.

Mrs. Stone knelt in front of Rebecca and said, "So, you're weak."

Rebecca shook her head, so Mrs. Stone said it again.

"My PawPaw said I'm able," Rebecca answered.

"Your PawPaw's an idiot. You're weak, and you'll always be weak."

Tears welled in Rebecca's eyes as she said, "My PawPaw's not an idiot."

Mrs. Stone's eyes flashed red. Her face clenched in anger and made her look even more like stone. She grabbed Rebecca's arm, took the paddle out of her desk drawer on the way to the door, dragged Rebecca to the bathroom, and paddled her with a hotheaded abandon that seemed to have no regard for the consequences for herself or Rebecca.

When it was over, Mrs. Stone knelt in front or Rebecca, grabbed Rebecca's upper arms, shook her, and said, "Stop crying, now! That is not what strong little girls do. You'll thank me for this one day. I'm going to make you strong."

Rebecca kept crying.

Mrs. Stone shook Rebecca again and said, "Grow up! Stop crying! I'm going to make you strong." She paused for a minute before she shook Rebecca again and mocked, "Little girls don't get strong by running to their Mommy and Daddy for help, not that those hillbillies could help you anyway. Tell them anything, and it'll be twice as bad the next time."

Rebecca opened her mouth to say something and quickly closed it. When she did, I saw the light go out in her eyes. It was like she became

164

a robot who dutifully followed this monster back to the classroom when her every instinct should have been to run.

When Clara picked Rebecca up after school, Rebecca kept walking very slowly. Dog and I trailed behind Clara and stayed close to Rebecca.

"Does your leg hurt?" Clara asked.

Rebecca shook her head.

"You don't have to act brave and strong when you're hurtin'. It's okay to admit if you're in pain."

Rebecca shook her head.

"I can tell by the way you're walkin' that your leg hurts," Clara said. "I'll carry you the rest of the way."

When Clara picked Rebecca up, she held Rebecca in a hug and put her arms under Rebecca's butt. When she did, Rebecca started screaming and kicking until Clara was forced to put her down as she asked several times, "What's wrong?"

Rebecca wouldn't answer no matter how many times Clara asked that question. She trailed silently behind Clara all the way home. Dog and I continued to stay close to Rebecca. When we got home, Rebecca lay on her side on the floor in front of the television. When it was time for supper, she said she didn't feel like eating and asked if she could go to bed.

Clara lay a hand on her forehead and said, "You don't feel warm, but I can tell you don't feel good. Go on downstairs and go to bed. If you don't feel better soon, maybe you should go to the doctor."

Dog and I followed her downstairs and lay with her as she slept on her side all night. We watched the next morning while she gathered her clothes and carried them upstairs instead of waiting for Clara to get them for her like Clara usually did. Rebecca went in the bathroom off the kitchen, locked the door, and washed and dressed herself. Being a ghost, I was able to go through the door. I immediately knew what she was hiding while she ignored Clara knocking on the door. Her butt was covered with bruises that were such a dark purple they almost looked black. In addition to the bruised areas, welts were beginning to form.

When Rebecca came out of the bathroom already dressed, Clara asked, "Why did you dress yourself this mornin'?"

"PawPaw said I'm able."

"I reckon he was right. You did a good job. Did you brush your teeth?"

Rebecca nodded.

"I think you still need me to comb your hair and fix it though. I'll do that after you eat breakfast. Mitchell ate his while you were gettin' dressed. He's watchin' TV. Your cereal is already in a bowl on the table. I'm just goin' to go get my shoes on while you eat." Clara left the room, walking on feet that were bare like they usually were when she was at home.

While she was gone, Rebecca stood next to the table and ate her cereal. She was finished by the time Clara returned with a brush. Clara sat on one of the kitchen chairs, and Rebecca stood in front of her while Clara combed Rebecca's hair and put it in a ponytail.

When Clara was done, she said loud enough for Mitchell to hear her, "Come on, Mitchell. We need to leave now."

While they waited for Mitchell to come to the kitchen, Rebecca went to the bathroom and picked up a sweater she carried up from her bedroom.

When she carried it out of the bathroom, Clara asked, "Why do you have your sweater? It's still pretty warm outside."

Rebecca shrugged.

"Why don't you leave it here?"

Rebecca hugged it tight and shook her head.

"Okay," Clara said. "We have to go before you miss the bus. You sure are in an odd mood this morning."

Clara herded the two children out the door and down to the bus stop. When the bus arrived, Mitchell sat in the front with some friends who immediately started doing some minor rough-housing with him. Rebecca walked to the last row of the bus, folded up her sweater, and sat on it. Tears welled in her eyes as she looked out the bus window and waved at Clara, so Dog and I both snuggled close to her.

That was the beginning of another pattern that was as predictable as the neighbors partying every night. Mrs. Stone systematically trying to erase the message that Rebecca was able, Clara being too tired from lack of sleep to realize that Rebecca's insistence on dressing herself was suspicious, Dog growling without effect at Mrs. Stone multiple times per day, and me repeatedly whispering the promise in Mrs. Stone's ear that I would be waiting for her when she got to this side. A few times, I smelled the whiskey that she kept in her desk drawer on her breath when I leaned in close enough to whisper my promises.

The only peace Rebecca saw that year was when a student teacher named Miss Ally joined the class for an internship. Clara usually waved at the children as the bus pulled away in the morning, but one morning during Miss Ally's first week, Clara got distracted by the neighbors arguing and forgot to wave. Rebecca cried all the way to school. Dog and I tried to comfort her, but there wasn't much we could do. When she got to school, it was obvious she was trying to hold back her tears. She probably feared she would be punished for crying. No matter how hard she tried, the tears kept escaping.

Miss Ally knelt beside Rebecca's chair, rubbed her palm up and down Rebecca's back, and asked, "What's wrong?"

Miss Ally was young, tall, thin, and had long, straight, blondish-brown hair cascading down her back all the way to her waist. She was also warm and caring. When she touched Rebecca with warm, caring hands, Rebecca released a flood of tears and couldn't stop crying. It seemed that everything Rebecca held in during the first quarter of the year came out.

When Miss Ally couldn't get Rebecca to stop crying, she walked over to Mrs. Stone and asked, "What's wrong with her? Why is she crying like that?"

"Who knows? She cries all the time. She's a weak child. Maybe it was born into her to be weak when she was born crippled, or maybe something is going on at home. You should see those simpleton hillbilly parents of hers. I doubt either of them can even read, and that hillbilly drawl of theirs hurts my ears. Lord knows what the poor child goes through at home."

"Should we call Child Protective Services?"

Mrs. Stone swallowed hard before she stammered, "What good will it do? They need physical evidence before they'll intervene, and there are no bruises on the child. I've been suspicious a few times and checked, so I know they won't find any physical signs of abuse. Child Protective Services won't help her at all."

"Do you think we should call her Mom?"

"It can't hurt. We can't have her crying like this all day."

Miss Ally went over and knelt next to Rebecca again. She rubbed Rebecca's back for several seconds before she said, "You can trust me. I promise I won't get mad at you for telling me what's wrong. Maybe if I know what's wrong, I can help."

Rebecca looked at Miss Ally for the first time.

Miss Ally smiled and crossed her heart before she said, "Cross my heart. I won't get mad, and I won't tell anyone what you tell me. What's wrong."

Rebecca hesitated for a full minute before she stammered, "My Mom didn't wave bye to me this morning."

"Awww, I'm sorry to hear that. Does she always wave bye to you?"

Rebecca nodded.

"Is your Mom nice to you?"

Rebecca's tears slowed and she said, "Yes."

"Do you like your Mom?"

"I love my Mom!"

"Is your Mom ever mean to you?"

Rebecca shook her head.

"Is your Dad ever mean to you?"

Rebecca shook her head again.

"Is anyone ever mean to you?"

Rebecca looked at Mrs. Stone without saying anything. Mrs. Stone immediately jumped up, ran to the other side of Rebecca's desk, looked down at Rebecca, and asked, "This has been a rough day for you, hasn't it?"

Rebecca looked down without answering.

"Would you like me to call your Mom and have her take you home for the rest of the day?" Mrs. Stone asked.

Rebecca nodded without looking up.

Mrs. Stone looked at Miss Ally and said, "Please go to the office and ask the secretary to call Rebecca's Mom and have her pick Rebecca up."

Miss Ally nodded before she got up and left the room.

When Miss Ally was gone, Mrs. Stone leaned close to Rebecca and whispered, "I see you got your way today, but don't get used to it. That woman will only be here for one quarter, and then she goes back to school. When that happens, it will just be you and me again. Remember that before you say anything about me."

Rebecca nodded and started crying again. She was still crying when Clara got there.

When Miss Ally saw Clara's face in the window of the classroom door, she excused herself and went out in the hall to talk to Clara. Dog stayed in the classroom to protect Rebecca, and I followed Miss Ally into the hallway.

"What's wrong with Rebecca?" Clara asked when Miss Ally closed the door.

"She's been crying all day. She said she's crying because you didn't wave at her this morning when the school bus pulled away from your house."

"Oh, my word. She's right. I didn't wave at her. We wave at each other every mornin', but this mornin' I was distracted by the next-door neighbors arguin'. I had no idea it would upset her this much."

"It's not normal for something like that to upset a child this much. Is something going on at home?"

"Are you tryin' to say —"

"No, No. Nothing like that. Rebecca told me how much she loves you and how good you are to her, and you must be very close if you not waving upset her this much. I'm just wondering if there's anything else going on that might —"

"Well, actually there is. We live next door to people who party until late at night, and we don't get a lot of sleep."

"Have you called the police?"

"We used to, but they never did anything. Now, we try to ignore it. We're tryin' to sell our house. When that sells, we'll be movin'."

"I hope you sell it soon. Do you think that's enough to cause this cryin' spell?"

"Well, she's crippled, and she has a lot of doctor's appointments. She knows she's goin' to have to have surgeries. Maybe that has her upset, and it came spillin' out this mornin'."

Miss Ally took Clara's hand in her own and said, "You seem like a very warm and caring mother. I hope you're able to sell your house quickly and get that child out of here. I'll go get her now."

"Thank you," Clara said as Miss Ally entered the classroom and returned a few minutes later with Rebecca and Dog.

Clara knelt in front of Rebecca and said, "I'm sorry I didn't wave at you this mornin'. I was lookin' at the neighbors fightin', and I should have been wavin' at you."

Rebecca took Clara's hand and said, 'That's okay, Mommy. Let's go home."

When we got home, Clara told Rebecca to go take a nap before the noise next door started again. Rebecca was asleep when her head hit the pillow.

The next morning, Clara waved until the bus was out of sight even though Rebecca stopped waving and sat stoically on the back seat with Dog and me.

Shortly after we arrived at school, Mrs. Stone quickly took attendance before she said, "Excuse us for a minute, students. I need to have a word with Miss Ally out in the hall."

When Mrs. Stone grabbed Miss Ally's wrist and drug her to the hallway, Dog and I glanced at each other before we followed them.

When they were in the hallway, Mrs. Stone closed the classroom door, turned to Miss Ally, and asked, "What did you say to Rebecca's mom yesterday?"

"I let her know Rebecca was crying all day and asked if she knew anything that could be wrong."

"And, what did she say?"

"She said they have some noisy neighbors who keep the family from getting proper sleep every night. She also said Rebecca might be upset about an upcoming surgery the child has to have."

"That may be the case, but I feel I need to advise you to be careful about getting involved with these redneck families —"

"I think you're mistaken about Rebecca's family. They may be country people, but her mother seemed like a very nice, caring, and attentive mother."

"Like I was trying to say, don't get too involved with these redneck families. They all act the way they want to be seen in public, but you wouldn't believe the things that go on behind closed doors. Half of these children have alcoholics or drug addicts for parents, and most of them are from redneck mountain families. Rednecks saturated this area when some of the mines closed a few years ago. Most of them don't even know how to flush a toilet. That little girl will probably be married off to some old mountain goat by the time she's fifteen and living on welfare or worse, because these rednecks don't know how to make it in the city. Most people who live around here think they just need to go back to where they came from."

Miss Ally stared at Mrs. Stone with a dead pan expression and didn't say anything.

Mrs. Stone shifted on her feet and said, "Just mind what I'm telling you, and remember that I'm the person who'll evaluate your internship."

Miss Ally nodded one curt nod and both teachers entered the room. I followed them.

Although Rebecca's personality didn't fully re-emerge due to Mrs. Stones' continuing presence in the classroom, Miss Ally made Rebecca feel safe enough that some of her old self came back. Her love for books, writing, and drawing slowly returned over the next few weeks, and Eamon helped her reconnect to her love of animals.

CHAPTER FIFTEEN: BUNNY LOVE

The parties next door grew from late night adventures to all night adventures to weekend long adventures, so the family developed the habit of taking Sunday rides in the country to get away from the noise and stress. Dog and I were grateful to be in the back seat of the car with Mitchell and Rebecca and away from the noise.

Even though Eamon was so grumpy from stress, pain, and lack of sleep that I heard him confess to Clara a fear that he would become like his own father, he was able to show love for his family in ways his own father was never capable of. He knew Rebecca loved animals, so he often made stops at local farms during those Sunday rides to let Rebecca look at the animals through the fence. Some farmers didn't notice them, some ran them away, and some started a friendly conversation. When the latter happened, Eamon asked if his little girl could meet their animals that were friendly enough to be safe around children.

One day they met a friendly farmer who took them to his bunny hutches and let Rebecca hold a bunny. As Rebecca carried the bunny out of the barn and sat in the yard with it, Mitchell stood at the edge of the fence and watched. When the farmer came out of the barn, he looked at Mitchell and asked, "Would you like to hold one, too?"

"Naw," Mitchell answered. "This wasn't meant for me."

When the farmer walked away, Clara walked over to Mitchell, put her arm across his shoulders, and said, "You should hold a bunny, too."

"I'm not the one who likes animals. He never asks what I want to do. It's always about her."

"Don't you understand why?" Clara asked.

"Because I don't matter."

"That isn't true. She's crippled, and he's crippled. He knows her life is goin' to be harder than someone whose body works right, because his life has been harder. He told me that one night when you and Rebecca were in bed. He's scared for how her life is goin' to turn out, and he's scared that somethin' will happen to her when she has to have her operations. He cares about you, too."

"Yeah, sure. Her life's just goin' to be easier, because everyone will be treatin' her like he treats her."

"It rarely works that way outside a person's family," Clara said. "She needs all of us to be nice to her, because the world isn't always nice to crippled people."

"I guess you're goin' to tell me that's why Grandpa was so much nicer to her when he was alive, too."

"It was, but that doesn't mean he didn't care about you, and it doesn't mean your Daddy doesn't care about you. Maybe you can make some effort. Instead of gettin' mad and excludin' yourself, accept invitations to join them. That farmer just offered to let you hold a bunny."

"Yeah, right!" Mitchell said before he stormed back to the car.

A few minutes later, Rebecca came to the fence carryin' a mostly white bunny with a couple of black spots on it. She said, "Look what Daddy bought for me."

"What?" Clara asked. "How are we goin' to keep a bunny?"

"I'll build a hutch in the back yard — as far away from the neighbor's yard as possible. We can move it to that first-floor room in the winter." Eamon looked around for a minute before he asked, "Where's Mitchell? I was goin' to let him pick a bunny, too."

"He went back to the car."

"Oh," Eamon said as he handed a picture to Clara while lookin' at Mitchell standin' next to the car. "The farmer's wife took this picture with a camera she had that spits out instant pictures."

When Clara took the picture from him, he walked to the car.

Clara looked at the black and white picture of Eamon and Rebecca sitting next to each other while Rebecca held the bunny on her lap. Clara smiled and asked, "Did you see this picture yet, Rebecca?"

Rebecca snuggled her face against the bunny as she said, "Yes."

A few minutes later, Eamon and Mitchell returned from the car. Mitchell picked out a bunny that had so many black spots on its white fur that it almost looked like a black bunny with white spots. He was smiling as he carried it to Clara to let her see it.

As they walked to the car, Rebecca asked, "Why did you pick that one?"

"Because I don't want it to look anything like yours?" Mitchell snarled before he pushed her out of the way so he could get to the car first.

When they got home, Mitchell pushed Rebecca out of his way again so he could get to the house first. When Eamon unlocked the door, Mitchell went inside, carried his bunny to the basement, and left it there. Rebecca spent the rest of the evening playing with both bunnies.

The bunnies lived in the basement for the first month they had them. Every day, Dog and I watched Clara sweep up the bunny poop, mop the floor, and ask Eamon when he was going to build the hutches. The first few days she asked, he said he'd get to it. The following week, he snapped at her that he would get to it. The third week, he yelled at her to quit badgering him.

The fourth week, Clara was waiting at the table when Eamon got home from work. It seemed that Eamon could tell by the way she was sitting there that she had something to talk about, so he yelled, "Don't start badgerin' me about those bunny hutches again."

When we saw Eamon was angry, Dog and I stayed under the table.

"I didn't say a word about them."

"What are you sittin' there lookin' at me for? I can tell you have somethin' you want to talk about, and I'm not in any mood for it right now."

"Yes, I do have somethin' to talk to you about. Morgan called today. He wants to know if he can stay with us for a while."

"Why? He's got a good job down at that factory. What? Am I goin' to take care of your family now like I always took care of mine when I was a kid?"

"Emmett apparently got married last weekend when he went home to visit Ma and Pa. His wife is movin' in the apartment with them, so Morgan needs some place to go."

"Times sure are changin'," Eamon said, obviously calming down. "Remember when I first met you. You were livin' in that apartment across the street from me with both of your brothers. We got married and left Emmett and Morgan to find an apartment together. Now, Emmet's gone and got himself married again, and Morgan's all alone." He paused for a minute before he sat across the table from Clara and said, "Thinkin' about old times gets me to wonderin' about Mr. and Mrs. Williams. I wonder how they're doin'."

"I talked to Mrs. Williams on the phone last week. I'm sorry I forgot to tell you. She understood why we hadn't been able to visit in a while with everything we've got goin' on here with these neighbors and all, but she said they miss us. They want to see the children as soon as they can."

"How's Mr. Williams doin'?"

"Mrs. Williams said he seems to be doin' okay now that he's not workin' anymore. As long as he doesn't do too much and takes his medicine, she said he's pretty comfortable."

"That's good to hear."

"What about Morgan?" Clara asked. "Is it okay for him to stay with us?"

"I don't imagine he'll be here long. With you and Emmett married, I reckon Morgan will be the next one to get married."

"That would be a good thing. I think Morgan would make someone a fine husband."

Eamon shook his head and said, "I just hope Emmett's new wife works out better than his first wife. From what I hear, his first wife was so difficult that even your parents agreed to the divorce — and they don't believe in it at all."

"They probably just got married too young — they were both so young. I reckon it's been hard on the children though since the judge gave their mom custody. She can be mighty hard to get along with. I'm just glad me and Morgan were up here in the city when Emmett left her. Stayin' with us made it easier on him."

"I'm just wonderin' — your brothers didn't move out from our apartment until you were pregnant. Why does Emmett get so much more respect?"

"It seems she's already pregnant. I reckon they had to get married."

"Oh," Eamon said. After a long pause, he asked, "How did your Ma and Pa take it?"

"I reckon they're takin' it okay. The gossip on the mountain says he's already got a bastard son. I don't rightly believe it since he would've married whoever that baby's Ma is just like he married this one, but Ma and Pa have heard those rumors for years. I reckon they'll be okay with anything they hear now."

"Whatever's goin' on, this does leave Morgan needin' a place to live. I reckon he can stay here. He ought not to be livin' alone. Nobody ought to be livin' alone. Does he know we're tryin' to sell the house and might be movin'?"

"He knows. He said he'd move right along with us when we do."

"We don't know what kind of house we'll be gettin' when we move. We might not be able to afford a house that gives him his own room."

"He ain't goin' to be worryin' about that. He and Emmett both slept on cots in the livin' room the whole time they were livin' with me. Besides, him livin' with us might help us afford a house big enough for him to have his own room. He said he'd pay us $25 a week. I already cleaned out that far back bedroom on the annex. That's the only room in the house people don't have to be walkin' through to get to the other rooms, so I thought that might suit him best."

"A'righty then," Eamon said as he stood up. "Tomorrow's Saturday. I'll go get the makin's for that bunny hutch in the mornin'. He might not feel friendly about livin' with animals in the house."

"But, Saturday is — oh, never mind. I'm so used to takin' Rebecca to the doctor every Saturday that I keep forgettin' she only has to go every other week now. Yeah, we can build a bunny hutch tomorrow."

"We really should be goin' home more to see your Ma, but I'm scared I'm too tired to drive that far safely. Besides, those idiots next door will destroy this house if we go away for the weekend. Even when we're home, we have to clean up the mess they leave all over our yard after their wild parties. Imagine what they'd do to the place if they knew we weren't home for a whole weekend. We probably wouldn't even have a house to come back to."

"We'll get back down there more often once we get moved. Ma understands why we can't make it as often as we used to. Morgan went last weekend, and he'll be goin' again next weekend after he gets moved. It'll be okay."

When Eamon left the kitchen, Clara went to the phone and called Morgan to tell him he was welcome to move in with them. When the phone call ended, she started cooking supper.

The party next door started around the same time the family sat down to eat. They ignored it through supper, through the evening, while they tried to sleep, and the next morning when Eamon went to get the supplies for the bunny hutch. Around the time Eamon started building the hutch, the partiers got tired enough to go to bed. Most of them either went in the house or left, but some of them, as usual, fell asleep in the yard.

About an hour into building the hutch, a man emerged from the house next door, came up to the fence, and yelled, "Hey, could you keep that hammering down? We're trying to sleep over here!"

Dog and I both got very tense, but Eamon ignored him and continued hammering.

"Hey, cripple, I said keep the hammering down! We're trying to sleep over here!"

Eamon ignored him again.

"Hey, you crippled piece of shit, lay that hammer down now, or I'm coming over there and kicking your ass!"

Eamon threw the hammer onto the ground and stormed over to the fence. I stepped in front of him and tried to stop him while Dog ran to the fence and barked at the man, but Eamon walked right through me. Eamon was so angry that he not only looked bigger, but he also had less of a limp. He got to the fence, poked the man's face as he pointed at him, and said, "Bring your ass on over here and beat my crippled ass if you think you can! How fuckin' dare you tell me to keep the noise down when we haven't had a decent night's sleep since we moved in here, because you party all night long! Hell, you keep such night hours that after all these years of livin' next door to you, this is the first time I've ever seen your face! How about comin' out of your damn house durin' the day every once in a while and cuttin' your damn grass and cleanin' up the garbage you throw all over the yard? How about cleanin' up the garbage you throw in my yard?"

The man poked his finger at Eamon as he screamed, "You think we're the only ones who are difficult to live by! Every day when we're

177

trying to sleep, we have to hear your damn kids over in that yard making so much noise we can't sleep! Can't you keep your damn kids in the house every once in a while —"

Clara ran out of the house and stood in front of Eamon. She slowly pushed him away from the fence as she said, "Come in the house and ignore him. This isn't helpin' anything."

Eamon shook his fist at the man over Clara's shoulder and screamed, "Don't you bring my children into this, you stupid —"

"Come on inside," Clara interrupted as she led him toward the house.

When they got to the side door, Morgan was standing there holding a suitcase. As Clara and Eamon approached him, he asked, "What's goin' on?"

"You might want to think twice about livin' here," Eamon sneered. "Our neighbors are assholes."

Eamon stormed into the house. Clara and Morgan followed him into the living room with Dog and I close behind. Eamon changed the channel on the television as he stormed past it, sat on the couch between Mitchell and Rebecca, put his feet on the coffee table, and stared at the television screen. In one trip, he used the only three pieces of furniture in the room.

Mitchell gasped and said, "But we were —"

Clara ran to Mitchell, picked him up, and as she carried him to the door that the stairs to the first floor were behind, she said, "Never mind that now. You and Rebecca go downstairs and play with your bunnies, and I'll let you know when you can watch television again."

Mitchell started to argue. When Eamon started complaining loudly to Morgan about the neighbors, Mitchell stared at Eamon for a minute and apparently decided against it. He followed Clara's instructions to go downstairs without saying another word.

When Mitchell started walking down the stairs, Clara looked at Rebecca and said, "Come on, Rebecca. I need you to go downstairs, too."

While Rebecca walked toward the door, Morgan looked around the sparsely decorated room before he interrupted Eamon to say, "I left everything but my clothes over there for Emmett and his new wife, Sally. I thought they might need it. Do you need me to get any of it?"

"Naw," Clara answered. "If you bring anything over here, it'll just be more to move when we finally sell this house. There's a bed and a dresser in your room. Will that be enough for you?"

"That'll be enough for me. I don't need much." He glanced around the room and said, "I see you got a television set."

"Eamon has a new job workin' for some rich lady. She gave us her old set when she got a new one."

"That's right nice." Morgan stared at the show on the television screen for a few seconds before he asked, "So, what's goin' on with the neighbors next door?"

"Eamon may be right," Clara said. "You may not want to live here. Those people next door party all night and keep us awake. You may not get much sleep if you live here. Maybe you ought to go to Lana's instead."

"After they've kept us awake every night since we moved here, he just started a fight, because I was keepin' them awake durin' the day buildin' a hutch for Mitchell and Rebecca's bunnies," Eamon said.

"Maybe if you kept them awake durin' the day a little bit more, they'd sleep at night," Morgan said. "Let me unpack my things, and I'll help you finish that hutch. People like that are bullies. If they see more than one person out there, maybe they'll be less likely to start any trouble."

Dog and I went outside and watched Eamon and Morgan construct the bunny hutch. When they were almost finished, some of the young people who partied next door started to party again. Within half an hour, the party was roaring.

"I reckon we don't have to worry about botherin' them with our noise now," Morgan said as he hammered in one of the last few nails.

"I reckon not," Eamon said as he hammered a nail in, too.

A few minutes later the hutch was finished, and the two men sat it up on all four legs.

When they stepped back to look at it, Morgan said, "It looks good. I think we should carry it over and set it next to the annex's back door. It's not as noticeable there, and if anyone messes with it, I'm likely to hear it."

"How about if we set it along the side wall of the annex. You'll probably still be able to hear it if anyone messes with it, and it won't block that thin stretch of concrete where Clara hangs the clothes."

"That's probably a good idea. The children can see it from their play area, and if it's sittin' behind the picnic table, the neighbors might not be as likely to notice it."

Each man picked up an end, and they carried the hutch to the agreed-on spot.

Dog and I followed Morgan and Eamon through the back door of the annex and to the living room where Clara and Mitchell were watching television.

Eamon looked around the room and asked, "Where's Rebecca?"

"She's downstairs playin' with that stupid bunny again," Mitchell answered.

"Go get your bunny and tell her to bring hers up, too," Eamon said. "The bunny hutch is done."

Mitchell got up and left the room.

"Did the neighbors say anything to you while you were workin' on the hutch this time?" Clara asked.

"They didn't say a word. They're already partyin'. I doubt they even knew we were out there."

Mitchell ran up the stairs holding his bunny. While we waited, we heard Rebecca limping up the stairs. She emerged a few seconds later, hugging her bunny, who she named Flopsy.

"The hutch is done," Clara said.

"Can I keep Flopsy in the house?" Rebecca asked. "The neighbors might be mean to her like they were to Daddy."

"Bunnies are quiet," Clara said. "Those people only yell at people who are noisy."

Dog and I followed the family out to the bunny hutch. Eamon lifted the top, and Clara took Mitchell's bunny from him and sat it inside. Rebecca hugged Flopsy for a minute before she let Clara take her and put her in the hutch. When both bunnies were in, Eamon lowered the top.

"It's too high," Rebecca said. "How am I supposed to get Flopsy out when I want to play with her?"

"We don't want you to get Flopsy out by yourself," Eamon said. "Ask me or your Mom, and we'll get her out for you."

Rebecca dropped her head and shuffled to the back door with Dog and I close behind her. The rest of the family followed, whispering remarks about how she'd get used to it.

Just as Rebecca opened the door, the man who yelled at Eamon that morning yelled, "Hey, Buddy." Rebecca, Dog, and I looked at him, but the rest of the family ignored him and continued to walk toward the door. Just before we entered the house, the man yelled, "Hey, Man, I'm just trying to make amends for this morning." He reached his hand across the fence with a joint pinched between his fingers and said, "Let's lighten up together. Come on over and share this joint with me. Come on over and join the party. That'll work everything out."

The family walked into the house without answering him.

As usual, the party went on all night. Rebecca barely slept. I thought her lack of sleep was due to worrying about Flopsy as much as it was about the noise. My suspicion proved to be true. She got up when the noise next door stopped and walked through the sleeping house to go outside and check on Flopsy. Dog and I followed her. Flopsy must have been frightened by the party noise, because she was hunkered down in the corner of the cage and wouldn't come to Rebecca.

"Are you okay, Flopsy?" Rebecca asked.

When Flopsy didn't move, Rebecca climbed onto the picnic table, lifted the hutch top, and stretched over the side to get her bunny. As she pulled Flopsy out of the cage, her elbow hit the top and caused it to fall. The top fell on Rebecca's arms, but they weren't hurt, because Flopsy's head took most of the weight. When blood squirted onto Rebecca, she screamed and dropped Flopsy's limp body back into the hutch. When Flopsy yelped before she went limp, Dog fell onto the ground and started shaking. Rebecca stood on the picnic table looking at the blood on her arms and screaming. When she screamed, Dog crawled under the picnic table and hunkered down with his tail between his legs and his paws over his ears.

A few seconds later, Clara ran out the back door. When she saw Rebecca, Clara ran to her daughter, grabbed her into an embrace, and asked, "What happened?"

Rebecca kept screaming.

The man came out of the house next door and screamed, "I said something to your husband yesterday about those children screaming and keeping us awake during the day, and she's doing it again today! Shut that little brat up! People are trying to sleep over here!"

181

Clara looked at the man and screamed, "You shut up!" She bounced Rebecca on her knee as she asked, "How are you hurt? Where did the blood come from?"

About that time, Eamon and Morgan ran out the back door. Clara was still bouncing Rebecca in her arms and asking, "Where did the blood come from?"

Morgan cleared his throat and said, "Uhh, Clara."

Clara turned to him, and he pointed at the bunny hutch. Clara looked inside, gasped and said, "Oh my word." She sat Rebecca on the picnic table and asked, "What happened?"

Eamon gasped and turned away. He went over to the retaining wall and threw up in the grass before he plopped down on the wall. As he sat there, he put his face in his palms, started crying, and said, "That's what Dog looked like."

Dog went to Eamon, sat next to him, and leaned against his leg.

Rebecca's screams stopped, but tears continued to run down her cheeks. She stared straight ahead, and her eyes didn't move.

"I think she's in shock," Morgan said.

Clara shook her and asked, "What happened?"

Rebecca continued to stare straight ahead.

Clara carried Rebecca into the house and sat her on the couch. Dog returned to under the picnic table, but I followed them into the house and sat on the couch with Rebecca. Clara turned on the television, and after changing the channel several times, settled for a choir singing on a church show. She then went to the bathroom and got a wet washcloth and a towel, which she brought back to the couch and used to wash the blood off of Rebecca.

When Eamon got himself back together enough to come into the house, Clara asked, "Can you sit with her while I make breakfast for everyone?"

When Clara left the room, Eamon sat next to Rebecca. He put his arm across the back of the couch behind her and said, "I know how you feel. The same thing happened to my Dog once."

Rebecca leaned against him without taking her eyes off the television.

Rebecca wouldn't leave the couch to eat breakfast, lunch, or supper, and I wouldn't leave her side while she was in this state even though I was worried about Dog curled up under the picnic table. Rebecca just stared straight ahead all day.

After everyone went to bed that night to try to sleep, Clara made some chocolate pudding. She filled two bowls, carried them to the living room, and handed one to Rebecca as she said, "I thought we could have a snack together."

Rebecca took the bowl and set it on her lap, but she didn't eat any of it. She just kept staring at the television.

Clara sat next to Rebecca, took a bite of pudding, and said, "This is really good. You should eat something. Flopsy wouldn't want you to be hungry." Clara filled her spoon again, held it in front of Rebecca's mouth, and said, "Please take a bite." Clara pressed the spoon against Rebecca's mouth until she opened it enough for Clara to get the spoon in. After feeding Rebecca about three spoonfuls, she picked up her spoon and ate the bowl of pudding. About an hour after she ate the pudding, she fell asleep on the couch, Clara put a blanket over her and went to bed. Dog came in the house a few hours later and lay on the couch next to Rebecca.

Clara kept Rebecca home from school the next few days. Rebecca was eating a little, but she didn't talk again until Thursday. She stared at the television and her books, but I wasn't sure if she was seeing what she was looking at. Sometimes she stared at the same page for longer than an hour. The only thing that animated her was hearing the train whistle. She went to the window to see the train every time like she usually did, but she lumbered toward the window like a zombie.

Dog was also more reserved than usual, and he wouldn't leave Rebecca's side during those days. I was glad, because I didn't leave her side either. With Dog next to her, I could keep an eye on both of them. Considering what Eamon said after he threw up and collapsed on the retaining wall right after the accident, I wasn't surprised that he was also acting more reserved. I think this was reminding Eamon and Dog of the day Caelan killed Dog.

On Thursday morning, Rebecca came into the kitchen after everyone except Clara left the house and said, "I hurt Flopsy like Mrs. Stone hur —"

"What's that?" Clara asked.

"I'm worse than Mrs. Stone. I killed Flopsy."

Clara crinkled her brow before she knelt in front of Rebecca and asked, "Mrs. Stone killed something?"

Rebecca shook her head.

Clara pulled Rebecca into her arms and said, "Well, never mind that now. Thank God you're talkin'. I was startin' to think you were never goin' to speak again." After a long embrace, she looked into Rebecca's eyes and asked, "What happened?"

Tears streamed down Rebecca's cheeks again as she said, "I was tryin' to get her out, and the lid fell."

"Why were you gettin' her out of the hutch by yourself?"

"She was really scared. The noise from the neighbors had her so scared, she was shakin'. I wanted to bring her in the house and — but I killed her."

Clara hugged her again and said, "You didn't mean to. You were worried about her and tryin' to help her."

"The preacher said I was goin' to hell."

"What preacher?"

"The one on the television — after the people stopped singin'. He said anyone who kills will go to hell. I killed Flopsy."

Tears welled in Clara's eyes as she said, "He doesn't mean animals, and he doesn't mean accidents. God knows it was an accident. You were tryin' to help Flopsy and an accident happened. God doesn't send people to hell for that."

"Are you sure?"

"Yes, I'm sure."

That night when Eamon got home from work, the children had already eaten and been put to bed at what would normally be supper time in the hope they could get some sleep before the party next door started. Dog was curled up in bed with Rebecca, so I went to the kitchen when I heard Eamon come home.

Clara put two plates on the table and sat across from Eamon before she told him what happened.

Eamon looked at Clara and asked, "You don't think she's goin' to grow up to be like my Pa, do you? He crushed my Dog under a tree."

Clara laughed for a second and said, "Of course not. She was hurt so bad that she didn't talk for almost a week. It was an accident. I'm not at all worried she's goin' to be like your Pa. I'm worried that she's never goin' to get over what happened. She's still not herself."

Rebecca hadn't been in her first-floor room since the accident. The only time she left the couch was to go to the bathroom and to talk to Clara in the kitchen that morning. After Eamon and Clara were finished eating, Eamon went and sat on the couch next to Rebecca and Dog. I followed him and sat on the coffee table. I was watching the three refugees of violent animal deaths as they gathered in mutual understanding when I saw Flopsy appear for a moment. She materialized on the back of the couch and nuzzled Rebecca's face like Rebecca often did to her when her bunny body still had life in it. Flopsy only stayed for a few minutes before she went with the Angel.

As the Angel rose toward the ceiling, I remembered Rebecca's PawPaw Faolan saying at his funeral, "The gates of heaven are not locked." I jumped up and started to yell for the Angel to take me with her since I knew I could come back whenever I wanted. Before I did, I looked at the couch of pain in front of me and realized it wasn't time for me to go. I belonged here. After all, I was a victim of violent death as well. I sat on the couch next to Dog, hugged my knees, and resigned myself to stay here for a while longer. For all of us to be okay, this couch of pain needed to stick together.

CHAPTER SIXTEEN: THE LAST STRAWS

Rebecca returned to school on Monday. Clara met Rebecca, Dog, and me after school. As we walked home, she said, "When we get home, you need to be extra quiet. Your Uncle Morgan was hurt at work this morning and had to be taken to the hospital. Someone he works with brought him home. Something fell on his foot at the factory. He's in bed on pain medicine, and that medicine makes him tired. We need to let him sleep as much as he can today in case the neighbors keep him awake tonight."

Even though Morgan was on pain medication, the breakthrough pain was severe enough that he hobbled on crutches past the couch, where I sat with Rebecca, to get a beer out of the refrigerator several times that day. By that evening, the combination of beer and pain medication gave him a boldness that was out of character for him. Clara was at the sink washing the supper dishes when he walked past her toward the door without his crutches. I had a feeling trouble was brewing, so I followed him. When I realized what was about to happen, I tried to stop him, but my ghost body wasn't even able to slow him down.

Clara noticed him seconds after I failed to stop him. She dropped the dish and dishrag she was holding, ran to him, and asked, "What are you doin' walkin' without your crutches?"

"I'm not goin' to listen to that shit next door tonight. I'm goin' over there to beat the crap out of them and shut them up."

Clara jumped between him and the door, put her palms on his chest to stop him, and said, "You can't go over there. You're already hurt. You're not even supposed to be walkin' without your crutches, and you want to start a fight. They'll beat the stuffin' out of you."

"Get out of my way!" Morgan yelled as he tried to push her out of the way.

"No! I'm not movin'!"

Eamon came into the room and asked, "What's goin' on?"

Clara continued to hold Morgan back as she said, "He's tryin' to go next door and start a fight."

Eamon started pulling on Morgan from behind as he said, "You can't go over there. They'll beat the shit out of you."

"Get off of me!" Morgan screamed. "Get out of my way! You all just take too much shit off of people, and I'm stoppin' it now! This is just like when Eamon's family called all night cussin' Clara out, and you all just let them get away with it! Not this time! I'm goin' over there!"

Clara screamed in a hysterical voice, "You're not goin' out there! Please stop this!"

Rebecca entered the room and stood just inside the kitchen door hugging the book she'd been reading as she asked, "What's goin' on?"

Clara grabbed Morgan's upper arms, shook him hard, and yelled, "Don't do this in front of the children!"

Morgan stopped fighting Clara, looked at Rebecca, and returned to his room without saying anything.

When he walked past Rebecca, she looked at Clara and asked again, "What's goin' on?"

"It's okay now," Clara answered. "Go back to your book. Me and Daddy will take care of it."

"What's wrong with Uncle Morgan?"

"He's okay. Go read your book."

"But —"

Eamon turned and yelled, "Go read your book!"

Rebecca ran out of the room, and Dog followed her.

I stayed to hear Clara say, "Don't yell at her. She just started talkin' again."

"She's not the only one goin' through hell here!" Eamon yelled.

Clara sat at the kitchen table and said, "We've just got to get out of here."

"How? The house has been on the market for months, and we haven't even had one person look at it."

"Maybe we could sell it cheaper."

"You're not the one who goes out there and kills yourself workin' on crippled legs for every dime I bring into this house!"

"I don't know what we're goin' to do," Clara said as she shook her head.

Eamon sat across from her and said, "The realtor said we might have more luck sellin' it if we fix it up a little bit. I don't know what we can afford to do though."

"Do you think we could afford some paint? The realtor said if we'd put a fresh coat of white paint on the walls that might help. She said havin' color on the walls makes a house take longer to sell even if the colors are light like on our walls. I could do that durin' the day while the children are at school."

"You can't paint this whole house by yourself and do everythin' else you do when you're not gettin' enough sleep," Eamon said.

Before Clara could answer, the phone rang. She answered it and a few seconds later said, "Emmett. It's good to hear from you. How's married life." For several minutes, she listened, occasionally breaking her silence by saying, "Uh-huh!" After a long pause, she said, "I'm sorry to hear that. I'll have to talk to Eamon and call you back. Let me ask you first, would he be willin' to earn his keep? We need some help paintin', because we're tryin' to sell the house."

Eamon looked and Clara and asked, "What's that about?"

"Hold on a second," Clara said before she put her hand over the receiver. "It's Emmet. His son, Everett, is havin' a hard time gettin' along with Emmett's new wife when Everett's there for visitation. Emmett wanted to know if Everett could stay here on visitation weekends until they get this sorted out. He's afraid if he doesn't pick him up at all that his ex-wife will drag him back into court, plus he can come here and see Everett if we have him."

"Does Emmett know about the noisy neighbors?"

"I'll tell him," Clara answered.

"If he's okay with the noisy neighbors and Everett can help us paint, send him on over," Eamon said.

Clara returned to the phone and discussed the details with Emmett. It was soon agreed that Everett would start coming to Eamon and Clara's house the following weekend.

Clara removed the beer from the refrigerator and hid it under the picnic table in the back yard. When the reward of beer stopped being an incentive to leave his room, Morgan stayed in bed and did as the doctor had instructed. Clara made this easy for him to do, because she delivered his meals to his room three times a day. With that problem solved, the rest of the week continued as usual without any unexpected problems. I emphasize the word unexpected. The routine problems seemed to never go away.

Everett arrived on Saturday morning. It was amazing how much he looked like Emmett. The only difference in their appearances was Everett was tall, broad-shouldered, and heavier-set than Emmett. Other than that, they looked alike.

Dog and I watched Clara feed everyone breakfast before Eamon and Everett went to the paint store. When they returned, Everett helped Eamon carry the paint up the steps. They set it in the middle of the widest part of the concrete-covered back yard behind the kitchen.

While Eamon and Clara went into the house to plan how they were going to paint, Dog and I stayed in the back yard and watched Everett get the children playing in a way they hadn't played in a long time. Rebecca was on the tricycle, and Mitchell was pushing her all around the flat part of the yard. Not only were the two children having the rare experience of getting along, it was also the first time Rebecca smiled, much less laughed like she was doing then, since Flopsy's death. When Eamon and Clara came out of the house, Mitchell and Rebecca were going in circles around the paint cans. A few minutes later, they accidentally knocked one over and the lid came off.

Eamon ran at them as he screamed, "What the hell are you doin'? We couldn't afford that paint to begin with, and now you've gone and spilled one of them! I'm tired of this shit!" He stopped and looked at the spilled paint for a minute before he screamed, "Go and get a switch off that tree! I'm goin' to beat both of your asses!"

Rebecca immediately showed signs of labored breathing, and her skin glistened with sweat. She was so distraught that I listened to her thoughts, and I was not surprised to learn she was remembering what Mrs. Stone repeatedly did to her. I was surprised to learn that Rebecca was feeling grateful that Mrs. Stone did it in the privacy of the bathroom. Rebecca had lost sight of how wrong the unfair punishments were and was instead focused on how wrong she felt her reaction to them was. Mrs. Stone had shamed Rebecca so much for the natural reactions of begging, crying, and screaming that Rebecca felt that was the part that was wrong. The thought of Everett seeing her that vulnerable frightened her more than the punishment. The thought of Mitchell making fun of her for those reactions frightened her more than the punishment. Rebecca paced the yard while Clara tried to calm Eamon.

When Eamon continued to scream at the children, Clara lost her temper and yelled, "They're only children, and they made a mistake! My Mommy always told me not to beat children for every little mistake they make unless you want to make them so mean no one can control them, and she was right —"

"I got beat for every little mistake I made, and I'm not mean —"

Clara interrupted him to say, "Not all the time, but do you think you'd be yellin' like this if your folks had treated you better? Do you want your children to grow up afraid all the time like you were?"

Eamon sat at the picnic table, dropped his face in palms, and said, "I promised God I'd never hit my children if he'd get me out of that mess, and he got me out of it."

"The mess they made is easy to fix," Clara said. She tore a piece of cardboard off of a box some of the paint cans were in and scooped the spilled paint back in the can with it.

As Clara finished the job of returning the paint to the bucket, Everett walked over to Rebecca and said, "See, there was nothin' to get so upset about. Everything's fine."

I was still in Rebecca's head, so I heard her think before she walked away, "You haven't been through what I've been through."

After the spilled paint was returned to the bucket, Everett and Clara carried the painting supplies into the house through the back door. As they did, I heard Clara say, "We'll start in the front rooms, so Morgan will have time to get better before we disturb him working on the back rooms."

While Clara and Everett painted, Eamon got the beer from Clara's hiding place. Morgan heard the bottles clinking together when Eamon carried them to the refrigerator. While Clara and Everett faced the living room walls painting, Morgan went to the refrigerator unnoticed and got a few beers. When the Saturday evening party started next door, Clara had to drop the paint roller into the pan and run to Morgan to stop him from starting a fight with the neighbors again. Morgan allowed her to lead him back to his room so easily that everyone should have known he had a card up his sleeve.

The party continued until almost four o'clock in the morning. We didn't realize at the time that Morgan was awake, waiting for the party to end. When it did, Morgan gave the people next door enough time to fall asleep before he got up, snuck out the back door, took the metal lids off two garbage cans, went to the fence, and started banging them together. As he banged them together, he danced around in a way his injured foot couldn't have tolerated if he would have been sober and screamed, "Wake up! Wake up, everybody! It's a party! Wake up!"

Within minutes, people from both houses were coming outside saying, "What's goin' on?" and other phrases that had more expletives in them. Morgan ignored everyone and kept dancing, banging, and screaming. The neighbors came to the fence and screamed at Morgan to shut up, and Morgan mimicked each thing they said back to them. Everyone from our house, including Dog and me, stood in the middle of the concrete part of the yard and laughed.

When the neighbors got tired of being mimicked, they went in the house and called the police. When the police arrived, they did the same thing they always did. They politely asked Morgan to keep it down and left without doing anything. When the police car was out of hearing range, Morgan started his dance again.

Rebecca and Mitchell laughed, along with Dog and me, again on Monday. Morgan was doing the same thing when they left for school. Clara was obviously trying not to laugh while she chastised him for dancing on his bad foot while she led him back to his room.

Unfortunately, Dog and I saw Rebecca's laughter end when she learned Miss Ally's internship was over. Due to a bad review given by Mrs. Stone, Miss Ally returned to her studies earlier than anticipated.

As soon as Miss Ally was gone, Mrs. Stone started treating Rebecca badly again. The first day without Miss Ally, Rebecca was dragged to the bathroom again. This time, Mrs. Stone knelt in front of Rebecca after the beating and said, "You made Miss Ally think I was doing something wrong, and I don't appreciate that. I'm not doing anything

191

wrong to correct you. That's my job as a teacher. That's any adult's job. I'm making you strong. You'll be ready for the world when you grow up because of me. Now, stop crying!"

When Rebecca couldn't stop crying, Mrs. Stone grabbed Rebecca's crotch. Rebecca struggled to get away, but Mrs. Stone increased her grip until discomfort forced Rebecca to stop fighting. When Rebecca stopped fighting, Mrs. Stone said, "Look at me!" When Rebecca didn't look up, Mrs. Stone said it again in a stern voice. When Rebecca obeyed, Mrs. Stone said, "I've heard about the people from where you come from — incestuous fathers touching their daughters like this and worse. I know what your people are. I know what you are. If they can find any man they can pawn a crippled girl off on, you'll be pushing babies out of this by the time you're fifteen years old, and then my tax dollars will be supporting you and your brats like I'm supporting your family now. Teaching you is a waste of my time, because you'll never use what you learn if you're even capable of learning. If I make you strong, maybe you can be different. If I make you strong, maybe my children's taxes won't be supporting your babies like my tax dollars support your worthless family now."

When Mrs. Stone released Rebecca, Rebecca backed away with a look in her eyes that was similar to the look Dog used to have when Caelan cornered him.

Mrs. Stone revealing how she felt about Rebecca set the stage for the rest of the school year. Any offense in the class that Rebecca was even near was blamed on her. When the other students figured out that pattern, the bullies taunted Rebecca to make it look like she was involved in offenses.

By the end of the first week without Miss Ally, Rebecca wasn't talking again. She ate very little, stared at the television screen without responding to anything she saw, and only stared in the direction to the train whistle instead of going to window like she usually did. She showed no interest in books, writing, or drawing. She was so out of sorts that even Mitchell, who usually picked on her, brought his bunny to her and let her hold it.

The only thing that made Rebecca smile was Morgan banging garbage can lids every morning. Since Clara didn't intervene when he didn't risk his foot by dancing on it, he vowed to do it every morning until he was well enough to return to work. When he made this vow to the family, he laughed and said, "When I go back to work, there's always the weekends."

A couple of weekends after Miss Ally left, Emmett brought his new wife, Sally, when he came to visit Everett. Emmett thought it might ease some of the tension between Sally and Everett if more family was there, so he invited Lana and her children, too. When everyone arrived, the children went to the living room, and the adults got extra chairs from other places in the house and squeezed all of the adults around the small kitchen table. No one seemed to notice that Rebecca hid in Clara and Eamon's bedroom, so Dog and I spent the evening sitting on the bed with her. She had a book on her lap, but she spent most of the time staring at the wall.

A couple of hours after everyone arrived, she went to the bathroom in the annex to get a drink of water. Mitchell was leaning on the door frame waiting for her when she came out of the bathroom.

When she tried to walk past him, he stopped her and said, "Please tell me you didn't just drink water out of the bathroom faucet." She tried to push by him, but he grabbed her arm and asked, "Did you just drink out of the bathroom faucet?"

Rebecca nodded.

"Oh, no! Don't you know you're not supposed to drink out of the bathroom faucet?"

Rebecca shook her head.

"The plumbin' in the bathroom isn't for drinkin' water. It's only for bathin' and cleanin'. You're only supposed to drink out of the kitchen faucet. If you drink out of the bathroom faucet, you'll die." Rebecca jerked her arm free and ran toward the door, but he grabbed it again and asked, "Are you goin' to tell Mom?"

She nodded as she fought to get her arm away from him.

"There's no point in tellin' Mom. She can't do anythin' to help you, and you know how upset she gets. You don't want to get her upset like that, do you? Be a good girl and let Mom enjoy this evenin', because tomorrow she's goin' to be really sad when she finds you dead in your bed. Just go lay down and let it happen without botherin' anyone. You'll be with Flopsy soon, and it's a lot quieter in heaven than it is here — no more all-night parties. You'll be okay."

Tears poured out of Rebecca's eyes as she went to the first floor and lay on her cot. Dog and I followed her. At one point, she looked at me through her tears and said, "I'm goin' to miss my Mom, but Mrs. Stone won't be able to hurt me anymore." I gasped. I thought she had grown up enough that she was losing the ability to see me, but I thought she saw me in that moment — unless she was just talking out loud to herself. I rubbed her back until she cried herself to sleep.

When Rebecca woke up the next morning, she sat up and felt her arms and legs. When she realized she was still alive, she got up and went to the living room. Mitchell was sitting on the couch watching television. When he saw her, he pointed at her and laughed.

She ignored him and went to the kitchen. She sat at the table by herself and listened to Morgan's garbage can lid serenade. She continued to ignore Mitchell when he offered to let her hold his bunny. She ignored him no matter what he offered. He must have gotten bored, because he stopped picking on her for a while. I wished she could hear me, so I could remind her of that lesson the next time someone picked on her.

A few days later, I was sitting on the couch with Rebecca while Eamon and Clara were sitting at the kitchen table. I heard Clara ask Eamon, "Do you think she's stopped talkin' again because of that bunny? Do you think I should take her to the doctor?"

"I don't know," Eamon answered.

Rebecca must have heard them too, because she walked to the television and turned the volume up. I couldn't hear what Eamon and Clara said after that, but whatever it was, it may have been the reason Eamon came home from work the next day carrying a dog.

While Eamon carried a black dachshund into the house, he said to Clara, who was standing at the oven cooking, "I told Mrs. Reynolds about Flopsy and how Rebecca isn't talkin' lately, so she gave us this dog. It wandered into work a couple of weeks ago, and I've been feedin' it some of my lunch every day. Mrs. Reynolds took it to the vet and bought its license this mornin', so I could bring it home for Rebecca."

Clara smiled and said, "Take it in and give it to her. I'll do anything to get her to talk."

When Eamon entered the living room, Rebecca looked up from the television and smiled. Dog was laying on the couch next to Rebecca, and he jumped up and started wagging his tail so hard it was making his whole-body wag. While I petted Dog, I realized I was smiling, too.

Eamon sat the dog on Rebecca's lap and said, "She's for you. What do you want to name her?"

Rebecca petted the dog a few times before she answered, "Princess."

Royalty was brought into the house that day. With Princess' influence, Rebecca often recovered from Mrs. Stone enough over the weekend that she was talking to the family by Sunday. That was no surprise, because Princess made everyone smile at times when they felt they didn't have anything to smile about.

Every day, about five minutes before Clara left to pick Rebecca up, Princess ran to the door and barked as she ran in a circle. She wouldn't let Clara leave without her. Letting Rebecca hold the leash while they walked home seemed to help Rebecca no matter how bad her morning was. Princess did the same thing five minutes before Mitchell's school bus arrived at the end of the school day. Clara had to walk Princess down to the street where the bus dropped Mitchell off and let Mitchell hold the leash while Princess walked back up the steps. Princess usually spent the rest of the evening following Rebecca wherever she went.

On a Saturday about three weeks after Princess arrived, Eamon came into the living room and told Mitchell and Rebecca about teaching a dog to do tricks. He knelt in front of the television so the children couldn't see what they were watching and enticed Princess away from the couch with a treat. He tried to teach her to sit, but she wasn't understanding.

After about a dozen failed attempts, Eamon looked at Rebecca and screamed, "Quit makin' that noise. It's you makin' that noise that's keepin' her from learnin'."

"I'm not makin' a noise," Rebecca defended.

Eamon tried one more time to get Princess to sit and failed. He looked at Rebecca again and yelled, "Quit makin' that noise!"

Rebecca looked at the television screen and saw that the noise was being made by a swarm of cartoon bees who were chasing another cartoon character and making quite a racket doing so. Rebecca pointed to the television and said, "Look, Daddy, it's on television. It's not me."

Eamon yelled, "Shut up and stop makin' that noise, so I can teach Princess a trick."

Rebecca started crying and said, "It's the television. Look at the television, and you'll see it's not me."

Eamon stood up and yelled, "Rebecca, it's all your fault she didn't learn, because you wouldn't stop makin' that noise."

Eamon threw the dog treats on the floor and stormed out of the room. Rebecca sat on the floor and petted Princess while Princess ate the treats. When Mitchell got up and left the room, Rebecca whispered to Princess, "I'm sorry he got so mad when you didn't do the trick. Everything's my fault, because I'm crippled. Mrs. Stone said so."

When the children went to bed that night, Dog went to bed with Rebecca and Princess. I followed Eamon to the kitchen as he joined Clara at the table. While they sat there drinking coffee, the phone rang. Clara got up and answered it. After several one word starts to sentences she wasn't able to complete, she hung up the phone, looked at Eamon with an expression of shock on her face, and said, "I reckon your brother David and his family are comin' over tomorrow. He said he had such a good time when they visited a few weeks ago that he wants to make sure he doesn't lose touch. He didn't even give me a chance to get a word in edgewise."

Eamon looked at her for a long time before he asked, "Was he drinkin'?"

"I'm not sure. Maybe." She sat at the table again and said, "I guess I need to get some food together —"

"No! We didn't invite them, and remember how Bobby's wife raided our refrigerator before they left the last time — and all they did was talk about each other the whole time they were here. If they're goin' to come around here actin' like Regan, we're goin' to treat them like Regan. When they come around here actin' like they've got some sense, then we'll start cookin' for them again."

"I guess we'd better get to bed and try to get some sleep," Clara said as she picked up the coffee cups and set them in the sink. I think it's goin' to be a long day tomorrow."

Eamon and Clara both seemed upset about David coming to visit, so I stayed with them that night. After many hours of listening to the party next door, they both finally fell asleep — until a knock on the door echoed through the house very early the next morning.

Dog and I watched Eamon and Clara got dressed quickly as they tried to race to the knocks that were turning into urgent hammering.

196

When Eamon got to the door and opened it, he said, "I had no idea you were comin' this early."

Dog and I hid under the table.

"We thought we'd join you for breakfast," David said as he entered the kitchen with his wife and three boys following him.

They looked like a row of ducks following their Mama as they entered the house. David was the tallest and biggest. His wife was about two inches shorter than him, and the three boys were all about two inches shorter than the person in front of them all the way down the line. All of the males were husky and broad-shouldered, and David's wife was big without being fat — she looked like she was trying to keep up as a form of self-protection. They all sat at the kitchen table without being invited. When they were one chair short, it was the woman who stood.

Clara looked at Eamon. He rolled his eyes and nodded before she said, "We don't even have the children up yet. They haven't eaten. Let me get them up and dressed, and then I'll make a big pan of scrambled eggs and some toast."

"No meat?" David asked as Clara walked toward the kitchen door.

Clara turned to him and said, "We didn't know you were comin' until last night, and you got here so early this morning we didn't have time to get to the store. The only thing I have are eggs and toast or cereal."

David looked at the cereal boxes sitting on top of the refrigerator. He got up and walked toward them as he said, "Don't worry your little head. You go on and get them children ready, and we'll start with the cereal."

His wife opened several cabinets before she asked, "Where are your bowls?"

Clara looked at Eamon. He rolled his eyes and nodded again.

When Clara left the room, he said, "They're in the cabinet right next to the one you're in now."

When Clara came back a few minutes later with the dressed children and Dog, the cereal boxes were laying on their sides on the table.

"What about those eggs?" David asked.

Clara picked up one of the cereal boxes and shook it as she said, "It looks like all the cereal is gone. I'm goin' to go ahead and make those eggs, but my children haven't had anything yet. I'm goin' to have to feed them with the first eggs that are done." She looked at Eamon and asked, "Can you pour the children a glass of milk?"

Eamon nodded toward the empty carton on the table and said, "It's all gone."

Clara rolled her eyes, went to the refrigerator, and got out two cartons of eggs. As she scrambled them, she kept toast moving through the toaster. She had to fight to feed her children first. By the time she had them settled on the couch with a plate and a glass of water, David's family had eaten everything before Eamon and Clara got any breakfast.

When the children were finished, Clara said, "It's a nice spring day. Why don't y'all go out in the yard and get some fresh air while I clean up this mess."

David started to stand, but when he was halfway up he sat back down, looked at Clara, and said in an angry tone, "Are you accusin' us of makin' a mess?"

Clara cleared the table as she answered, "Eatin' a meal always makes a mess that needs to be cleaned up. Dishes don't wash themselves."

David nodded and got up, and his family followed him outside. Eamon and Clara shared a look of frustration before Eamon, Rebecca, Mitchell, and Dog followed them.

I stayed with Clara while she washed the dishes. When the dishes were clean and put away, she made a ham and tomato sandwich with mayonnaise with the last two slices of bread and sat it on the table for Eamon. She used the bread heels that were still in the bag to make a sandwich for herself. When she finished eating hers, I followed her as she joined the family. When she got to the back yard, Eamon was sitting on the retaining wall with David's wife. David and the children were throwing a ball back and forth.

Clara sat next to Eamon, lay her hand on his forearm, and whispered, "There's a sandwich on the table for you."

Before Eamon made it to the kitchen door, Morgan opened the back door, looked out in the yard, and said, "Oh, there's lots of people here today. I can sleep in." He screamed at the top of his lungs, "Make lots of noise, kids!" He closed the door and went back to bed.

Eamon was still laughing when he entered the kitchen.

While Eamon was gone, Clara tried to keep a conversation going with David's wife while they watched most of the children play ball. Rebecca sat on the picnic table and quietly watched. Shortly after Eamon returned and sat on the wall next to Clara, the ball hit David in the head.

David screamed like a woman in the last stages of labor, put his palm on his head, and yelled, "Who the hell threw that ball?"

David's wife went to him, looked under his hand, and said, "It ain't bleedin' or nothing. I think you're okay."

David pushed her away and screamed, "Who threw that ball?"

Rebecca ran to Clara, Mitchell pressed himself against the wall of house, Dog hunkered down under the picnic table, and I sat next to Eamon and hoped he could feel my ghost hand holding his hand and gain some comfort from it.

The neighbor opened his door and screamed, "Shut up! People are trying to sleep over here!"

David ran to the fence and screamed, "You shut up, you dumb SOB! It's the middle of a Sunday morning! Wake your ass up and get it to church!"

The neighbor stormed to the fence and yelled, "Don't you yell at me, and don't you tell me what to do. I'm tired of you people making so much noise during the day when we're trying to sleep."

Eamon stood up, which yanked his hand out of mine, and yelled, "Who the hell do you think you are to say that when you kept us awake most of the night last night?"

The neighbor shook his fist over the fence and screamed, "Then take your ass back in the house and get some sleep now."

When David turned toward Eamon's yelling, he saw his three boys huddled together, shaking, in the middle of the flat part of the yard. He ran toward them as he screamed, "Which one of you hit me with that ball?"

Eamon and the neighbor both stopped yelling and stared at David, and the three boys looked down and started shaking noticeably harder.

David grabbed the oldest boy's chin as he yelled, "Look at me when I'm talkin' to you! Who hit me with that ball?"

"I don't know."

David grabbed the oldest boy's arm and threw him in the direction of the steps as he yelled, "All of you get your asses to the car!" As the oldest boy walked toward the stairs, David pushed the two younger boys in that direction. His wife obediently followed without being told to.

When they got to the street, David started yelling again.

"I wonder what he's goin' to do to those poor boys," Eamon said as he walked to the other side of the house with me following close behind. We stood at the top of the hill and watched as David ripped a medium-sized limb off a tree. His wife was already in the passenger seat, and the boys were lined up just behind the driver's side in the same way they had been lined up in the kitchen.

"Well, come on, get in the car!" David screamed as he waved the limb around. As the boys filed to the back door of the car, David hit each of them multiple times with the limb.

When Rebecca heard the screams of the first boy, she ran and stood next to Eamon. She watched as the second boy got hit while he got in the car and while the slightly rotted limb exploded as it broke on the third boy's back.

Rebecca grabbed Eamon's leg. Eamon looked down at her, and their eyes met. I didn't have to read their thoughts to know what they saw in each other's eyes — they saw their own eyes looking back at them. They understood each other. Eamon had been hit many times by unfair parents, and Rebecca had been hit many times by an unfair teacher.

Eamon picked Rebecca up and carried her to the house even though holding her additional weight made him limp more. I followed them. As we walked past Clara and Mitchell, Eamon said, "Let's go inside and try to forget this mornin' ever happened." Clara took Mitchell's hand and led him toward the kitchen door. When the family got to the kitchen door, Dog came out from under the picnic table and ran after us.

As we walked past the fence, the man next door said, "Wow! Just Wow!" He shook his head and said, "Thanks for going in and being quiet, so we can sleep." He walked away from the fence, but he turned back and said, "I'll try to get my people to keep the noise down tonight."

Eamon nodded, and we all went into the house. Once we were inside, Eamon sat Rebecca on the couch, and Clara led Mitchell to sit next to her. As Eamon and Clara left the room, Clara turned on the television. When Rebecca saw it was a television preacher, she got up and changed the channels until she found a cartoon before she returned to the couch. Both children stared at the television without blinking for a long time.

Eamon and Clara went to the kitchen. Eamon sat at the table while Clara made a pot of coffee. When the coffee was ready, she poured a cup for both of them and joined Eamon at the table.

Eamon took several sips of coffee before he said, "Livin' in this house is drivin' us all crazy. We need to move. I'm goin' to call the realtor tomorrow and tell her to sell this house for whatever she can get for it."

"Whatever you think is best," Clara said as she stood up. "Those pain pills must really be workin' for Morgan — or he's so exhausted his body finally gave up and let him sleep no matter how noisy it's been this mornin'. He hasn't even had breakfast yet. I'm goin' to go see if he wants a ham sandwich for breakfast." She stopped at the kitchen door, turned, and said, "We don't even have any bread left. They ate us out of house and home." She looked at the top of the refrigerator and said, "There isn't even part of a box of cereal left."

"There isn't any milk left even if there was cereal," Eamon said.

"What am I goin' to feed Morgan?"

"I think I saw a can of corned beef hash in the cabinet. Why don't you give that to him, and we'll go to the store this afternoon?" He paused for a minute and asked, "Do we have enough money to go to the grocery store?"

"We've got enough to get a few things. I'm goin' to go see if Morgan wants to get up and eat now."

Eamon nodded as she left the room.

I don't know if it was Eamon's body language or that I'd never seen him give up the fight before, but I felt like I should listen to his thoughts and learn why he was willing to sell the house for whatever they could get out of it. When I entered his thoughts, he was thinking about his behavior of the past few weeks. He yelled at his children when they spilled paint and would have broken his promise to God and beaten them if Clara hadn't stopped him, he yelled at Rebecca the night Morgan tried to beat up the neighbors, and he yelled at her about a noise the television was making when he tried to train Princess. He hadn't listened when Rebecca told him the noise was on the television, because as a child, he was always afraid of what his father would do to him if he failed — that fear stayed with him and caused him to lash out at his child when he failed to teach their dog a trick.

I understood his thoughts, but he couldn't understand them or his options enough to bring them to the surface and resolve them — or even to know he could apologize to Rebecca. Unresolved fear still caused him to act from his animal brain, and his brain stem was telling him to run by putting this house on the market for whatever he could get out of it. If he would have been able to go deeper into his thoughts and resolve old conflicts, he would have found more peace in his life, but he wasn't capable of doing that yet. If he would have been able to apologize to Rebecca, he would have learned that most people, especially children, are so forgiving that he no longer needed to be afraid to make a mistake. How could he know these things? Not only was he never taught these things, but he grew up among an entire culture that didn't know these things — a culture that lacked the simple skill of apologizing, because apologies were seen as a sign of weakness. All he knew was something had to change even if he didn't fully understand how or why, so he resigned himself to listen to his brain stem and run.

Clara called the realtor the next morning. The realtor hung a reduced-price shingle on the existing sale sign that afternoon. Two weeks later, the house sold — just in time for the school year to end and Morgan's foot to be healed enough that he could help them move. Not only did they almost break even on the sale, but the whole family was able to laugh all the way to the bank. When Eamon and Clara met to sign the closing papers, they learned that the people who lived next door bought the house, because they found it impossible to sleep during the day with such noisy neighbors living next door to them. Since it appeared no one who lived next door ever went to work, Eamon assumed the money for the sale came from illegal activity, but that wasn't his problem any more. He just wanted to get his family and himself away from them.

CHAPTER SEVENTEEN: FAIRYLAND

Eamon and Clara rented the first house they looked at even though it was too small for their family, much less Princess, Morgan, and Everett's frequent visits. They took it because the property was surrounded by trees, which reminded them of the mountains, and the landlady was willing to give them a month to month lease, which would allow them to move immediately when they found a house they could afford. Even though the house was too small for their family, it wasn't a problem, because the children were often in the yard.

I couldn't believe the family still wanted to buy a house after living here, because this place was perfect. Dog and I once sat with Rebecca while she read a book about a fairyland to Princess, and that book described this place. From the moment Dog and I followed the family down the narrow stairs that cut through the bushes that separated the property from the street above, I felt like we were descending into a magical place. At the bottom of the stairs, you couldn't tell you were in the inner city anymore. This place was so well-hidden that dangerous people were not likely to find it. There were beautiful flowers covering the small hill on the yard side of the bushes, and there was greenery surrounding the entire lot. To the far right of the lot sat a small cottage that was tucked into the forest's edge. In the middle of the lot sat a matching cottage. The property felt like a refuge of peace after all we'd been through at the old house. This would be the perfect place to spend the summer after a very difficult year.

An old woman sat on a rocker on the porch of the cottage that was tucked into the forest's edge. When she saw us, she got up, wrapped her shawl around her shoulders, picked up her cane, and walked toward us. She was short, portly, and her still-dark hair was in a bun. She looked harsh, but the twinkle in her eyes told me that, in her case, looks were deceiving.

When she reached Eamon and Clara, she said, "You didn't tell me there were children." Mitchell and Rebecca both stood obediently in front of their parents. She looked them up and down and said, "The house is really too small for children. They look like a well-behaved lot though. I guess since you'll only be here month to month it can work. Follow me, and I'll show you the house."

We all followed the old woman into the house. When we entered, I realized she was right about the size. The front door led into a small square kitchen, and all of the rooms were connected through a circle of doors that took them through four perfectly square rooms that created a perfectly square house. The layout was similar to our old house minus the annex, but it was much smaller.

I think Rebecca would have been happy to sleep in the yard to accommodate the space concerns inside the house. From the moment the family moved in, she wandered around the yard experiencing a seemingly mystical connection to nature. It seemed like the land was so magical it made her forget she was handicapped. Her limp and leg deformity didn't slow her down at all, but I guess they never really had. She investigated every form of plant life she found and sat at the edge of the foliage and talked to animals that looked out at her from the safety of their hiding places. Sometimes her soothing voice coaxed them out to receive a snack or petting. There was an abundance of snails, so she collected them in a shoe box that she carried with her every place she went.

Dog and I tried to stay with the family member who needed us the most. After the family moved here, we stayed home all of the time. It was the first time either of us ever felt at peace, so for the first time in either of our existences, we stayed here to take care of ourselves. We weren't being lazy. We watched out for Rebecca. She seemed to need it since Mitchell constantly antagonized her. Princess watched out for Rebecca, too, so we were a happy foursome. We found our own souls being nurtured and healed by this magical land.

One day when Rebecca was collecting snails, she wandered close to the landlady's house. The only time we saw the landlady was when she sat on the rocking chair on her porch. On that day, the landlady, leaning on her cane, walked over to Rebecca. Princess and Dog watched the landlady closely, and they growled when she got close.

Rebecca was on her knees at the edge of the yard like she had been the day she was caught feeding Lucky Charms® to the child next door at their old house. What she said when she saw the landlady revealed that similarity hadn't been lost on her either. The front of her body was in the foliage picking up a snail. When she emerged from the greenery, she saw the shadow over her and looked up. Seeing the landlady made Rebecca jump and fall backwards, which knocked the box of snails over. When she fell, Princess and Dog started barking at the landlady. Even though Rebecca hadn't spoken to anyone outside the family since Mrs. Stone had abused her, her fright caused her to say, "I wasn't givin' away our food. I promise."

"Why would I care if you were feeding someone? Feeding people is a nice thing to do." Rebecca started to sit up, but the landlady said, "Be careful. You don't want to crush any of the friends you spilled. Let me help you." She used her cane to lower herself to her knees. When she was on her knees, she gingerly picked up each of the snails and returned them to the box. While she worked, she said, "My name's Matilda. What's your name?"

Rebecca didn't answer, but Princess sniffed Matilda. Princess must have liked what she smelled, because after the snails were in the box, she allowed Matilda to pet her while Matilda looked around for any missed snails.

After a moment of looking, Matilda said, "I think it's safe to get up now."

Rebecca sat up and dusted herself off. She smiled at Matilda, but she didn't say anything.

Matilda put the lid on the box and handed it to Rebecca as she asked, "Why do you put them in the shoebox?"

Rebecca didn't answer. She just looked down at the shoebox that she sat on her lap.

"Not much of a talker, huh?," Matilda asked as she petted Princess again. "That's okay. I go for long periods of time without talking to anyone myself. I think I understand. I used to put snails in shoe boxes too."

Rebecca's face lit up, and she looked at Matilda.

"I put them in shoe boxes when I was a little girl, because I thought they were beautiful," Matilda said. "I liked to look at them. I also liked figuring out how to take care of them. It made me happy when they were happy."

Rebecca watched her own hand rub over the top of the box as she stammered, "I just love them."

"I'm glad to see you poked holes in the top of the box. Did someone tell you they needed to breathe?"

Rebecca nodded as she said, "My Mom."

"Are you feeding them?"

"I pick leaves from all around the yard and put them in the box, but I don't know if they're eatin' them."

"Do you see any holes in the leaves where they are chewing on them?"

"On some of them."

"Recognize what leaves have holes in them, and then only put those kinds of leaves in the box. You might try some lettuce or other vegetables from your house. If you see chew holes in them, keep putting that kind in." Matilda picked a dandelion, pulled the leaves off, and handed them to Rebecca as she said, "I've noticed them eating the leaves of these yellow flowers, so I think it would be good if you put some of those in your box every day."

Rebecca smiled, took the leaves, and put them in the box before she asked, "Will they still eat the leaves after the flowers become wishes?"

"What do you mean?"

Rebecca touched the yellow leaves of the flower with her index finger as she said, "These yellow leaves turn into a white puff ball. You make a wish and blow on the puffball, and your wish flies away."

Matilda smiled and said, "I don't know. I think they will still eat the leaves of the wishes, too. Just watch to make sure there are holes in the leaves where they are eating. If there are no holes, you need to find something else for them to eat."

Rebecca nodded as the old woman asked, "Do you give them water?"

"I sprinkle water on the leaves. I'm afraid they'll drown if I put a bowl of water in there. My Mom got me a baby chick for Easter once. He drowned in his water bowl."

"I think they'll like having water sprinkled on the leaves. Do you do it every day?"

"Yes, Ma'am."

"It sounds like you're a good friend to the snails. Will you keep them forever?"

"I don't know."

"I think one way to be a good friend is to let them go when you're ready to. They used to live in the wild, so they'll probably be happy to go back to it one day."

Rebecca hugged the box and said, "But they love me."

"They will always love you even when they aren't with you."

"Like my PawPaw loves me from heaven?"

The old woman smiled and said, "Yes, just like that. Love never dies."

Clara called for Rebecca and Mitchell. When Rebecca didn't answer, Clara walked to the corner of the house where she could see Rebecca and yelled, "Rebecca, it's time for lunch."

"I have to go," Rebecca said as she stood up.

Matilda stopped petting Princess and used her cane to lift herself to her feet. When she was halfway up, Rebecca asked, "Do you need me to help you?"

Matilda shook her head before she got the rest of the way up. When she was standing, she said, "Enjoy your lunch, keeper of the snails. I will talk to you another day."

Rebecca smiled and nodded before she went to Clara with Princess, Dog, and me following close behind.

As Clara and Rebecca walked side-by-side to the front door of our house, Clara asked, "What was that old woman sayin' to you?"

"Her name's Matilda. She told me how to feed the snails."

"Did she now?"

"She said they like the leaves on those yellow flowers."

"You really should let them go," Clara said as they entered the house. "They're nasty little creatures, and I'm sure they don't like livin' in a box."

Rebecca sat at the kitchen table with the box of snails on her lap.

Clara sat a sandwich and a bowl of soup in front of Rebecca before Clara said, "Be careful of that old woman. We don't know her, and she ain't family."

Dog lay under Rebecca's chair, Princess lay at her feet, and I sat on a step ladder chair that usually sat just inside the front door.

"She seemed nice," Rebecca answered.

"They all seem nice — until they aren't," Clara said. "I made your favorite, split pea soup. Do you want some crackers for it?"

Rebecca nodded as she took a bite of her fried bologna and cheese sandwich. Clara sat a bowl of crackers in the middle of the table and went to the door and yelled for Mitchell again. Rebecca was crumbling crackers into her soup when Mitchell came in a few minutes later and sat at the other side of the table. Clara sat a sandwich and a bowl of soup in front of him before she sat her own food on the table and joined them.

As they ate, Mitchell said, "I saw you talkin' to that old woman."

Rebecca nodded as she took another bite of her sandwich.

"You really should stay away from her," Mitchell said.

"Why?" Rebecca asked before she pulled her soup bowl closer to herself and took a bite of soup. "She was really nice."

"She's a witch. She's only bein' nice, so she can get you to her house and throw you in the oven like she did Hansel and Gretel."

Rebecca stopped eating and looked at Clara. Clara nodded and said, "Like I said, they're all nice until they're not. You really should be careful of strangers."

"But, she's not a stranger."

"We've lived here for a month," Clara explained. "We really don't know her."

"What was she talkin' to you about?" Mitchell asked.

"She told me how to feed my snails."

"She should have told you how to get rid of them," Mitchell said. "They're gross, and I'm sick of lookin' at them."

Rebecca lay her hands on the box and said, "They're mine."

Mitchell looked under the table and said, "You're so gross! They're in your lap right now, aren't they? You're even eatin' with those bugs. That's gross! You're gross! Get rid of them!"

Rebecca looked at Clara and said, "Mom!"

"He's right. You shouldn't have snails at the table."

Mitchell said in a spooky voice, "I saw a huge one without a shell on it the other day crawlin' around outside in the yard. I bet it's their mom or their queen or something. I bet she's lookin' for you. She's probably mad that you took all of her babies. Maybe that old witch that lives next door cast a spell to make one of them really big, because she's mad that you're puttin' the snails from her yard in your box."

"That's not true!" Rebecca argued. "She told me how to take care of them."

"So you won't hurt them, because they're her babies."

Tears welled in Rebecca's eyes as she looked at Clara again and said, "Mom!"

"Maybe you should let them go," Clara said. "They would be happier in the yard where you found them, and maybe that big snail Mitchell saw was their mom lookin' for them."

Rebecca was crying so hard when she took the next bite of her sandwich that she had a hard time swallowing, so she fed the rest of her sandwich to Princess by tearing off one bite at a time and reaching it under the table when no one was looking.

After lunch, Rebecca, Princess, Dog, and I stayed in front of the house. Rebecca peeked around the corner several times and quickly retreated to the front of the house when she saw the Matilda rocking on her porch.

Rebecca was sitting at the picnic table in front of the house playing with the snails in their box when Eamon got home. Princess came out from under the table to greet Eamon, but she stopped when she got halfway to him. This made Rebecca look at him.

His hand was wrapped in gauze, and he was carrying a brown paper sack in his other hand. He was limping worse than usual and looked pale and sweaty.

"Daddy, what's wrong?" Rebecca asked.

"I hurt my hand at work today?" he answered as he entered the house.

"We should have gone with him today instead of staying with Rebecca," I said to Dog as Rebecca, Dog, and I followed him.

Clara was standing at the stove cooking. When she turned and saw him, she turned off the burners, went to him, and asked, "What happened?"

Eamon sat at the kitchen table, and Clara sat next to him. Rebecca, Princess, Dog, and I stood inside the front door as Eamon said, "I don't know how it happened. I was tryin' to make a new leg for an antique table I was fixin' for Mrs. Reynolds, and a huge splinter of wood just broke off and went all the way through my hand. Mrs. Reynolds told the gardener to take me to the emergency room, and I was there for the rest of the day."

Clara wiped a lock of hair from his forehead and said, "You're clammy, pale, and shaky. This must have really taken its toll on you."

"I guess it did," Eamon said. "I'm goin' to go out front and sit at the picnic table. I just feel so nervous and shaky."

"Do you want something to drink or eat? Do you think that will help?"

"I think a beer might help. Will you bring one out for me?"

Clara nodded and went to the refrigerator while Eamon carried the paper sack outside to the picnic table and sat down. He sat the sack on the table and started unwrapping his bandage with shaking hands. Our group of four followed him. Rebecca, Dog, and I sat across from him, and Princess lay at his feet. Clara joined us a few minutes later, set an opened beer in front of him, and sat down next to him.

Eamon stopped unwrapping the bandage long enough to take a drink and said, "The doctor told me to change the bandages every few hours. There are clean bandages in that bag."

Clara took over unwrapping the bandage as she said, "Your hands are shakin' too bad to do that yourself. Let me do it."

When the bandage was removed, Rebecca and Clara both gasped when they saw how big the hole in Eamon's hand was. Eamon looked away while Clara put the ointment that was in the bag on the wound and re-wrapped his hand.

While Clara worked on Eamon's hand, he pulled a pack of cigarettes and matches out of his shirt pocket with his good hand and said, "I just can't seem to quit shakin'. Maybe a cigarette will help calm me down." He pulled a cigarette out of the pack, put it in his mouth, opened the matches, pulled off a match with one hand, and tried to strike it while holding the pack between his palm and little finger. When he couldn't do it, he asked Rebecca to light the match for him. Once his cigarette was lit, he took a long drag off of it before he drank almost the whole can of beer in one drink. A few minutes later, he said, "I think I'm startin' to feel a little calmer now."

Clara cut the tape she wrapped around his bandages and said, "The bandage is changed. Is that comfortable? It's not too tight, is it?"

Eamon shook his head as he said, "No, it's just fine." He took another drink that emptied the can and crushed it with his good hand as he asked, "Can I have another beer?"

Clara nodded as Rebecca said, "I'll get it." Rebecca limped quickly into the house and returned a few minutes later with a can of beer.

When Eamon finished the second beer, he looked around the yard and said, "I think I'm feelin' better now. It sure is pretty out here. I'm just goin' to sit out here and enjoy this yard for a while."

"Since you're doin' all right, I'm goin' to go inside and finish cookin' supper," Clara said.

Eamon looked around and said, "It's goin' to be a shame to move away from this place."

"Let's stay here forever then," Rebecca said.

"We can't," Eamon said as he turned to Rebecca. "It's too small for us, and it doesn't belong to us. Neither set of your Grandparents ever rented. A man should own his own land, put down roots, and get to know the land so well it speaks to him. We'll own our own land again one day soon."

"This land speaks to me and Princess," Rebecca said.

"Me too, but we don't own it and it ain't for sale." He touched the top of the box and asked, "What do you have in there?"

"Snails."

"Can I see them?"

Rebecca opened the box.

Eamon looked inside and said, "They're kind of slimy. Don't you think they're a little gross?"

Rebecca giggled and said, "They're not gross at all, Daddy. They're really pretty. Look how pretty their shells are, and the trail they leave when they crawl sparkles. One of my books said fairies ride them. They live with fairies."

"Have you ever seen a fairy in that box?"

"Not yet, but I will."

"I hope you do," Eamon answered as he gently touched the shell of one of the snails. "Just don't go believin' everything you read in books. You might end up gettin' yourself disappointed."

"Matilda told me how to take care of them."

"Who's Matilda?"

"That lady who lives in the house next door."

Eamon looked at her and asked, "What were you doin' at that old witch's house?"

"Why do you and Mitchell say she's a witch?"

"She's odd. She sits on that porch by herself all day and rarely talks to anyone. She dresses funny. She always wears long black skirts and has that black shawl wrapped around her shoulders — and that black hat with flowers on it she wears any time she goes out. Animals that should be wild come and sit on the porch with her. I bet she rides that broom that's always leanin' against the porch railing.

"She was really nice to me today."

"People are always nice — until they're not."

"I reckon," Rebecca said as she put the lid back on her snail box.

A few minutes later, Clara came to the door and said, "Dinner's ready."

Eamon turned to her and said, "I'm not hungry just yet. I think some of this medicine is makin' my stomach odd. Y'all go ahead and eat, and I'll eat later."

"Come on, Rebecca," Clara said before she went back in the house.

Rebecca picked up her snail box and followed Clara. Princess continued to lay at Eamon's feet. Dog and I were so worried about him that we stayed with him too. He sat at the picnic table and smoked cigarettes while everyone else ate. After Clara put the children to bed, she returned to the picnic table.

When she sat down, Eamon said, "It's the darndest thing. I started to feel better after I drank those beers. I've been sittin' out here relaxin', nothing to make me nervous at all, and I'm startin' to shake and feel clammy again.

"It's been a long day for you," Clara said as she stood up. "I'm goin' to make you a plate, so you can eat and go to bed. You probably need some rest."

Clara returned a few minutes later with a plate of salmon patties, fried corn, sliced tomatoes, and a piece of cornbread. A few minutes after Eamon finished eating, Clara said, "You look a lot better now."

Eamon looked at his hands and said, "Yeah, I'm not shakin' anymore. I do feel a right smart better."

"Why don't we go to bed? I'm sure you'll feel a lot better in the mornin'."

Princess, Dog, and I followed them into the house. Princess and Dog went to Rebecca's bed, and I started to follow Clara and Eamon to their bed — until I saw Rebecca, Princess, and Dog tip-toeing across the kitchen and out the door. I followed them.

Rebecca snuck to the edge of the house and peeked around the corner. She held Princess while she sat on the grass and watched Matilda rock on her rocking chair. About half an hour passed before a raccoon came out of the woods and went to Matilda. She reached into a bowl that sat on a table next to her rocking chair, took something out of the bowl, and threw it to the raccoon. The raccoon sat on its haunches and ate the treat before it climbed onto Matilda's lap and got another treat.

Rebecca gasped and whispered, "She really is a witch!"

Rebecca limped to the picnic table with Princess close at her heels, took a cigarette out of the pack Eamon left lying there, and stared at it for a full minute before she said, "Maybe they'll make me feel less nervous, too."

Rebecca picked up the matches and went to the end of the yard farthest from Matilda's house. The first time she tried to light a match, Princess pushed the matchbook with her nose and kept Rebecca from lighting it. Rebecca turned away from Princess and succeeded at lighting the next one. She lit the cigarette, took a drag, and started coughing. After three drags and three coughing fits, she stared at the burning cigarette until it was almost burned away before she said, "Princess, why would I get in trouble for bein' bad if Mommy and Daddy caught me smokin', but Daddy smokes. Is he bad? Is that why he yells sometimes? That preacher on TV said we need to save people from bein' bad. I need to save Daddy from bein' bad."

Dog and I knew Eamon didn't need to be saved from being bad. We were here to save him from bad people hurting him again. I wished she knew that, so she wouldn't feel like it was her job to save him. Bad habits were just bad habits. Everyone had at least one. Uncle Teagan told me true evil often looked beautiful. He said the bible described the devil as beautiful and that made sense, because people would run from him instead of to him if he was really ugly. I knew Uncle Teagan was right. Evil was charming. That was the one thing that devil of a preacher back home on the mountain taught me.

She threw the cigarette and match into the grass and went in the house. Fortunately, the grass was green and damp with dew, and the cigarette soon fizzled out without any harm being done.

Princess, Dog, and Rebecca slept in Rebecca's bed, and I went to be with Eamon. I was still concerned about his injured hand.

CHAPTER EIGHTEEN: HOUSE NUMBER TWO

Dog and I were very happy during the magical summer living in the fairy land with Eamon's family. Every weekday we were surrounded by nature. After the family got settled in, we were surrounded by the beauty of the mountains every weekend when we, accompanied by Everett who was still staying with us on the weekends, visited Darina. The exception was the one weekend per month when Rebecca had a doctor's appointment. On doctor's appointment weekends, we visited Mr. and Mrs. Williams even though Everett usually chose to stay home and watch television.

At least one weekend a month, all of the children were at Darina's house at the same time. The grandchildren played together, the men fished together, and the women worked together to garden, cook, and give Darina's house a good cleaning. On the weekends when fewer family members were there, gardening, cooking, and cleaning were the only activities from that list that continued. The men sat on the porch and talked while Rebecca curled up in her Grandfather's rocking chair with Princess and quietly listened. On Saturday night, Darina treated everyone to takeout from the only restaurant in town, The Dairy Bar, which would be eaten on the porch.

On the weekends the family visited Mr. and Mrs. Williams, Mr. Williams usually held Princess while he listened to everyone else's conversation with the radio playing softly in the background. He was getting too weak to do much more, and we were all worried about him. Mrs. Williams was getting older too, but she was still energetic. She always made supper and served hot chocolate after supper to celebrate a weekend of being together. Although the game was often Go Fish now that there were children, they usually still played cards after supper – at least until Mr. Williams got so tired he had to go to bed.

It seemed like some magic was being yanked away from us when the school year started. The night before the first day of school, Rebecca stopped talking again. She remained mute the next morning as she got ready for school, ate breakfast, and even when something terrified her on the way out of the yard.

Rebecca was holding Princess' leash and leading the way as Clara, Mitchell, Dog, and I followed her toward the steps. When Rebecca was about to step onto the bottom step that led us out of fairy land, a giant leopard slug slithered across it. She stopped and froze. Everyone was behind her, so we couldn't see what made her stop. When Clara gently nudged Rebecca, her breathing became heavy and her skin gleamed with sweat. It seemed as if my ghost ears could even hear her heart beating faster.

Mitchell nudged her harder than Clara had and said, "Get out of the way!"

Rebecca stumbled toward the slug. She would have fallen on it, but she grabbed a tree branch as she screamed. When she stumbled, we saw the back end of the slug moving into the bushes.

Mitchell laughed and said, "See, I told you I saw the Mom lookin' for her babies. She's mad that you put them in a box, and she's goin' to get you."

Clara gasped and said, "Maybe you should let them go."

Rebecca was crying as she dropped Princess' leash, ran to the picnic table as fast as her club foot would let her run, picked up her box of snails, ran to where the giant snail had slithered to, and dumped the whole box into the foliage. She continued to cry during the long walk up the isolated hill they lived on to the more populated street at the top of the hill that was a straight shot to her new school.

When they arrived at school, Clara took Mitchell to his classroom before she took Rebecca to hers. Unlike Mitchell's classroom, Rebecca's new teacher was waiting at the door to greet her students as they entered the room. Rebecca didn't even look at the new teacher much less answer her when the teacher said, "Welcome to my class. My name is Mrs. Abel. What's your name?"

If Rebecca would have looked at Mrs. Abel, she would have seen that her new teacher was a beautiful woman with ivory skin, light green eyes, and black hair that was cut to her shoulders, flipped up at the ends, and stacked in a near-beehive behind bangs. A dark-blue hairband that matched Mrs. Abel's dress separated her bangs from the lifted part of her hair. She was about 5'4" tall, which seemed short standing next to Clara, and had a small waist that complemented an hour glass figure. Most importantly, Rebecca would have seen that those light green eyes sparkled, which proved that the big smile she gave each new student and their parents was genuine.

Mrs. Abel knelt and petted Princess while Clara said, "I'm sorry she didn't answer you. Her name is Rebecca."

Rebecca went into the room, sat at the seat that had a folded name tent with her name on it, and stared straight ahead. Dog and I followed her. Dog lay under her chair, and I stood behind her. When Mrs. Abel stopped petting Princess, Princess started pulling at the leash like she wanted to stay with Rebecca too.

The classroom had squares that were made by four desks being pushed together around the periphery of the room rather than rows of desks. After everyone assigned to Rebecca's square was seated, Rebecca ignored them. When the student sitting across from her smiled, Rebecca looked down.

Mrs. Abel watched Rebecca for a minute before she looked at Clara and said, "It's okay. The first day of school is always hard, especially when a student is attending a new school. The principal told me Rebecca is new to this school."

"Yes, she is," Clara answered. "We just moved into this neighborhood over the summer."

"I'm sure she'll be fine. Just give her a few days."

"I'm sure you're right," Clara answered as she stuck her head in the door. She called Rebecca's name several times before Rebecca looked at her. When Rebecca looked, Clara waved. Rebecca waved tentatively before she returned to staring at the top of the desk again.

A few days didn't bring any change in Rebecca's behavior. Dog and I stayed with her in the hope that she would feel us enough to find some comfort from our presence — after all, it hadn't been that long since she was young enough to be able to see us. Rebecca didn't respond to Mrs. Abel when she stood in the middle of the classroom teaching in a manner designed to get the class to interact. When recess was called, Rebecca stayed in her seat. Mrs. Abel had to bring

Rebecca's lunch bag to Rebecca's desk to get her to eat, and sometimes she still didn't eat or ate very little. She didn't even respond to Clara bringing Princess when Clara came to walk the children home from school.

Mrs. Abel became so concerned that she asked another teacher to watch her class during recess, so she could sit with Rebecca and talk to her. This developed into Mrs. Abel eating lunch with Rebecca. Every time Mrs. Abel sat with Rebecca, she talked about many things that might be entertaining to a child and asked questions throughout the conversation to try to get Rebecca to talk. She asked if Rebecca's Mommy and Daddy were nice to her so many times that after several days Rebecca finally nodded.

That night, Mrs. Abel called Clara. Dog and I stayed close enough to the phone to allow us to hear both sides of the conversation.

"Hello," Clara said when she picked up the phone.

"Mrs. Teague?"

"Yes, who is this?"

"This is Rebecca's teacher, Mrs. Abel."

"Is something wrong?"

"Well, maybe. Rebecca won't talk in my class. She sits and stares at the wall almost like she's in shock or something. I'm not sure what to do. I've finally gotten her to the point where she'll nod or shake her head to answer yes and no questions. She nodded to let me know that you and your husband are good to her, so please don't think I'm accusing you of anything. I just wonder if she's had anyone be mean to her or had any traumatic experiences."

Clara paused for a minute before she said, "Well, last year she accidentally killed her pet bunny. She dropped the cage door on its head and killed it. She didn't talk for quite a while after that happened."

Mrs. Abel's voice registered shock as she asked, "She hasn't talked since then?"

"No, no. She started talkin' after about a week, but she had periods of time for the rest of the year when she didn't talk much. We thought it might still be about the bunny."

"Does she talk at home?"

"Well, yes, she does. She had spells last school year where she didn't talk much, but even then she talked some. She talked like

218

normal over the summer." Clara paused for a minute and then said, "You know, she stopped talkin' the night before she was supposed to return to school. She slowly starts talkin' on the walk home from school, but she stops talkin' every mornin'."

"Did something happen at her old school last year?"

Clara paused for a minute before she said, "Not that I'm aware of. We moved away from our old neighborhood, because we had noisy neighbors who were drunk and high all the time. Maybe one of them did something to her, but I watched her awful close when we lived there. I don't think she ever was around them."

"Maybe it was just the trauma of being exposed to all that chaos, especially if she's a sensitive child."

"She is a sensitive child. I sometimes think she feels everything everyone else is feelin', and I didn't think she'd ever get over that bunny dyin'."

It was Mrs. Abel's turn to pause before she asked, "Whatever happened, she obviously needs some help."

"I took her to the doctor, and he said physically everything seems to be fine. He recommended we take her to a counselor, but we can't afford that. You see, she's also handicapped. She was born with a clubfoot. That's why she still wears those white, high top, lace-up shoes even though she'd dearly love to have shoes like the other girls wear. My husband is handicapped himself and almost workin' himself to death to make ends meet, so we have to do what we can do one step at a time. We have to get her legs fixed first, and then we'll consider counselin'."

"Oh, my. I didn't realize things were so hard for your family. Technically, I'm supposed to call in the school counselor, but if she recommends you get outside counseling and you can't, there's a chance you could be reported to Child Protective Services. I saw it happen to another family once. I don't want to put you through that when you're already dealing with a handicapped husband and a handicapped child. Let's see if we can pull her out of her shell first, but if it doesn't work, we'll eventually have to take her to the school counselor."

Clara nodded and said, "Thank you. I'd hate to have Child Protective Services called on us. We really are doin' the best we can do."

Mrs. Abel paused for a full minute before she asked, "Do you think maybe children made fun of her at her old school for being crippled and wearing orthopedic shoes? Do you think that could be part of the problem?"

"Do they make fun of her at your school?"

Mrs. Abel paused again before she said, "Mrs. Teague, children will be children. I've heard some of them making fun of her, but not because she's crippled. I don't think they know she's crippled, because she never leaves her seat for them to see her shoes or her limp. They make fun of her for being so quiet. They say mean things like she's too stupid or too stuck-up to talk. I talk to them about it every time I catch them, but I'm sure I don't catch them every time. I'm sure that isn't helping her any."

"Oh —"

"Do you work outside the home, Mrs. Teague?"

"No."

"I would like to recommend something. Can you come here each day at lunch and work with her with me? I sit with her at recess and lunch and talk to her and ask her questions. Just today, she got to the point where she'll nod or shake her head to answer me. I've noticed you two make sure you wave at each other every morning, so I'm assuming you're close. Maybe she would talk faster if you were involved. Could you come and sit with us at lunch every day? I think it would be best if you packed a lunch for yourself and ate with us, so it just looks like we're all having lunch together. That might help her feel more at ease. Oh, and if you agree, can you please leave your dog at home when you come at lunch time? The dog might be a distraction."

Clara backed up her yes answer by arriving at lunch time the next day with a packed lunch and no Princess, although there was a dog there since Dog and I sat with Rebecca during all of those lunches. Everyone sat at Rebecca's square of desks and ate together. Clara and Mrs. Abel shared stories and asked Rebecca what she thought about them. Rebecca would answer yes and no questions with a nod or a shake of her head. After a few days, Rebecca laughed at a funny story Mrs. Abel told about how her dog reacted to a bath. Rebecca laughed several more times over the next few school days.

At the end of the second week, Mrs. Abel gave Clara, Rebecca, and herself a chocolate chip cookie from a tin she brought to share that day.

220

Rebecca looked at Mrs. Abel for the first time as she took the cookie. Rebecca continued to look at Mrs. Abel's as she asked in a low whisper, "Are you goin' to hurt me?"

"I'm sorry, sweetheart. I couldn't hear what you said," Mrs. Abel answered.

Rebecca looked at the table and asked, "Are you goin' to be mean to me?"

Clara lay her hand on Rebecca's back, leaned close to Rebecca, and asked, "Did you ask if she was goin' to be mean to you?"

Rebecca nodded.

Mrs. Abel started rubbing Rebecca's back as she asked, "Why would I be mean to you?"

Rebecca continued looking at the table as she said, "Because I'm bad."

"You're not bad," Clara said.

"Why do you think you're bad?" Mrs. Abel asked.

"Because I'm crippled," Rebecca stammered.

"That doesn't make you bad," Clara said. "Mrs. Williams said it makes you special."

Rebecca looked at Clara and stammered, "That's what PawPaw said, too." Tears welled in her eyes when she mentioned her PawPaw.

"Then why do you think you're bad for bein' crippled?" Clara asked.

"Mrs. Stone said I was."

"Who is Mrs. Stone?" Mrs. Abel asked.

When Rebecca didn't answer, Clara said, "Mrs. Stone was her teacher last year."

"Why would she say that?" Mrs. Abel asked.

"She said I was weak and she was goin' to make me strong."

"You are not weak!" Clara said.

"Then why did Mrs. Stone do —," Rebecca started to say.

Clara and Mrs. Abel both paused for a long time before Mrs. Abel asked, "Then why did Mrs. Stone do what?"

"I can't tell you," Rebecca said as tears streamed down her cheeks. "She said it would be twice as bad next time if —"

Rebecca couldn't stop crying. She was still crying when the other children returned to the classroom.

Mrs. Abel looked at Clara and said, "Take her to the nurse's office. It's in a room in the administrative office area, right next to the principal's office. I'll join you in a minute after I get my classroom settled and get another teacher to look in on them."

Clara led Rebecca out of the classroom and to the administrative offices with Dog and me close at their heels. After we went through the door to the administrative office, we had to walk past the principal's office to get to the nurse's office. As we walked past the principal's office, Rebecca froze. Clara couldn't get her to move. Since I knew what Mrs. Stone had done to Rebecca, I knew Rebecca was staring at the paddle laying on the Principal's desk. She started breathing rapidly before she passed out.

"Someone help her!" Clara screamed.

The nurse ran out of her office, looked down at Rebecca, and asked, "What happened to her?"

"I don't know," Clara answered. "Mrs. Abel told me to bring her down here, because she couldn't quit crying, and now she passed out."

The nurse picked Rebecca up and carried her into the nurse's office. She lay Rebecca on a couch, grabbed a bottle off the shelf next to the couch, and placed it under Rebecca's nose. A few seconds later, Rebecca gasped and coughed her way back to consciousness.

Mrs. Abel entered the room just as Rebecca was waking up. She ran to Rebecca's side and asked, "What happened?"

"I don't know," Clara answered as the nurse helped Rebecca sit up. "She just passed out."

After Mrs. Abel explained the conversation they had in the classroom to the nurse, the nurse sat on a stool in front of Rebecca and asked, "Was your teacher at your old school mean to you?" Rebecca didn't answer, so the nurse continued, "You go to a different school now. That teacher can never get near you again. You're safe. Was your teacher at your old school mean to you?"

Rebecca nodded.

The nurse rubbed Rebecca's handicapped leg like her PawPaw used to rub it and said, "Your teacher was wrong to be mean to you. Can you tell me what she did to you? I promise she'll never know you told. I just want to help you feel better."

Rebecca looked at the nurse's hand as it ran up and down her handicapped leg and said, "You're touchin' my leg."

The nurse removed her hand and said, "I'm sorry. I didn't mean to make you feel uncomfortable. I wanted to comfort you so badly that I started doing it without thinking. I won't do it again."

"Did it make you sick?" Rebecca asked.

"Why would it make me sick?"

"Mrs. Stone said my crippled leg made her sick, but my PawPaw rubbed it like that and it didn't make him sick."

"Is Mrs. Stone your old teacher?" the nurse asked.

Rebecca nodded and said, "She said I was weak, because I'm crippled. She hit me to make me strong."

Clara gasped and asked, "Is that why you wouldn't let me help you get dressed anymore? Did you have bruises?"

Rebecca started crying again and curled up on the couch in the fetal position.

The nurse looked at Mrs. Abel and asked, "Can you stay with Rebecca for a few minutes while I step outside and talk to her mother?"

Mrs. Abel nodded and sat on the stool when the nurse stood up.

The nurse placed her palm on Clara's back and led her to the hallway. When they got to the hallway, the nurse asked, "When did Rebecca stop letting you change her clothes?"

"I don't remember exactly, but it was durin' the last school year. She came upstairs one mornin' carryin' the clothes she wanted to wear that day and locked herself in the bathroom to change herself. At first I thought it was odd, especially since she wouldn't answer when I knocked on the door. I assumed I was just bein' worrisome when she came out dressed as nicely as if I had helped her and seemed to be okay. I didn't think any more about it — until just now when she said Mrs. Stone hit her. When she said that, I remembered how odd I thought the sudden change was before she proved to me she could dress herself, and I wondered — I don't know, I just wondered. Maybe I should have —." From there, Clara's tears spoke more than words could convey.

The nurse sent Rebecca home for the day. As Clara, Rebecca, Dog, and I walked home, we saw a For Sale sign on a house a couple of blocks before the corner of the street where we were renting. The bottom of the 'For Sale' sign had a sticker on it that said 'Reduced

Price.' Clara stopped and looked at it for several minutes before they continued walking home.

Rebecca was so out of sorts for the rest of the day that Clara had to carry her when she went to get Mitchell at the end of the school day. I wished I could help Clara carry Rebecca, but my ghost body wouldn't allow that. All Dog and I could do was walk with them.

When Eamon got home from work that night, the children had already eaten. Mitchell was in the living room watching television, Rebecca was sitting at the picnic table hugging Princess and staring straight ahead like a zombie, and Clara was standing at the sink washing dishes. When Eamon walked in, Clara dropped her dishrag and made Eamon a plate.

After she sat his plate on the kitchen table in front of him, she sat across from him and said, "I think I found a house for us to buy."

"Really?" Eamon asked

"We walk past it on the way to and from school every day. I think this is the perfect house, because Rebecca would still go to the same school. Rebecca finally talked today after all these weeks of me and Mrs. Abel talkin' to her, and she said Mrs. Stone at her old school was mean to her. Her new school will be lookin' into it. It's just that Mrs. Abel is so nice, and the nurse seemed to be very nice, too, and the neighborhood is very quiet when I'm walkin' her to school."

"Our old neighborhood was quiet in the mornin', because everyone who was up all night was sleepin' then."

"I would just hate to take her out of this school since Mrs. Abel is bein' so nice to her. If we buy that house, she'll be able to stay in this school. Plus, the sign said reduced price, so maybe this can help us get back on our feet."

Eamon took a couple of more bites before he said, "Get the phone number off the sign when you walk the children to school tomorrow. You can call the realtor and set up an appointment for this weekend. We'll skip a weekend goin' home to take a look at it. I'm assumin' your brothers will be goin' to help your Ma like they usually do."

Clara got the phone number the next morning. She was standing by the phone getting ready to call the realtor when it rang. When Clara answered, the school counselor was on the other line.

"I was wondering how Rebecca's doing," the counselor said.

"She seemed a little worn out yesterday afternoon, but she was fine by bed time. She was doin' so good this mornin' that I went ahead and took her to school. She actually seemed to want to go to school this mornin'. She took a moon pie to give to Mrs. Abel."

The counselor laughed before she said, "Mrs. Abel told me about the moon pie. That was cute. Mrs. Abel also said she seems to be doing better in class today — said she's talking and participating a little bit.

"That's good."

"I think Rebecca had what we call a flashback yesterday, and that's why she was crying and passed out. I recommend you take her for counseling."

Clara swallowed hard, started to shake a little, and had tears welling in her eyes when she said, "I already talked to Mrs. Abel about that. You see, Rebecca's handicapped. It takes everything we have to come up with the money to pay for her doctor visits and operations, because her father's handicapped, too. I don't think we can afford counselin' until the medical treatments for her clubfoot are over. We'll be happy to use the money we're usin' for her current medical bills to take her to counselin' once her clubfoot is better."

"But you are providing the medical treatment for her clubfoot?"

"Yes, we are."

"And she is seeing a doctor regularly?"

"Yes."

"What is her doctor's name?"

"Dr. Stark."

"You don't have medical insurance?"

"No, we don't."

The counselor paused before she said, "You seemed like a very concerned mother when you were in the school office yesterday, and you're obviously meeting her physical needs. I really do believe you're doing the best you can. I'll keep an eye on her here at school. If I see any of her problems returning instead of improving, I'll call you again, and we can figure it out from there."

Clara sighed and said, "Thank you. I appreciate that."

When Clara hung up the phone, her hands were still shaking. She took several deep breaths before she looked at Princess and said, "I thought she was goin' to call that child welfare place on us." She took several more deep breaths and got a drink of water before she stopped shaking enough to call the realtor.

The realtor was in the office when Clara called, and they set up an appointment for Saturday morning. The realtor was already waiting at the house when the family, accompanied by Dog and me, arrived. We did a quick tour of the house, and at the end of the tour, Eamon said it was up to his wife. Since Clara wanted the house, they sealed the deal with a handshake. In that moment, it seemed they would finally be starting the life they had worked so hard to achieve since they left the mountains.

During the drive home, Rebecca said, "I don't want to move."

Clara looked at Rebecca in the back seat and said, "We always knew we'd be movin' when we found a house. Don't worry. You'll still be goin' to the same school. Mrs. Abel will still be your teacher. Not that much will change."

When they got home, Rebecca sat at the picnic table and picked at splinters sticking out of the wood. When Clara opened the front door for the rest of the family to enter the house, Princess came out and lay at Rebecca's feet. Dog lay under the table with Princess, and I sat with Rebecca. At least an hour had passed when Matilda came to visit, carrying the discarded snail box.

"Hello, Keeper of the Snails," Matilda said as she approached Rebecca from behind.

Rebecca jumped and turned to look at Matilda, and Princess came out from under the table to be petted. Matilda petted Princess for several minutes before she walked the rest of the way to the table.

"May I join you?" Rebecca just kept staring at her, so Matilda said, "I'll take that as a yes." Matilda sat across from Rebecca before she set the box on the table and said, "I found your box by the steps. I know you love your snails, so I wanted to make sure you're okay."

Rebecca stared at her.

"I see you've been crying, little one. Are you okay?"

Rebecca nodded.

"Cat got your tongue?"

Rebecca touched her tongue before she shook her head. I remembered Eamon doing the same thing the first time he met Mr. Williams and thought, 'Like father, like daughter."

Matilda laughed and said, "I can see you're having a sad day. Is it because of the snails?"

Rebecca shook her head.

"Whatever it is, I'm sorry you're sad. I can see you don't want to talk right now, so I'll leave you to your thoughts. You know where I live if you ever need someone to talk to." Matilda gave Princess one more vigorous pet before she used her cane to help her stand. As she walked past Rebecca, she said, "I saw one of your snails crawling on a blade of grass. He was glowing with the love you put in him, so I know they'll be okay. Now, you know it, too."

Rebecca looked up at her and smiled, and Matilda walked away.

Rebecca smiled as she stared for several minutes at the last splinter she pulled out of the table top. When she dropped that splinter onto the pile in front of her, she got up and ran as fast as her club foot would let her toward Matilda's house with Princess, Dog, and I following her. When she got to the other side of our house, a noise that was probably an animal in the woods made her look toward the back of the house. There was a rolling swarm of caterpillars climbing the wall. They were the same kind of caterpillars that had been in her dream at the old house. The look on her face let me know she remembered that dream, too.

Rebecca looked toward Matilda's house, and Matilda waved. Rebecca instinctively raised her hand but didn't move it to wave back, because she was looking at the caterpillars again. After a full minute of standing there with her hand in the air, Rebecca ran into our house and to her bed as fast as her crippled leg could run. Princess, Dog, and I ran after her. When she got to her bed, she pulled a small, brown suitcase out from under it and started packing her few belongings.

Princess, Dog, and I sat on the bed and watched Rebecca. As Rebecca packed, she said, "Princess, Matilda is a witch. A raccoon sat on her lap, she made a snail get really big, and she made the caterpillars in my dream real. I thought she was nice, but she's a witch."

Clara came up behind Rebecca and asked, "What are you doing?"

Rebecca didn't answer. She just kept putting her things in the suitcase.

Clara sat on the bed next to the suitcase and asked, "What are you doing?"

Rebecca kept packing without answering.

Clara grasped Rebecca's hands, but Rebecca yanked them away and started packing again as she said, "You threw caterpillars at me."

"When?"

"You and Mitchell."

Clara laughed and said, "I never threw caterpillars at you. You must have had a bad dream. Are you already gettin' ready to move?"

Rebecca nodded.

"You're goin' to need clothes for this week. We aren't movin' until next weekend."

Rebecca closed the lid of her suitcase, lay on the bed, and hugged Princess. Rebecca wouldn't answer anything Clara said to her, so Clara put the suitcase under the bed, covered Rebecca with a blanket, and left the room. Rebecca fell asleep hugging Princess.

CHAPTER NINETEEN:
THE OTHER MEANING OF NUMBER TWO

The new house was a long three by three, which meant it had three rooms in a row on the first floor and three rooms in a row on the second floor. It was built like a child might create a toy house by placing three square boxes in a row and then placing three square boxes on top of those. There was a stairway between the front and middle rooms, so the only rooms that had a door were the front ones. The back room on each floor could only be accessed by walking through the middle room. From front to back of the house, the first floor held the bathroom, living room, and kitchen. The second floor held three bedrooms. All of the matching houses on the street were close together, so they only had windows on the left and back walls, apparently for privacy. There were two unique features in these six square rooms. One was that the bathroom was a stone utility room that was under ground, because the house was built into a hill in the front. It had a small pink-tiled room sectioned off for a private bathroom area. The second one was that the living room had an entrance to a large walk-in closet that extended under the stairs.

The second floor appeared to be the first floor since the front of the house was built into a hill. The thin porch on the front and left side of the house was surrounded by a black railing that looked like it wasn't sturdy enough since the porch on the side of the house was on the second floor. The fragile railing was a concern since the second story entrance was at the far end, which was the highest end, of the porch. To the left of the porch was a set of stone stairs that led down to the side yard and the first story entrance. The first story entrance was directly below the second story entrance. There was a storage area under the porch between the house and those stairs. Other than a stone wall where the first floor was coming out of the hill, the house was covered in medium-gray stucco siding.

The kitchen had a back door that opened to a yard that was the width of the narrow house, the narrow porch on the left side of the house, and the stairs next to the porch. The porch and stairs were the width of the side yard, and the back yard extended to the street behind it. About halfway down the back yard was a retaining wall with steps to the right of it that led to the next level of the long yard. There was a tall chain-link fence separating the yard on the left, but there was no fence separating the yard on the right.

Everett spent the first weekend in the new house with them, but the stress of moving revealed a conflict they had been ignoring while they lived in the peace of the fairyland. Everett ate a lot and especially drank a lot of milk. A gallon of milk a day wasn't unusual, and the family couldn't afford that. While Clara tried to figure out the grocery budget they could afford with the house payment, she complained to Rebecca. Out of the mouths of babes – Rebecca recommended that Clara ask Emmett for some money. Even though Clara learned a long time ago not to be that direct, Rebecca's advice seemed so logical that Clara followed it. Instead of understanding the request for what it was, Emmett took it as a complaint about Everett coming. He started keeping Everett at home on the weekend. The new house looked like it was going to be a place only for those who lived there all the time.

Since there wasn't a fence separating their yard from the house on the right, Mitchell and Rebecca were soon playing with the six children who lived there. Those children ranged in age from Rebecca's age to a sixteen-year-old. The children all seemed to enjoy the increased play area two yards created, and they all seemed to enjoy having Princess playing with them since the neighbor children didn't have a dog. I enjoyed watching them, especially since Dog was running and playing with them. The fact that they couldn't see his ghost body didn't deter his enthusiasm.

The innocent playing convinced Clara it was safe to let her children go into the neighbor's house. She didn't realize letting her children go in their house was going to pile a second conflict on top of the one she just had with Emmett. A few weeks after they moved in, Rebecca found herself sitting around the neighbor's coffee table while the sixteen-year-old daughter, Tessa, and her friends passed a joint and drank beer. Dog and I were trying to supervise, so Dog growled at Tessa when she gave Rebecca a can of beer. Rebecca took one drink and spewed it onto her clothes and the round coffee table they sat around. Everyone laughed at her, so she left in embarrassment and went home with Dog and me at her heels.

When Rebecca got home, she found Clara in the utility area of the bathroom hanging clothes. Clara smelled beer on Rebecca, so she smelled Rebecca's breath and asked, "Did you get in your Daddy's beer?"

Rebecca shook her head.

"Then why do you smell like beer — and what is that other smell?"

"Cigarettes."

"Your Daddy smokes cigarettes, and they don't smell like that." After a long pause, she asked, "Did you smoke cigarettes?"

"Tessa tried to get me to. I didn't like how the smoke in the room was makin' my throat feel, so I didn't do it."

"Tessa next door? Did she give you the beer?"

Rebecca nodded.

"You and Mitchell are not goin' to play over there anymore. Do you understand?"

"But, I like the other kids —"

"I don't care. You're not goin' over there anymore. Understand?"

Rebecca nodded.

Later that day, some of the younger children from Tessa's family knocked on the door and asked Rebecca to come out and play.

"I'm not allowed to play at your house anymore," Rebecca said. "Tessa gave me beer, and my Mom's mad."

That seemed to be all that was needed to separate the two families. All of the children stopped talking to each other, and the parents never discussed the problem.

The next Saturday was Rebecca's monthly doctor's appointment, so the family stayed in the city and visited Mr. and Mrs. Williams as usual. Since that was the first weekend home since they moved into the house, it was the first weekend they got to experience the wild parties that went on at Tessa's house on Friday and Saturday night.

Eamon and Clara called the police when the party was still going on at three o'clock in the morning. Just like in the old neighborhood, the police didn't do anything, and the party started again as soon the police left. Either the police told Tessa's family who made the call or they assumed correctly, because the second stage of the party included people throwing beer bottles at the front of Eamon and Clara's house and screaming, "Rat!"

Eamon and Clara spent another night at the kitchen table drinking coffee and getting no sleep, just like at their previous house. The conversation I overheard let me know they were starting to blame themselves since this was the second time they lived next door to partying neighbors.

When you're a ghost like Dog and me, you see things differently. In my last moments of life, I blamed myself and the blood moon I was staring at for my death. In death, I came to realize it was my abusive parents who killed me and Dog. That is why Dog and I knew we needed to stay and protect Eamon. If I would have continued to think it was the blood moon that killed me, I would have gone with the Angel a long time ago.

Eamon and Clara were still living in the human world where it can be harder to see the big picture. It can be even harder to see the big picture when a person is surrounded by constant stress. When they started having some of the same problems in the new house they had in the old one, they didn't realize it was because that's what happens in poverty neighborhoods where there's a lot of crime, alcohol, drug abuse, and, quite frankly, the desperation that leads to those things. Even seeing it on the news every night didn't help them understand that, because the people on the news were a distant unknown — those people on television were living it in their own little corner of the world.

Eamon and Clara didn't understand that the remedy to their problems was out of their reach. They needed to have enough money to allow them to have better options to choose from. Lack of education combined with physical handicaps and illness is not a formula for creating better options — especially when people come from places where options were so rare they didn't even know what that looked like or, in some cases, that they even existed. They were forced to grab onto whatever they could grab onto within their limited resources and hope for the best.

Since there were only two houses isolated from the rest of the neighbors on the street their first house was on, Eamon and Clara missed one good thing that can happen in an under-privileged neighborhood. When there are a lot of neighbors close enough that you can get to know them, you soon learn that most of them are good people who are just as scared as you are. When word spread through the neighborhood that Tessa's family was throwing beer bottles at Eamon's and Clara's house, the good neighbors knew someone in their home had taken a stand and were receiving retaliation. This marked us as good people, so the good neighbors reached out to us. Clara was invited to walk her children to and from school in a large group of women who walked together for safety, which meant Dog and I got to walk with them as well. Unfortunately for Princess, the ladies recommended that Princess not walk with Clara any more for Princess' safety since she was a small dog.

All of the women in the group, who jokingly called themselves The Street Walkers, were from families where the woman nurtured the children and took pride in their home, the fathers worked for a living, and whether they attended church or not had values that focused on keeping their homes pure — which meant among many things drug free. All of them were traumatized by the small number of families in the neighborhood who earned their living from drugs, prostitution, or abusing the system, so they learned to stick together. Despite the problems living in a poverty area often brings, there was a lot more good here than in the old neighborhood.

The mothers in The Street Walkers benefitted the neighborhood in many ways. It soon became apparent that Mrs. Abel was with child. When she announced her maternity leave, the mothers planned a baby shower for her last day in the classroom. Dog and I were excited to watch, because we had never been to a party like it before.

During the party, Mrs. Abel approached Clara and said, "I'm really going to miss Rebecca — and you. I just want you to know that I'm not sorry about how things turned out, and I would have done it all again."

"What do you mean?" Clara asked. "You're goin' on maternity leave, right?"

233

"Oh, my," Mrs. Abel said as she laid her palm on Clara's arm. "They didn't tell you?"

"Tell me what?"

"Oh my word. I thought they would have told you since it was about Rebecca and all."

Clara looked concerned and said, "Please tell me, especially since it's about my daughter. I have no idea what you're talkin' about."

"Oh, my goodness. I thought they told you. They investigated Mrs. Stone. I don't know what happened to her, if anything, but they let me go. My pregnancy is just starting to show. They're saying I'm on maternity leave to save me the embarrassment of everyone knowing."

Clara gasped and asked, "Why?"

"They said I was wrong to have handled it the way I did. They said I should have brought Rebecca immediately to the nurse or counselor or called Child Protective Services instead of handling it myself the way I did."

Tears welled in Clara's eyes as she said, "I'm so sorry. I don't understand. You helped her. Everything you did helped her."

"It's okay," Mrs. Abel said as she ran her palm up and down Clara's arm. "I didn't follow procedure, but I don't feel bad about that. I did what I thought was best for her instead of dragging strangers in when she was already so scared —"

"What can I do to help?"

"Nothing. I don't want you to do anything. That might make it worse, maybe even for Rebecca. I know you just bought a house, so she'll have to attend here for a while. Don't make any waves. I didn't lose my license. I can still teach. Maybe this is a blessing in disguise. I will take a year or two off to be with my baby, and then I'll look for another job. It'll be okay."

"I'm so sorry. I wish you only the best."

"When I start to apply for a job, may I use you for a reference? I'm not sure what kind of reference this school will give me?"

"What's a reference? What would I need to do?"

"I would put your name and contact information on my job application, and the new school would call and ask you if you think I could do a good job."

"Yes, yes," Clara said as she nodded. "Yes, you can use me as a reference. I'll tell them what a wonderful teacher you were for my daughter."

Mrs. Abel hugged Clara and said, "I'll miss you and Rebecca. I wish you both the best." She then walked away quickly with tears in her eyes.

While The Street Walkers, which included Dog and I, walked home from the party, Clara approached one of the ladies she was starting to get close to and said, "Marjorie."

"Yes," Marjorie said as she turned away from another mother she was talking to.

Clara moved closer to Marjorie and whispered, "What does Child Protective Services do — you know, if a report is made?"

"They'll investigate, and if there's a problem, they'll take a person's kids from them. Are you planning on reporting your neighbors?"

"Oh, no, I don't think so. I was just wonderin'."

"Take my advice. Don't report them. If you do, they'll do a lot worse to you and your family than throwing beer bottles at your house."

"I won't. It's better not to make waves."

"No one would blame you if you did. You don't just live next door to people who take drugs like most of us do. You live next door to the people who sell them. I made the mistake when I first moved here of going to their house to complain to the mom about them exposing my kids to drugs. When they answered the door, I could barely breath from the cigarette and pot smoke that wafted out into my face. When I asked for the mom, a whole group of hippies who were doing all kinds of drugs around the coffee table in the front room told me she was dead. When I say all kinds of drugs, I mean it. There were needles and lines of cocaine on a mirror sitting right out in plain sight, and they were passing a joint around while they were talking to me. One of them went to get the dad, and he came to the door and offered to sell me drugs before he even knew what I was there for. When I said his kids offered drugs to my kids, he told me he didn't see what the problem was. I walked away so mad I could have hurt one of them, but I can't go to jail when I've got kids to take care of. That's the only reason I walked away."

The lady Marjorie was talking to said, "I think it's our moral obligation to report people like that even if it does mean we'll make them mad. Both of you should report them if you've seen drug use."

Marjorie laughed and said, 'When you've lived here long enough to learn how things work, you'll think differently, Katie."

I was a little surprised Marjorie was the first mother Clara was getting close to. Even though Marjorie was about Clara's age, she seemed to be the opposite of Clara in many ways. Clara was tall and had an hour glass figure and Marjorie was tall and thin. Clara kept her hair short and permed while Marjorie's hair was long, black, and looked a little stringy on the ends when she didn't put it in her normal ponytail. Clara always wore dresses and Marjorie always wore dress slacks and a t-shirt. When they socialized, Clara always had coffee and Marjorie always had tea. Clara now bought tea at the grocery store for when Marjorie visited. The only thing the two women seemed to have in common was their mothering style — but in a poverty neighborhood with drugs that was probably the most important thing. Both women were fiercely protective mothers even though Clara was normally a very passive woman, which is another way Marjorie was different. Marjorie said whatever she thought and didn't care how anyone took it. As I watched them talking that morning, I tried to figure out why two such different women were becoming friends. As I thought about it, I realized that Marjorie was a lot like Clara's sister, Lana. Maybe that was the attraction.

The next night while Clara was making supper, someone banged on the upstairs door. Clara and I ran upstairs to answer it. When Clara opened the door, Tessa's dad was standing there. Before Clara could say anything, he yelled, "You dumb bitch! I know you're the one who called Child Protective Services on us. Believe me, I'll never forget it! You'll regret the day you called! We're goin' to make your life a living hell, so you'll remember not to report us ever again! You won't get away with this!" He stormed off the porch before Clara could say anything.

Clara didn't tell Eamon when he got home from work, because she hoped it would blow over if nobody did anything to make it worse. She learned the next morning that it wasn't going to be that easy.

The next day while we walked to school, The Street Walkers had to surround Clara, Mitchell, and Rebecca, because all of Tessa's relatives were trying to get to them. I understood why the Moms recommended Clara not walk with Princess any more — as small as she was, she might have gotten hurt in this melee. I stayed inside the circle of women who surrounded my family, but Dog was on the outside of the circle barking at the aggressors. Once Tessa's family realized they couldn't get through The Street Walkers, they stopped pushing, stayed outside the circle, and screamed names at Clara, Rebecca, and Mitchell.

From the middle of the circle, Marjorie asked Clara, "Did you call Child Protective Services after I told you not to?"

"No, but they think I did," Clara answered. "The dad knocked on our door last night and accused me of it. He stormed off before I could say anything."

Marjorie put her arm over Clara's shoulder and whispered, "I bet Katie made the report after what she said the other day." Marjorie removed her arm and continued, "She shouldn't have done that, and she especially shouldn't have let someone else take the fall for her when she did. You don't ever report anyone in this neighborhood. To be honest, they don't give a damn if their kids get taken from them — that'll just be one less responsibility they don't want anyway. They're scared of getting arrested for selling drugs, so they'll do anything to shut up a person they think might get them caught."

Clara swallowed hard and asked, "Do you mean this is never goin' to end?"

Marjorie shrugged and said, "I don't know. I hope it does, but it'll probably go on for a while. They're sending you a message. Trust me — listen to it."

Clara nodded.

"You're really goin' to need some support to survive this neighborhood now. We'll come to your porch every morning and pick you up. Don't leave the house until we get there. We'll walk you all the way to your porch in the evening, too. You also need to start coming to church. We all attend that white church on the hill that we pass every day. We'll pick you and your family up at nine-thirty Sunday morning. Services start at ten o'clock. I don't know how anyone could survive this neighborhood without God and prayer."

Clara nodded and said, "Okay, but I don't think my husband will come."

"Why?"

"He had a bad, uhm, well, he's handicapped, and it's hard for him to walk that far."

"None of us have cars, or I'd offer for one of us to pick him up. If you want, we can make sure you all get safely to his car —"

"Let's start with me and the children goin' and then we'll figure it out from there."

"Okay. We'll pick you and the children up at nine-thirty Sunday morning."

CHAPTER TWENTY: GOOD, BAD, OR INDIFFERENT?

The retaliatory harassment continued in the same way through autumn. It might stop for a day or a week, but it always returned. Dog and I were happy to witness The Street Walkers keeping Clara, Mitchell, and Rebecca safe every time we walked to church or school with them. The winter months gave everyone some reprieve from the vengeful neighbors — the bad weather must have impacted them more than their desire for revenge. No one knew what was going to happen now that spring was returning. As I watched the children play on the school playground on the first nice day of spring, it seemed that none of them cared what might happen during the walk home. They all seemed to be ecstatic. As usual, Dog was running and playing among them. In spite of her limp and the high-top shoes she still had to wear, Rebecca was playing, too, when the principal came out of the building carrying a chapter book and yelled for Rebecca.

Rebecca froze and stared at him for so long that he smiled big and said, "Come on. You're not in any trouble."

Rebecca walked toward him very slowly, and I followed her to make sure this principal wasn't going to hurt her like Mrs. Stone had done. When she got to him, she said, "Yes, Mr. Claus."

"Would you be willing to read to that group of teachers standing over there?" Mr. Claus asked as he pointed toward a group of teachers standing at the edge of the playground.

Rebecca smiled and nodded, so he lay his hand gently on her upper back and led her to the teachers who were assigned to be playground monitors that day. When they got to the teachers, Mr. Claus said, "I know you don't believe me, so I'm going to prove it." He handed the book to Rebecca and said, "Go ahead and show them how good you are at reading."

As Rebecca took the book, one of the teachers said, "That's four grades above her reading level — she won't be able to read that for a couple of —"

Rebecca opened the book and started reading. All of the teachers jerked their heads in her direction and listened while Mr. Claus stood above Rebecca with a big smile on his face. She sped through the first chapter of the book. When she got to the second chapter, she looked up at Mr. Claus and asked, "Should I read another chapter?"

The teachers were still staring at her, speechless, as Mr. Claus answered, "That's enough, I think. Thank you for reading to us."

Rebecca handed the book to him, and he said, "I think your fine reading should be rewarded with something. You can keep the book."

Rebecca smiled big and asked, "Really?"

Mr. Claus nodded and said, "Yes. You can play with your friends again now."

As I followed Rebecca back onto the playground, I heard one of the teachers say, "That's amazing!"

Rebecca didn't return to the game she had been playing. Instead, she sat next to the school building, leaned against the wall, and read the second chapter in her new book. I sat next to her and read over her shoulder. The night Clara gave Rebecca the notebook of paper Mrs. Reynolds sent home with Eamon, I started watching over Rebecca's shoulder when she wrote. Combine that with paying attention when she read out loud or sounded out words, and I was learning to read. I couldn't keep up with Rebecca, but that didn't stop me from trying. She was already on Chapter Three when their short recess was over.

When the bell rang, Rebecca was so lost in the book that she didn't hear it. When a teacher walked by, she smiled and said, "Rebecca — Rebecca —" When Rebecca continued reading, the teacher tapped her shoulder and asked, "Rebecca, did you hear the bell?"

Rebecca jumped and answered, "No."

"The bell rang. You need to go back to your class."

Rebecca and I followed the teacher to the group of students who were crowded outside the door waiting to enter the building. As the crowd moved slowly toward the door, Lisa, the class bully, moved closer to Rebecca and said, "I guess you think you're pretty special now, don't you crip?"

Rebecca looked at her and sincerely asked, "Why would I think I was special?"

Lisa laughed and said, "I bet you think you're better than us cuz you can read so good."

"So what? You can read, too. We can all read."

Lisa pushed Rebecca with her shoulder as they entered the building. Rebecca stumbled. As she regained her balance, I looked at Dog and said, "I guess there are Regan's every place."

As The Street Walkers walked home from school, Rebecca showed the book the Principal gave her to Clara. When Marjorie heard what Rebecca was saying, she congratulated Rebecca on being such a good reader, took the book, and passed it around the group as she shared with everyone how proud she was of Rebecca. When the book finally made its way back to Rebecca, Marjorie said, "You have to read some scriptures in church on Sunday. Do you think you can do that?"

Rebecca looked at Clara before she said, "I don't know."

Marjorie looked at Clara and said, "If I pick out a Psalm, would you mind if she reads it in church on Sunday? If she can read this book, she can read a Psalm."

"I don't mind if she doesn't mind."

"Do you mind?" Marjorie asked.

"I can try," Rebecca stammered.

"I'm three years older than her," Mitchell said. "Why aren't you askin' me to read?"

Marjorie looked at Mitchell and said, "You can read too if you want to. Would you like me to pick out a Psalm for you to read?"

Mitchell nodded.

Marjorie looked at Clara and asked, "If I stop by your house to help the children pick out a Psalm, do you think your husband could give me a ride home when he gets home?"

"I'm sure he would, but he often doesn't get home until after supper time."

"Oh — well, maybe I can just call you on the phone when I get home."

Marjorie did call later that evening.

"Hi, Clara," Marjorie said when Clara answered the phone. "Good news. I think I found the perfect Psalm for Rebecca to read on Sunday. Psalm 117."

Clara picked up the Bible she had laid by the phone and said, "Let me look that up." When Clara found the Psalm, she said, "I think that one's too easy for her. Do you have another one in mind?"

"Well, uh, no. I don't have another one in mind. Do you have any recommendations?"

"She really likes Psalm 6."

"She already has a favorite Psalm?" Marjorie asked, surprised.

"Yes, she does."

"And you feel confident she can read it without any problems?"

"I know she can," Clara answered and smiled proudly.

"Okay, Psalm 6 then."

"What one do you have for Mitchell?"

"I thought Psalm 92, since he likes music."

"Okay. I'll make sure they both practice." Clara paused for a few seconds before she said, "This is the first time they've read the Bible in church. I talked to Eamon, and we agreed we would get them both their own Bible. I'm goin' to stop at the bus stop on the way back from droppin' the children off at school tomorrow and catch a bus downtown, so I can shop for a Bible for them."

"I think that's an excellent present. The Street Walkers will wait with you at the bus stop until you're safely on the bus."

Dog and I were worried about Clara traveling alone when we followed Rebecca into the school building the next day. Fortunately, she took a bus that reached her return stop around the same time The Street Walkers were coming to pick up their children at the end of the school day. I was relieved to see her standing with the other Moms when Dog and I followed Rebecca and Mitchell out of the school building.

As we walked home, Mitchell and Rebecca kept asking her what was in the bag she was carrying.

"We'll open it when we get home," Clara answered each time.

Marjorie came closer to Clara and asked, "Why don't you just give it to them?"

"I don't want to make the other children in our group feel left out since they didn't get anything today."

"All of these children go to church with us, and part of being a Christian is being happy for other people when something nice happens to them."

Clara shrugged and said, "Okay," before she pulled the Bibles out of the bag and handed them to each of her children.

Both Bibles were about six by nine inches, vinyl covered, and had a zipper to protect the pages inside. The only difference was Mitchell's had a black cover and Rebecca's had a white cover.

Mitchell looked at his, handed it back to Clara, and said, 'I don't need it until Sunday."

Marjorie took his Bible from Clara, unzipped it, opened to the Psalm he was supposed to read on Sunday, and said, "Now is a good time to practice. Can you read your scripture for us, please?"

"But, it's not Sunday."

Clara looked at him and said, "Please do what you're told."

Mitchell took the book, grudgingly, and said, "But, I don't like to read."

Clara looked at Marjorie and said, "They have different gifts. He really likes music. We're tryin' to figure out a way to get music lessons for him. He wants to play the guitar."

Marjorie smiled and said, "It's good to know how to do many different things. If you'll read this for me, I'll let you borrow my son's old guitar until you can get one of your own."

Mitchell took the Bible and read his Psalm as the group continued to walk up their dangerous street together. Marjorie had him read it half a dozen times before she said, "Do it just like that on Sunday morning, and you'll do just fine."

Marjorie kept her promise. She brought the guitar the next morning. It traveled to the school and back and was waiting on Mitchell's bed when he got home. He sat on his bed strumming the guitar for the rest of that night, for hours every night that week, and most of the day on Saturday. He was so enamored with it that Clara barely got him out of the house in time to meet The Street Walkers to walk to church with them on Sunday morning.

When the Sunday school classes returned to the sanctuary, Marjorie gave Mitchell a brief introduction. The congregation clapped as he stepped up to the dais and again when he stepped down after his reading.

Before Rebecca stepped up to the dais, Marjorie introduced her by taking a full minute to rave about how good Rebecca was able to read at her young age and how her principal gave Rebecca a book earlier that week to reward her for reading so well. Rebecca proved this to be accurate when she breezed through her Psalm without a problem. The congregation clapped for a much longer time than they clapped for Mitchell when she stepped down from the dais, and several members took her hand and told her what a good job she did as she returned to her seat.

When she was seated between Clara and Mitchell again, Mitchell said, "Geez. You were talkin' so fast no one could even understand you."

Rebecca looked at Clara and asked, "Did I read too fast?"

"Everyone clapped," Clara said. "We need to be quiet now. The preacher is talkin'."

Tears rolled down Rebecca's cheeks as Mitchell kept intermittently whispering, "That was horrible." — "You were talkin' too fast." — "Do you even know what you read?" When the congregation laughed at a joke the preacher told, Mitchell said, "They're laughin' at you for talkin' too fast."

I lay my hand on her shoulder from where I sat in the pew behind them, but she didn't feel it. She wasn't aware of Dog's front paws on the back of her pew as he tried to cheer her up either.

As we left the church that morning, Marjorie knelt in front of Rebecca and said, "You did a very good job. Would you be willing to read again next Sunday?"

Rebecca swallowed hard and said, "I read too fast," and walked toward the door to go outside.

Marjorie looked at Clara. The two women shrugged before they ushered the children who walked with The Street Walkers out of the church.

When we got home from church, Eamon was on the phone. When Clara entered the kitchen where the phone hung on the wall, Eamon said, "Hold on, Mom. Clara just got home, and I'm sure she'll want to talk to you."

He handed the phone receiver to Clara. She took it and then stood there with her arm extended looking at him like she didn't know what to do with it.

Eamon whispered, "Please, I can't stand to talk to her anymore."

Clara put the receiver to her ear and said, "Hello."

"Hello. This here's Eamon's Ma. David done told me how he comed by your house not so long ago, and Regan done told us about that big party ya had. If'n you're goin' to start bein' with the family, I would think your children's Grandparents would be where you'd start."

"We didn't plan either of those things, or we would have invited you."

"It's easy to say that now. I want to see them grandchildren of mine. David said y'all said that girl of yours would be havin' an operation when she was eight years old. We want to see her before she goes under the knife, just in case anything should happen to her that would keep us from ever seein' her again."

"The doctors have decided to do the first operation this summer while she's out of school. She'll be goin' in the hospital in a few weeks when school's out, so she'll have the summer to recover and return to school in the fall. She'll be fine. Nothin's goin' to happen —"

"So, you're sayin' we can't be seein' her?"

"That's not what I said."

"Good, then we'll see you on Sunday next."

They did see them the next Sunday. Like dutiful parents, they drove their children to see their Grandparents right after church. Of course, Dog and I went along. When we arrived, the entire family was on the side deck.

After Eamon parked, we all sat in the car for a long time staring at the deck.

"I hope they don't start talkin' about everyone like they did at our house," Clara said.

"They will," Eamon said as he removed the keys from the ignition. "Let's just go on over and get it over with."

When we got to the deck, Mabon was sitting at the picnic table. She stood and looked over the deck railing when she saw Eamon, Clara, and the children and said, "Oh my word, they actually did come. I wasn't really expectin' it to happen. Well, come on up and get yourselves a plate of food. We didn't spend all this money on food to have it go to waste. Someone may as well eat it."

Everyone was either sitting around the picnic table that was covered with food or on folding chairs that littered the deck and yard. They were all eating, and they continued to eat as they looked up at Eamon and Clara and nodded or said hello.

Eamon, Clara, and the children walked up on the deck stairs with Dog and me following close behind. Eamon got some folding chairs that were leaning against the house and opened them for Clara, the children, and him to sit on at the end of the picnic table. He lined the chairs up in a row of four. He and Clara sat on the end chairs and sat Mitchell and Rebecca on the middle ones between them. Dog lay at Eamon's feet, and I stood behind him. Rebecca had been having such a hard time lately that we were spending more time with her, but we instinctively knew that in this environment, Eamon needed us the most.

Mabon said, "Y'all think ya be too good to be sittin' at the table with us."

Eamon glared at her and said, "We're fine right here. We're already settled."

"You mean to tell me y'all didn't bring no food to add to the pot luck?"

"We thought we were just comin' to let the children visit their Grandparents," Clara answered. "We didn't know there was goin' to be a big party or food. We ate before we left the house."

Mabon laughed and looked around at everyone at the table as she said, "Well, people've got to eat anyway, haven't they?"

Everyone at the table started laughing.

"Well, go ahead and eat then," Eamon said. "Ain't no one stoppin' ya."

Everyone got quiet and returned to eating.

Eamon and Clara sat silently for a long time at the end of the table before Regan and her son came up the deck's stairs and stopped at the top. Regan looked Eamon up and down before she said, "Well, I see you finally came out to see your Ma and Pa."

Everyone else at the party was wearing casual clothes, but Regan wore a fancy, pink dress that was formfitting to about halfway down her thighs and then flared out into a skirt that went to her knees. The fabric looked like chiffon, and it had small, pink sequins all over the bodice. Her son wore a light gray, three-piece suit with a white shirt and a wide necktie that was a darker shade of gray. He was about Rebecca's age. He kept fidgeting with his clothes, but Regan didn't get the message that he was uncomfortable.

Eamon nodded.

"Have you met my son yet?" Regan asked.

"Naw," Eamon answered. "Is he Louie's?"

"Who else would he belong to?" Regan huffed.

"Lord only knows."

"Pleased to meet you," Clara looked at Regan's son and interjected. "These are my children. This is Mitchell, and this is Rebecca. What's your name?"

Before he could answer, Regan said, "You just said they're your children, Clara. Does that mean they're not Eamon's?"

Eamon stood as he said, "You know damn well they're my — "

Clara lay her palm on Eamon's arm. He looked at her and his children, stopped mid-stand, and sat back down.

Regan looked at Mitchell and Rebecca and said, "Why don't you go out in the yard and play with my son — whose name happens to be Larry," she added as she looked at Clara.

Mitchell crossed his arms across his chest and said, "I don't want to play." He leaned back in his chair and kept his arms crossed.

Rebecca looked at Clara and asked, "Can I go play?"

"As long as you stay where I can see you."

As Rebecca left the deck with Larry, Regan said, "Poor little crippled girl. I bet everyone just makes fun of her like they did you, Eamon."

"Not anyone with any sense," Clara said as she put her arm across the back of Mitchell's chair.

Rebecca stopped at the bottom of the steps, looked at Regan, and said, "I'm able. My PawPaw said so."

Caelan stood up from the chair he was sitting on in the side yard and said, "I nary said such a thing."

Rebecca looked at him and said, "Not you. My PawPaw."

"I am your PawPaw!" he said as he walked toward her.

Rebecca swallowed hard and froze. Larry grabbed her hand and held it as Caelan loomed over the two of them from the top of the deck steps and said, "I am your PawPaw, and you'd know that if'n yer Pa ever brought ya around to visit."

Clara stood up and started walking toward Caelan as she said, "Rebecca, why don't you and Larry go on and play." The two children ran to the end of the deck as Clara yelled, "But stay where I can see you."

Dog stayed with Eamon, but I followed Rebecca to make sure she would be okay. The two children went to the corner of the deck by the front of the house. They sat in the grass in a small patch of shade the afternoon sun was allowing the deck to create. Larry pulled some baseball cards out of his jacket pocket and showed them to Rebecca. When they looked at all of them, the two children started using the cards to pick up ants that were bustling around them, so they could watch them walk across the cards.

They played that way for about a half an hour before Rebecca said, "I have to go to the bathroom."

Larry pointed toward the front of the house and said, "Go in that door by the carport. When you are inside, go down the hallway near the door. You'll see the bathroom."

When Rebecca started walking toward the front door, I saw Caelan, who had returned to his seat at the picnic table, crane his neck to watch her. He got up and entered the house through the door on the deck. Even though he was old, Rebecca's crippled leg made her slow enough that he was standing in the middle of the living room when she got inside the house.

She looked up at him and stammered, "I have to go to the bathroom."

"I reckon I'm only your PawPaw when you need something."

Rebecca swallowed hard and said, "I don't need nothin' but to go to the bathroom."

Caelan stepped between her and the hallway and said, "If'n ya can get around me without me grabbin' ya, ya can go to the bathroom. It's just down that hallway right there. Do you think you can get there before I stop ya?"

Rebecca started shaking. When Caelan approached her, she tried to run around him. She was almost to the hallway when he grabbed her arm. She wiggled until she pulled away. She ran to the front door, but before she could open it, he grabbed her arm again.

As she wiggled, Caelan grabbed one of the needles off the top of the short curio cabinet that sat just inside the front door. As he held it in front of Rebecca's face, he said, "Stop wigglin', or I'll poke ya with this. Your Grandma's a diabetic, and her medicine's in here. If I shoot it in ya when you're not a diabetic, it'll kill ya. Is that what you want?"

Rebecca stopped wiggling and shook her head.

"Good," Caelan said as he shook the arm he held hard enough that it shook her. "Now, who is your PawPaw?"

Tears welled in Rebecca's eyes as she stammered, "You are."

"Who is that other man you called PawPaw?" Rebecca started crying, so he shook her arm again and said, "Answer me!"

"He's in heaven."

Faolan was right — the gates of heaven are not locked. I saw Faolan materialize between Rebecca and Caelan. Somehow, he made the side door to the house swing open with a loud bang, and the wind seemed to carry a feeling that gave Clara a warning.

Clara jumped up, looked over the railing where Larry was playing, and yelled, "Where's Rebecca?" Larry kept playing, so she yelled, "Larry!" When he looked at her, she yelled, "Where's Rebecca?"

"She went to the bathroom," he answered.

Clara ran in the side door, saw Caelan kneeling in front of Rebecca, and yelled, "What's goin' on?"

Caelan returned the needle to the top of the curio cabinet and said, "I was just talkin' to Rebecca about what it will be like when she goes in the hospital this summer. I was just lettin' her know that shots ain't nothin' to be afraid of." He squeezed Rebecca's arm tight and said, "Tell your Ma that's what we were doin'."

Rebecca nodded as she crossed her legs and started bouncing up and down.

"Do you still need to go to the bathroom?" Clara asked as she walked toward Rebecca.

As Clara approached, Caelan whispered to Rebecca, "If you say anythin', I'll shoot that medicine in yer Ma too."

Rebecca swallowed hard.

When Clara got to them, she took Rebecca's hand and led her toward the hallway as she said, "Let's go to the bathroom."

When they came out of the bathroom, Caelan and Mabon were both standing in the living room. Clara led Rebecca out the front door, probably because going out the side door would mean walking past them, but Mabon said, "Wait a minute!"

Clara and Rebecca stopped right in front of where Faolan was standing. He wrapped his arms around them both.

When they stopped, Mabon and Caelan approached Clara as Mabon said, "We almost never see these children. Why don't ya let that lil' girl spend the night with us tonight, and ya can pick her up in the mornin'."

"She has school tomorrow."

"She can miss one day," Caelan said.

Rebecca grabbed Clara's dress and hid behind her as Clara answered, "She needs to go to school. I can't be pullin' her out of school for no reason."

"I'm sure she'd rather spend a night with her Grandparents than go to school," Mabon said. 'No child likes school."

"She does," Clara said. "She's very smart. She gets sad when she has to miss a day. Just last week the principal gave her a book for bein' such a good reader, and that led to her readin' a Psalm in front of the church at her young age."

"That's the problem with these damn young'uns nowadays," Caelan said. "They forget their roots. They think they're better than where they come from." He craned his neck to look around Clara, stared into Rebecca's eyes, and said, "Ya think you're somethin' special, because ya can read so good, don't ya? Ya walk around on yer high horse and wonder why people be mean to ya. H'it be because they can see ya think you're high and mighty. H'it be yer own fault. Yer too big fer your britches. I never went to school. I never read a word in my life, and I turned out just fine. Ya ain't no better than your roots."

Rebecca started pulling on Clara's dress so hard that she was almost pulling her over. Clara looked down at Rebecca peeking around from behind her dress, crinkled her brow, looked at Caelan and Mabon suspiciously, and asked, "Do you want Mitchell to stay, too?"

"Oh, no, no, there's no need for that," Mabon answered. "Just let the girl stay tonight, and Mitchell can stay another time."

"Why don't you want Mitchell to stay?"

"We're old," Caelan answered. "We can only keep up with one child at a time."

Clara pried Rebecca's hands off of her dress, picked Rebecca up, and walked out the front door as she said, "She won't be stayin' here."

When Clara and Rebecca left the house, Faolan disappeared.

As I followed them out the door, I heard Caelan say, "No wonder she thinks she only has one PawPaw."

Clara carried Rebecca back to where Larry was still playing with the ants and sat her down next to him. I followed Clara back to the deck. She moved her chair to the top of the steps and watched Rebecca and Larry as they played.

Eamon moved his chair next to hers and asked, "What's wrong?"

"I'll tell you when we get home."

Caelan and Mabon came out the side door and sat at the picnic table. They kept giving Clara dirty looks, but they didn't say anything.

About a half hour later, Regan walked up the deck steps again. When she was about halfway up them, she looked at Larry and screamed, "Boy, what the hell are you doin' sittin' in the dirt while you're wearin' your Sunday best?"

As Regan stormed down the steps and across the yard toward Larry, Eamon whispered to Clara, "They were all makin' fun of you for bein' over-protective when you didn't know where your child was, but it's okay for Regan to scream like a crazy woman because her child gets his clothes dirty. Thank God we don't see these people much."

When Regan got to Larry, she yanked him up by his arm so hard that she tore the back of his jacket at the arm seam. As she dusted the dirt off the seat of his pants much more roughly than she needed to, she saw the tear and screamed, "And you tore it, too." She started beating him as violently as Mabon had beaten Eamon the day she left him handicapped.

Rebecca's eyes got really big and she started shaking before she got up, ran to her parents, sat on Eamon's lap, and buried her face in his chest. She was crying uncontrollably.

Eamon stood and walked toward the car with Rebecca in his arms as he said, "Come on, Clara. Get Mitchell and let's get outta here."

Mitchell was still sitting on the chair with his arms crossed. Clara grabbed his hand, and they followed Eamon to the car with Dog and me close behind them. Everyone was watching Regan beat Larry, without helping him I might add, so no one seemed to notice when we left.

As our car pulled out from in front of their house, Eamon said, "We're never comin' back here again."

"You won't hear any argument from me anymore," Clara answered.

When we drove away, Rebecca was sitting on the back seat with her books between her and Mitchell. She couldn't see us, but Dog and I were sitting on them. About halfway home, we moved out of the way when Rebecca pushed the books onto the floor. I listened to her thoughts and learned she was remembering what her grandfather said about it being her fault people were mean to her, because she had forgotten her roots when she learned to read so good. She hoped people would be nicer to her if she stopped being so good at reading.

She left the books on the floor when we got home and went into the house. Instead of reading a story out loud to Princess before she went to bed like she usually did, which meant Dog and I didn't get to hear it either, Rebecca retrieved a stuffed purple donkey from the storage items under the steps on the first-floor landing. It had been following the family for so long no one even remembered where it came from. Rebecca hugged it all night that night and for many nights to come. Princess compensated for the loss of her nightly story by laying her head on the donkey and using it for a pillow.

CHAPTER TWENTY-ONE: THE FIRST OPERATION

Rebecca continued to ignore her books and the binder of her writing. The only thing that got her attention was the purple donkey even though it was so ragged there was barely enough fabric to hold the stuffing inside and it was doubtful it would survive a needed trip through the washing machine. On the day she was supposed to leave for the hospital for her first operation, she cried and hugged the donkey the entire time Clara was preparing for them to leave.

Princess followed Rebecca around and tried to make her feel better, but Rebecca didn't seem to be aware of her. Because of that, I was sure she wasn't aware of Dog and me as we tried to comfort her, too.

When Clara had Rebecca's suitcase filled, Rebecca sat on the bed next to it and lay the donkey on top of its contents. Clara removed the donkey and lay it on the bed. Rebecca picked it up and put it back in the suitcase, and Clara pulled it out again.

Rebecca picked it up and hugged it as she said through her tears, "I'm takin' him with me."

"You can't take him," Clara said as she closed the suitcase and latched it.

Rebecca curled up on the bed in the fetal position, hugged the donkey, and cried. Princess jumped on the bed, snuggled close to Rebecca, and lay her head on donkey.

Princess and Dog lay on the bed with Rebecca while Clara carried the suitcase downstairs. I followed Clara, trying to think of a way to get her to change her mind about the donkey. She carried the suitcase into the living room, sat it on the floor next to the television, sat on the couch next to Eamon, and said, "I had to bring the suitcase downstairs

253

to keep her from puttin' that tattered old donkey in it to take it to the hospital with her."

Eamon looked at her and asked, "Why don't you just let her take it?"

"You know how people are. We have to work ten times harder to prove ourselves than other people, because we're poor and don't have much schoolin'. The last thing I want to do is have her go over there carryin' a worn out, old, stuffed animal that announces to everyone we're poor. I'm already worried she won't get as good of care as other patients because of that. Don't you remember how that doctor talked to us when we took Mitchell to the emergency room when he was a little? How that doctor talked to you when you tried to find out why you get shaky and sick when you don't eat regular? He told us to go back to the mountains. Don't you remember how that nurse acted when we took Rebecca over for her pre-admission testin' and had a problem fillin' out some of the paperwork — and then it got worse when we told her we didn't have insurance? I'm afraid they aren't goin' to treat her as good as the other patients."

Eamon nodded.

Rebecca entered the living room, crying and hugging the donkey, and said, "I'm takin' him with me."

"You can't take him," Clara said.

Rebecca was crying even harder when she went back upstairs.

Eamon looked at Clara and said, "If it means that much to her, you should let her take it."

"I hate that she even has to go over there. Those people at that hospital aren't like us. They're outsiders. They don't get us, and we don't get them. I just want them to think she's like them, so they'll take good care of her."

"Dr. Stark has proven to be a good doctor."

"We didn't know that right away. She's been seein' him since she was born. Now we know we can trust him. We don't know those other people."

"I think we're goin' to look worse to them if she goes into that hospital screamin' and cryin' like that."

Clara sat quietly for a long time before she said, "Okay, I'll go tell her she can take it."

I followed Clara upstairs.

Rebecca was laying on hers and Eamon's bed with Princess, Dog, and the donkey when Clara looked in the door and said, "We're leavin' in five minutes, and you can take your donkey."

Rebecca sat up, smiled, and asked, "Really?"

"Yes, you can take it."

Rebecca petted Princess until they were ready to leave, and she gave Princess a big hug when they were leaving the house. Dog and I followed them to the car and rode in the back seat with Rebecca and Mitchell. When we got to the hospital, it was mid-afternoon. We went to a desk in the lobby, and Clara let the receptionist know Rebecca had arrived.

The receptionist was cold but efficient. She waved toward the two chairs that sat in front of her desk to invite them to sit down before she picked up the phone and dialed a couple of numbers. Clara sat down and lifted Mitchell onto her lap and Eamon sat down and lifted Rebecca onto his lap as the receptionist said into the receiver, "We have an admission. Can you please send Marcus down with the wheelchair to take her up to her room?"

When she hung up the phone, the receptionist explained the paperwork required in such detail that Marcus was there with the wheelchair before she got finished. He helped Rebecca off Eamon's lap and onto the wheelchair. He then stood behind the wheelchair and waited while the nurse finished her explanations and passed the clipboard of paperwork to Eamon as she said, "Just sign each place there is an X and initial each place there is an arrow."

Eamon took the clipboard and looked at it for several seconds before he said, "I can't read or write."

Marcus snickered.

Clara gave Marcus a dirty look before she took the clipboard from Eamon and said, "I can sign them."

Clara signed and initialed so quickly that the receptionist asked, "Don't you want to read them all first?"

"That's okay," Clara said as she continued to sign. "You explained it all very well."

When Clara handed the clipboard back to the receptionist, the receptionist looked at Marcus and asked, "Will you please take Rebecca and her family up to her room now?"

Eamon, Clara, and Mitchell followed Marcus as he pushed Rebecca toward the elevator, and, of course, Dog and I followed them. Dog and I had already decided we were staying with her the entire time she was away from home.

When they got to the room, Clara said, "It looks like you're goin' to be the only one in this room. It's small and only has one bed. When I had you and Mitchell, I was in a room with another woman. I guess they do things different nowadays. It's already been eleven years since Mitchell was born and eight years since you were born, Rebecca. I can't believe how fast time goes by. Are you goin' to be okay bein' alone all night by yourself?"

Rebecca nodded.

A pretty nurse entered the room. She was a petite blonde who was wearing bright red lipstick that seemed out of place with her white nurse's uniform and cap. She flirted with Marcus while he was leaving the room before she said, "Hi. My name is Stella. I overheard what you were saying, and I wanted to say I'm sorry about the accommodations. We're full to capacity. We don't even have a bed open for any emergency admittances. There may be people waiting for a long time for rooms in the emergency room tonight. This is the only room we had to give her." She winked at Rebecca and said, "That means you can watch anything you want on television."

Rebecca smiled.

Stella spent a few minutes explaining everything the family needed to know before she said, "I'm sorry, but we are awfully busy this afternoon. I'm going to have to go check on some other patients. Is there anything you need before I go?"

When Clara shook her head, Stella left.

Eamon and Clara stayed with Rebecca until visiting hours were over and Stella told them they had to leave. As they left the room, Stella instructed them to be back when visiting hours started at eight o'clock the next morning, so they could have a few minutes with Rebecca before she was taken down for her surgery that was scheduled to begin at nine o'clock.

After they left, Dog lay on the bed with Rebecca, and I sat on a chair next to the bed. She lay flat on her back with the blanket pulled up to her neck, holding the donkey in such a way that it's head stuck out from under the blanket like her own head did. It was obvious she was frightened, so I listened to her thoughts.

Even my ghost eyes had tears welling in them as I listened to what she was thinking, 'I want to go home. I don't want to be away from Mommy. Mommy told me I'd be okay, but she told me I'd be okay the first day I went to school. I wasn't okay. Mrs. Stone really hurt me. If I would have known what I did wrong, I would have stopped doing it, so Mrs. Stone would have stopped hurting me. I didn't know. What if I do something wrong here, because I don't know it's wrong? What will they do to me?' Tears welled in her eyes as her thoughts shifted to home, 'What if the neighbors hurt my Mommy while I'm here, or my Daddy, or Mitchell, or Princess. What if our neighbors come here to the hospital to hurt me? Mommy isn't here to protect me. The Street Walkers aren't here to protect me. What if Grandma and Grandpa come here while I'm asleep? Mommy isn't here to protect me. Daddy isn't here to protect me. What if they hit me like Aunt Regan hit Larry?' She hugged the donkey closer as she thought, 'What if it hurts to get an operation? I wonder if it will hurt? Will it hurt bad? I want to go home.'

Rebecca was still awake at seven o'clock the next morning when the nurse came to get her ready for surgery. The nurse was a large, black woman whose skin was so dark it contrasted the white of her uniform in a complimentary way that made her look very pretty. She was so large she looked like she was about to bust out of her tight uniform — the buttons over her large chest were straining and about to pop off. She seemed to have a hard time moving, but she found enough mobility to do her job and do it well. She got Rebecca out of bed and into the bathroom within a matter of seconds.

When they got in the bathroom, the nurse said, "My name's Maggie. It looks like I'm goin' to be your nurse the whole time you're stayin' here, well, durin' the daytime anyway. I'm here for the next five days. We're goin' to get to know each other really good before you go back home."

Rebecca smiled at her.

"Let's get you a shower and a clean night gown before you go down for your surgery. You'll have a cast on afterwards, so it'll be a while before you can get a bath or shower again. You'll be washin' off with a basin and a washcloth for the next few weeks I'm afraid. Is that okay with you if I help you get a shower?

Rebecca nodded.

The nurse opened the shower door, turned on the water, and tested it for temperature for several minutes before she said, "Okay, let's get that nightgown off."

The bathroom door was slightly ajar when Marcus came in and said loudly, "Maggie."

"Yes, yes. I'm in the bathroom."

Marcus looked through the bathroom door just as Maggie was taking Rebecca's hospital gown off. The nurse continued her task as she looked at Marcus and asked, "What do you need?"

"I was wondering if she was ready to go down yet?"

"No, no, Lord no," Maggie answered. "Take Mr. McClure down first. I'm gettin' this child a bath, and her parents are goin' to be here at eight o'clock to see her before she goes down."

Marcus continued to stand in the doorway and watch the nurse undress Rebecca. He was the opposite of the nurse in every way. He was tall and thin, and the white shirt, pants, and lab coat he wore all seemed too big for him. His sandy brown hair and light-colored skin blended into the uniform to give the impression that he was disappearing into it.

When Rebecca was undressed and getting into the shower, Maggie glanced at the door and said, "Marcus, quit standing there leering. People are going to think you're an old pervert or something. Mr. McClure's surgery is scheduled for eight o'clock. You'd better be getting him down there."

Eamon and Clara arrived just as Maggie was getting Rebecca back in bed. She looked at them as they entered the room and said, "Well, look here, Rebecca. You've got some visitors. I'll bet this is your Mommy and Daddy." She tucked Rebecca in, smiled at Eamon and Clara and said, "She just got a bath. She'll only be able to take sponge baths for a few days, so I thought that might be a good idea. You're a little early. Visitin' hours don't technically start until eight o'clock, but heck, rules are made to be broken, right? Go ahead and enjoy some time with your daughter. I'll leave you all to visit for a while before Marcus comes up to get her and take her down."

Eamon and Clara both thanked Maggie as she left the room.

When Maggie got to the hallway, she met Marcus coming to get Rebecca. She stopped him at the door and said, "Her parents just got here. Let's give them a few minutes to visit. Come on down to the nurse's station with me, and you can take her down about 8:15."

As they walked away from Rebecca's room, Marcus said, impatiently, "Don't these hillbillies know we've got schedules to keep? I've got other patients to transport."

When I heard Marcus call my family hillbillies, I wondered what else he had to say. I left Dog with Rebecca and followed them to the nurse's station.

"They actually got here early," Maggie said when they got to the nurse's station. "Visitin' hours don't technically start until eight o'clock. You've got plenty of time to give them a few minutes and still get all of your patients down in time.'

"Whatever you say."

"I'll just be glad when that child's surgery is over and she can relax. Stella was her nurse last night. She said that child was so scared she lay awake all night, said she was wide awake every time Stella checked on her. I gave her a bath this morning, because I thought the warm water might soothe her and being busy with something might take her mind off it. A bath is always a good idea anyway right before gettin' a cast."

Marcus cleared his throat before he said, "Lord only knows what might be happening in that hillbilly family to make that kid afraid. Did you see her parents? Her Mom's still wearing a feed sack dress, and her Dad looks like an old farmer. I brought her up from the receptionist's desk yesterday — those two couldn't even sign her admittance paperwork. And, did you see that raggedy old stuffed animal that kid's carrying. I bet you dollars to doughnuts that we never get paid for this bill. I don't know how Cincinnati got all these damn hillbillies, but they need to go back to where they came from. They make decent people look bad."

Maggie huffed before she said, "I don't know about all of that."

Marcus continued to talk bad about Rebecca and her family. Maggie kept looking at her watch like she couldn't wait to get away from him.

At a quarter past eight o'clock, Maggie interrupted Marcus mid-sentence to say, "Maybe we ought to go get her now."

Maggie came out from behind the nurse's desk and walked to Rebecca's room with Marcus pushing the transport bed behind her — and me walking beside Marcus trying to figure out a way to trip him with my ghost foot.

When they entered Rebecca's room, Maggie said, "Marcus is here to take you down for the operation. In just a few hours, this will all be over, and I promise to give you some ice cream when you feel like eatin' it."

Maggie and Marcus moved Rebecca to the transport bed, and Eamon and Clara followed it to the swinging double doors that led to the operating room. They were stopped at the doors and instructed to wait in the nearby waiting area. After Eamon and Clara said some encouraging things to Rebecca, they joined Dog and me in that waiting area. They chose the seats that were farthest away from the many other families waiting to hear about their loved ones operations. All of the families sat in their own isolated groups and didn't talk to anyone outside those groups.

When three hours passed without hearing anything, Eamon got fidgety. Clara looked calmer, but her wringing hands revealed she was as nervous as Eamon was. By the time another half hour passed, Eamon was pacing back and forth even though his limp, getting worse with each step, revealed how much pain he was in. After four hours, he sat next to Clara and said, "It shouldn't take this long. It's been four hours. Somethin's wrong. What if somethin's wrong with her? What if she doesn't make it?" By the time he ranted that way for another half hour, he was starting to shake.

Clara lay her hand on his and said, "I think it's just too hard on you to wait like this, and to be honest, you're makin' me worry more when I'm sure we don't have anythin' to be worryin' about. Why don't you go and get some lunch and go back to work to get your mind off of it. By the time you pick Mitchell up from Lana's house and get back to see her tonight, she'll be safely in her room."

"What if somethin' happens — "

"Nothin's goin' to happen. Just go on back to work to get your mind off it, and you'll see tonight when you come back to visit that she's just fine."

Eamon nodded, kissed Clara, and reluctantly left.

260

As he walked down the hall, he saw a vending machine. He got a candy bar and ate it as he walked to their car. By the time he got to the car, he stopped shaking.

Clara sat there for two more hours before the doctor came to the door of the waiting room and said, "Mrs. Teague."

"Yes, yes," Clara said as she got up and walked to the doctor.

When she got to him, he said, "Your daughter's fine. She came through the operation with no problems. She's in recovery now. She should be back in her room in a couple of hours. Have you eaten lunch?"

Clara shook her head.

"There's a cafeteria down the hall. Why don't you go have some lunch and by the time you get to her room, she'll probably be up there."

"Thank you. Thank you. Yes, I'll do that. I have to admit, I was startin' to worry. The operation took a lot longer than I thought it would."

"Didn't anyone tell you?" the doctor asked.

"Tell me what?" Clara asked as she shook her head.

"I'm so sorry. It was a long operation, but we didn't get started until about eleven o'clock. We had some scheduling problems. I'm sorry no one told you."

Clara nodded, and the doctor walked away. She went to the hospital cafeteria and ate a sandwich like the doctor recommended. After she ate, she passed a gift shop on the way to Rebecca's room. There was a table inside the window that had gift boxes stacked in a way that resembled the tiers of a wedding cake with merchandise displayed on each tier. On the top tier was a white planter that was shaped like a poodle and had a plant growing out of its back. After looking at it through the window for several minutes, she went in and looked at the price tag.

Clara stared at the price tag for a while before the cashier walked over to her and asked, "Can I help you with something?"

"No, thank you. It's a little more money than I can afford to spend right now."

"You're in luck. Everything in the window is half price today. Does that help?"

Clara looked down at a sign that was taped to the edge of the table and verified the sale, smiled, and said, "I'll take it."

When Rebecca returned from surgery, the poodle was sitting on the table next to her bed. After Marcus and Maggie transferred her from the transport bed to her hospital bed, she looked over at the poodle, smiled, and said, "That's pretty." She fell asleep a few seconds after she said it.

By the time Eamon and Mitchell got there that evening, Rebecca was becoming less groggy. She had been too tired to eat supper when it was delivered, so Maggie set it aside and brought it to Rebecca just before her shift ended.

As Maggie set the tray on the bed table in front of Rebecca, she looked at Clara and said, "She should be okay through the night. The doctor prescribed something for pain, just enough to take the edge off, so she shouldn't have any discomfort. She'll be on it while she's here and probably for a week or two after she goes home. She might be a little groggy on it, but since it's a low dose to take the edge off, she probably won't experience much grogginess. Just don't be alarmed if she does."

Clara nodded, and Maggie left the room.

Maggie kept the promise she made when Rebecca was leaving for surgery. She brought ice cream. There was an ice cream cup and a spoon on the tray for each member of the family. It was good that Maggie did that, because Eamon was starting to shake again before he ate it. The family's successful operation celebration of sharing ice cream seemed to calm him down and stop the shaking. As usual, Dog and I stayed with Rebecca when visiting hours were over and the night-shift nurse asked the family to leave.

Each day Rebecca was in the hospital, Clara and Mitchell stayed with her from the beginning to the end of visiting hours, Eamon came to visit her each night, and Dog and I stayed with her around the clock.

By the second day after Rebecca's surgery, Maggie was helping her walk to the bathroom instead of bringing the bedpan. On the way back from the first trip to the bathroom, Maggie looked at Clara and said, "She's makin' good progress. She'll probably get to go home soon."

When Maggie got Rebecca in bed, Mitchell pulled himself out of his boredom, sulking, or whatever caused him to sit quietly with his arms crossed over his chest while he was at the hospital and said, "I've got a story to tell you. Now that school's out, the neighbors are noisy every night like they were at the old house. Uncle Morgan got mad again and started doin' the garbage can lid dance. Well, Tessa's family don't take crap like our old neighbors. A bunch of them ran at Uncle Morgan and started beatin' him up —" Mitchell started laughing. Even when he continued the story he was giggling as he talked. "Well, Uncle Morgan hit Tessa's dad on both sides of his head like the garbage can lids were cymbals, and it knocked him out. The family stopped hittin' on Uncle Morgan to drag Tessa's dad back to their house."

Rebecca giggled for a few seconds before she looked at Clara and asked, "Is Tessa's dad dead?"

"No," Clara answered. "We saw him go to work the next day."

"Is Uncle Morgan okay?

"He's fine," Clara answered. "And, he won't be doin' that anymore. He understands that it won't work at this house like it did at the old one."

"But, he's okay?"

When Clara nodded, Rebecca started laughing and said, "I wish I could have seen Uncle Morgan do that to Tessa's dad."

For the rest of the evening, the family was relaxed and shared jokes and funny stories thanks to Mitchell redirecting everyone's tension with his story about Morgan. Rebecca seemed much less scared than she was when she arrived by the end of that second day. Even when Maggie's shift was over and Eamon, Clara, and Mitchell were ushered out at the end of visiting hours, Rebecca seemed content to be alone in her room with Dog, me, the purple donkey, and the poodle Clara gave her. Instead of having the covers pulled up to her chin, she was sitting up in bed, playing with her donkey while she watched television, and smiling. Dog was lying next to her, and I was sitting on the edge of the bed watching her smile.

She fell asleep on top of the covers with the television still on. Around midnight, the night-shift nurse checked on her. After taking Rebecca's vitals and giving her some medicine, the nurse helped Rebecca get tucked into bed with the donkey and turned the television off. Dog snuggled up against Rebecca again when the nurse left, and I sat in the chair next to the bed.

Shortly after the nurse left, Marcus entered the room dressed in a nice pair of rust-colored dress pants and a black dress shirt. His hair was slicked back, and he reeked of cologne. He was carrying a teddy bear. Rebecca was still awake from the nurse's visit, so she stared at him from the moment he entered the room. He held the teddy bear out as he walked toward her and said, "I think I'm right that you and I have become buddies the last few days. Buddies do nice things for each other. I thought a teddy bear would make you feel better."

Rebecca took the bear when it got close enough for her to reach it, but she held it at a distance and continued to stare at Marcus without saying anything.

Marcus smiled and said, "Maggie told me you're walking to the bathroom by yourself now. She asked me to come in and help you go tonight."

"I don't need to go."

"Stella won't be back until three o'clock in the morning, and I know how she is. She's cute, but she's lazy. She won't be back here one minute before she has to do her three o'clock rounds. You don't want to have to wait until three o'clock in the morning to go to the bathroom, do you?"

"But, I don't need to go."

"I'm supposed to take you at midnight, so you can sleep through the night," he said as he pulled the covers off of her. When she resisted his attempt to help her out of bed, he crossed his arms over his chest and asked, "Am I going to have to get the doctor?"

Rebecca looked so frightened that I listened to her thoughts. She was so afraid the doctor would punish her like Mrs. Stone did if she didn't do what she was told that she swallowed hard and let him help her out of bed. Dog was growling at him the whole time.

When she was out of bed, he gave her crutches to her, picked up the remote and turned the television on, turned the volume up a little, and helped her walk across the room to the bathroom. I had a bad feeling about him, especially after the mean things I heard him say the morning of Rebecca's surgery, so I followed them into the bathroom. My concern increased when Marcus locked the door once they were inside. Rebecca was trying so hard to lean the crutches against the wall and turn around without falling that I don't think she noticed. She grabbed onto the back of the toilet to help herself turn around, and Marcus touched her.

Rebecca froze so stiff that not only did she look like a statue but I wasn't sure she was breathing. I listened to her thoughts: 'No! No! No! This place is like school. No! Mommy left me at school and Mrs. Stone hurt me! No! This man is going to hurt me the same way Mrs. Stone did! NO! NO! NO!' Marcus pressed the front of himself against her back and wrapped his arms around her waist as he bent her forward. I was still in her thoughts: 'He's bending me over! No! No! No! He's goin' to hit me like Mrs. Stone did! No! My leg already hurts, so this is really goin' to hurt this time. NO! NO! NO! NO! NO!'

Marcus revealed the ways he intended to hurt her when he treated her body as if she were his bride on their wedding night. When Rebecca responded to the pain, Marcus said, "Shut up and take it, or I'll make sure I hurt you even worse. It's up to you how much you suffer. If you make a fuss or fight back, I'm really going to hurt you bad."

When he said that, Rebecca's thoughts were gone. I couldn't listen to them, because it was like she disappeared — like she wasn't there. I didn't want to see what happened after that, and I will never talk about it beyond what I've already said here — not that anyone could hear my ghost voice if I did. Now that I've had more time to come to grips with what I witnessed, I understand why Rebecca disappeared. I understand why she didn't want to remember. I didn't understand then.

As I ran through Rebecca's mind looking for her, I was remembering the day my mother had killed me. I fought. I fought the entire time she dragged me to the barn. I tried to crawl out of the barn and escape when she returned to torment me. I didn't stop fighting until my body expired. I didn't freeze and let it happen like Rebecca was doing, and in the moment, I was angry at her for not fighting. I chased her through her mind. I looked for her. I screamed her name. I begged her to fight back. I antagonized her to try to make her so angry she would fight back. In hindsight, that was a mistake. When I found her, she was plenty angry — she was just projecting it onto herself.

I found her, because she came back to her body due to a drop of blood her physical eyes saw on the bathroom floor. When her body and spirit were reunited, she passed out in Marcus' arms. He picked her up and carried her to her bed, unaware that Dog was standing at the end of the bed snarling at him. When he lay her on the bed, he

265

closed the door to her room and started cleaning her up with hypocritical tenderness.

Rebecca was as gone when she passed out as she was when her spirit separated from her body, but I continued to listen to her thoughts anyway. When she woke up, Marcus was finishing the job of cleaning her up. She tried to scoot away from him, but he grabbed her leg and said, "Where are you going? We're buds. Remember, I brought you a teddy bear. If something is wrong here, it's your fault. You accepted the Teddy Bear. You shouldn't have accepted the Teddy Bear if you didn't want this to happen. This is all your fault."

Dog stood next to her, growling at Marcus through bared teeth.

Her thoughts told me that her gut was telling her to scream for help, but her mind was being charmed by him like a mouse being charmed by a snake. Part of her surrender was her fear of the outrage she would probably be exposed to if she defended herself — remembering Regan beating Larry reminded her of that possibility. The other part of her surrender was being angry at herself — blaming herself just like Marcus told her to do. I guess she had been charmed by a snake in human clothing enough times that she felt she must be doing something horribly wrong since she kept being the mouse.

Rebecca stared at him while she was thinking these thoughts, so he said, "Don't look so hurt. You can't tell me this is the first time this happened to you. I've seen that hillbilly family of yours. Everyone knows you hillbillies do this to each other all the time. I wasn't trying to hurt you like they do though. I was just trying to show you how much I care about you. That's why I brought you a teddy bear."

Other than blinking her eyes once, Rebecca didn't move.

"Don't stare at me like that," Marcus snapped. "I also know you hillbillies protect each other. I'm not goin' to have your daughter-fucking Pa at my door with a shotgun, because I touched what was his. I'd hate for it to come to that since we're buddies and all, but if you tell anyone what happened here tonight, I'll have to kill your folks. It would break my heart to have to do that since you're my buddy. You won't make your buddy have to do that, will you?"

When Rebecca didn't answer, he grabbed her shoulders, shook her, and asked, "Will you?"

Rebecca shook her head.

"It wouldn't do you any good to tell anyone anyway," Marcus said as he pulled the blankets up over her, lay the teddy bear he gave her next to her, and gathered the laundry he made while he cleaned her up. "Your folks couldn't help you if you told any more than they helped you tonight. They can't even help themselves. I saw them when you checked in. They couldn't even write. They probably can't read either. What's your prairie mom in her feed sack dress goin' to do to protect you or herself? What's your crippled Pa who can't hardly walk goin' to do to protect you or himself? I know where you live. It's in the papers we tried to get your parents to sign when you checked in. If you tell them anything, I'll be forced to come to your house and shut you all up. I don't want to have to do that to my buddy or my buddy's family. You won't make me have to do that, will you?

Rebecca shook her head.

Marcus carried the wash tub to the bathroom and emptied it in the sink. When he returned, he put the dirty laundry in it and said, "You're not going to say anything and force your buddy to hurt someone are you? We're buds. Remember, I gave you a teddy bear. We're buds, right?"

Rebecca's thoughts let me know she wanted to nod so he wouldn't get mad at her lack of response and hurt her again, but she was so petrified she could no longer move.

Marcus came to the edge of the bed and kissed her on the forehead. He didn't seem to see how her body went stiff the moment he touched her. He smiled at her and said, "See you later, buddy," before he went to the door. When he opened it, he stuck his head out and looked up and down the hallway before he went to the door across the hall that led to the stairwell.

When he left the room, Rebecca pushed the teddy bear off the bed.

Dog quit growling and lay next to Rebecca.

Rebecca lay awake all night thinking things along the lines of, 'Why did he do that to me? Was I bad? I must have been bad. I must be really bad. Mrs. Stone hurt me. The neighbors always try to hurt us. We have to walk with The Street Walkers to be safe. Lisa always picks on me at school. Now this man hurt me. I must be really bad. Everyone wants to hurt me. I'm bad. Are The Street Walkers bad, too, since they like us? What if someone finds out he did this? Will The Street Walkers be able to keep my Mommy and Daddy safe if he comes to our house?'

After a pause, 'Oh no! I killed my bunny. I am bad. I'm really bad. I killed my bunny. I need to stop being bad. If I stop being bad, people will stop hurting me.'

When Stella checked on Rebecca at three o'clock, Rebecca acted like she was asleep even though she needed to go to the bathroom. Stella turned down the volume on the television and left the room without disturbing Rebecca. By four-thirty, Rebecca needed to go so bad that was the only thing she was thinking about — that and how afraid she was to ask anyone to help her. Listening to her thoughts let me see an image of her deflecting the touch of other people even though she wasn't putting it into words. By five o'clock, she was fidgeting to try to keep from pee'ing in the bed. When she feared she couldn't hold it, she thought, 'What will they do to me if I ask to go to the bathroom? What will they do to me if I can't hold it, and I pee in the bed?' That thought was more frightening than being touched, so she reached for the nurse call button. Reaching caused her to stretch in a way that made it impossible for her to hold it anymore, and she pee'd in the bed. Her thoughts then shifted to how she was going to hide it.

Dog moved to the foot of the bed to avoid the mess, but he didn't leave her. For the rest of the night, Rebecca lay in her pee and thought things along the lines of, 'What are they going to do to me when they find this? Maybe they won't notice. If they notice, what will they do to me? Will they punish me like Mrs. Stone did?'

When Maggie came in at seven o'clock in the morning to check on Rebecca, she noticed the bed was wet and said, "Oh, my word, child! Why didn't you call someone for help?"

Rebecca shrugged.

"Oh, my word! We've got to get you cleaned up! You can't lay in this mess so soon after surgery."

Maggie helped Rebecca onto the chair next to the bed. When Maggie started to slide Rebecca's hospital gown down her shoulder, Rebecca grabbed it and said, "I'll do it."

"You are an independent one, aren't you?" Maggie said.

Rebecca pointed to her suitcase, and as Maggie retrieved it, she said, "You want to put your own clothes on today? Are you sure? It's going to be harder maneuvering to go to the bathroom if you have to pull a nightgown up? That's why I left you in a hospital gown up till now."

Rebecca nodded.

"Do you want to wash yourself, too?"

Rebecca nodded again.

Maggie went into the bathroom and filled a wash tub with water. She sat it on the bed table with soap, a towel, and a washcloth and then lowered the table for Rebecca to be able to reach it. While Maggie changed the bed linens, Rebecca washed herself and put on a pair of underwear and a nightgown Clara had made for her.

Shortly after Rebecca was dressed, Maggie said, "I'll be back in a minute. I have to go down to the linen closet and get you a pillow case. There don't seem to be any more in this room."

When Maggie left the room, Rebecca picked up the teddy bear Marcus gave her. She ripped the seam on its back open enough to stuff the bloody hospital gown inside the bear. She then threw the bear into the garbage can.

After Maggie returned and put the pillowcase on, she asked, "Do you need anything else?"

Rebecca nodded and said, "To go to the bathroom."

Maggie got Rebecca up on her crutches and helped her walk to the bathroom door. When they got to the door, Rebecca said, "I can go by myself."

"Okay, if you're sure," Maggie said. "I'm goin' to leave the door ajar so I can hear you, and I'll be right out here. Let me know if you need anything."

Halfway to the toilet, Rebecca stopped and started breathing really heavy. She started to go back to bed without going to the bathroom, but I was still in her thoughts and was hearing the memory of Marcus' threats making her afraid someone would find out what he did if she turned back. She continued to walk to the toilet, but her breath became heavier and her skin became clammier with each step. After she was done, she put some toilet paper in her underwear and returned to her bed. Dog and I both lay on the bed with her.

Shortly after Clara and Mitchell arrived, Rebecca kicked the covers off her legs enough to see a small blood stain on the cast near her ankle. When she saw the stain, her memory returned to the blood stain on the bathroom floor that had brought her spirit back to her body after Marcus abused her, and she screamed while she pointed at it. Her screaming brought Maggie to the room before Clara had time to press the nurse call button.

Maggie took Rebecca's hands, put her face in front of Rebecca's and said, "Look in my eyes, sweetie." She kept repeating that until Rebecca was looking into her eyes and stopped screaming. When Rebecca stopped screaming, Maggie asked, "What's wrong?"

Rebecca stammered, "Blood."

Clara interjected, "She was pointin' at her cast."

Maggie continued to hold Rebecca's hands as she looked at the cast. When she returned to looking in Rebecca's eyes, she said, "Sweetie, it's okay. That happens sometimes. It's just a little spot, so I'm not worried about it. I know it will be okay. I will have the doctor look at it, but I know it is okay. I see that happen all the time." Maggie nodded her head as she asked, "Do you understand?"

Rebecca started nodding in unison with Maggie.

After Maggie left the room, Rebecca lay flat on her back, holding donkey. They were both covered up to her chins. Any time a nurse wasn't working with her, she was staring blankly at the television. She stayed that way until she was released the next day. Her mind was full of thoughts such as: 'I'm bad. That's why that man hurt me. I hope Mommy never finds out. She got mad when I knew that boys and girls looked different under their diapers. She'll know I'm bad if she finds out. She might throw caterpillars at me again or put me in the pot of stones. She might send those army men to get me. That man said he'd kill her if she finds out. I hope she doesn't find out. I hope Daddy never finds out. That man said he'd kill him too. That man knows where I live. What if he comes to hurt me again? What if he comes to hurt me again and kills Mommy and Daddy like he said he would do? What if The Street Walkers can't protect us? What if he helps the drug dealers next door act worse to hurt me more? What if I'm so bad people never stop hurting me? Mrs. Stone hurt me. Is this my punishment for killing my bunny? Is this my punishment for feeding the baby next door when I was little? Is this my punishment for keeping the snails in the box when their Mom was looking for them? Is this my punishment for being friends with the witch who lived next door to us? Are the caterpillars going to come for me again when I'm dreaming like they did on the side of our house? I'm bad. That

270

preacher on television said people go to hell if they're bad. Am I going to go to hell? I don't want to go to hell.'

Her thoughts never went to the one place I wanted them to go to — 'I HATE THAT MAN!' If she hated him, she would protect herself instead of blame herself. As long as she blamed herself, I was afraid more people like him would hurt her.

Before the doctor signed her release papers, he pulled Maggie aside outside Rebecca's door, and I was able to hear him when he said, "She seems healthy and is recovering nicely, but her lack of responsiveness has me concerned. She acts like she's in a daze."

"I think she's just a very shy child," Maggie answered. "She was like that the first night she was here, maybe through the first day. Then, when she got to know me, she was very friendly – not talkative, she was never talkative, but friendly. Then, all of the sudden yesterday morning she was back to the shy child she was when she first checked in. I think the surgery may have traumatized her a bit and that may be what caused her to start being shy with me again. When she saw the blood on her cast, it scared her so badly she started screaming."

"I saw that on her chart," the doctor answered. "I took a look at the blood on her cast, and everything's fine."

"I thought it would be."

The doctor signed a paper on the clipboard he was holding as he said, "I'm signing her release papers. Just emphasize to her parents that if she doesn't act like herself once she gets home, they should take her to their family doctor."

Eamon, Clara, Mitchell, Dog, and I were all there when Marcus came with the wheelchair to take Rebecca down to the lobby. As he entered the room, he looked at Rebecca and said, "Hi, buddy. Good to see you again. Sorry you're going home. We're all going to miss you." He then looked at Eamon and Clara and said, "We became good buddies while she was here."

"That's good to know," Clara said.

Rebecca became a mute, clammy statue as Marcus pushed her to the front of the building where Eamon's car was waiting for her. I didn't notice she'd been holding her breath during the last seconds of the trip — until she released it when Marcus went back into the building.

When we got home, Clara made the couch that was closest to the walk-in closet into a bed for Rebecca, because she needed to be on the same floor as the bathroom. There was another couch along the wall that separated the living room from the kitchen, so the family still had a place where they could sit and watch television or visit with Rebecca.

Rebecca lay on the couch day and night for two weeks, getting up only to go to the bathroom. She stared at the television, hugged donkey, and ate what was given to her, but she didn't talk, look at her books, or write in her binder even though reading and writing could have eliminated some of her boredom and given her an escape from the memories of what had happened in the hospital that wouldn't leave her alone. I hoped she might return to reading and writing when she got the ruler out of the pencil bag inside her binder, but she only used it to stick down her cast to scratch the itching that her thoughts let me know was a recurring problem. Even though Clara talked to Rebecca several hours each day like she had with Mrs. Abel the last time Rebecca stopped talking, Rebecca didn't answer with more than a nod or a shake of the head.

After a couple of weeks passed, Clara said, "I know havin' this operation has been very hard on you. Because of that, you deserve something really nice. If I could make anything you wanted for lunch, what would it be?"

Rebecca looked at her lap and said, "A chicken spread sandwich on toast."

When Clara brought it to her, Rebecca said, "Thank you."

From there, she spoke a few more words each day until she was talking normally by the time school started. Unfortunately, she wasn't talking about what she needed to talk about, but at least she was talking. What she needed to talk about was summed up in the one thing she wrote in her binder that summer: Everything is mixed up. I feel different. When will I feel like I did before?

CHAPTER TWENTY-TWO: GROWING UP FAST

Rebecca's summer proved to be difficult. In addition to recovering from the surgery, she kept getting hives. Every time her prescription ran out, the hives returned. As is common for people who don't 'have medical insurance, the doctor didn't test for allergies or ask about her emotional state – he just kept her medicated. As if that wasn't enough, she began to have a mild form of whatever caused Eamon to shake so often.

Unfortunately, her second-grade school year proved to be just as difficult, maybe even more so. This worked to Rebecca's advantage, because the quiet and reserved nature she had adopted since her hospital stay appeared to be the result of new traumas; therefore, old traumas were not suspected and didn't have to be revisited. I'm not saying this was a good thing. I'm only saying it allowed Rebecca to survive in the only way she felt she could after what had happened to her.

When Rebecca returned to school, she was still on crutches. This made it even more important that we walk with The Street Walkers for protection, especially since Tessa's family threatened to ramp up their harassment when they saw Rebecca was vulnerable. Dog and I, of course, walked with them and stayed with Rebecca at school — we weren't going to leave her alone while she was still recovering.

When Dog and I followed Rebecca into her second-grade class on the first day of school, my ghost heart stopped — the teacher reminded me of Mabon. She was a small, thin, old woman who wore her hair in a tight bun that made her wrinkled face look even older, and she carried a ruler around bouncing it off of her palm in the same manner Mabon had done with a stick right before she had killed me.

Although I don't remember a single child being punished all year, the whole class was terrified of this teacher, and it was apparent by the end of the first week of school. Even though she was a horrible teacher who had them sitting at their desks all day doing busy work, the entire class obediently sat with their heads bowed in a studious manner. Even when the monotony of her teaching style became too much for their young bodies and minds, the only evidence of this was the students becoming subtly fidgety.

Rebecca, on the other hand, didn't even allow herself to fidget. I listened to her thoughts frequently, so I knew she was afraid to fidget. Her thoughts were a combination of memories of Mrs. Stone and fear this teacher would treat her as badly, fear that the drug dealers would kill her Mom or Marcus would kill her parents before she got home from school, fear of her next hospital stay — basically, just fear. She was the epitome of the phrase "scared stiff."

A few days after the school year started, Clara made a follow-up appointment for Rebecca's hives. Clara made an appointment for herself for the same day. During Clara's appointment, the doctor confirmed that Clara was pregnant.

News of the pregnancy somehow got back to Caelan and Mabon. A few days later, they were waiting in their car in front of Eamon and Clara's house when the family returned home from the grocery store. Caelan and Mabon got out of the car when Eamon pulled in behind them.

"What are you doin' here?" Eamon asked as he got out of the car.

The rest of the family got out of the car, with Clara helping Rebecca since she was still on crutches. All of us, including Dog and me, stood next to the car as Mabon said, "We heard tell Clara was in the family way again. We figured we'd have to come down here to offer our congratulations considerin' the way y'all ran off from our house the last time you were out without sayin' a word."

"You've got to be kiddin'," Eamon said.

"Grandparents ought to know their Grandchildren," Caelan said. "Since we hardly even know them two you've already got, we figured we'd get involved with this one early on. Hell, you wouldn't even let that girl of yours spend the night the last time y'all was at the house. Y'all act like we're some kind of disease or something."

"It ain't born yet," Eamon said. "Come back in seven months."

"There ain't no point in standin' here on the street bickerin' in front of the children," Clara said. "Why don't you come on down for a cup of coffee, and we can talk while the children go upstairs and play."

"Hell," Caelan said. "You can't even leave them in the same room with us when we come to visit."

Eamon walked to the back of the car and opened the trunk. Everyone except Rebecca took as many bags of groceries as they felt they could carry and started carrying them toward the steps without anyone responding to Caelan's remark. Clara directed Mitchell to go down first, and she went in front of Rebecca and waited at the bottom of the steps in case Rebecca stumbled. Dog and I went in front of Rebecca for the same reason even though we knew our ghost bodies couldn't help. Rebecca went down next, and Eamon walked patiently behind her.

When Rebecca was about halfway down the steps, Mabon said, "They just coddle these children. If that were a child of mine, I'd take your belt from around your waist, Caelan, and beat her with it until it toughened her up. She could walk faster than that if she wanted to, but actin' like this gets her all this attention."

I saw Eamon's hands tighten into fists and his respiration get faster, but he didn't say anything until Rebecca was safely at the bottom of the steps. When she was at the bottom, Eamon stopped so that he blocked the steps and said, "You go on in the house with your Mother, Rebecca. I'll be in in a few minutes."

While Clara helped Rebecca get to the house, Mabon said, "It's goin' to be hard to get in the house to get that cup of coffee your wife offered if you don't get out of the way."

When Clara and the children were inside the house with the door closed, Eamon turned to them and said, "It's bad enough that you crippled me up for life and no one will talk about it, but you ain't goin' to come down here and threaten my children, especially not my crippled child. You need to go home! Now!"

"Jesus," Caelan said. "We was good parents. The Bible itself says to spare the rod is to spoil the child. You're raisin' yourself up a passel of spoiled brats around here, so I'm just as glad y'all don't come around for us to have to watch it. Them children of yours are goin' to grow up to be nothing but pure shit unless you start disciplinin' them with the rod once in a while."

"Get the hell off my property!"

"What the hell," Caelan said. "Your wife invited us in for coffee. We're family —"

"Those people who just walked into that house are my family! You need to go home! Now!"

"But —" Mabon started to say.

"Don't finish that sentence," Eamon warned. "If you're not off my property in ten seconds, I'm callin' the police. I'm sure they'll be right happy to hear about all the bruises on Regan's boy and all them drugs David's sellin' and —"

"Fine," Caelan said as he grabbed Mabon's arm and led her up the stairs. When they got to the top of the stairs, Caelan looked down at Eamon and said, "We don't need the likes of you anyhow. Thank God the good Lord gave us some decent children. We told Pastor Skaggs back home that you weren't nothing but trouble, and we was right. We seen it comin' then. You know what's waitin' for you in eternity since Pastor Skaggs couldn't never get through to ya. Now, on top of everything else, you're disrespectin' your folks. You know what the Bible says about honorin' your folks. You done broke two commandments here today. You disrespected your folks and you did it cuz they was tryin' to follow what the Bible says about disciplinin' young'uns. We nary need to be worryin' about you. God's got your punishment a-waitin'. Come on, Mabon. We're gettin' out of here."

"Good riddance," Eamon said as he carried his groceries into the house.

The wounds of Mabon's harsh words about Rebecca were still fresh enough when Caelan called two months later that, when Clara knew it was him on the phone, she coldly said, "What do you want?"

Caelan tearfully said, "I wanted to let y'all know Mabon passed away this mornin'."

Clara paused for a minute before she stammered, "What from?"

"Her diabetes — somethin' about her diabetes."

"I am always sorry to hear when anyone passes away."

"The information ought to be in the paper tomorrow. Can you read? Will you be able to read the information for the layin' out for Eamon?"

"Yes, I can read."

"Will y'all be comin' to the layin' out and the funeral?"

"I have to talk to Eamon about it. Probably we'll come."

Caelan hung up.

Clara stared at the phone receiver for several minutes before she hung it up. She returned to the living room and would have missed the couch when she sat down if she wouldn't have been holding onto its arm.

Rebecca was still recuperating on the other couch. She looked concerned and asked, "Mommy, what's wrong?"

Clara shook her head like she was trying to get cobwebs off of it before she answered, "Mabon just passed away."

I sat on the couch next to Clara. I didn't think my ghost body could experience so much emotion — and I didn't expect to feel sad. And happy. Sad and happy at the same time? How could that be? I was glad she might finally be getting hers for what she did to me and Eamon, and sad to think of her suffering because of all of her sins. Suddenly, I was just sad. Was anyone bad enough to deserve what Pastor Skaggs told us people like my Ma would get when they died? Now that those I loved were safe from her abuses, safety allowed me to realize that she only acted like that because she was hurting really bad inside. Her Daddy abused her. Caelan raped her and only married her because he got her pregnant. Caelan loved another woman while he was married to her. Caelan beat her. Now that we were safe from her, I could see that she did the horrible things she did because she was hurting inside. Should someone be punished eternally for hurting really bad inside? Every person or animal who died in this family came to say goodbye before they went with the Angel, or refused the Angel to stay like Dog and I did. Mabon hadn't come to visit, and I hadn't seen the Angel come to get her. Did that mean she went to a bad place to get punished, or did it mean the Angel picked her up some place else? Maybe the Angel picked her up at Caelan's house. I lay on the couch next to Clara and cried. Dog left Rebecca's side and came to lay with me. I wrapped my arms around him and hugged him for the first time since he became a ghost. He snuggled into my hug.

Rebecca sat up straighter and asked, "Are you okay? You're scarin' me."

Clara shook her head again and answered, "Yes, yes, I'm okay. I'm just a little shocked. I just never imagined either one of them would die. I guess I thought they were a force of nature or something. And, Caelan, he was cryin'. I think he was cryin' anyway. His voice sounded strained. I didn't know he could cry."

Clara stood and said, "I'd better get up and get supper started. Your Daddy's goin' to be home soon, and I don't know how he's goin' to take this. He likes banana puddin'. I'll make him some banana puddin' to help cushion the blow a little bit."

When Eamon got home, Clara was putting supper on the table. She helped Rebecca into the kitchen, and they all sat down and ate without saying anything to Eamon about Mabon. After supper and dessert, everyone went to the living room to watch television. After Clara had Rebecca comfortably settled on her couch, she went to the kitchen and returned a few minutes later with a bowl of banana pudding.

Clara stood in front of Eamon and handed the pudding to him before she said, "You might need two desserts after what I have to tell you."

Eamon sat the bowl on the coffee table and asked, "What's wrong?"

"Caelan called today —"

"What the hell does that ol' —"

"Calm down until you hear what I have to say."

"What is it?"

"Mabon died this mornin'."

Eamon gasped and tears welled in his eyes.

"Are you okay?" Clara asked.

Eamon shook his head several times like Clara did right after she heard the news before he said, "I don't know. I don't know what I'm supposed to think or feel."

Clara sat next to him and lay her hand on his knee before she said, "I didn't know what I was supposed to think either. I don't think I yet know what I'm supposed to think." After a pause, she said, "Caelan wants us to come to the funeral. I told him it's up to you."

Eamon shook his head again and asked, "When is it?"

"He said the whereabouts will be in the newspaper tomorrow. Marjorie gets the newspaper delivered to their house. I'll call her tomorrow and ask her to tell me what it says. You can decide then what you want to do."

They did attend the lay out, with me and Dog in tow. When we entered, every person in the room stopped and stared at us as we followed Eamon to the coffin. At first, I thought everyone was staring, because Rebecca was on crutches. Then, I heard the whispering; "What a good son to come after what she did to him." "I can't believe he came after what she did to him." "Does he remember that she was the one who did this to him?" "He shouldn't have to limp up to that coffin to see her like that; he was born a healthy child." Suddenly, it dawned on me that everyone in the family knew what happened when Eamon and me were children, and they had acted like they hadn't known — but why?

Clara helped Rebecca to a chair and gave her a book to look at while she walked around the room with Eamon. Rebecca looked at her Grandfather, remembered what he had said about her reading, and sat on the book instead of reading it. She watched her parents talk briefly to most of the relatives before having a cup of coffee in a small room directly across from where she sat. When Eamon and Clara left that room, the family, Dog and I went home without saying goodbye to anyone.

On the way home, Eamon stopped at a liquor store for the first time and bought a bottle of whiskey. When we got home that night, the family sat around the living room watching television like they always did — except this night Eamon was drinking whiskey instead of having his normal snack of cornflakes with sugar and milk.

After the third drink, he put his elbows on his knees and dropped his head into the palms of his hands. As his arms to held his head up, he cried and said, "Clara, what if she's in hell? What if there's somethin' I should have done to change her — to help her? What if it's my fault she went to hell? Maybe I should have stayed closer to her, and maybe I could have saved her. I bet she's in hell, and there isn't anythin' I can do about it now."

Clara patted his leg and said, "Eamon, you shouldn't talk this way in front of the children, and Rebecca sleeps here. Let's go upstairs and talk about it."

"I'm okay," Eamon said. "I don't need to talk anymore. I got it out of my system. You and Mitchell go ahead and go to bed. I'm goin' to sit here and have another drink, and then I'll be up."

"Are you sure?"

Eamon nodded as he poured another drink.

About a half hour later, he fell asleep on the couch that sat along the kitchen wall.

Rebecca got so good at using her crutches that she was able to get up, go to Eamon's couch, lift his feet onto it, take his shoes off, and cover him with her blanket. When she returned to her couch, she lay under the blanket that usually was under her. This ritual and sleeping arrangement continued several nights a week for the remainder of the school year.

Around the time Rebecca got off her crutches, Clara's pregnancy began to show. She didn't allow this to slow her down from keeping up with The Street Walkers as they walked their children to and from school and church. Even as her pregnancy progressed and her belly got bigger, Clara still kept up.

Even though Rebecca was happy about the new baby, this added another item to her list of fears. When I listened to her thoughts, she was afraid her Mom wouldn't be able to keep up with The Street Walkers while she was pregnant and would get hurt, that her family wouldn't be able to keep the baby safe from the neighbors when it was born, that something bad would happen to Clara while she was pregnant or delivering the baby, or that something would be wrong with the baby – she didn't want the baby to be born crippled like she was and have to be in hospitals with people like Marcus.

It wasn't only concerns for Clara and the baby that made Rebecca's list of fears longer. She was also concerned that her Grandmother was meeting some horrible fate in the afterlife and that Eamon being aware of that was going to make him go crazy. Between those daily trips to and from school that required The Street Walkers to keep a handicapped child and a pregnant woman safe, the evenings brought to life Rebecca's concerns about Eamon. Fortunately, Rebecca being off crutches meant she could go upstairs and escape the dance Eamon was doing with his demons, but that didn't mean she wasn't affected by it.

Eamon was drinking enough to get drunk and pass out at least three nights a week by the time Thanksgiving rolled around. One night, in a drunken stupor, it seemed like he was aware of me — he was looking right at me while he bared his soul of sins that were not his own. As he looked at me, he slurred, "Maybe Ma beat me and left me crippled, because I was a bad child like she said I was. Maybe Ma was just doin' what the Bible says and tryin' not to spoil me. If that's the reason, maybe she's in heaven right now. If that's not the reason, maybe she's in hell right now. If she did this stuff because she's just mean, then she's in hell. I don't think no one deserves to go to hell. I don't want her to be in hell even if she did make me crippled. I don't want no one to be in hell. I reckon I was just a bad child. She was beatin' me so she wouldn't spoil me. I was a bad person. I yelled at her the last time I saw her. I sent her away. I told her to get off my property. Surely, she's in heaven, and I'm the one goin' to hell for bein' such a wicked child. There's no hope for me now."

He poured another shot and continued, "What if she is in hell for all she did? It's all my fault if she is. I'm the reason she's there if she is. It's the stuff she did to me that put her there. If she hadn't done that stuff to me, she might be in heaven. It's the stuff she did to me that made her bad. I'm the bad one. If I wasn't bad, she wouldn't have done that stuff to me."

He shook his head like he was trying to get cobwebs off of it and said, "But, if she beat me because I was a bad child, then did she kill Juanita because Juanita was a bad child? If Juanita was a bad child, does that mean she's in hell? But, if Ma beat her just out of meanness, does that mean Ma's in hell? The way I see it, one way or another, one of them is in hell. Either Juanita's in hell for bein' a bad child, or Ma's in hell for bein' mean to a good child."

Tears rolled down his cheeks as he continued, "One way or another, one of them is sufferin', and there ain't a thing I can do to make the sufferin' stop."

He wiped tears from under his eyes and said, "There ain't never been nothin' I could do to make the sufferin' stop, even when they was here on this earth and sufferin'. Why does God make people be born to never have a minutes peace from sufferin' no matter how much others try to make the sufferin' stop?"

He drank another shot and passed out on the couch — again.

A few weeks before the baby was due, Darina came up from the mountains to help. Eamon somehow found the strength to stay sober while she was visiting. She did most of the housework the last few weeks Clara was pregnant, and when Clara went into labor, Darina, Dog and I stayed with the children while Eamon drove Clara to the hospital.

While Clara was in labor, Darina remained patient while Mitchell argued that the new baby would be a boy and Rebecca argued that the new baby would be a girl. When they got a call from Eamon telling them the baby was a boy, Mitchell ran around the house hooting and dancing a victory dance while Rebecca sat on the couch and cried.

Princess jumped onto the couch and nudged Rebecca. Rebecca didn't quit crying as she hugged Princess and whispered into Princess' ear, "I hope this brother is nicer than the one I've got."

None of Rebecca's fears about the pregnancy happened. Clara gave birth to a healthy little boy, and Clara and the baby were both fine. Eamon and Clara named their new son Stewart.

It was late in the day when Clara came home from the hospital. She came home to many members of her family waiting anxiously to see the new baby. They sat around the living room not saying much to each other, yet they stayed until ten o'clock that night. It was obvious Clara was so tired she could barely sit in the chair and hold the baby anymore.

Rebecca opened her mouth and said one unintelligible word. When everyone looked at her, she covered up her mistake with a fake yawn. Her thoughts told me that she wanted to say, "Can't you all see she's tired — go home." She stopped herself from saying it, because she had learned a long time ago to keep her mouth shut and be invisible. She curled up on the end couch cushion with Princess and fought to stay awake until she fell asleep before everyone left.

When Stewart came home, Princess adopted the role of protecting him. She took up residence under the baby bed Marjorie loaned Clara for the living room during the day and under the baby bed that was in Eamon and Clara's bedroom at night. She stormed out barking and growling at anyone who came near the crib who wasn't living in our house.

Darina was going home the Sunday Stewart turned four weeks old. All of the family who lived in the city came to Eamon and Clara's house on Saturday to see her before she left. When the children saw how protective Princess was of Stewart, they teased her. They kept approaching the crib and acting like they were going to touch Stewart to get her to run at them — until the fateful run when she yelped and fell down onto her side whimpering. Dog ran to her and was laying by her side before Eamon and Clara got there. Darina spent her last night in the city tending to Stewart, so Clara could sit up with Princess and try to keep her comfortable.

Morgan drove Darina home the next day while Eamon and Clara looked without success for a veterinarian that was open on Sunday. By the time Clara contacted Mrs. Reynolds' veterinarian on Monday morning, they couldn't get medical care for Princess until Monday afternoon. Mrs. Reynolds gave Eamon the afternoon off to take Princess to her appointment.

The veterinarian diagnosed Princess with a slipped disk and told Eamon that other than a very expensive operation, there was nothing they could do for her. Eamon brought Princess home and discussed the options with Clara. They tried through the next day to find a way to come up with the money for the operation, but they couldn't. In the meantime, Clara spoiled Princess by giving her scraps of meat from the table and petting her while sitting with her on the bed of blankets they made for her in the corner. Princess was so loyal to the family that she didn't stay on the blankets like the vet wanted her to do. She kept dragging her back legs as she tried to follow the family around. When she did that, it was obvious she was suffering. Eamon and Clara were forced to admit they couldn't come up with the money for the operation on any timetable that would justify them allowing Princess to suffer. Eamon took Princess back to the vet and had her euthanized. Dog went with them.

I stayed home hoping I could be a comfort to the family. There's an odd feeling in a house when everyone is waiting for news that a beloved dog has been euthanized and it's over. I guess that feeling is there any time someone is waiting for bad news. It felt like the air got heavy, the clocks slowed down, and no one had the heart to do anything except surrender to the inevitable by stepping away from all of our usual activities and waiting.

Rebecca was sitting on the couch rocking back and forth instead of being stiff and stoic, so I knew she was really hurting. Her thoughts told me that this child who had such a hard time being angry at anyone but herself was angry at her parents. Despite everything she'd been through, this was the worst pain Rebecca had felt — mostly because it was a pain she couldn't separate from her body to avoid, because grief was too long lasting. Since she had no place else to project her anger, she projected it onto her parents for not doing what a school friend's parents did. When that friend's dog died, her parents hid it from her and bought a dog that looked like it to try to protect their daughter from the pain. It hadn't worked. Rebecca knew that the little girl was aware the new dog was not her dog and got angry at her parents for lying to her and trying to trick her, but Rebecca couldn't acknowledge that part of the story yet. She just wanted something to make the pain go away.

I knew Princess was gone before Eamon got home to give the tearful family the news. Princess' ghost stopped by to say goodbye before she went with the Angel. I was happy to see she wasn't suffering anymore.

Everyone had their way of dealing with the pain. Eamon began to drink again when Darina was gone, and his drunken talk was filled with the added concern about where Princess and Dog went after they died. Clara focused on helping everyone else through their suffering even though she was walking around in a daze that was a combination of grief and exhaustion from taking care of a newborn. Mitchell took his frustrations out on Rebecca by picking on her even more than usual. Rebecca returned to reading books and writing in her binder.

I listened to her thoughts. She finally realized Caelan had been wrong. People weren't mean to her because she could read so good they thought she was uppity. Since she stopped reading, Marcus had hurt her, Caelan and Mabon had come to her house and hurt her, and she still believed her parents had hurt her by not trying to hide Princess' death with a replacement dog. She realized there was no good reason to stop reading and writing. She regretted she had not read stories to Princess for several months. She wondered if Princess missed those stories. She got a book and her binder out from under her bed and read a story to Princess' ghost, drew pictures of Princess, and wrote notes to Princess in her binder. I had no way of letting her know Princess went with the Angel. Faolan said the gates of heaven weren't locked, so maybe Princess was hearing Rebecca.

The night Princess went with the Angel, Eamon's grief caused him to get very drunk again. I guess Rebecca needed someone to grieve with, because she came downstairs to be with him when he cried out in his sleep after he passed out. She sat on the cold linoleum floor near his feet and listened as he said, "Sinead. Sinead."

"Who's Sinead, Daddy?" she asked.

Apparently, her question made it into his unconscious mind, because he sat up, looked at her through glazed eyes, and choked out of a throat that was raw with cigarettes and whiskey, "Sinead?"

"It's me, Daddy," Rebecca said.

"Sinead? I'm sorry I didn't save you."

"It's me, Daddy. It's Rebecca."

"Sinead, I was so afraid! I'm sorry I didn't save you!" he said before he closed his glazed eyes and began to snore.

The following morning, the family tried to go on as if nothing had happened, but the next few days made it very apparent something had. Being in a daze caused Clara to repeatedly put out food and water before she remembered Princess was no longer with them. Every day, the children came home from school looking for her before they remembered she was gone. Eamon repeatedly called for Princess when he came home from work before he remembered. After a couple of weeks like that, Rebecca's thoughts revealed she realized no dog could replace Princess, and the last thing she wanted was for any dog to try. She was grateful her parents hadn't tried to trick her like her friend's parents did. She released her anger and allowed herself to feel the pain.

A few weeks later, someone gave Eamon a dog. It was a hundred-pound Golden Retriever named Shecky. Eamon built a dog house and tied Shecky in the back yard. I was never sure if he handled it that way due to the size of the dog or due to his fear that he would get that close and that hurt again if he brought another dog in the house. Even listening to Eamon's thoughts didn't answer that question, because Eamon wasn't sure of the answer himself. His grief over Princess was so intermingled with his grief over Dog that he was forced to push all of it down just to get through the days. Part of his confusion was the guilt he felt for loving Princess so much when he hadn't been able to save Dog, and part of it was guilt that, in the end, he hadn't been able to save either one of them. He was becoming a master of owning sins that were not his own. Fortunately, Shecky remained unharmed in the backyard even if the neighborhood was bad, maybe because Eamon built the dog house next to the fence that was on the other side of the yard from Tessa's family's yard.

The family was just starting to come to grips with their grief about Princess when the school year ended and it was time to schedule another operation for Rebecca. Just like last time, everyone agreed that it was better to do it early in the summer, so she would be mostly healed by the time she returned to school. Therefore, Eamon and Clara took her to the hospital the Monday after school was out.

Before the last hospital stay, the tension about whether or not Rebecca could take her stuffed donkey seemed daunting, but it was nothing compared to the conflict the family faced as they prepared to leave for the hospital this time. Rebecca was bound and determined not to go, and it took Eamon and Clara both to carry her kicking and screaming to the car. The fight continued as they struggled to carry her into the hospital. A doctor had to be called to the lobby to give her a shot to calm her down.

The doctor kept Rebecca medicated until she was taken down for surgery the next morning. Just like the last time, Eamon and Clara sat in the waiting room until the surgery was over. About four hours after she was wheeled through the swinging double doors that led to the operating rooms, the doctor came out and said, "Mr. and Mrs. Teague."

Eamon and Clara went to the doctor, and he asked, "I'm sorry, but is there any medication your daughter is on that you neglected to tell us about?"

"Why?" Clara stammered.

"We're having a bit of a problem waking her up from the anesthesia."

Grabbing onto the doorframe was the only thing that kept Eamon from collapsing. He held himself up while Clara stammered through her tears, "No. No. We told you everythin'." Clara's whole body shook as she asked, "Is she goin' to die? Is she dyin'?"

"We're doing everything we can. We'll let you know when we know more." The doctor said and went back through the double doors.

Clara went to Eamon, and when she touched him, he fell into her arms and screamed, "What if she doesn't make it? We never got her baptized. What if she goes to hell with my mother?"

Clara slumped over onto him as she held him, and they both wailed.

I followed the doctor back to the operating room. When we got there, I saw a man standing on one side of the transport bed Rebecca was laying on, and he was doing things to her that I didn't understand. I did understand what the nurse standing on the other side of Rebecca was doing. The nurse was holding Rebecca's hand and saying in a loud voice, "Rebecca! Can you hear me? Come on back, honey. Rebecca! Come on back!"

When I saw Faolan, Princess, and Flopsy standing along the back wall, I went into Rebecca's thoughts, and I searched until I found her. She felt like she was floating in limbo, in a light blue something, and there was a bright white light off in the distance. I didn't remember seeing anything like this when I had died, so I didn't think she was dying. She had no thoughts. She just was. I don't know how else to explain it. She just was. I felt she either had to come back or eventually go on. I just knew she couldn't stay like this forever. I screamed her name — and I screamed it again — and I screamed it again. After screaming her name several more times, I saw a glowing white man appear next to Rebecca.

He gave her a push and said, "You have to go back now. It's not your time."

As Rebecca floated toward me in a manner that looked like a person floating on their back in a river, I got a flicker of her thoughts. There was something there to read. She was hearing the nurse. She heard her name. She heard it again. She started moving faster, through the blue — toward the nurse's voice. Every time the nurse called her name, her thoughts let me know she heard it. After that, Rebecca's thoughts revealed what seemed like a long fight to get to that voice. At the end of that fight, Rebecca opened her eyes.

"Oh, praise God," the nurse said before she turned to the doctor and said, "Doctor, we've got her."

I felt my ghost body exhale the breath I'd been holding without even knowing I'd been holding it. She would still be with us to live another chapter of her life.

Thanks to Religious Recovery Press for publishing the first book in this series.

Religious Recovery Press is now a 501(c)3 Non-Profit Publishing House. We decided that "The Blood Moon Series" is not a 501(c)3 book series, so I changed publishing houses. I still strongly support their literature and recommend it for any readers who need help recovering from religious abuse.

Following are the books currently published from *ReligiousRecoveryPress.org*

(available on Amazon)

Every Path Leads Home, Opening to Your Spiritual Journey
By: Wayne Holmes

Strength For The Journey Home
By: Wayne Holmes

Set Your Course
Daily Lessons into Spirituality
For the Religious Recovery Program
By Wayne Holmes

About Rhonda Partin-Sharp

Rhonda comes from an Appalachian lineage. Her memories combined with stories she heard of previous generations have nurtured her as a storyteller. Although she received higher education in literature and writing and worked as a writer in various non-fiction forms, she feels her heart is what made her a storyteller, and her heart is tied to the mountains that were the lifeblood of many generations before her. *Escape Under A Waning Crescent Moon* is the second book in a series that tells a story of the trials many people faced as they migrated from the Appalachian Mountains – in this case the story of how an abused child who was escaping began to repair their broken heart.

In her early years, Rhonda often found herself surrounded by troubled people. She had to learn that not all people had needs as great as her parents and the friends from her culture she often helped. She also had to learn that women were not required to put their needs and their family's needs second to other people's wants in order to be right with God. These lessons helped her start learning to stop extending compassion and/or understanding to people who cherished chaos above healthy relationships. This change began when her counselor recognized that Rhonda's personal key to healing was for Rhonda to understand that people see in others what they are themselves; therefore, Rhonda had to stop assuming all people were as accepting, compassionate, and helpful as her lineage and life experiences had taught her to be.

During the two years since the first book in this series was released, Rhonda has expanded on those lessons. She experienced opportunities to practice setting boundaries, and she did so instead of becoming codependent or enabling like she would have done in the past. She has even stronger boundaries than she had when this series began, and this has blessed her with even stronger relationships.

Her old boss, Rosemary, who is mentioned in the Acknowledgements for this book, helped Rhonda get started on the road to letting go of cultural and religious submission teachings for women and developing stronger boundaries. Rosemary told her when the journey began that she would reach her goals by peeling away layers like peeling away the layers of an onion, stating that Rhonda would encounter resistance with each layer and thus must become strong. Rhonda said she peeled away a huge layer of the onion during the time she wrote this book. This has greatly increased her happiness, even in the face of trials such as grief over the loss of her friend Linde Grace and others during this same timeframe.

She hopes that her writing – this book and other books that are in the works – will help others achieve the same successes and happiness. She desires to pay it forward.

**Book Three in The Blood Moon Trilogy
is planned for release in 2019.**